Fearless

Fearless

Book II in the Survival Race Series

K. M. FAWCETT

Best Wishes,

K. M. Fawcett

FOREVER
YOURS

New York   Boston

Copyright © 2014 by K. M. Fawcett
Excerpt from *Captive* copyright © 2013 by K. M. Fawcett
Cover design by Melody Cassen
Cover photography by Stock by Getty Images
Cover copyright © 2014 by Hachette Book Group, Inc.

Forever Yours
Hachette Book Group
237 Park Avenue
New York, NY 10017
hachettebookgroup.com
twitter.com/foreverromance

First published as an ebook and as a print on demand edition: January 2014

Forever Yours is an imprint of Grand Central Publishing.
The Forever Yours name and logo are trademarks of Hachette Book Group, Inc.

The publisher is not responsible for websites (or their content) that are not owned by the publisher.

The Hachette Speakers Bureau provides a wide range of authors for speaking events. To find out more, go to www.hachettespeakersbureau.com or call (866) 376-6591.

ISBN: 978-1-4555-2819-6 (ebook edition)
ISBN: 978-1-4555-7578-7 (print on demand edition)

To Scott, my best friend, my love, and my partner in everything.

I could not write a better hero than you.

Acknowledgments

If it weren't for authors Cathy Tully, Chris Redding, and Stacey Wilk, I would have given up a long time ago. Thank you for being more than a critique group. You are truly Gems.

My appreciation and gratitude goes out to knife maker Jim Hammond for permission to use the Flesheater name, Sensei A. J. Advincula for teaching me how to use the Flesheater knife he designed, and Cheryl Willis for answering my horse questions. Any errors in the book are my own.

Thank you beta readers Margaret Smith, Craig Smith, and Leslie Sauerborn for your honest feedback. My deepest thanks goes to Doug Moran for beta reading (more than once), brainstorming sci-fi elements, and answering my panicked phone calls. This story is better because of you.

Of course, there would be no book if it weren't for my agent Michelle Grajkowski, my editors Lauren Plude and Megha Parekh, and the entire Forever Yours team. Your belief in the series and hard work has made it all possible. Thank you.

Scott, Gregory, and Julie: I can't thank you enough for your love, encouragement, and patience—and for eating a lot of take-out—while I was off in my own world writing.

To the readers: I am truly grateful for your amazing support of *Captive*, and for requesting more Survival Race books. I hope you enjoy the new adventure and romance in *Fearless*.

Fearless

Chapter One

Guided by the light from Hyborea's two crescent moons, Kedric crept through tangled jungle vegetation with gladiator stealth. He crouched behind a tree trunk and motioned for his troops to surround the targeted village. A hundred men would be in position before dawn broke in fifteen minutes.

Advancing this deep into the savage's territory had been easy. Too easy. After their last raid, the tribe's leader should have built defenses. That's what Kedric would have done. But Kedric was an alpha gladiator and the Highland warlord. These people knew nothing about fighting. There wasn't a trap or a sentry anywhere, not even atop their newly constructed bell tower. The thatch-roofed platform appeared unmanned. What good was a warning bell if no one was there to ring it?

Ignorant fools.

What had he expected from primitives who lived in grass huts, hunted with spears, and prayed to the aurora tropicos? Those lights weren't Protecting Spirits. They were electromagnetic fields. Forces of nature. Science. *That's* what protected their island from Hyboreans.

His skin crawled and jaw clenched. If it weren't for the Hyboreans, he wouldn't have to capture these savages in the first place.

But he had a plan that would end human suffering.

A warbling birdcall signaled the first troop was in position. It wouldn't be long before he heard the others' signals.

Kedric almost felt sorry for his enemies.

They'd no idea war was imminent.

* * *

Myia couldn't sleep. She should have been able to conquer her emotions by now, yet here she was on her eighteenth birthday—the most important day of her life—and she couldn't calm her nerves enough to sleep through the night.

The rope frame creaked beneath her as she got out of bed. She padded barefoot across the dirt floor to the hut's only window.

A crack of orange sunlight separated the forest from the still-starry heavens where the Spirits danced in a display of red-and-green lights. But today, they weren't weaving and swaying with their usual harmonious grace. The lights clashed and crashed into each other as if doing battle.

They appeared as restless as she was. Surely they weren't reflecting her anxiety over today's vision quest.

What had upset the Protecting Spirits?

If she could relax, she could alter her state of consciousness and ask them. But that was her whole problem, wasn't it?

A shaman must maintain inner serenity, her father had instructed time and time again.

She closed her eyes and inhaled sticky humidity and the sweet, dusty scent of dried herbs, thatch, and soil. She tried concentrating on her breathing like she'd done so many times in the past, but it was no use. Excitement and apprehension had hijacked her tranquillity.

How would she ever become a full-fledged shaman if she couldn't quiet herself?

She was doomed to fail her vision quest.

And disappoint her father.

Her body grew heavy with the thought. Although she'd never be as wise and knowledgeable a healer as he, she wanted nothing more than to follow in his footsteps. She'd do her best to try.

As if summoned, her father rushed into her hut. Something was wrong. He never rushed. "Myia"—his voice remained calm—"sound the bell. The Highlanders are coming again."

Not wasting the precious seconds it would take to slip on her moccasins, she raced out the door, weaved between huts, fire pits, and water barrels toward the village center. After the last attack, the remaining men began constructing the bell tower and only finished it yesterday. No one had been assigned to stand watch yet.

It was up to her alone to sound the alarm.

Heart pounding, she scrambled up the twenty rungs of the ladder, praying the structure wouldn't collapse. The wooden platform seemed to sway, or perhaps the height made her dizzy. She gripped the half wall to steady herself, and her eye caught movement through the jungle below. The Highlanders had the village surrounded and were quickly advancing.

She gripped the mallet's thick handle and swung hard, striking the bell with all her force. A deep metallic ring reverberated inside her body and ears, nearly deafening them from a warrior's shriek below.

The vegetation emitted menacing screams that grew louder as more and more warriors joined in the war cry. Despite the summer heat, icy chills slid down her spine.

She repeatedly struck the bell as the village came alive. Men and women fled their homes with small children and babies in their arms. The older children ran close behind their mothers.

From her vantage point, she could see what they couldn't: the surrounding invaders moving swiftly through the vegetation toward them.

Tears blurred her vision. If she hadn't been so self-absorbed, so wrapped up in her own concerns, she could've received the Spirits' warning before her father had. She could've sounded the alarm sooner. Her friends and neighbors might have been able to escape into the jungle.

Instead, they were ambushed.

The bell clanking and ringing in her ears couldn't drown out their frightened screams as the Highlanders captured them. There wasn't much of a fight. Hers were a peaceful people. They didn't train for battle as the Highlanders did.

The warriors who didn't lay in wait surged into the village and raced to specific huts as if they had been targeted before the attack. One raced for her tower.

Tamping down her fear, she took a deep, cleansing breath, preparing herself for the confrontation. Once the Highlander touched her, her spirit would enter his and she'd heal his angry heart.

Assuming she could remain calm and at peace with the world.

This would be so much easier if she weren't whacking the heck out of an upside-down metal bowl and the tower wasn't shaking from the warrior climbing the ladder.

"Spirits, fill my heart with peace and tranquillity to help my people." She closed her eyes and struck the bell with an even tempo. The rhythm of it wasn't relaxing her. No power surged through her body.

A fist encircled her biceps stopping her arm midswing. Her eyes opened to a familiar face she hadn't seen since the first raid on their village. "Lem!"

"Myia." He released her arm and embraced her. The gesture lowered his defenses, and his emotional brew of resentment and excitement flowed into her.

The last time their souls had intertwined she'd helped him grieve the loss of his mother. "I'm so relieved you're alive. Everyone sent to negotiate our people's return had been captured."

"Not captured. Liberated." He glanced over the half wall before pulling her to the floor as he crouched. "Stay down. It's best if no one sees us talking."

"But the warning bell."

"It's too late."

He was right, of course. The Highlanders had already invaded, and by the sounds of the chaos below, the villagers were defending themselves as best as a peace-loving people could against warmonger aggression.

"Are the Highlanders forcing you to capture your own people?"

"They aren't forcing me. I volunteered. I've come to save you."

"Me?"

"Not *you* exactly, but the bell ringer."

"Lem, take my hand. I can heal the hostility in your heart."

"It's not hostility. It's determination. I want to bring our tribesmen to the Highlands."

"Why? Why would you capture your own people?"

"Life is so much better there. The Highlanders are so advanced and smart. They have technology. And the food! Myia, there's so much to eat all the time." Lem certainly didn't appear to be starving. In fact, in the few weeks he'd been gone, he looked to have been well nourished and filled out his nearly six-foot frame. "They have medicines, too. Powerful medicines that could have saved my mother. Our people fear the unknown. By bringing them to the Highlands, we help them see the light. After a few days, they don't want to leave."

Not want to leave? Not want to return to their homes and families? He was talking nonsense. "Take my hand and I'll heal your heart."

"I don't need healing. I know the truth."

"What truth?"

"That the Hyboreans capture humans. They keep them caged as pets. They force men to kill each other for sport. Kedric, our leader, believes we can defeat them and free the human race."

Poor Lem. Only two years younger than she, he'd been easily led astray. "Your so-called *leader* has captured you. *He's* kept you caged behind stone walls. *He's* seduced you with food and technology and brainwashed you to attack your own people. Look." She pushed aside some thatch in the half wall, making a hole. "Your brethren run in fear for their lives and their families. How could you have become a part of this?"

"But they won't be harmed. Kedric only needs more men for his army. We can't fight the Hyboreans without them."

"They won't be harmed, yet they are made to join an army and forced to kill? Do you not hear the foolishness of your own words? Your leader is no better than a Hyborean."

He had no counterargument. "I-I never thought of it like that."

Myia's fingers entwined with Lem's. She breathed in deeply, silently calling upon the Spirits to give her strength to calm his heart and fill it with peace.

"Myia," he whispered.

"Shh. Let the grace of the spirit world reveal what is truly in your heart. You aren't a soldier. You don't slay other creatures for war. You're a spiritual being who lives in peace, harmony, and balance with all life. Let the Spirits breathe the love and goodness you knew back into your soul."

Her spirit flowed into his body. "Thank you for your trust, Lem."

It didn't take long before his thoughts dissipated from Highland madness to the old, peaceful village life. His spirit had a strong and deep connection here. His subconscious knew what was right and what was wrong. Unfortunately, his conscious mind had been under the influence of the Highland lord the past few weeks. But now that she'd reminded him who he was, he was ready to return to his true essence.

This was what shamanism was all about. Healing a man's soul. Restoring his balance and harmony and joy.

Reawakening his essence.

When she finally separated her spirit from his and rejoined the physical world, mournful sobs had taken the place of the screams and warriors' shouts from earlier. How many villagers had been taken away this time?

"I'm sorry, Myia." Lem wept.

It was a natural response to enlightenment. Tears were the body's way of purging ego.

The planks beneath her vibrated as though someone was climbing the ladder. The tower couldn't possibly hold any more weight.

"Myia!" The fear in her little sister's voice sent shivers down her spine.

She crawled to the edge of the platform and peered over. "Don't come up, Kimi. The tower can't hold us all."

"Come quickly. Father's been injured."

Myia turned back to Lem. She didn't want to leave him while he was so vulnerable, but Father needed her.

"Go," he said. "I'll be all right."

She touched his shoulder in thanks. Lem would be all right. He needed time to reflect on all he'd been through in the last month. She'd check on him later.

As soon as hard ground met the soles of her bare feet, Myia sprinted after her sister. When she saw two women carrying her father into his home, she paused. It wouldn't do anyone good to see a shaman-aprendi in a state of panic. She wiped her eyes and then calmly walked to the door.

Once inside, she knelt at his bedside. "I'm here, Father." Her voice was low, quiet, and far more at peace sounding than she felt. Outwardly masking her feelings was the easy part. She'd had eighteen years to perfect that skill. The trouble was quelling them on the inside.

How could she be a true shaman when she couldn't control something as simple as her own emotions?

Father didn't speak. Nor did he open his eyes, yet somehow his hand found her fingers and he squeezed them in reassurance. Their spirits didn't connect. He would want to meditate first.

"His shinbone is broken," Kimi said.

Myia forced her tears back and nodded. She had to be strong for the group. They would look to her for guidance and strength. It would help no one to blubber all over her stoic father.

With a fortifying breath, she let go of his hand and then took command of the room. In all the time it took to cleanse his wounds, set poultices, and dress his injuries, his breath remained steady and strong.

The fact that he hadn't spoken in over an hour didn't concern her. He would speak when he had something to say. And she knew he'd have nothing to say until he finished meditating on this morning's invasion.

His tranquillity was admirable. Awe-inspiring. Even in the most trying and troubling times, he could be still, reflect and receive the Spirits' wisdom. Would she ever be able to do the same?

When she finished administering to his injuries, he intertwined his fingers with hers. His despair gushed into her soul. His heavy heart was burdened not with his own ailments, but with the attack, and worse, the betrayal of his own people. They'd taken up arms and fought back when he'd instructed them to hide. Apparently the villagers had spent the last month secretly practicing hand-to-hand combat. But their skills had been no match for the Highlanders. Engaging in battle only caused them greater suffering.

She hated feeling her father's anguish over the tribe's path to becoming a fighting people. Once a nation became ruled with anger and hatred for another nation, there would be no bringing peace and spirituality back.

"I see your thoughts and fears, Father. You rest and leave the villagers to me. When you are well, you will see each and every heart in our nation healed."

"No, my child."

"Father?" She hadn't expected him to voice an answer. He'd been too weak; his spirit too dim. Had her anger at the Highlanders clouded her ability to read him clearly?

She must get control of her feelings.

It took all his strength to speak. It would have been less taxing for his spirit to communicate directly with hers, but she sensed his desire for all in the room to hear his words.

"Heal the…Highlanders." His breathing labored. "Only then…will we…have peace."

In order to heal the Highlanders she'd have to leave the village. Leave Father. What if he got worse while she was away? He was getting up there in years, and his body didn't recover like a younger man's. He needed her here to care for his wounds, both the physical and spiritual. "I can't go. The people here need me. *You* need me. If I step foot beyond the Highland walls, I'll never be set free."

"You will…once you heal…their people."

How would she do that from a prison cell or a dungeon? Surely those barbarians would keep her locked away. Or maybe they would get rid of her body altogether. How much help could she be to anyone on this island if her soul joined the Protecting Spirits? Without her father or her to link the physical world with the spiritual, there would be no healing. No enlightenment.

What would happen to the people of Pele if left to rule by ego?

"Start with their leader." Father spoke slowly, taking many breaths between his words. "His heart has a great wound. Mend his spirit, and he will stop the attacks."

How could she possibly do that? She wasn't a full shaman. She had to pass the initiation test, and she'd yet to begin her vision quest.

It would take the greatest strength coming from the greatest inner tranquillity in order to heal the warring heart of an alpha gladiator leader who was hell-bent on taking all their men for his army. The fool couldn't win against the Hyboreans. They were an advanced race, indigenous to this planet. And the Peletians were either escaped refugees or descendants of escaped refugees. They were only a few hundred strong.

"I can't leave you, Father. You need me to help heal you. You're too weak to do so on your own."

"You must…heal…the nations. That is…most important."

"But—"

"You will not fail." Faith in her flooded his soul in a powerful surge. He believed in her abilities wholeheartedly. Whether that was due to prophecy or blind faith she couldn't be sure. She only knew it was unwise to argue with the most astute elder shaman in Peletian history. Especially when he was her father and suffered from a broken leg and a broken heart.

"Yes, Father. I will heal the warriors' hearts." It wasn't a lie. She would do everything in her power to uphold her vow. She just wasn't as confident in her abilities as he was.

His lips pulled into a smile before he closed his eyes to sleep. As peace entered his soul, she withdrew her spirit from his.

"Kimi, I need you to take care of—"

"I will. I've been studying the herbals. I can nurse Father back to health."

She cupped her little sister's cheek. Though Kimi was only fourteen, she was smart and capable. "I know you can."

By the bright morning sunshine filtering in through the window,

Myia estimated about eighteen hours of daylight left. It should take about fifteen hours to hike the mountain to the Highland kingdom, assuming she didn't run into any trouble.

If she were to arrive before dark, she best get started.

It didn't take long to gather supplies, kiss her father and sister good-bye, and bid farewell to the few villagers who'd escaped the attack.

Funny, whenever she'd imagined today's journey into the jungle, she had thought it would be for her vision quest. She'd no idea she would be on a journey to heal the Highland warlord's heart.

Assuming he had a heart to heal.

Chapter Two

Kedric left the welcome center satisfied with the freedom speech he'd addressed to the newcomers. He'd delivered it in front of the glass wall providing Highland Castle as a backdrop. The late-day sun glinting off the silver mineral in the gold-and-red-striated stone blocks never failed to amaze and impress the savages.

He headed down the gravel road through the middle of town past the little shops and markets that had closed early this evening. The entire kingdom was home preparing for tonight's banquet.

He had reason to celebrate.

The day had been successful. He'd counted twenty-seven men and boys who would serve him well in his army. Plus, the men taken in the last raid had collected their wives and children. That totaled sixty-three new people whom he'd personally inspected and welcomed to the Highlands.

The first day was always the most difficult for them. Many of the savages were frightened and on edge, which was understandable. Capturing them wasn't the best way to win them over, but it seemed to work. Experiencing was believing, and once the savages experienced the land of abundance, they realized their village leaders kept them in poverty.

He'd given everyone a choice to leave the Highlands or collect their families and return. Their choice alone proved his plan was in everyone's best interest. His steps grew lighter thinking about the family reunions.

He turned down the narrow, rocky path toward the ferry dock where the motorboat waited to take him to Discovery Island. Hopefully, the science team would give him good news as well.

Today's raid yielded no casualties, minimal wounds, and only one deserter. The young soldier named Lem. The villagers wouldn't have killed him in the raid. They weren't hostile. Though some had fought back this time. Obviously they'd been training, which only provoked his warriors and resulted in more people being needlessly hurt.

There had to be a better way to collect those savages.

When he'd brought food and technology to the leaders of each village, they'd refused it and threw him out. Apparently, maintaining authority and power over their nation was a greater priority than meeting their people's basic needs. Thus, the only course of action was to "escort" the people to civilization.

It didn't take more than a day before the villagers' eyes opened to a better way of life. They had clean water and plenty of food. Medicine and education. How many people had personally thanked him for bringing them and their families here?

"Another rousing speech." Griffin's mocking tone spiked the hair on Kedric's nape. Arms folded, the lanky fop leaned against a tree about twenty paces away. He'd been at the welcome center when Kedric left, so he must have run like hell through the jungle. He moved to block the path.

Kedric stopped a few paces away and scanned the woods. He listened for the rustling of leaves, the snapping of twigs, or the breath of men waiting in ambush.

He saw and heard no one. "Out of my way, Griffin."

"How can you lie to the villagers like that? Promising them a better, easier life in the Highlands while you brainwash them to join your army? How do you live with yourself, Kedric?"

"That's *Lord* Kedric." Before the king had died two years ago, he'd named Kedric successor to the throne instead of his only son, Griffin. Kedric didn't tire of Griffin's narrowing eyes and reddening face.

"My father was an escaped gladiator. Of course he'd choose brawn over brains."

Kedric snorted. The king chose him because he shared his vision of destroying Hyboreans and freeing humankind. "Step aside. I've a nation to run. I don't have time to waste on the likes of you, aye?" *Aye.* It was the only word left in his vocabulary that paid homage to his earthly ancestry.

Griffin's mouth clamped shut. His jaw muscles shifted as if grinding his back teeth. Head cocked, eyes skyward, he shook his head in obvious pride-swallowing contempt. Whatever he wanted was more important than a condescending comeback. He met Kedric's eyes. "I want my job back. Reinstate me to the science team."

"Piss off." He shoved past Griffin.

Griffin caught up and matched him stride for stride down the steep, rocky path toward the ferry dock. "You need me, Kedric. You know you do."

"What I need are researchers. Not a lying, manipulative bastard who hides vital secrets from his leader."

"Watch yourself, Kedric."

The menace in Griffin's voice stopped him cold. Reaching beneath his king's robe where his dagger hung under his arm, he faced his enemy. He would only unsheathe the weapon if forced to use it. "You challenging me?"

Griffin's pupils dilated as he eyed Kedric's hand beneath the robe. "I'd be a fool to fight a gladiator."

Griffin knew damn well he'd be sent to his ultimortem within seconds. Hatred darkened his muddy irises as he stared Kedric down before retreating out of striking distance. Kedric released his grip on the hilt. He was about to continue downhill when Griffin pivoted around.

"Understand this, *lord*." His fevered glare bore through Kedric. "There's more than one way to dethrone a king."

* * *

Twenty minutes later, inside Discovery Island's research facility, Kedric donned a skintight thermal suit, and then entered the forty-foot-square refrigerated room where two Hyborean captives—each twice the size of a full-grown man—sat with their backs against a wall. The one within arm's reach had charcoal-gray matted fur; the other was shit brown. Both reeked of sweat and that spicy anise scent inherent to the humanoid species. Their beady black catatonic eyes stared out into space as if peering into another dimension.

They had arrived in their subaquatic three months ago to poach humans for their black market blood sports. They must have thought they could get in and out before the island's low electromagnetic forces scrambled their brain waves.

Griffin had been chief scientist then. He'd convinced the team to keep the Hyboreans a secret and built the frozen habitat. When Kedric found out, he banned the chief traitor from Discovery Island and took over the research.

"Magnificent creatures, aren't they, my lord?" The awe in Finn's voice irritated him.

"You'd think differently had you been beaten, starved, and tortured for their pleasure." He never missed an opportunity to paint the ugly truth in all its gory detail. "You understand they force men to slaughter each other and then reawaken them for sport, aye?"

"Yes, my lord."

He nudged a furry charcoal leg with his boot. "Hyboreans think they're so clever with their survival races and their genetic experiments." And their incessant blood draining. "Well, look who the lab rat is now."

Kedric was damn lucky to have escaped the abuse at HuBReC, the Human Breeding and Research Center. Though if it weren't for his friend and fellow gladiator Max, he never would have reached freedom.

An ache stabbed his heart like it always did whenever he thought of his friend's sacrifice. After trekking three months through frozen terrain, fighting off wild creatures, and nearly drowning when they capsized in the ocean, they were one river crossing away from the refuge's electromagnetic safety.

If only Xanthrag hadn't tracked them, but the survival race master refused to be denied his prized alpha champion. Trapped on the rocky cliff of Sanctuary River, Max's odd green eyes shone with a last-ditch effort of determination. *I better not live to regret this*, he'd said to Kedric, and then willingly raced to his slaughter, knowing damn well Xanthrag would chase the champion gladiator over Kedric. His heroics enabled Kedric to flee to the refuge. Alone.

A knot formed in his gut. Why did Max sacrifice his freedom for him?

Kedric itched to plunge his dagger into these two creatures' black hearts in Max's honor. But he had other plans for the beasts.

He strode off to the conference room.

Finn entered after him and then found his place at the long knee-high table with three other scientists. Kedric knelt on a pillow at the head of the table and glared at the expectant faces. "Gentlemen, give me some good news."

"Our tech-rings are complete, my lord," chief scientist Dunna said. Pride shone in the old man's wrinkled face. "They look identical to the headbands the Hyboreans wear."

"Do they work? Can you control the beasts?"

"The electrical impulses are successful in stimulating parts of their brain. We've been able to switch on and off their aggression, directional movement, even sexual arousal."

What the hell kind of experiment was that? "Perhaps your time would be better served discovering how to control the Hyboreans, not artificially stimulating their erections."

The other three scientists sniggered.

"Yes, my lord."

"The question is, can you make the Hyboreans operate the subaquatic?"

Dunna cleared his throat and scratched his balding head. "That's the problem. Though we can stimulate particular neural pathways to get a general response, we can't figure out how to control them to do specific movements or tasks. In essence, we can lead a Hyborean to the subaquatic, but can't make him drive." He chuckled.

Kedric scowled. "Do you find this amusing because I sure as hell don't. I charged you with the most important task in this war and all I'm getting are one-liners."

Dunna's gaze dropped to the table. No one said a word.

"Every day those monsters torture innocent men, women, and children for their perverse pleasure. How is our army going to stop them if we can't travel to Handakar City? We have their subaquatic in our possession, but can't pilot it. Hell, we can't even open the damn door." His hammer fist struck the table and echoed in the silence.

Every piece of Hyborean technology was controlled telepathically, but no man or man-made machine could mimic the complex Hyborean wavelengths. Without a quick and efficient way to get to HuBReC and back, how the hell was he going to save his family? If the subaquatic couldn't be piloted, he might as well stop training his army.

Dunna's dejected headshake wasn't promising. "We've tried using sound and flashing lights to alter Labrat's brain waves. The flashing lights caused seizures."

"Is there permanent damage?" There were only two Hyboreans in captivity. He couldn't afford to lose one.

"No, my lord."

"Good. So is that it then? You have nothing more for me?"

The men exchanged nervous glances before Wren swept the mop of brown hair out of his eyes and spoke up. "My lord, we're also working on an imagined speech project."

"What's that?"

"Imagined speech is thinking in the form of sound. It's the voice you hear in your head while reading silently to yourself. The human brain generates word-specific signals before sending electrical impulses to our vocal cords. If we analyze these imagined speech signals and translate them into distinct words, we can send the signals through the control device to the Hyborean's tech-ring. If we're successful, we can produce synthetic telepathy."

"That's brilliant."

"It would be if it worked," Dunna mumbled. His bony fingers pushed a pencil behind his ear.

"Why won't it work?"

"My lord," Wren interrupted before Dunna could answer. "The tech-rings have the ability to transmit the signals, but we're still identifying the neural patterns unique to individual words."

"You're missing the point, Wren." Dunna leaned forward and his pencil fell to the table. Either his ears were too big or he needed more hair to keep it in place. "Imagined speech won't work on Hyboreans because they don't speak. Not our language nor any other because they have no voice box to make sounds. Our word-specific neural signals have no meaning to them. They communicate telepathically through feelings and senses."

"That's your hypothesis," Wren spat. His brown hair fell into his eyes, and he swept it aside before continuing. "You don't know for a fact that they use feelings. They may have their own complex form of telepathic language."

"I do know for a fact. I lived with Hyboreans. When they communicate with each other, humans can sense their emotions. Our brains decipher those emotions based on our own individual experiences. Some people may interpret the communication as an imagined sound or a feeling. Ergo, Hyboreans communicate through sensory telepathy."

Kedric slapped his hand on the table to gain their attention. "Gentlemen, we're getting off topic. I don't care how the Hyboreans communicate with each other. I want to know how we implant our thoughts into their minds so they do as I command. What about teaching them our language first so they can understand imagined speech?"

Finn spoke up. "I'm afraid that won't work, my lord." Though the youngest member of the science team, his medical knowledge was far superior to anyone else in Pele.

"Why the hell not? They're advanced beings. Surely they have the brain power to learn English."

"Their cognition is impaired," Dunna answered. He turned his attention to Kedric. "My lord, the Hyboreans can move, eat, and maintain normal body functions due to the autonomic nervous system performing below the level of consciousness. However—and this is the whole point my colleague fails to acknowledge—the Hyboreans cannot learn or decode speech signals while their conscious is asleep."

Kedric scratched his stubble as he processed the scientist's information. "Let me get this straight. The Hyboreans' lack of cognitive function means we can't teach them language and thus can't use the computer to control them with synthetic telepathy."

"Correct, my lord."

"Dammit. Two chronic sleepwalking Hyboreans and an unusable watercraft does not a secret weapon make."

"Then I propose we focus all our efforts on *my* research." That would be the chief scientist's erection-stimulating research. Fantastic. "I need Wren and his team working for me. Not wasting their talents on Griffin's—"

"Griffin!" A flush of hot adrenaline set his heart pounding.

"Yes. Imagined speech was his—"

"Consider the imagined speech project canceled. Wren, your team will assist Dunna with electrical brain stimulation."

"But—"

"Do I make myself clear?"

Beneath that mop of hair, Wren glared at Dunna. "Yes, my lord."

"Keep researching, gentlemen. I don't care how long it takes. Find a way to control those animals' minds."

Chapter Three

Kedric stepped from the master bath with a towel around his waist and ambled to the stone ledge of his bedroom window four stories above the castle courtyard. Below, servants bustled about preparing for the banquet that would start when the sun set in an hour. Luna Major and Luna Minor peeked through the aurora tropicos.

If only the science team had better news. Controlling the Hyborean poachers had been his first real hope for waging war. Now it appeared the two creatures were useless, and he was back at the beginning.

Footsteps echoed in the hallway outside his door. Its unhurried pace and uneven cadence belonged to an older gentleman with a bum leg, Andrei. He'd been the previous king's chief manservant and refused to retire when Kedric was crowned. It's a good thing, too. Under Andrei's management, the castle ran as smooth as a new blade.

Andrei knocked twice while opening the door. "I apologize for the interruption, Lord Kedric. A woman arrived at the main gate seeking an audience with you."

"Refugee?"

"No. A shaman from the lowlands. She wishes to heal you."

"Heal me? I'm not sick."

He shrugged in apology. "That's what she told the gatekeeper."

"She alone?"

"Yes, my lord. She'd been detained at the gate while guards patrolled the perimeter. They've found no sign of any of her tribesmen. They brought her to the castle."

"Send her in."

"Yes, my lord." Andrei bowed and then left.

What a fortuitous circumstance. A shaman was a holy leader. That had to be worth a good ransom to the villagers. Perhaps he could exchange her for the rest of the lowland men. He donned only his breeches before the door opened again.

Andrei held it open for a soldier who carried in an unconscious woman draped over his arms. Her limbs dangled. Her limp head exposed the creamy skin of her neck. The ends of her long raven hair dragged across the floor as the soldier approached.

Red-purple bruises colored a swollen eye. Blood was smeared across her mouth and chin from a split lip. "What the hell happened?"

"She's been wounded, my lord," the soldier said.

"Wounded? She's been beaten. What could this little bitty pacifist possibly have done to warrant a gladiator's fist?"

"A guard claimed she'd grabbed hold of his hand and began working some magical voodoo. He retaliated. Apparently with a little more force than was necessary."

Magical voodoo? Ignorant asshole. "I want the name of the guard who struck this woman."

"It's Robarts, sir."

"Take him into custody until I question him." He'd deal with Robarts later. Right now he had to figure out what to do with the girl.

"Yes, my lord. Shall I bring her to the doctor on my way?" He indicated the girl with a head nod.

The soldier would have to cross the courtyard where the newcomers were beginning to gather for the celebration. It wouldn't do to have them see their pillar of peace—a young female, no less—injured and limp in the arms of a Highland warrior. That image would not endear him to the savages.

"No. Put her on my bed."

After the soldier obliged, Kedric dismissed both of the men. The door closed behind Andrei with a click.

Kedric moved to the bedside and stood over the woman. Girl actually. Maybe ten years younger than himself. The sound of fingernails scraping his stubbly chin filled the quiet room as he scrutinized her unconscious body.

If he was to ransom her to the savages, her wounds would be sure to anger them. A wounded spiritual leader might be enough to cause the villagers to retaliate. It didn't take much to turn peaceful men into warriors. He knew that firsthand.

No, if he were to give her back to her people, she must be uninjured and fully restored to health. No one could believe her story of being struck by a Highlander. He didn't need a civil war to break out before he started a revolutionary one.

There was only one way out of this mess.

He had to get rid of the evidence.

Dammit. There really was nothing else he could do. Only three others would question it. The guard who struck her, the soldier who'd carried her in, and Andrei.

He'd tackle that problem after he and his dagger dealt with this problem.

Kedric locked his bedchamber doors and drew the thick draperies over the windows. He glanced over his shoulder to be sure he was alone.

No one could witness this.

He retrieved his weapon from the unlit fireplace's mantel and withdrew the dagger from its sheath. Although the hilt's design and blade's weight felt comfortable in his right hand, it would never equal the Flesheater knife he had lost in the escape from HuBReC.

Back at the bed, the mattress sunk beneath his weight, and the girl's hip gravitated toward his. She didn't stir. She'd been knocked out pretty hard and was unlikely to rouse any time soon. Good. That would make this so much easier.

Another glance over his shoulder.

No one was there.

He exposed the underside of his left forearm and drew his blade across the soft flesh barely feeling a sting. A thin, red line materialized. He squeezed the skin around it, forcing out more before it coagulated. He wiped the blood onto his finger and then applied it to her black eye.

He made a second cut on his arm, squeezed more blood onto his finger, and worked that into her split lip.

It took six more incisions to produce a thick enough coating over her wounds. Within half an hour, the bruise around her eye would vanish and the split lip would mend. By the time she roused, she'd have no trace of swelling or pain.

And he'd have no trace of the eight slash marks on his arm.

Kedric yawned. He'd been awake for nearly forty-eight hours, traipsing back and forth through the jungle with captured villagers, spending the rest of the day personally overseeing them, plus the science team meeting. And now he'd cut himself to heal this girl.

Could he feel any more drained?

Though exhausted, he couldn't allow himself to fall asleep. If she woke up before healing completely, he'd have to prevent her from looking into the mirror. She'd scream at all the blood on her face, and that would cause unwanted attention from the castle guards and Andrei.

He had to keep watch over her, which wasn't a terrible thing. After all, he enjoyed the way her breasts rose and fell beneath the buckskin bikini top. It was damn hypnotic. He forced his closing eyes open.

While her breasts were perfect, the rest of her was too damn skinny. Her ribs were visible. They protruded through her dust-covered skin.

Just like Tess's had.

Strength drained from his heart. All that remained was the same sad, hollow feeling he always got whenever thoughts of his sister slipped past his guard. He'd been too exhausted to harden himself from the pain.

And the guilt.

He reminded himself it wasn't his fault. Not really. It was the damn Hyboreans. But that didn't stop the hurt. Or the vision of Tess's skin so pale, so sheer that her veins were visible. She'd always been frail. Weak. Always needed protection.

But now—

Dammit. He had to stop this line of thinking. So what if this little shaman girl was just as frail and weak as his sister. He was the warrior. He controlled his emotions. He could bury and guard his secrets from everyone.

Including himself.

A warlord had to keep his eye on the future. Not be reminded of the past whenever he saw a sickly young woman.

When this girl woke up, he'd make certain she ate a big meal. Then he'd send her to the shower to scrub the day's travels from her sun-darkened skin and wash the brambles from her tangled hair. He pictured her in the steamy water, her body naked and wet. A surge of energy pumped through him. Waking him. Thank goodness for that. He'd been on the verge of sleep again.

He'd give her proper clothes of the Highland clan. Savage women's eyes always lit up when they first laid eyes on the colorful silk skirts and tops. They also enjoyed adorning their bodies and hair with jewelry and beads and little tinkling bells around their ankles.

This young woman needed no adornments. What she needed was a little meat on her half-starved bones. If the lowlanders continued their primitive ways, they would all die of starvation and disease.

He'd hate to send her back to that fate.

Better to have her fall in love with the Highlands like everyone else did. Once she realized how much better the Highlands were, she could go back to each tribal village and convince the people to join his kingdom. This could be the break he needed. With a shaman on his side, he'd have no need to raid the villages.

Energized by the thought, he got off the bed and went to the master bath for a wet washcloth, soap, and a towel.

His wounds had healed. Hers were sure to have healed as well.

He returned and washed the blood from her face. The bruise was gone and the lip had mended. No one would believe a Highlander had hit her, except for the guard, the soldier, and Andrei. But the guard would believe she'd healed herself with voodoo, he'd assign the soldier to a lookout on the other side of the kingdom, and Andrei could use a couple of days' vacation.

Satisfied with his plan, he snapped off the lightstick on the bedside table and then lay down next to her on the king bed. A few minutes of rest would do him good. He needed to recharge before giving this evening's speech.

He breathed in her scent of fragrant rain forest and sweat that clung to her drab clothes. The shaman and her people were desperate for a better way of life, and he was desperate for manpower.

There was no way this plan would fail.

* * *

Myia opened her eyes. Everything was dark save for a crack of light that appeared to be coming from beneath a door. Where was she? What happened?

At the gate, she had touched a guard's hand. His aura had been so dingy, so murky, it practically cried out for healing. She'd entered his soul. He'd cursed. That was the last thing she remembered.

Had he hit her?

Though she felt no pain, he must have knocked her out hard. If not, she would've awakened on the ground with Highland soldiers looming over her. But her backside lay cradled on something soft.

A bed.

She'd been taken to a bed softer than any she had ever lain upon. A light blanket covered her. Deep, heavy breaths came from a body sleeping at her side. Heat radiated off of it. So did a faint glow of light. But the color of the person's aura wouldn't be visible until all her senses fully returned.

The body's very large silhouette was twice her size and smelled of soap and man.

She tamped down the urge to jump out of the bed and scream. That reaction would only wake him up, causing more uncertainty to this already-perplexing problem.

A true shaman must remain calm in the world. Emotions got in the way of correctly assessing situations.

Who was this man?

She blinked until her eyes focused. His aura light grew bright enough to see his long red hair.

Only one man in all of Pele had been described with hair the color of fire. Lord Kedric. The warlord king of the Highlanders.

When she'd set out to attain an audience with him, this wasn't a scenario she'd envisioned. Heat blazed through her veins like molten lava. Who would've suspected he'd sleep with her?

The barbarian.

Though he didn't appear barbaric now. A calm, blue aura enveloped him. Blue, thank the Spirits, was not the color of a satiated violator of women.

Her anger only slightly lessened.

How could this male sleep peacefully after storming into her village at dawn's first light and capturing her people? And why was she lying next to him?

Calming breaths, Myia. Calming breaths. She had to become tranquil…like this warrior was right now.

Hmm…

At the moment, Kedric wasn't a fierce warrior. He was vulnerable. Without his defenses, she would be able to connect to his spirit and enter his soul without a fight. It might be wrong of her to take advantage of him while sleeping, but hadn't he taken advantage of her village and her people while they were sleeping?

How could the tribe survive when the Highlanders kept attacking them and the neighboring villages? They captured hunters and fishermen, leaving women and children to go hungry. They took away her people and are doing who knows what to them.

Fire coursed through her again, and an intense desire to smack sense into the barbarian burned inside. But acting on that kind of passion had always caused her more trouble. How many times had her father said, *Anger is futile at best. At worst, counterproductive.*

If she were to become the full shaman she so desperately wanted to be, she had to remain at peace with the world.

More deep breaths of the sweet night air relaxed her enough to calm the anger inside. She had come here to heal the Highlanders. This moment was the perfect opportunity to do that.

Quietly, gently, she slipped her fingers into Kedric's large, callused hand and concentrated on going deep inside herself to the place of tranquillity. The place where her spirit could mingle with other Spirits. To be one with the world around her.

With the power of the surrounding Spirits, she channeled her energy into Kedric's body.

It was time to take a deep look into his soul.

And repair it.

"Thank you for your trust," her spirit said in good faith.

On the surface layer, he was a strong man with many responsibilities. He was the leader of his people. He ruled with power and conviction. He provided for his people. Typical of any leader, but she needed to go deeper to see what was in his heart. Even as he slept, there were thick layers like rock walls hiding his true essence. He must have spent many years building these walls, which meant he was covering a great pain. A deep hurt. Possibly guilt. Possibly—

Strong fingers tightened around hers. Her spirit ripped away from the stone wall and was purged from his body with abrupt force.

He rolled atop her, his weight pinning her to the bed. He captured her other hand with his. No amount of pulling or struggling would free her hand from his paws. His grip only tightened. Though there wasn't enough light to make out the color of his eyes, there was no mistaking the anger smoldering in them. Her heart raced. Pinned beneath his full weight, she had no leverage to move her body or legs.

There was no point in struggling. She couldn't move—well, except for the involuntary shaking.

Angry red streaks snaked through his aura. "What manner of trickery is this?"

"Get off of me, barbarian." Name-calling? Really? Had her father taught her nothing?

"Barbarian? That's funny coming from a savage."

She gasped. "Savage? You're the one on top of me."

"As I recall, I wouldn't be on top of you if I hadn't needed to protect myself from your tricks."

"I am a spiritual healer. I only wanted to repair your soul. You must release my people."

"They're free to go at any time. They choose to stay."

His weight was crushing her, making breathing difficult, but she refused to let him see her discomfort. If she could calm herself enough, her spirit could reenter his, and she could try healing him again. This might be the only chance she got before he…What would he do to her?

She didn't sense anything evil, vile, or malicious. Murder wasn't present in his aura. The only thing she perceived was arousal. Typical male. Perhaps she could use that to her advantage.

There were three occasions when a person's spirit was the most vulnerable: during sleep, during illness, and during sex—so she'd been told.

"You've invaded our peaceful village and took our people against their will. Forgive me for not believing you." Her words were angrier than she wanted them to be. What happened to her shamanic training?

"Seems we have a lot in common, you and I."

"We have nothing in common, barbarian."

"Did you not invade my body against my will?"

"To heal your spirit."

"So you say, savage."

Would he stop calling her that? She was not a fierce, violent person. She was tranquil and at peace with the universe, dammit.

Well, at least she strove for peace.

"However," he continued, "you needn't concern yourself. My spirit requires no healing."

"So say you. But our spirits have met, and yours told me it hid a deep wound. Let me back in. Let me into your body to heal you."

His smirk surprised her. What could he possibly find so humorous?

"If anyone enters another's body, it will be me." His warm lips pressed against hers. As if to prove his point, his tongue coaxed hers to open for him.

She'd been kissed before, but not from a man so dangerous and commanding, or so good at it.

Well, she wasn't about to waste the opportunity to do what she came here for, especially since nothing in his aura indicated malicious intent. His spirit simply sought to demonstrate his male dominance in a kiss. Nothing more. Ha. He'd learn who the dominant one was when she connected with his spirit again.

She opened her mouth and kissed him back. His pause indicated surprise. He'd obviously expected her to resist. When she didn't let up, his jaw relaxed and his kiss deepened. She couldn't deny the freedom her soul felt.

But she'd come to heal his heart, and as much as she would like to give in to the pleasure she was receiving, she needed to heal him first.

Again retreating to that tranquil place in her mind, her spirit gathered energy and flowed from her body into his. Her spirit didn't get further than the impenetrable stone wall before it was thrown from his body again.

His lips were off hers, the weight of his body disappeared. The influx of warm night air came as a relief.

"Savage," he boomed. "Stay out of my body."

"If you enter my body, barbarian, rest assured I *will* enter yours."

Chapter Four

She'd invaded his body. That skinny little lowland savage lying helplessly in his bed just entered his body as easily as if she'd entered a room. How was that possible?

There was no such thing as voodoo or magic as the guard had claimed. Everything had a logical explanation. A scientific explanation.

It could very well be hypnosis. Or a mind control trick. Or perhaps her ability came from being a gen-alt. A genetically altered human.

Like him.

No matter how she slipped inside his mind, one thing was for certain. She would not be doing it again. No wonder why his guard had lost control and struck her.

His stomach turned. As much as her ability freaked him out, he would never hit the weaker sex. Though there was nothing weak about a girl who made an alpha gladiator—the Highland warlord, no less—jump out of his own bed as if he'd been attacked by a saber-toothed smilodon.

He took the lightstick from the bedside table, snapped it on, and scrutinized her as she sat up, eyes rapidly blinking against the bright light. He twisted the base to dim it to a comfortable intensity.

Her eyes—free of swelling or redness—grew wide with awe and curiosity, obviously seeing artificial light for the first time. Like an eager child, she took the lightstick into her hands and played with it. The light dimmed and brightened. It snapped on, off, on, off.

The strobe effect gave him a headache. "It's a lightstick," he said, a sense of power surging through him once more. She might be a genetically altered shamanic leader among her people, but here in his Highland domain, she was an ignorant savage and he was king.

The beam found his eyes, blinding him. "Cut it out."

"What a clever invention," she said with laughter in her voice. She'd blinded him on purpose. He grabbed the lightstick away from her. "State your name and business, savage."

"My name is Myia. I'm a shaman-aprendi in the lowland village you attacked today. I'm here to heal your soul."

Remembering her invasion into his soul, he almost took a step back, but he was a gladiator warlord so he took a step forward instead. He glared down at her with a menacing scowl meant to frighten her. "I told you, I don't need healing."

She looked so small and frail sitting there in his oversized bed, but she didn't appear afraid. She didn't recoil as he'd hoped. She seemed very calm.

Damn, that pissed him off.

"Of course you need healing." Her voice sounded so sweet, so innocent, so matter-of-fact. "And once you are healed, you will let my people go."

He had to laugh. This girl was too young and too naive to understand to whom she dared speak. Though, he must admit, he enjoyed her honesty. He'd had so little of that in his life. "I will?"

"Yes. Because I'm not leaving until you've been healed and all of my brethren join me on the walk home."

"Perfect. You've made my job easier. You see, I'm not allowing you to leave until you become a Highland brethren and join my army." Now it was her turn to laugh. It was a sweet sound. An honest sound. A giggle. "Do I amuse you, savage?"

She had the nerve to nod her head. "Yes. I am a shaman-aprendi. A pacifist. You must know that I most certainly will not join your army."

"You needn't take up arms for my cause. You will simply live here in luxury a few days and come to realize that the Highland way of life is the best way of life. Then you will make a trip back to the villages and convince the lowlanders to come here, too."

Anger flashed in her eyes. Her expression changed from amusement to displeasure too quickly for someone who claimed to be a pacifist. She threw back the sheet and got out of bed. "I will never encourage my people to abandon their happy homes and peaceful lives to become warmongers."

"Is that what you think we are?"

"Yes. Your nation is spiritually corrupt."

"You say this knowing that some of the people here were once villagers like yourself?"

"You've enticed them with your riches and reconditioned their beliefs."

"I don't tell them what to believe. They can figure out for themselves that running water is better than carrying buckets from a stream, that medicine is better than herbal remedies, and that a kingdom with waste disposal is better than hiking into the jungle to crap in a hole."

"You take away their freedom and make them fight."

"They fight for freedom. For all mankind."

Her eyes squinted in confusion. "I don't understand."

"You will, savage. In time. But first let's get you fed and cleaned up." He retrieved a large silver circle from atop a chest of drawers and set it on his head. He placed the wire hanging from the ring into his ear. "Andrei," he spoke to no one. "I need food brought up to my room. A little of everything from tonight's feast. Some clothes for the shaman. And some adornments, perhaps something for her hair."

Who was he talking to? No one else was in the room with them.

Kedric removed the ring from around his head and tossed it back where he'd found it before turning a satisfied look on her.

"You may keep your riches, barbarian. They won't seduce me."

* * *

Bare chested, he sauntered toward her with a bold confidence and self-assurance she'd never witnessed from any man. His raw power set his aura aflame. Intensity and danger smoldered in his eyes, sparking something deep inside her most private place.

"Oh, you'll be seduced all right. Sooner or later everyone is."

Had he meant seduced by the Highlands or seduced by him? Heat spread through her body and radiated into her aura.

She could barely breathe.

He came within arm's reach, but no closer. Their auras mingled. Sparks of electricity flashed through her like lightning through the Spirit Lights. She alone would be able to feel the sizzling heat passing between them.

She should stop reading their auras. But the intensity of this connection was like nothing she'd ever had the pleasure of experiencing.

And she didn't want it to end.

Selfish desire was dangerous. It made a person lose focus. It disengaged them from the spiritual world. Heck, it disengaged them from the physical world.

How had she so easily fallen into that trap? If Kedric touched her right now, she'd be at his mercy. Her ability to enter into his soul and heal it was gone. Her throat dried.

How could this man affect her so?

"Do I make you nervous, savage?" His smug expression irritated her. He knew he ruffled her, and it obviously pleased him. The arrogant— She was not about to use profanity. He wasn't worth it.

Besides she hadn't been the only one ruffled this evening. The warlord had nearly jumped out of his skin twice tonight. She might not be in the right state of mind to commune with his spirit, but he didn't know that.

She straightened her spine and stepped into his personal space, deeper into his aura, and reached for his hand.

Kedric's abrupt about-face startled her. "Come." Anger stained the word so unlike the cocky arrogance from a moment ago. Like a man on a mission, he strode across the room, opened a door, and snapped on a lightstick. "You will use the master bathroom. I'll send someone up to show you how the shower works and help you dress. Food will be brought up. You will remain in my room and wait for my return."

He was leaving? Now? But she hadn't done what she came here for. "Where are you going?"

He returned to the bedside table to retrieve a sheathed bladed weapon and then tucked it into his waistband. "To a banquet welcoming our new arrivals."

If she went to the banquet, she could begin healing her tribesmen's fears. Excited by the idea, she followed him to the bedchamber's door. "I'm a new arrival."

He turned on her so quickly she recoiled. "You're not invited." He exited, slamming the solid oak door behind.

It was not going to be an easy task healing the warlord's heart.

At least she was stuck in his bedchamber and not in his dungeon. Perhaps this time alone was what she needed to regroup. She could commune with the Spirits tonight and regain her control and her vision.

For now she'd check out her surroundings. She pushed back the heavy drapery from a stone window that was taller than she was. Luna Major and Minor hung in the sky, and the Spirit Lights had settled from their earlier distress into harmonious movement, as if dancing to the music from below.

There were only three visible sentries standing watch on the gold-and-russet castle walls, which enclosed an astounding area the size of her entire village. The courtyard housed lush gardens, white stone carvings that miraculously shot arcs of water into man-made pools, and trees with little white lights that appeared to twinkle every time a gentle breeze tickled their leaves. Miniature lightsticks perhaps?

Five lengthy banquet tables that must have been able to seat a hundred people each were spread over a great lawn. Covered dishes filled the tables from end to end, awaiting the guests to be called to banquet. The scent of roasted meats and other savory foods she didn't recognize wafted up to her, making her stomach growl.

Hopefully she wouldn't have to wait too long for dinner. For some reason she felt hungrier than ever before.

Must have been the day's hike to get here.

Men and women twirled in front of musicians in a blur of vivid colors she'd never seen outside of nature. Couples strolled arm in arm along the cobblestone paths. Children raced around, laughing and throwing balls back and forth. She recognized some in the crowd from her village. They wore no shackles nor chains, only radiant Highland silks and smiles befitting a celebration.

The splendor of it all was beautiful. Alluring.

A contrivance of temptation meant to seduce her people.

The bedchamber door opened as someone tapped on it. "Hello, miss." A woman in her early twenties bounded into the room, her curly brown hair bounced around her square-shaped face. A pile of sheer, rose-colored veils peeked from the top of the wicker basket she carried.

Myia nodded in greeting.

"May I present myself? I'm Naomi, castle dressmaker." She bowed. Naomi placed the basket on the bed and emptied it of clothing, bottles, and hair combs before buzzing around the room, opening and closing drawers, gathering shirts and vestments, which she refilled the basket with. "I've never met a shaman before, miss."

"Please, call me Myia. And to tell you the truth, I'm merely a shaman-aprendi. I have yet to take my vision quest."

"Don't sell yourself short, my dear." She picked out some shoes from a closet and then carried everything to the door. "You must have some powerful magic to have riled up Lord Kedric so. He about left for the celebration naked." She opened the door and handed the basket to a man waiting outside.

Myia would have smirked, but the fact was she'd been so riled by Kedric she had forgotten he'd been wearing only pants when he left.

"I brought you soaps and perfumes and everything you could possibly need for a makeover. Let me see your fingernails."

She moved to where Naomi stood and offered her hand. Naomi's soft fingers turned her callused hand over and back as she examined them. Myia had never given much thought to her fingernails before, but as she observed the short, chipped, and dirty nails when contrasted against Naomi's long, clean, and painted ones, heat crept up her neck.

Naomi tsked. "Well, no worries. We'll get you cleaned up and made over in no time. If Lord Kedric was riled before, wait until he sees you tonight." She winked.

Myia couldn't help but like this woman. She didn't need to read her aura to know she possessed honesty, genuineness, and a heap of sass.

Two knocks came at the door as two men entered with trays of food, which they placed at an empty round table. Was this where Kedric and his family shared their meal? After they set up the table, they left. Surely they would come back and share this food with Naomi and her. But Naomi insisted all this food had been brought for Myia alone. If she had a week to finish it, she'd never be able to eat it all. There was enough to feed her entire village. Literally. Hopefully it wouldn't go to waste.

After her delicious meal, Myia stood in the bathroom astonished that water as warm as the island's hot springs poured from a spout on the wall. Another ingenious invention, though she wasn't sure she felt as clean scrubbing in the waterfall as she did scrubbing in the hot springs. After washing her hair, she made sure she washed again with the conditioner Naomi had instructed her to use. She said it would remove the tangles and make her hair shiny and easy to comb.

Though skeptical, she decided to give it a try. The humidity tended to frizz her hair, and anything that might help was worth trying.

When she finished and dried off, she slipped into a soft, white robe that must have been Kedric's since it hung to her ankles and nearly wrapped around her twice. It reminded her of being a little girl playing dress up in her father's ceremonial robe.

An ache stabbed her heart at the thought of her father. She hoped Kimi wasn't having trouble caring for his leg. An infection at his age would be very dangerous.

Maybe she should return home tomorrow and check on him.

No, that would undermine her sister. At nearly fifteen years old, Kimi was almost a woman. She did well with herbal remedies and didn't need her big sister checking in on her. Besides Myia had promised not to return until she healed the warlord's heart and he freed her people.

Though if her people were given bathrooms with hot showers and, what was that word, oh yes, *toilets*—which, at the push of a button, disintegrated the waste put into it—she could understand the difficulty in giving that up. They were very convenient innovations, indeed.

She left the master bathroom, as Kedric had called it, to find a little table set up in his bedchamber. A small bowl of water, bottles of lotions and little paints, and some other tools sat atop it. Another bowl of warm water rested on the floor by an empty chair.

"Have a seat." Naomi indicated the chair opposite her. Put your feet in there and let me have your hands. I'm going to do your nails. Pick a color."

Myia looked down at her fingernails still chipped but scrubbed clean. "If you don't mind, I like the color they are."

The disappointment was evident in Naomi's sigh. "Okay. I'll give you a clear coat, then. Maybe next time, you can try a color."

As the night went on, Naomi clipped and shaped and painted her nails, gave her fragrant lotions to smear all over her body, and plucked her eyebrows.

"Is all this really necessary?" She wanted to enjoy the laughter and music outside. Maybe even twirl across the floor a time or two. This makeover was ridiculously painful.

"Trust me. As soon as Kedric takes one look at you, he will be at your mercy."

At her mercy was good. Repairing his soul would take time enough; she'd rather not waste another minute with his resistance, too.

Naomi helped dress her in the sheer silk veils the women in the courtyard wore. The three shades of rose silk were beautiful. Much too delicate for the labor the village women did. Her buckskin top and skirt were more practical.

From a band that fit low and snug around her hips, the rose veils hung to midcalf length. Two thin, bejeweled chain belts hung scallop-like around her hips. Her thighs peeked through slits in the veils as she walked.

Braided silk covered her breasts in a halter bikini style like she'd worn many times in the village, only village clothing had never been made of such feminine material. More thin, bejeweled chains fringed the bottom of the halter top. When she moved, they swayed against her ribs, tickling her. She had to admit that the outfits worn by the Highland women were very pretty and feminine.

If there was one thing she would like to bring back to her village, it was this lightweight clothing that swayed around her body as she walked, creating a wisp of breeze, rather than the drab colors and fibrous hemp of the clothing the lowlanders wore.

Dear Spirits, what was she saying?

Could it have been that simple to be seduced?

Chapter Five

After four hours mingling with and winning over his new countrymen, Kedric bid Andrei good night and climbed the steps to his room. He'd gotten a second wind for the celebration, but now exhaustion from the past few days had caught up with him.

Though most people had turned in for the evening, some were still out there partying and would most likely greet the dawn.

Nothing interested him more than falling into his bed and sleeping until midday tomorrow.

He entered his room to find the shaman girl sitting on the window ledge, her profile to him. Her long, silky black hair had been braided and adorned with pearls. She glanced at him. Her beautiful sun-darkened face glowed. Her eyes held a dreamy gaze.

His breath caught.

By the time he closed the door and turned back to her, she was off the ledge and gliding toward him. Her swaying hips sent the skirt of veils swishing side to side. Her bare legs and thighs peeked out from the sheer material as she moved.

This was not the same savage girl he'd left hours ago. This was a Highland woman.

A very sexy Highland woman. With painted red lips that he desired to taste as he'd done earlier.

It would be no effort to cross the room, take her into his arms, and kiss her again. Why shouldn't he? He ruled this kingdom and she was his prisoner.

Her tongue darted out and moistened her lips.

The temptress.

She knew exactly what she was doing sauntering up to him looking sexy as hell.

If he were to prevent her from invading his body, he didn't dare touch her.

In fact, he wasn't going to give her the satisfaction of a compliment on her appearance.

"You enjoy the celebration, savage?" He sidestepped her, but not before seeing the flash of anger in her eyes. Apparently, she didn't like being called a savage. Good. He headed for the closet and shrugged out of his king's robe.

Behind him he heard her intake of three slow, deep breaths.

"The food was delicious. Thank you." There was no hostility in her voice. In fact, she sounded genuinely grateful, which made him feel like an ass. He hung up his robe. "And the music was wonderful. Music is a big part of my culture, but I've never heard instruments like yours. And the dancing—" Enthusiasm filled her words, and by the light rustling sound behind him, he knew she had spun around in a circle. "Oh, the dancing was marvelous. I wish I could have experienced it all from the courtyard."

He sat on the cushioned stool near the closet, pulled off his boots, and peeled off his socks. "You weren't dressed for the courtyard."

"I am now."

He turned his head to catch a glimpse of her in her party dress. Her cheeks were aglow with joy. Eagerness filled her eyes. "You want to go to the celebration." It wasn't a question. The answer was evident by her body language.

"Very much so."

This was excellent. His plan was working already. She wanted to join his people in the festivities. Ironically, they were celebrating the very thing she claimed to have come to the Highlands to undo. He thought winning her over to the Highland way would have taken longer, but within four hours, she was already hooked.

He'd have his army in no time.

"Okay, then. You may join the party. I'll call Andrei to escort you down."

"You mean you won't take me?" Why did the disappointment in her big golden eyes leave him cold? It should have boosted his ego. Instead, he wanted to reach out and comfort her.

It must be the alcohol.

And exhaustion.

His defenses would be back after a good night's sleep. Right now he needed her out of his room and out of his sight.

"I was hoping I could dance with you. You seem to be quite good at it."

Had she been jealous watching him twirl the ladies around the dance floor?

"I saw the delight you brought to one young lady in particular." Her eyes shone with tenderness. And was that admiration? He didn't deserve admiration. "The others ignored her, but you didn't. You took the time to make her night special."

She was referring to Milly. His twelve-year-old buddy. Sweet kid. Very friendly. But unfortunately was often left out and teased due to her genetic deformity.

It wasn't something his blood could fix.

He'd tried.

He shrugged off her praise. "It was just a dance or two."

Her eyes glistened as if holding back tears. He didn't deserve the warmth radiating from her smile. "It was so much more than that. Your kindness brought joy to an aching spirit. I have hope for you."

His fingers itched to trace her cheek. And he would have, too, if she didn't use the opportunity to enter his soul. She'd claimed to want to heal him, but for all he knew she wanted to plant some mind control thoughts into his head. Until he knew for certain what her true intentions were, he would not touch the vixen.

"It was just a dance," he said again and then peeled off his tunic and tossed it on the stool. "When you've finished in the courtyard, Andrei will show you to your room."

"But I thought—"

"That you'd stay in here with me?" He stripped off his pants right down to his underwear. "I'm flattered, but no."

"You barbarian. I most certainly didn't expect to share your room. I merely thought you wouldn't want me out of your sight. You know, for fear that I might heal the aggression in your people's hearts."

He couldn't help but laugh. Her honest spunk was like nothing he'd ever before experienced from a woman. Savage Myia would not back down nor be intimidated by the nearly naked Highland warlord.

Sure, nudity was commonplace among the peoples of Pele, but usually when he removed his pants in front of a woman, it elicited some sort of reaction. A gasp. A blush. A glance of approval. Something. Undressing in front of this woman hadn't that desired effect.

Damn, she irritated him.

After a quick tech-ring call to Andrei, it wasn't long before two abrupt knocks came at the door as it opened. Andrei entered and his eyes lit up at the sight of Myia. A broad grin spread across his face. "You look stunning, miss. It is my pleasure to escort you to the courtyard."

Andrei—who had spoken of his exhaustion only minutes ago when they'd ascended the castle steps together—perked up as if someone shoved ice down his shirt back. Kedric's jaw clenched. Maybe he should get dressed and take her to the celebration himself.

Andrei squinted as he inspected Myia's lip and eye. "Your face, miss. It has—"

"Makeup," Kedric interjected before Andrei could finish his sentence. How had he forgotten he was to keep his manservant from Myia? Where was his head today? "Wonderful stuff. Can hide any fault or discoloration."

The horrified expression on Myia's face pained him like a kick in the balls. She'd no idea he was talking about the black eye and split lip he had healed.

Andrei's expression changed to one of sympathy. He held out his hand to the shaman. "Are you ready, my dear?"

Her posture straightened, and with head held high, she placed her hand in Andrei's and nodded. For the first time since she woke up from his bed, Myia remained silent.

Heat crept up Kedric's neck and face.

He felt like the king of crap.

* * *

As Andrei escorted her out of the barbarian's bedchamber, Myia couldn't help but think of those last hurtful words.

He'd wanted her to become a Highlander, yet when Naomi physically transformed her into a beautiful Highland lady, he barely noticed. He never said a word about her appearance. Except that makeup could cover her faults.

"Are you okay, miss?"

"Please, call me Myia."

"Don't fret. You look beautiful regardless."

Regardless of what? Kedric's callous words or her homeliness?

She had to snap out of this. She wasn't here for more than a day, and already she'd lost her spiritual way. She'd known better than falling victim to pride and vanity. Those two emotions walked hand in hand with dejection and poor self-esteem. How many times had she healed the same hurt in others?

Her own soul needed repair now.

As she descended the steps in a steady, quiet rhythm of moccasins on stone, she inhaled three deep cleansing breaths. She turned inward to her spiritual place. In her mind's eye, she saw herself in her buckskin clothes back in her village where she belonged.

"Your body is nothing more than a temporary home for your spirit," her image said. "Body does not define you. Spirit does. Keep your body clean and healthy to protect your spiritual dwelling. If caring for the dwelling becomes more important than caring for what dwells within, balance is lost and disharmony results. Return to balance."

She'd been a fool to expect Kedric to be at her mercy because of her appearance. It didn't matter what she dressed in, she would heal his heart because of her spirit, not her body.

By the time Myia entered the courtyard, peace had entered into her heart. A sure sign that balance had been restored.

The courtyard was amazing—the colors, the smells, the sounds. Oh, to be walking beneath the twinkling tree lights. To feel the energy of the people who were still dancing and milling about. She smiled at the other guests she passed.

Andrei brought her to a table with sweets. "Would you care for some dessert, miss?"

"I'd love some. And please call me Myia."

He handed her a beautiful plate made from some kind of white clay, which she piled high with many unusual treats. Everything here was so unique, so different from the bamboo plates and bowls she was used to.

It didn't make them better or worse. Just different.

This proved her balance had returned. The things around her weren't good or evil. They simply were.

After tasting these delicious-looking pastries, she'd dance to the Highland music. It wasn't better than lowland music and it wasn't worse. It just was.

Andrei sat on a pillow at one of the long knee-high tables and yawned.

"There's no need to stay at the party with me," she said. "You should go home and rest. I'll be fine."

"I can't, miss. Lord Kedric entrusted me to watch over you." He covered another yawn. "Go ahead and dance. I'll be right over here."

He'd be asleep in less than five minutes, which was just as well. She could enjoy the party, and he'd get the rest his body desperately needed.

On the dance floor, Myia twirled a few times to the music. She moved her hips and arms and let herself feel the lively beat.

"Excuse me," a deep male voice said behind her.

She turned to face a handsome young man no more than a few years older than her. He looked dashing in his black trousers and red silk shirt. He was a few inches shy of six feet and thin. His brown hair was short on the sides and longer on top with little spikes going this way and that. It appeared messy yet neat at the same time and didn't move in the warm breeze.

"I haven't seen you in the Highlands before," he said.

"I just got here."

"The Highlands must be so overwhelming and frightening to you."

"Not at all. I find it very exciting."

"I'm relieved to hear that." The genuineness in his grin spread all the way to his dark brown eyes. "May I present myself? Name's Griffin." He bowed.

"Myia, shaman-aprendi." She returned the bow.

"Would you care to dance, Myia?"

"I've been watching, but I'm not sure I know how."

"I'll teach you."

Before she could reply, his large, warm hand pressed against the bare flesh of her lower back. He held up his other hand waiting for hers. When she placed her hand in his, he stepped to the side and led her through one of the dances she'd watched Kedric perform earlier.

Before she knew it, she was twirling and laughing and finding her rhythm. After a few turns around the dance floor, another gentleman cut in and whisked her off for another turn.

She had no clue how long or with how many men she'd danced, but she was out of breath and asked for a drink. Her first partner, Griffin, obliged and escorted her to a table with alcohol.

"I'm a shaman-aprendi. These aren't the spirits I engage in." She giggled. Alone. Why did no one ever get her sense of humor?

Griffin led her to another table with a large bowl almost the size of a cauldron filled with red liquid. "Would you like some punch? There's no alcohol."

When she nodded, he ladled some into a glass goblet and then handed it to her.

The goblet was absolutely beautiful and much heavier than any glass she'd held before. She lifted it up to the lightsticks twinkling in the trees. The cut patterns in the glass caught the light, and colorful rainbows glinted off it.

He chuckled. It was a pleasant sound and not at all unfriendly. "It's crystal. The man who makes these is a master craftsman. You should see his other work in the marketplace sometime." He clearly enjoyed teaching her about this strange and wonderful new place, and she appreciated his patience. She also appreciated the fact that he made no mention of the countless times she'd stepped on his toes while dancing. Either he was a gentleman or he hadn't felt her moccasins on his hard shoes. She'd go with gentleman.

"It's beautiful," she said of the crystal goblet.

"Not compared to you, Myia."

Her cheeks warmed and she was sure they turned as red as the silk shirt he wore. No man had ever called her beautiful like that. It wasn't the word so much as the way he spoke it; soft and tender as if he'd reserved it for her alone.

Though she accepted the compliment, this wasn't the Highlander she wished had given it to her.

The punch was sweet and cold and possibly the most delicious thing she'd ever tasted. Well, next to the chocolate Andrei had introduced her to. Glancing past Griffin, she spotted Andrei across the courtyard, where she'd left him an hour ago. He was sound asleep with his head on folded arms on the table. People moved about him, but no one bothered him.

"I'm glad you joined the party, Myia. When I saw you sitting in the castle window earlier, I feared Kedric had locked you away. I trust he's treating you well?" Griffin's aura darkened, indicating ill feelings.

Apparently eliciting ill feelings in people was something Kedric excelled at. She should help Griffin find peace. "How about a stroll through the courtyard? I'd like you to tell me a little more about yourself and how you came to the Highlands."

When he crooked his arm toward her and held an expectant expression on his face, she shook her head. "I'm sorry, Griffin. I'm not sure what—"

Before she could finish, he tucked her arm through his. "This is how Highlanders stroll."

She liked strolling, only again found herself wishing it were with a different man entirely.

Chapter Six

Kedric couldn't sleep. He'd tossed. He'd turned. He'd kept storming to the windows. How dare that savage dance with all those men? She was a shaman, not a castle wench. Men had lined up waiting for their turn with her. Had she any clue what her body did to them every time she moved? She'd teased them. Aroused them.

Aroused *him*.

He hadn't been able to stop watching. Even when he moved from the window, the image of her in the arms of all those men was seared into his mind. He'd thought about going down there and dragging her away from the party.

But he'd wanted this. He'd wanted her to be seduced by the Highlands. What better way than by this celebration?

It wasn't the celebration. It was the company.

Didn't she know what kind of men stayed out partying through the night? Rowdy, horny drunkards. That's who.

And manipulative bastards, like Griffin, who were trying to steal his throne.

He'd wanted her to have a great time here. He'd wanted her to see the Highlands as her new home. Yet here she was having a great time and he was miserable. Why the hell did it bother him so much?

Naked, he rolled out of bed and stormed to the window again. There were less than twenty people in the courtyard now. Myia wasn't among them.

She wasn't on the dance floor. Or by any of the food tables. Had she turned in for the evening? Wait. Was that Andrei asleep at a banquet table? He was supposed to keep an eye on her. Where was she?

He saw them in the shadows, sitting at the edge of a fountain, their hands intertwined, their foreheads touching so intimately.

Myia and Griffin.

Kedric charged out the door.

* * *

Myia's spirit entered into Griffin's body, and in the darkness she conjured her fantasy image. People could relax and better open up if they could view her like they could in a dream. A diaphanous image materialized next to her. "Thank you for your trust, Griffin."

His fantasy image nodded, took hers by the arm, and together they strolled through a dark corridor in his soul. The two of them came upon a large solid door.

"You keep your pain locked behind this door," her fantasy image said to his. She'd seen this before. Everyone had some kind of barrier. A locked door was a very common symbol.

"I can trust you with this, can't I, Myia?"

"Of course. I want to heal your pain. I will keep your secrets."

"But who heals your pain? Who keeps your secrets?"

"You're trying to distract us from what's behind this door. I'm here to heal *your* pain. Open it to me, Griffin. You needn't fear me."

His fantasy image's eyes narrowed. He considered her for a moment before giving a reluctant nod.

She had his trust now.

He pressed a shoulder against the heavy wood door and shoved. Slowly it opened.

Like lightning through the sky, her spirit ripped through his body. His forehead was off hers. His hand yanked painfully out of her grasp. The connection was shattered.

She opened her eyes and was greeted by a man's naked groin. She gasped. "Kedric?"

He'd pulled Griffin by his throat to his feet. "Keep your hands off what doesn't belong to you."

"I didn't know she was yours," he wheezed.

"Taur-shit." Kedric punched Griffin, who stumbled backward into the fountain. The splash soaked Myia.

She didn't have time to offer Griffin assistance before Kedric lifted her over his shoulder and carried her back to the castle.

"You barbarian. What on Hyborea do you think you're doing?"

"Protecting you." He took the stone steps two at a time, which might have been impressive if she weren't dangling upside down, blood rushing to her head, and scared her skull would crack open if dropped.

Inside, Kedric opened one of the doors she'd passed after leaving his bedchamber. It was a much smaller room than his, though still larger than her village hut. He dumped her off his shoulder and onto a soft bed. She untangled her limbs and veils, and righted herself.

Kedric stood there watching her with arms crossed over his chest and anger in his eyes. At least she assumed anger was in his eyes. She couldn't meet his gaze while gawking at his male parts. She swallowed.

"What in Spirits' name were you doing with that bastard Griffin?"

"I was starting to heal him until you—"

"He wasn't looking to be healed. He was looking at your breasts. You, my dear, are too innocent to understand the desires of men."

"I understand men's desires. I am eighteen after all."

"You understand nothing."

"I understand you're not angry with me." That quieted him down. He stood there shamelessly naked, looking mighty fine in all his muscular glory. Well, he looked mighty fine minus the scowl. "What's bothering you, Kedric? Let me heal you."

"Nothing is bothering me."

"Really? So, is it customary for a Highland warlord to storm into the courtyard naked, hit a man, and then carry off a woman over his shoulder?"

"You'd be surprised how often that happens."

Public nudity may be prevalent in her culture and his, but in this particular case she doubted his words.

She got off the bed and reached for a hand still folded over his chest. "You're so on edge. Let me help you find balance. Please."

His head snapped up like he'd just thought of something important. "What was in Griffin's soul?"

"What?"

"What did you see in Griffin's soul? What *healing* did he require?" He said the word with contempt, making her bristle.

"That is between him and me."

"And now me. Tell me what you saw."

"It's not my place to reveal the secrets of those I help. Of course, I really didn't have a chance to heal him, did I?"

"Infuriating woman."

Again, she reached for his hand, but he stormed out of the room.

On the other side of the closed door, something turned and clicked into place. She didn't need to check the doorknob to know she'd been locked inside.

* * *

"Rise and shine, sleepyhead." Naomi's voice roused Myia from her dream. A wonderful dream in which she and Kedric danced beneath the Spirit Lights.

It had felt so real, like it could have been a true vision. She'd smelled the honeysuckle in the gardens. She'd felt the muscle of Kedric's shoulder beneath her palm as they swayed in time to the slow music. His body, warm and solid, pressed against hers. His mouth slowly drew closer and closer to her lips. She'd closed her eyes preparing for the kiss that was unfortunately interrupted by Naomi.

"You woke me five seconds too early. On second thought, maybe ten." Her cheeks warmed. She sat up and stretched her arms as Naomi set two plates on a round table filled with breakfast foods.

"Hmm. You must have had a nice dream. Anyone special? Lord Kedric perhaps?"

This probably wasn't a good topic of conversation to have with one of the castle workers. She climbed out of bed and headed for the bathroom.

"Your silence incriminates you, Myia," she said loud enough to be heard through the door. "I hope he was tender in your dreams. Rumor has it he was fierce last night. I heard he grabbed you out of the arms of another man. Slugged him good before carrying you off to his bedchamber to ravish you. I heard he made you come harder than the Peletian rains."

Her gasp had Naomi chuckling on the other side of the door.

"Okay, so maybe I started the last rumor. But what did you expect me to believe?"

Myia exited the bathroom. "As you can plainly see by the fact that he locked me in this windowless room rather than taking me to his, Lord Kedric most certainly did not ravish me."

"No." Naomi's aura glowed with mischief. "I can plainly see Lord Kedric didn't ravish you by the disappointment on your face."

Naomi was incorrigible. Myia knelt on a floor pillow at the breakfast table. "You set two plates. Will you be joining me for breakfast, then?"

"Don't change the subject. You want that hunky gladiator. Admit it."

"I want to *heal* him. So he stops capturing my people. But how can I heal him when he won't even touch me?" She buttered a pastry roll a little too hard, and pieces flaked off onto her plate.

"He touched you last night. Carried you right over his shoulder."

Myia glanced at her out of the corners of her eyes. "Were you there? You seem to know everything that happened."

"The castle help has been gossiping about it all morning. I heard every last juicy detail right down to the shape of Lord Kedric's familial birthmark on the crease of his thigh. Or," she spoke more to herself, "would that tender spot be considered the hip? Whatever it is, it's beyond me why anyone would look at his birthmark when they could have been ogling the king's jewels."

"Naomi, please."

"Sorry." She snickered and cut a piece of cheese for her cracker.

An uneasy feeling crept into Myia's stomach. Gossip could be hurtful. Gossip about one's leader could be damaging. If he were upset about it, maybe he'd let her inside him to heal that one thing. Start off slowly. Build trust—

"Back to the healing," Naomi said after chewing. "Why didn't you do that when he had you over his shoulder?"

"I wasn't in a tranquil state of being at the time. Besides, his guard was up. I can't heal someone if they don't let me in. And trust me, Kedric won't let me anywhere near him."

"I know a way to get him to let down his guard. Dance for him. Seduce him."

"He's too smart to fall for that. Besides, my moral compass does not condone trickery."

"He's a male. A virile alpha male. Dance for him, and watch his guard shatter into a million little pieces."

Myia piled her favorite fruit onto her plate. "Even if I tried, which I won't, it wouldn't work anyway. Kedric didn't even look at me when he came back from the celebration last night. You said he'd be at my mercy. The man never even commented on the beautiful Highland clothes you gave me."

"It's not what a man says or doesn't say that counts. It's what he does. Lord Kedric knocked out your suitor in a fit of jealousy. It's as clear as your empty juice glass that he wants you. If you perform this dance for him, he'll beg for your touch."

She wasn't so sure about that. Kedric would see right through that ploy. "Seducing him so that I can connect with his spirit is dishonest. I don't do dishonest."

"So tell him exactly what you're doing while doing it. If he knows the consequences but touches you anyway, he'd have done so by his own choice."

"True." Energy surged through her, renewing her with confidence and hope. Maybe Naomi was on to something. This might actually work.

"Of course, you'd better make sure you're ready for the consequences when he accepts your dance."

She steadied her goblet as she poured juice from the carafe. "What consequences?"

"He might rock your world so hard you'll forget to commune with him on a spiritual level."

Liquid splashed down her fingers from her overfilled glass. She righted the carafe and grabbed the linen napkins to wipe the mess on the table and her hand. "I want to heal him, not have sex with him."

"Oh, honey, the dance I'm about to teach you is the ceremonial mating dance."

Her throat dried.

"You can't perform it and then not follow through."

"Don't you have a different dance you can teach me? Like a ceremonial friendship dance?"

Chapter Seven

With wooden dagger in hand, Kedric lunged at his opponent. He hadn't planned on coming down to the training field today, but his pent-up frustration needed relieving. What better way to do that than by knife fighting multiple attackers?

He blocked and countered one man and slashed at another.

That shaman was more trouble than she was worth. She'd only spent two hours in the courtyard last night and already "healed" three of his staff members.

A wooden blade came straight for his heart. He parried it and countered with a roundhouse kick into the soldier's gut.

First, Chef hadn't reported for kitchen duty this morning because he needed to work out some family problems, whatever that meant. Kedric had to eat cold cereal and call in another chef.

Then his ferryman decided to leave his post so he could propose to some girl, causing three of his scientists to be late to work, which in turn postponed his secret weapons check.

To top off the day, one of the castle guards felt his talents could be better utilized as a teacher and asked to be transferred.

How could he run a kingdom if no one would do their assigned jobs?

Was she deliberately trying to ruin him? He'd had enough shit to deal with from that power-hungry Griffin.

The thought of that asshole laughing with Myia and holding her on the dance floor set his teeth grinding. He lunged and ripped through his opponent's guard. The soldier hit the ground hard.

Myia had no idea what kind of scum Griffin was or that he'd threatened to overthrow Kedric. Or did she?

Could she be working for him? They seemed very close last night with their foreheads touching and their hands intertwined. Were they lovers?

Another blow to his opponent's head. Another knockout.

His thoughts were not only irrational, they were ridiculous. She was a shaman. She wasn't plotting with Griffin to take over his throne. She was doing what she thought was right. Helping to heal people's emotional wounds.

She'd even refused to divulge Griffin's wound, which was another thing pissing him off today. If he knew his enemy's weakness, he could crush him.

Shit. That logic went both ways.

Griffin was a master manipulator. It wouldn't surprise him in the least if the scum tried tricking Myia into finding out and revealing his own weakness.

If anyone knew that, he'd be overthrown in an instant and his army would be gone. And so would the last chance of saving his family.

In a clash of wooden knives, the last soldier standing fell off-balance. Kedric took him down and simulated a stab up under the ribs. Had the attack been real, the blade would have pierced the man's heart.

The fight was over.

And so was Kedric's problem. He'd have to keep Myia under close surveillance and far away from Griffin.

* * *

Kedric pulled a white loose-fitting shirt over his head. A pirate shirt, Max would have called it. His gut clenched whenever he thought of his gladiator friend from Earth. And invariably their escape from HuBReC.

"This army's for you, too, Max."

Kedric would free him along with the rest of mankind. That is, if Xanthrag hadn't already tortured him to ultimortem.

Blood pumped hot through his veins. The cold shower he'd just taken hadn't cooled him down for long. The Hyboreans had to be stopped. And he was the only one with the guts and the army to kill the bastards.

Damn, he'd been too volatile lately. He couldn't build an army and lead his people while feeling this way. Somehow, he needed to relax.

Could a shaman enter a soul and heal only one thing? Could Myia lessen his anger? He dismissed the thought. Whether she could or not didn't matter. He couldn't risk her stumbling upon any weaknesses.

Or worse, he couldn't risk her discovering his strength.

He ran a comb through his long, wet hair and then plaited it before leaving for Myia's chamber. He opened the door to an empty room. Checking the bathroom gave the same result. Where was she?

If she were with Griffin, he'd break the man's—

What the hell has gotten into him lately? *Get control of yourself, Ked. You're still king. Act like it.*

After retrieving his tech-ring, he placed it on his head, inserted the earpiece, and pressed the comlink button. "Where is the shaman?" he asked as soon as his manservant answered.

"Naomi took her into the town for the day. She wanted to show her the kingdom."

"Who gave her permission to do that?"

"I did, my lord. You said you wanted her to fall in love with the Highlands. She couldn't very well do that locked in a room all day."

She also couldn't cause trouble if locked in her room all day. "Find her and bring her to me. I'll be in my office. And send up some lunch for us." *If there's even a cook left in the kitchen.*

"Yes, my lord."

Thirty minutes later, Kedric sat on the edge of his office desk, masking his frustration on an entirely different matter. General Sebastian's militia report.

"We're completely wasting our time training the savages." The disgust in the general's voice rang as clear as the glass in the man's spectacles. "They are *not* warriors."

"They're not warriors *yet*. It's your job to turn them into soldiers. My concern right now lies with C and D companies. Are they ready for combat?"

"No." The word came out quick and sharp.

"General, A and B companies can't attack the Hyboreans alone. I need more manpower."

"I'm sorry, but those men"—Sebastian spat the word—"are inept with a sword. And their hand-to-hand combat skills are a disgrace. They need more time."

"They've been training for a year now. How much more time do they need?"

"With all due respect, my lord, these men were Highland civilians turned soldiers. They'd never trained to fight before you conscripted them into your army. They lack the killer instinct bred into gladiators like us."

"Don't give me that taur-shit. There are no bad soldiers under a good commanding officer." Kedric strode to the general and stared down the elder man. Although Sebastian had experience as a survival race gladiator, he hadn't been at the top of his game in a long time. "Perhaps our problem doesn't lie with the men but with their commander."

"I've been acting general for a week now. If the problem lies with the commander, then the blame lies with the late great General Bathas."

Kedric had to restrain himself from decking Sebastian. How dare he spit out Bathas's name as if it were a piece of rotten meat. Not only had he been a great military leader, he'd been a great friend and the only person on this island Kedric had ever trusted with his life.

His gut churned. His legs itched to move. He wanted to look away, but he couldn't display any weakness, remorse, or guilt over his friend's murder.

"Bathas built this army from the first man. Now it's your turn to continue the legacy he left behind. If you can't prepare the men for war, I will find someone who can. Do I make myself clear?"

"Yes, my lord."

"You're dismissed."

General Sebastian gave him a curt bow before exiting the room.

Kedric stared at the closed door for a moment. Whose side was Sebastian on anyway? His or Griffin's?

He moved to the window overlooking the training field where his A team wielded their swords. They were an impressive group of warriors, but they didn't respect Sebastian.

The general might have been a decent gladiator in his day, but he didn't make a good leader. He lacked the skills necessary to rally the men, to get them fired up, to make them feel invincible and capable of doing more than they'd ever dreamed possible like Bathas had.

His gut tightened again. He mentally beat the guilt into submission, reminding himself that Bathas had to die. His ultimortem had been for the greater good.

Even if it did leave the army with an unimpressive general.

He had to find someone else to train his men. Someone fierce. Someone with more experience.

If only he could go out there and train them himself. But if he pulled a stunt like that, Griffin would jump on his throne before he could assemble the troops. There was no way he'd let that bastard take over the Highlands.

Two knocks rapped on the door before it opened. Two men with trays of food acknowledged him with a bow before setting up the table with lunch.

His stomach growled in anticipation.

"Enjoy your meal, my lord," they said and bowed before leaving. Andrei entered through the already opened door. Something seemed different about him. Was he smiling? He never smiled. Not since Kedric claimed the throne two years ago after the king's death.

More guilt tried rearing its ugly head, but Kedric beat it into submission before it had a chance.

"My lord, may I present Miss Myia, shaman-aprendi." His bow was deep and dramatic.

What was with all the fanfare? Oh, fantastic, she must have *healed* Andrei, too. "Thank you, Andrei. See to it we aren't disturbed." The man bowed again and then with a regal air exited the room.

At least a staff member displaying pride in his work was an improvement over staff members who didn't show up. He turned his attention to Myia, who was waiting patiently for him to speak.

She was wearing that same sexy getup from last night, but he could have sworn the skirt rested lower on her hips today. Much lower. And he couldn't help but notice how her breasts filled out the halter top.

A purple-and-white flower clipped back one side of her straight hair. The rest hung loose down her back all the way to her calves.

How had he forgotten how beautiful she was? He cleared his throat. "Are you enjoying yourself in the Highlands?"

"Oh yes. The people have been very friendly and very open to my help. I've already healed a dozen men and women."

Fantastic. What more damage had she caused to his precariously balanced kingdom? "Right, well, that's what I wanted to talk to you about. You see, half of those people didn't show up to work today because they were implementing your help. The kingdom can't run efficiently when people aren't adhering to their duties."

"Oh, I never meant for anyone to shirk their responsibilities. Only that if they had a problem, they should work it out as soon as possible."

"Next time, tell them to work out their problems as soon as possible *after* work hours."

"You seem tense." She sashayed toward him, hips swaying and veils covering and then uncovering bare legs. "Would you like me to help calm your emotions?"

"No."

"Are you sure? I can help you take the edge off. I promise I won't delve any deeper into your soul than you permit. So you can keep all your deep, dark, painful secrets locked away from me."

Her words weren't mocking. They were sincere. As if it were natural to have deep, dark, painful secrets. As if everyone had them. "That's quite all right. Are you hungry?"

"No, thank you. I'm still full from breakfast. But you go ahead."

Holding his disappointment in check, he moved to the low table where the midday meal had been set out for them, and then sat on a floor pillow. Her refusal to share in the spread wouldn't stop him from eating. After that miniscule breakfast this morning, he'd been damn hungry. He piled the meat onto his plate. "I knew you'd like the Highlands," he said between bites of chicken.

"I've learned much from my morning here. The women have taught me a dance. Shall I demonstrate it for you?"

"I don't think that's a good idea." He'd seen enough of her dancing last night in the arms of every man who had asked. At least she hadn't mentioned the celebration or asked why he'd slugged Griffin. He wasn't about to bring it up, either. "Take a pillow and eat with me."

She didn't move except to shift her weight from foot to foot, seemingly wanting something but hesitant to ask. Most people requesting an audience with him demonstrated the same nervous behavior. What did the shaman desire?

Myia's eyes closed. She inhaled deeply and then swayed her hips provocatively. Her leg, right up to the uppermost part of her thigh, peeked out between the translucent veils. Her arms rose slowly over her head lifting her breasts in a most pleasing manner.

"Very nice. Please sit. Eat something." He bit into a chicken leg, trying not to notice the way her hips circled round and round as she turned. Her back was to him now. Her ass gyrated. With arms still over her head, she glanced over her shoulder but didn't make eye contact.

Blood pumped through him, making him hard. Did she have any idea what she was doing to him?

She turned to face him again and reached her arms, one at a time, out to him and then curled them toward her body, silently calling him to her. Inviting him to—

Dear Spirits, she was performing the mating dance!

He dropped the chicken onto his plate. "Myia, stop. You don't know what you're doing."

"But I'm performing the movements precisely how I was taught."

Aye. Aye, she was. And performing them all too well. "That's not what I meant. Those women shouldn't have taught you this. It's a ritual dance. There is a very specific meaning to it."

"Oh. I know." She bit her lower lip as her arms kept reaching for him and pulling back.

"You do? Do you understand what you're offering me?"

Her gaze dropped to the floor, unable to meet his eyes. "I do," she whispered. She bent over to untie a veil on her hip, giving him a splendid view of her cleavage.

Distracted with carnal urges, he took a moment to realize she'd been fumbling at the knot. Finally untied, the veil floated to the floor revealing her lean, sun-bronzed leg.

What would it feel like to have that leg wrapped around him as he thrust deep inside her? Desire and need coursed through him. His penis strained against his trousers. "Why are you doing this?"

"Isn't it obvious? I'm seducing you with my body."

He slapped his forehead and ran the hand down over his face. She was so damn innocent it pained him. "I know you're trying to seduce me. Why?"

"Because you refuse to touch me. I can't heal you unless you touch me. Touch me, Kedric."

Those words, spoken softly from her lips, were an invitation his cock begged to accept. It wouldn't take any effort to carry her upstairs to his bed, rip the silk from her body, and make love to her. Hunger consumed him, and he reached for her but then remembered what she'd threatened about entering his body.

He couldn't risk that. She wanted to heal him, but if he exposed his pain, he'd expose his secrets.

And that could never happen.

"You freely admit to this ploy?"

She frowned. Her eyes narrowed, drawing her brows together. "It's not a ploy. You know exactly what I want. And you know exactly what will happen if you accept my body. As do I." Her voice quavered. She cleared her throat and began untying another veil, hand trembling.

Clearly she wasn't ready for what she was offering him.

"The choice is yours," she said.

"It's hardly a choice when you tempt me so."

"Have you not admitted to tempting me with your *sinful* foods, your *alluring* clothes, and your *hot, steamy* showers?"

Her word choice and gyrating hips were driving him nuts.

"You wanted me to love your kingdom so that I would run home and betray my people in order that they may fight in your army and die. If losing my virginity will stop your war and your hatred, it is a small price to pay for the lives of my people and yours."

His body and jaw tensed. His people's lives—*all* people's lives—was precisely what the army intended to save. He shot to his feet. "I'm shocked at you. You're a shaman. A spiritual leader. And yet you will sell your body like a common harlot." The surprise and hurt in her eyes pierced his heart.

At least she'd stopped dancing.

"I'm giving my body selflessly to save lives. Don't you see? Healing you will heal the nations."

He stepped into her personal space to intimidate her. Though how intimidating could he be when she knew he feared touching her? "You want to find my weakness. Your goal is to stop my mission. You fail to realize my destiny is bigger than the nations of Pele. With the Hyboreans dead, this army will save thousands. It will *free* thousands."

In one step, she pressed her body to his, searing him with her warmth. Her breasts were soft against his ribs. Her palms caressed his shoulders, making him wish he hadn't been wearing a shirt. He shuddered, enjoying the friction of her hands rubbing up and down his arms, and then over his shoulders again. She smelled so good he wanted to explore every inch of her perfumed body. Wanted to sheath himself inside her hot, wet—

"No." It took every ounce of self-control to pry her hands from him and toss them aside. He stepped away, his cock straining against his pants in protest.

"Your aura betrays you, Kedric. You want me. It's obvious you do. Let me love you. Let me heal you."

"Two can play this game, savage. I will prove to you what true evil my army is up against and will win you over to my side. Then, when you realize my soul needs no healing, I will take you to my bed."

Chapter Eight

Myia's mouth dried, and her core grew wet. Kedric's bed was exactly where she wanted to be. Except he wouldn't bring her there until she joined his army, which essentially meant she couldn't sleep with him unless she failed her quest.

This was so much more difficult than she'd ever imagined.

How could her dance of seduction not have worked? She'd done everything the women told her to do. He even lusted for her. Anyone could see that. Well, anyone who could read auras anyway.

The man glowering before her was one tough nut to crack.

He sauntered back to his place at the table and took up his fork. "I'm curious about your look of blatant disappointment. Perhaps you desired more than healing from me." He filled his smug mouth with a forkful of meat.

The urge to push him over ran much too strong. She inhaled some cleansing breaths. She needed to come up with a new tactic. But what? He wanted to win her to his side. Maybe if she agreed to consider his point of view, she could find another way to enter his heart.

"Either sit and eat with me, or leave and let me eat in peace. Standing there eyeing me like that is making me nervous."

She very much doubted she made Kedric nervous. She doubted anyone made him nervous. He was the most self-assured, confident—and arrogant—man she'd ever known. And unfortunately, not one to give in to temptation. His willpower was strong.

Admirably so.

Perhaps joining him was the answer. If she could understand what made him tick, she could figure out how to get him to trust her.

She sat on the pillow across from him and filled her plate with some fruit, cheese, and chocolate. How she loved the taste of chocolate. Eventually, when she returned to her village, it would be with a recipe for making chocolate.

"Now then." His tone sounded much more calm and composed than it had been a moment ago. No anger. No smugness. "How is it that you can touch me but not enter my body?"

Her gut tightened. Drat. She shouldn't have caressed him while seducing him. But he'd looked so good with those muscular arms and broad shoulders that she'd wanted to know what they felt like. They were wonderful—firm and solid.

"Do you have to be holding the person's hand in order to connect with them?"

She shook her head. "No, but it works best that way. Hand holding is a physical symbol of trust and acceptance. When two people hold hands, their fingers intertwine. They become one. Spiritual energy can easily pass between two beings that have become one."

"If holding my hand wasn't necessary to make a connection, why didn't you enter my body when you had the chance?"

"You didn't give me permission. If I tried, you would've only tossed me out again."

"I didn't give you permission while I was sleeping, yet you entered."

He had to bring that up, didn't he? She bit into a cube of cheese, gaining some time to think. What was the use? The right thing was to apologize for her unsolicited intrusion. "I'm sorry I—"

"I don't want an apology. I want to know how you did it."

"Oh. Well, sleep lowers one's defenses."

"How so?" His eyes gleamed with excited curiosity.

She never imagined the warlord would be so interested in the workings of shamanism. Most people weren't. It was nice to discuss her gift with someone other than her father. "Think of your spirit as your kingdom. While awake, your conscious mind acts as a sentry protecting your kingdom. Your sentry has the power to escort your visitor only to the places you allow them to see. While you're sleeping, though, the conscious mind isn't present to stand guard. Anyone with the ability can slip into your unconscious mind and gain access to your spirit."

"Sleeping renders a person vulnerable."

"Yes. Which is why many Spirits visit their loved ones in dreams."

"Tell me, when else is a person vulnerable?"

"During illness, exhaustion, any time the body or the mind is weak."

"Any other times?"

Heat crept up her neck and spread into her cheeks. Unable to meet his eyes, she examined her halved fruit with its juicy purple flesh and seeds spilling onto the plate. Passion fruit. How apropos. "During sex."

"Aye. I figured that one." Kedric wiped his mouth and fingers on a cloth. "Can anyone learn how to make this connection?"

"Why do you ask?"

He reclined back, propping himself on his elbow. The casual yet appealing position contrasted with the intense interest in his gray eyes. "Mind reading could come in handy."

"This isn't exactly mind reading."

"You just said you slip into the unconscious mind to do your thing. Sounds like mind reading or mind control to me."

"Then you have no understanding at all."

"Enlighten me."

Enlighten him? That was exactly what she'd been striving to do ever since she woke up in his bed. Only he didn't want to be enlightened. He'd used the phrase *mind control*. Kedric probably wanted this information for military purposes. "You don't care one bit about making a spiritual connection, do you? You want a weapon."

"You read my mind." The conceit in his smirk irritated her.

"You're not funny. I take my gift very seriously and you mock me. You ask questions not because it interests you, but because you're power hungry and want to learn how to use it to your advantage. Thank the Spirits it doesn't work that way."

"Then tell me how it does work."

Refusing to talk, she pushed her food around on her plate. She should leave. She should just get up and walk out the door. Maybe keep walking right out of the kingdom. Go home. It wouldn't be that difficult. So what if Kedric got angry. He was never going to open up to her anyway. She was never going to heal the nations.

"I'm waiting."

For all she cared he could keep on waiting like that, all relaxed on his side as if too important to sit up while conversing. As she unfolded her crossed legs to stand, she remembered the vow she'd made to her father. She'd promised not to go home until she healed the nations.

At this rate she'd be stuck here forever.

She huffed through her nose and recrossed her legs. "Communing with another spirit is a gift you're born with. It takes many years to train and develop fully. You can't just wake up one day and say, 'Gee, I'd like to know my enemies thoughts. I think I'll get the shaman girl to teach me how to read them.'"

"I'm sensing hostility."

"Ooh, well, it seems you can read minds after all." She slapped a hand over her mouth, but it was too late to take it back. Why was she being disrespectful?

His sniggering surprised her. "Your sincere and candid words are refreshing, albeit at times unexpected coming from the mouth of a spiritual healer."

"I'm sorry. I shouldn't have—"

"Don't apologize. But do keep the sarcasm to a minimum in front of my countrymen, aye? I have an image as warlord to uphold."

She nodded. What had gotten into her?

"I'm still very interested in your ability. You said before that once the conscious mind is relaxed, you could communicate with the unconscious mind. Is the unconscious mind and the spirit one entity?"

"No. But they are interconnected."

"How so?"

"The mind can control or protect the spirit, and sometimes the spirit can control or protect the mind."

He seemed to be processing her words, but by the expression on his face she wasn't explaining well enough. She needed to start at the beginning.

"The spirit, or the soul, is at the core of one's being. To reach it one must pass through the conscious and unconscious layers of the mind. The problem is the conscious mind is deceptive. Rarely does it reveal our true selves to others. In fact, rarely does it reveal our true selves to, well, ourselves. If I'm going to reach the spirit, I need the conscious mind to relax. That only happens if the person I'm healing is willing to let me in."

"Or if they are in one of the aforementioned vulnerable states."

Would he let that go already? "Correct."

"Which is why you didn't try to connect with me earlier. I was neither vulnerable nor willing."

"Yes." Well, that and the fact that she'd been so preoccupied feeling his muscles that she didn't even think about releasing her spirit into him. She bit into sweet chocolate and chewed slowly giving her heated cheeks time to recover. "Once the conscious mind is relaxed, we get to the second layer; the unconscious mind. This layer is protective. It can repress thoughts and feelings or use other techniques to cope with pain or sorrow of the spirit. While the unconscious mind is truthful, it still may be untrustworthy, for a person may have faulty beliefs. Only the spirit is truly honest."

"I'm not sure I understand."

"For example, I've healed a woman who didn't want to marry. She was nasty to men. She didn't take care of her body so that they would find her unattractive. Her unconscious mind told me she was not worthy of love. Though this thought was truly her belief, it was untrustworthy. It was faulty. Everyone deserves love. When I talked with her spirit, I learned she suffered abuse by a man she'd loved, and she feared that happening again. Therefore, her unconscious mind had created a protective belief—not worthy of love—and the conscious mind did everything to make that belief come true."

Kedric sat up. "Did you reprogram her thoughts?"

"I don't understand what you mean by reprogram. But I did heal her."

"How?"

"I helped her to see and listen to the truth of her spirit. Not the faulty protective nature of her unconscious."

"Essentially, you showed her other thoughts and she was able to act on them."

"Yes." He understood this better than she'd thought. Maybe now he wouldn't be afraid of her healing touch. Excitement coursed through her. She never would have guessed that explaining how shamanism worked would open him up to spiritual healing.

"Were you successful in changing this woman's behavior?"

"I was. Yes."

His aura crackled with excitement. "This is incredible."

Pride washed over her.

"Can you talk to other beings?"

"I can communicate with anything that has a spirit."

"Even animals?"

"Sure, but it's more difficult as they don't think the same way we do or use language. That connection is more sensory and relies on feelings and visions and scent memory."

"This is amazing. You're amazing. Thank you." In one movement he was on his knees, leaning across the table, pressing his lips against hers in a hard, quick kiss that ended before she had a chance to react.

Shocked, she stared at him as he rushed to the door.

"I have to do something. Finish eating. I'll be back later. Hopefully, with good news."

He disappeared faster than the tingling sensation on her lips.

Chapter Nine

The scientists have been gathered, Lord Kedric." The assistant opened the door to the meeting room where five scientists seated on pillows around a knee-high table discussed their work.

The chatter died down as he took his place at the head of the table. "I've good news, boys. I know how to make the mind control device work."

The room erupted with gasps and chatter. "Silence," he boomed. The men stopped talking and sat with excited, expectant gazes fixed on him. "We've been trying to communicate with the wrong part of the brain. We can't speak to the conscious mind. Or the unconscious mind. We need to speak to their spirits like a shaman would.

"How?" Dunna asked. "They don't think on the same wavelength as we do."

"We must use the visions of our imaginations as well as our feelings to make our thoughts theirs. If you want them to sublimate the subaquatic's door, try visualizing the door turning from its solid state to vapor, visualize them stepping through the cloud, create their desire to do this by feeling the true desire to do this within yourself. Transmit *that* through the tech-ring."

"We are to pretend we want something, and they are to carry it out?"

"Aye. We are planting a spiritual desire so that they can act upon it."

"Synthetic telepathy," Wren said, nodding his head.

"That seems so basic and simple," Dunna said. "Will it work?"

The room erupted in excited talk. Scientific words Kedric had heard but wasn't sure the meanings of were tossed around. Some men seemed enthusiastic and some doubtful but still open to experimentation. Twenty minutes later, he concluded the meeting to let them get to work on designing a new experiment.

This had to work.

If the science team couldn't figure out how to plant thoughts into the Hyboreans, he knew a shaman-aprendi who could.

* * *

When Kedric had mentioned a boat would ferry them to Discovery Island, she'd imagined a canoe. What awaited them at the dock was something entirely different. It wasn't a hollowed-out tree. It was some kind of metal, long and wide enough to seat four people across each of its three benches.

The day was warm and the inlet calm.

The captain held out his hand and helped her inside. Seawater lapped against the sides as the weight from the boarding passengers rocked the vessel. It wasn't long before the boat came to life and started moving.

"It's a motor," Kedric said. The word meant nothing.

The boat pulled away from the dock slowly at first, and then when they'd passed a buoy on the sea, the motor roared louder and the wind whipped back her hair, giving her a sensation of flying over the waves. It was liberating yet terrifying.

Her arm shook from her tight grip on the railing. Her breathing exercises weren't calming her fears. How could they when salty sea air whipped at her face? Turning away from the wind only caused her hair to sting her eyes.

The boat quickly cut through the sea leaving a large white-water V trailing behind. She'd never seen such a thing. Every now and again a sea spray would mist her as they rose and fell over the ocean during the eight-minute ride to Pele's smaller island.

As they neared the shoreline, the ferryboat slowed once again.

Two men covered neck to toe in white waited for them on a dock. Their peculiar costumes clung tightly to every curve of their bodies. It was as if they'd fallen naked into a barrel of white paint.

When the boat was properly docked, Kedric got out before her and offered her his hand. Apparently, he'd overcome his fear of touching her. That was a step in the right direction.

She placed her hand in his. The last time their fingers intertwined had been in his bed. Her heart flipped in response to the memory. His grip tightened, and she felt his strength as he pulled her onto the wooden platform.

Disappointment came when he let go.

The men in white greeted Kedric with a respectful bow. "Lord Kedric," they said in unison.

"Gentlemen." They straightened again after the acknowledgment. "Myia, I present Chief Science Officer Dunna and Technology Officer Wren. Gentlemen, I present Myia, shaman-aprendi."

The two of them bowed their heads in greeting.

"Is everything ready?" Kedric asked the men.

"Yes, my lord. We've got them set up in the Yard."

"Excellent. Lead the way."

Myia's legs felt heavy and odd walking on land again, like they were still bounding up and down as they had been in the boat. The sensation tripped her, but Kedric caught her in his strong arms and sparks electrified her aura. He steadied her and didn't let go of her hand as they followed the two painted men up the path toward a large white building.

Her hand fit comfortably in his. Like they were made for each other. Like they belonged together.

Too bad the walk wasn't longer.

The unusually smooth building walls shimmered in the sunlight. What material could it possibly be made from? It was neither wood nor stone. In fact, it was nothing she'd ever seen before, not even in the Highlands.

Inside, Kedric led her down a long corridor, passing many closed doors on either side of them. Wren opened the last door, and Kedric motioned for her to enter the small room before him.

Hanging on wall pegs were some kind of full-body white clothing like the scientists were wearing. "Surely Highland men haven't the ability to shed their skin like a serpent."

"If I didn't know better, boys, I'd think she just called us all snakes."

Dunna and Wren chuckled.

"You're used to Pele's tropical climate. The beasts behind this door are from the arctic region. These thermal suits protect us from the freezing temperatures we've artificially recreated inside." He handed her a one-piece suit from the wall.

The scientists, already in appropriate dress, entered the room. A blast of freezing air slapped her skin before the thick door clicked back into place behind them.

Not only did the Highlanders have the ability to chill food, they had the ability to freeze entire buildings. Perhaps that's why the walls, both inside and out, appeared to shine like white crystals.

Kedric turned away from her to peel off his shirt and pants. She unwrapped the sarong from her hips, feigning disinterest in his naked body. She tried averting her eyes but couldn't stop glancing back at him, hoping to catch another glimpse of his glorious sex.

Heat flushed over her body.

What was wrong with her? It's not like she'd never seen nude men before. By Spirits, she'd even seen Kedric naked. So why was she this enthralled with watching the muscles of his backside as he stepped into his pants?

Because his body is beautiful. Magnificent.

She swallowed. The pounding in her ears couldn't be her heartbeat. Could it? Her head swam with dizziness.

Something had her unbalanced today. Yes. That was it. She was out of balance. Probably due to seasickness. Her equilibrium hadn't yet returned. She'd be back to normal in a few moments.

Turning away, she squeezed her eyes shut. It was no use. His image was seared into her brain. She couldn't stop seeing him no matter how much she focused on changing clothes.

When she turned back around, his intent gaze made her stomach tighten. She checked her suit to be sure she put it on correctly. "Do I look okay?"

"You look better than okay. You look like you've been dipped in white chocolate." His tongue darted out to lick his lips. His eyes glazed over with hunger. If she *had* been dipped in white chocolate, there was no doubt he would've devoured her on the spot.

Her mouth went dry. She shifted weight to the other leg. Kedric had been right; these thermal suits really did keep a person warm. In fact, she was burning up.

"Come." He held out his hand to her, and she slipped her palm into his. "I want you to see this." They stepped through the door into a frigid room that did little to cool her flesh.

White fog swirled around her head. "My spirit," she cried and covered her mouth to prevent it from leaving her body. Was this her punishment for lusting after the man she had been sent to heal? She wasn't worthy of her shamanic training.

"It's okay, Myia. It's only your breath. You can see it in the cold."
He, too, made fog as he spoke. Then he exhaled a big cloud to
demonstrate.

She uncovered her mouth, blew a short breath, and was rewarded
with a little cloud of smoke.

Dunna laughed. "Congratulations, Myia. You've been in the research facility for less than five minutes and have successfully exper-
imented with science. Perhaps you'd like to join our team. It's very
exciting."

"Aye." Kedric slapped Dunna's back. "If by exciting, you mean
stimulating erections."

Pink crept into the scientist's cheeks matching his pink nose.

"Look around you, Myia." Kedric spoke with pride. "This is our
Yard."

The stark room was as long and wide as it was high. If four gladiators stood on each other's shoulders, the top man still wouldn't be
able to touch the ceiling.

Contrary to being called a yard, the giant gray room contained
no dirt, grass, or anything else that would be found under the sky.
In fact, it contained nothing but four scientists, some large silver
rings—like the one Kedric used to talk to Andrei—on a cart with
wheels, a stepladder, and two furry lumps in the room's far corner.

"Bring the creatures here," Dunna said to two of his men. They
nodded and hurried across the room. Dunna and Wren each placed
a silver ring on top of their heads and adjusted the bands to fit comfortably across their foreheads.

A jingling sound drew her attention to the giant, furry humanlike
creatures being led by chains attached to collars around their necks.

She'd never seen such large animals. Were these the great creatures she'd heard stories of? The creatures that inhabited Hyborea.
The creatures who had poached humans and other life from the
planet called Earth. She bit back the fear racing through her veins.

"I take it you've never seen a Hyborean before."

"Not even in a drawing." Her breath came out as a whisper.

Their auras were too dim to read. Although she'd no experience perceiving the Hyborean essence, she could tell they weren't acting like their true selves.

The scientists unhooked their chain leashes and set up a stepladder next to one. Since no anxiety registered from any of the men, Myia tried quieting her apprehension. She stepped closer to Kedric, though. Just in case. "How can they be in Pele? The Spirit Lights protect us from them."

He turned to face her. "I don't want to upset you, but it's time you understood what the lights in the sky really are."

Ah, so that's why his eyes filled with pity. The leader of the "advanced" society must educate the ignorant savage girl on her foolish beliefs. Well, it wasn't the first time someone had tried to explain the physical manifestation of the Spirits. "Enlighten me, oh, wise one."

His eyes narrowed at her flippancy. He didn't admonish her for breaking her sarcasm promise. A fact that amplified her regret over voicing said wiseass comment. Why couldn't she keep her big mouth shut around him?

Perhaps he'd accept a big, bright smile as a peace offering.

He only shook his head in resignation. "We call the lights aurora tropicos. It's a phenomenon that occurs due to the strong electromagnetic fields on this part of the planet. The colored lights are created from electrons and gases. Dunna could explain the science to you."

Explaining the science didn't change the fact that the lights were indeed spiritual energy. She held her tongue. It would do no good to argue. An open mind was the only path to figuring out how to fulfill her goal.

"But the important thing to know is that while the electromagnetic or EM fields are harmless to humans and animals, they aren't to Hyboreans. The fields disrupt their normal telepathic brainwaves causing confusion, pain, and even death."

"You mean those poor creatures are in pain?"

"No, unfortunately." She didn't like his callous tone. "The EM field on this smaller island isn't strong enough to hurt them. It does, however, interfere with their brain waves. It alters their cognition."

"How so?" A bad, queasy feeling roiled her stomach.

"It shuts off their conscious thought."

This couldn't be going where she feared it was going. Her pulse quickened.

"In our efforts to control the Hyboreans, the science team created a tech-ring with the ability to stimulate certain parts of the brain to elicit certain behaviors. For example, aggression."

Her fingers tingled. This wasn't good.

"However, they were unsuccessful in making the beasts do any specific skill. To follow directions. They didn't know how to communicate with the Hyboreans. Until yesterday."

An undertow dragged on her soul. She glanced at the scientist securing a tech-ring on top of the second Hyborean's head. "You've created a mind control device?"

"Aye. But they didn't work until—"

"I told you how to communicate spirit to spirit." If she were in quicksand, she couldn't sink any lower. Kedric had been right; she was an ignorant savage. All those questions about her ability had nothing to do with understanding shamanism so that he'd feel comfortable with her healing powers. How could she have been such a fool?

Zapped of strength, her knees gave way and she stumbled backward.

Kedric caught her arm and steadied her. "Are you okay?"

Her stomach clenched, and she wrapped her arms around her

belly to ease the ache. "Y-you used me. You used my knowledge to control those poor creatures' minds."

His mouth slackened. A single red eyebrow rose. "Poor creatures? Pay no heed to the stupor they're in now. When these beasts are conscious, they are murderers. Torturers. These two came here to capture humans for their blood sports."

He wasn't even sorry. He gave no apology for the Hyboreans' mistreatment.

"We're ready, my lord."

Kedric's shoulders pushed back. He gave a nod. "How about a dance, boys?"

The Hyboreans turned to each other, assumed a formal dancing position, and began to glide with more grace than she'd imagined ten-foot-tall creatures could possess. The sight was more than odd.

The scientists whooped with joy. One of the Hyboreans stopped, which tripped the other. Both animals fell.

"Concentrate!"

"Yes, my lord." Wren closed his eyes presumably to focus his thoughts into the mind control device. The Hyboreans righted themselves and resumed dancing.

"This is ridiculous," Myia cried. She wanted to go to the Hyboreans. Alleviate their humiliation.

"You're right about that. How about a fight, gentlemen?"

The brown Hyborean punched the gray one's face. The gray ducked and rammed into the other's belly, pushing the animal backward.

The two scientists without tech-rings laughed and shouted, "Give 'em a left. Strangle the beast." They took bets on which one would be the victor.

"Stop this! Stop this madness. How dare you enslave another living being like this and make them attack one another?"

"How dare I?" Kedric turned on her, his gray eyes filled with fury.

His aura flamed with red-hot anger. Hatred and testosterone radiated off him.

The intensity of his rage frightened her. She'd never seen him so volatile, so explosive, so…so…barbaric.

"How dare they pit human against human and make them fight to the death against nature and beast and each other in their survival races? How dare they make us kill other men and torture us if we don't?"

"These are living creatures with a life and a spirit and—"

"They're fucking poachers, Myia. They may have advanced technology and godlike powers in medicine, but they are savage animals that thrive on watching humans fight to the death. They deserve no sympathy and will get none from me."

"Kedric, you're very upset. Your hatred is talking. This isn't you." She reached for his hand. "Let me heal you—"

He yanked his hand free. "There is no healing from the knowledge that mankind is enslaved."

She backed away from him.

He stepped closer. "You were born on Pele. You know nothing of the tortures your fellow man endures on this planet. They can't even escape the pain and agony through death. Not when the Hyboreans keep reawakening them. Do you know what that means?"

Her head quivered no. She was too scared to shake it fully.

"It means the bastards bring them back to life only to torture them further. It is a living hell you can't even begin to fathom."

"I'm sorr—"

He didn't let her finish. "Imagine you're a gladiator in the survival race. The last thing you remember is a blade across your throat. The next is reawakening on a table with arms and legs strapped down."

He gripped her hand, preventing her from backing away farther. His eyes were wild. His breathing labored. This was not the man she knew. The light in his eyes had turned off as quickly as pressing the bottom of a lightstick. Some ugly, hidden demon from within had taken over.

"Imagine a Hyborean's scalpel cuts into your skin just above your wrist restraints. The monster takes hold of your flesh between its leathery fingers." He pulled her thermal suit away from her wrist in demonstration.

She glanced at the scientists for help, but Dunna's and Wren's eyes were glazed over in deep concentration. The other two were jumping and hollering and punching the air as the Hyboreans fought.

"Your flesh burns while it's peeled away from muscle. You scream for your ultimortem as you watch yourself get skinned alive."

The thought made her dry heave. "Kedric, please. You're scaring me."

"No, Myia." His voice was cool, icy. "You've no idea what it's like to be scared."

Chapter Ten

The slap across his cheek had been hard and quick and unexpected. Tears shone in Myia's horrified eyes.

The instant he released her wrist and thermal suit, she sprinted for the door. What the hell had come over him?

He hadn't lost control like that in years. Not since his first year in the refuge. Safety had changed him. He'd buried his inner beast. He'd learned how to behave like a civilized man in society. He'd even become the leader.

But here in this room amid arctic temperatures, Hyborean scents, and fighting beasts, the old gladiator mentality had resurfaced.

With such a lack of control, it was as if he'd never escaped HuBReC.

"That's enough," he bellowed in an effort to release some of this anger. "We don't want them to kill each other before the war."

The beasts dropped in their places.

"See what you can do with them on the subaquatic. If they can't sublimate the door or pilot the craft, we're back at square one."

"Yes, my lord," Dunna said.

Kedric left the Yard through the thermal suit room they'd entered. Myia's clothes were still in their neat pile on a bench. She'd made a beeline for the front door no doubt.

What would he say to her?

He'd wanted to win her to his side. He'd wanted her to fear the Hyboreans. But she feared him instead.

All he'd accomplished today was creating sympathy for those beasts.

There was no point in searching for her in any of the other rooms in the building. She'd been so frightened she would've run as far away from this place as she could.

He knew he'd find her on the dock.

Spirits help him if she convinced the ferryman to take her back to the mainland. If word got out that he harbored two Hyboreans on the little island, the kingdom would erupt in panic.

He ran down the path to the dock. The ferryboat was still there, but a sight far worse hit him like another slap across the face.

Myia was in the arms of the ferryman. His legs raced faster. He would deck the guy for putting his hands on her. Dammit, that was the response of a gladiator. He'd already hit Griffin. He couldn't hit another subject. He was lord. He was supposed to be above that behavior.

Kedric slowed his pace. He walked the rest of the way in order to collect his thoughts.

Her head was on the ferryman's shoulder and he was rubbing her back. He heard her sniffle into the young man's shirt. Why did it bother him that the ferryman was about her age?

"There, there, miss." The man glanced up when Kedric's boots hit the dock. "Seems she had a fright, my lord, but wouldn't say what happened. Must be pretty bad to ask me to leave you behind and ferry her back to the mainland. I told her I couldn't do such a thing."

"You did right, son. Thank you." Kedric turned his attention to his savage little shaman. "Myia."

The tight thermal suit couldn't hide her back stiffening or muscles tensing in response. Her fear of him pierced his heart. "Come with me." When she didn't turn around, he softened his voice. "Please."

A sniffle and an eye wipe later, she turned to face him. They didn't speak as they walked back to the building. There was nothing to say to her out here anyway. A private room where they could talk intimately would be better.

She kept two steps behind him. Even when he slowed for her to catch up, she slowed, too. The woman couldn't stand to be next to him.

It bothered him more than he cared to admit.

Back inside the building, he brought her into the meeting room so they could talk without being disturbed. The scientists should be off testing their newly acquired skills on the Hyboreans and the sub-aquatic.

Myia sat on one of the floor pillows and folded her legs to the side. Still looking down, her long black hair hid her face.

He joined her on the floor, sitting next to her within arm's reach. "I want to apologize for my behavior in the Yard. I don't know what came over me. I—"

"Is that why you think I'm crying?"

That whispered response wasn't one he'd expected. "Isn't it?"

With chin still hanging practically to her chest, she shook her head no. She sniffled again.

He couldn't talk to her like this with her hair a black veil covering her face. He parted the strands like a curtain and lowered his head to hers. "Please look at me."

When her eyes, red from crying, met his, his heart nearly burst at the pain and anguish he saw in them. Was there anything worse than a woman's tears? "I'm so sorry for scaring you. I wasn't myself in there."

"I know that, Kedric. I know you bear a deep hurt. I appreciate your apology and accept it wholeheartedly."

"You do?"

"Of course. I see your sincerity."

"Then why do you still shed these tears?"

She wiped her eyes on the back of her gloved hand. "I've lost my way, Kedric. I came to the Highlands to heal your heart's fears. But all I have managed to do is allow my fears to take over mine."

"Please don't cry, Myia. Anyone would be frightened of an alpha gladiator telling them stories of torture while demonstrating it on their thermal suit. I was a complete ass. You have every right to be scared."

"You don't understand. Although I was scared of you in that moment, I also knew that your behavior was due to a great suffering. A great fear. I have been in these positions before. Well, maybe not quite as intense, but as a shaman-aprendi, I should have taken the opportunity to heal your hurt. I should have healed your fear. But instead I-I raised my hand to you in violence." The tears started again. "I've never struck anyone before. I've disgraced myself and all the spiritual healers who've come before me."

What the hell? "Am I understanding this correctly? You're not upset with what I did to you. You're upset because you slapped me?"

She nodded. "I'm so unbalanced. My father never should have sent me here. I'm so out of my element. I'm not worthy of the title shaman-aprendi."

"Myia." He chuckled. "It was just a slap. One I deserved...and needed."

Her sharp gaze met his. Tears shone in her suddenly sobered eyes. "No one deserves an act of violence. No one."

"But you woke me from that haunting nightmare. You actually helped me."

Her expression told him she wasn't buying it.

"Would it help if I told you I forgive you?" Though in his book she didn't need to be forgiven for anything, he hoped it would ease her conscience.

"That does lighten my heart some." By the sound of her words, it didn't lighten it by much.

"What else can I do to make you feel better?"

"There is nothing." Her words and slow headshake was a response of dejection. She had given up. On what, he wasn't exactly sure. But there was something about her that seemed to have been snuffed out. What could he do to raise her spirits?

Of course. Her *spirit*.

"You wouldn't be feeling this way if it weren't for me." He rubbed his stubbly chin. "I'm going to ask you something, and I want the truth." Why he added the last bit he wasn't sure. She'd been nothing if not truthful. At times, painfully so.

"Of course."

"Can a shaman heal a part of a person? I mean only one specific hurt that person tells them about? They wouldn't go snooping around in places they aren't welcome, would they?"

Her eyes lit up. Enthusiasm replaced her earlier depression. "Yes. A shaman would respect a person's privacy. Especially if you're willing, I mean, *a person* is willing to be healed."

"I've been very angry lately, Myia. You said you could take the edge off. Would you?" He never imagined a woman's smile could be so big or brighten up an entire room. It was as if twenty lightsticks had been lit. Or maybe it was his heart that her smile brightened.

"Oh yes. That's the whole reason I came to the Highlands." She faced him full on and settled into a crossed-leg seated position with a hand in the air, waiting for him to take hold of it.

Damn, did he really want to do this? He trusted her enough with the small hurts. It was the deeply buried hurts he didn't. If she entered his soul and he suddenly thought about those things, would she know? Then there were the nightmares from HuBReC. If they resurfaced again, she'd be terrified. No way would he expose her to that misery.

"Kedric?" Her voice was tentative. "Are you having second thoughts?"

"No, I'm having unsuitable thoughts. There's nothing in this soul inoffensive enough to share with you."

The sweet sound of her chuckle was a much-needed reprieve from her weeping. "You wouldn't believe the things I've seen, Kedric."

"Really? Like what?"

"You're stalling."

"Aye, I am."

She waited patiently for his hand.

He couldn't procrastinate any longer. He'd promised to let her heal him, and in doing so, she'd heal. That was the true goal here. He pressed his gloved palm against hers. The material made intertwining their fingers difficult. "This would be so much better if we were out of these thermal suits."

She gasped. By the shock in her eyes, she must have thought he'd meant they should get naked right here, right now. "I didn't mean we should strip off our clothes... Though now that I'm thinking of it, it doesn't sound like such a bad—"

"Kedric would you please focus?"

"I was focusing. You distracted me."

"Of course." By her unenthusiastic tone, she'd only said the words to placate him.

Her eyes closed, and he felt a presence—her spirit—inside his body. He tried to relax at the invasive sensation. It wasn't painful at all. On the contrary, it was actually kind of peaceful.

He closed his eyes, and in the darkness he saw Myia. Her white thermal suit illuminated the field of black around her. Then his own image materialized next to her.

"Thank you for your trust, Kedric." As spirit Myia spoke, the words came to him through his mind. His physical ears heard nothing. Could this be the phenomenon the scientists had been discussing? Communicating with imagined speech.

Though he was aware of her spirit inside him, he was also aware of the physical surroundings outside his body, though to a much lesser extent.

"What hurt do you want to show me?" spirit Myia said.

Somehow his image was able to easily reply, "You mean you can't find one and heal it?"

"Not with the barriers you've created." Her upright palms indicated the darkness around them.

Upon a closer look, he realized they were standing in the midst of four stone walls. His barriers. Perhaps this healing thing wasn't so bad after all.

"You are my guide here. I will see nothing you don't want me to. Use your spirit to call upon your pain and it will appear in this space."

Okay. He was ready to do this. "I want you to heal—"

The meeting room door burst open. He heard two sharp knocks as someone rushed in.

His eyes opened and he felt Myia's spirit vanish.

"Lord Kedric, come quickly," Dunna cried. "We've done it!"

Chapter Eleven

Myia was the last one to descend all 125 flamestone steps to the cavernous basement running the entire length of the science center. The damp underground chamber must have been somehow carved from the island. The gold-and-red bands in the walls and floor indicated natural rock. The ground gently sloped downhill from the base of the stairs, becoming sand and then ocean.

Chained to the cavern walls, an enormous and mostly submerged machine took up the majority of the space in the cave. Small waves lapped against the machine, crashed onto the beach, and echoed off the cavern walls.

"What is it?"

"That is the Hyboreans' subaquatic." Kedric must have seen the confusion on her face because he explained, "It's a boat that can be submerged beneath the water's surface. It travels very quickly. A journey that would take a man three months to walk would only take a subaquatic eight hours."

If his eyes hadn't been so serious, she would have thought he was spinning outlandish tales. How could something travel so fast? Then she remembered the stories about Hyboreans traveling to other planets. Those machines must be able to soar at unimaginable speeds. These creatures were truly remarkable.

It killed her to see them reduced to slaves controlled by the silver headbands on Dunna's and Wren's heads.

The scientists marched them to the subaquatic. A section of the wall began to vanish into swirling smoke. How could that be? How could something as firm and solid as a wall have the ability to turn to smoke before her very eyes?

The Hyboreans had done nothing. They simply stood there, yet somehow she knew they were responsible for the supernatural transformation. "They possess magical powers."

"Technological power," Kedric said.

"Can technology cause a wall to disappear?"

"It didn't disappear. It sublimated. Whatever material their doors are made from has the ability to change directly from a solid into a gas without first becoming a liquid."

"How? I didn't see them use a device to do this."

"They control their technology with telepathy. Stay here with Finn. You three"—he pointed to Dunna, Wren, and the last scientist whose name she didn't know—"come with me. Let's see what this thing looks like on the inside."

Her heart pounded. One by one, the Hyboreans, the scientists, and Kedric disappeared through the white swirling cloud. The cloud crackled like the sound dry, brittle herbs make when crushed as it solidified into place again.

"Will they be safe in there?"

"They'll be fine. Though they could be gone for hours. I'm sure there are plenty of cool things to investigate on board."

She saw the longing in Finn's pale face and blue eyes and knew he wished to be part of this great discovery. "I'm sorry you have to stay with me rather than go with the team."

"Don't think anything of it. They wouldn't have taken me on

board even if you weren't here. Someone has to stay on the outside. That job falls to me since my specialty is in medicine rather than technology. Besides, I'm the lowest man on the totem pole."

She perked up at the mention of a totem. "What animal is your spirit guide?"

"Uh. I don't have one. That was an expression from Earth. It means I don't have as much experience as the rest of these old geezers."

"Oh, I see." She tried not to let the disappointment show. It would have been nice to have a friend in the Highlands who was in touch with the Spirits. She missed discussing all things sacred. Especially with her father whose conversations were wonderfully enlightening.

After a mental prayer for his health, she turned her attention back to Finn who had his hand pressed against the subaquatic's door. It appeared as solid as any wall. "Are you from Earth?"

"No. Alex Graham was. He had unusual sayings for everything." Finn scribbled something on his notepad. "Have you heard of him? He used to be a scientist here."

She shook her head no.

"He spent forty years in the Highlands inventing so much of the technology and luxuries we enjoy. Only he called it reinventing. I don't care if his gadgets are all commonplace on Earth; I think he was a brilliant, brilliant man." An air of sorrow surrounded Finn as he spoke fondly of the man with two names.

"Was?"

"He died about a week ago."

Her heart went out to Finn for the loss of what sounded like a mentor and friend. "I'm so sorry."

"We all are. Come upstairs. I'll pour you some coffee and tell you all about him."

"Shouldn't we wait for the others to return?"

"If we waited that long, we'd die of starvation." He chuckled. "That's another of Alex Graham's sayings."

She glanced at the subaquatic. It seemed very quiet inside the big machine. What were they doing in there? What did it look like? Would Kedric tell her what he saw?

Following Finn to the top of the stairs, she heard his winded breath. "Alex Graham engineered what he called an elevator for this place. It uses a pulley system that would take all of us up and down without having to use the steps."

Having the ability to go up and down steps without walking sounded wonderful. "Too bad it never got built."

"It will one day. The blueprints for that and many of his other reinventions are in his office. I wish he'd lived to see the mind control devices work. He would've loved to have witnessed the sub-aquatic doors sublimating."

They entered the kitchen, and Finn told Myia to have a seat while he prepared the coffee.

"You were very fond of Alex Graham," she said.

"He was like a grandfather to me. Missed his family terribly. Always talked about searching for a way home to his wife and children. He was in his seventies—probably a great grandpa by now—but never once gave up on his dream of going home. Never took another mate. Isn't that amazing?"

"True love certainly is." She hoped someday she could find love. Perhaps after she returned to her village.

So why did Kedric's image pop into her head?

"He thought when they captured the Hyboreans and their craft, he'd be able to engineer a way back to Earth." Finn placed steaming coffee cups on the table and knelt on the pillow across from her.

"I feel your pride and happiness when you think of him. He must have been very special to you."

"He was."

She wrapped her hands around the mug, testing the temperature. It was too hot to hold. "Can I ask you something, Finn?"

"Fire away." He didn't say it, but she knew the odd expression was another one of Alex Graham's.

"You're a man of science. What are your feelings about using this technology for war?"

"I'm all for it."

That surprised her. "Really? You're okay with using mind control to enslave the Hyboreans when they could very well have family missing them, thinking they're dead, the same as Alex Graham's family presumably did?"

"The Hyboreans abducted Alex Graham from Earth. He told me some terrible stories about his experience with them and how he escaped to the refuge on Pele. If he could contribute to the freedom of mankind, he was all for this war. And so am I."

"That makes three of us." Kedric entered the kitchen and poured himself a mug of coffee. "Finn, the team has some things to show you on the subaquatic."

"Yes, my lord." In his excited rush to get to the watercraft, Finn's bow resembled a head nod. He was out the door in seconds.

Across from her, Kedric sat on Finn's pillow. "We can make the Hyboreans power up the craft. After we've tested all its capabilities, I expect we'll be piloting it around the world in a month."

He certainly seemed pleased with himself. She on the other hand wasn't. In fact, she really didn't want to hear any more about it.

"A three-month journey by foot will now only take eight hours. With our Hyborean henchmen, we'll be able to get into the city, attack, and get out before they even know what hit them."

"Are these two Hyboreans and your army prepared for opposition?"

"They will be." He gulped his coffee. If it was as hot as hers, his throat must be blistering right now. He wiped his mouth with his fingers.

"Please don't do this."

"I have to."

"Think about what you're fighting for."

"I do." His voice turned grave. "Every day."

"Don't you find it a little, I don't know, ironic that you fight for freedom, yet enslave these captives?"

"These creatures don't deserve pity, Myia. They deserve death or worse."

"It breaks my heart to hear you say that."

"And it breaks mine to know my father and sister are still in captivity."

A gasp escaped her lips. He hadn't told her that before. No wonder he was so passionate about this war. He wanted to free his family. She cocked her head to scan his eyes for the feelings hidden inside. Her heart ached for him, yet she could not condone his cause.

"I will destroy every last Hyborean who ever kept a human as a pet, a gladiator, or for body parts. I will free mankind. But this planet is immense and our numbers are few. I can't fight without more manpower. I need your men, Myia."

"What makes you think you can win against the Hyboreans? Even if every man, woman, and child on Pele joined your army, there would be less than a thousand people to fight your battle. The Hyboreans populate the planet. Your mission will fail. Every last one of your soldiers will be killed or captured. Do you want to be responsible for that?"

"My mission won't fail. My men are well trained. And we have our secret weapons. We can set our explosives and retreat to Pele where the Hyboreans can't follow."

She placed her hand over his. "We have a good life here on Pele. We are protected from the Hyboreans. Don't strip that away from those who live here. My people want peace. Don't lead them to their slaughter like the livestock I've seen in your pasture."

His free hand covered and held hers. "If you don't convince your people to come to the Highlands, I'll be forced to keep bringing them there myself. That will take more time and increase the risk of needless casualties. The best for all involved is for you to convince your men to live with us so that I can convince them to fight the Hyboreans. Please."

A rush of adrenaline set her midsection tingling. "I will never convince anyone to join an army that will lead them to their slaughter." Rather, she'd do everything in her power to convince his soldiers to abandon his army.

There was a heap of work ahead of her if she were to heal this entire kingdom hell-bent on fighting a losing battle.

Chapter Twelve

Kedric paced the stone floor of his office like a caged alpha gladiator. Why was that woman being so damn difficult? Why couldn't she see things his way? If she stood for peace and love, why would she be against creating a world where humans could live in peace? A world without Hyboreans.

The woman drove him crazy. And not just by opposing him. There was something else about her. Something drawing him to her no matter how hard he resisted.

Perhaps it was the way her gold eyes sparkled like flamestone. Or how her beautiful face lit up after helping someone. Or her innocence when being brutally honest.

She had fire and passion. He'd gotten a taste of it the night he'd kissed her in his bed. And he couldn't stop thinking about wanting to unleash that passion again. What he wouldn't give to take her into his bed and make her his own.

But her spirit had violated his and begun to chip away at the barrier placed around his heart. That wasn't for anyone to open up. No matter how much he desired her, no matter how much he lusted after her body, no matter how deep he wanted to bury himself inside her, she would only bury her spirit deep inside him. And that was something he couldn't allow to happen.

He thought after escaping HuBReC, he'd be free of torture.

Apparently not.

No wonder her people hadn't come for her. If she had the same effect on the lowland men, they were glad to be rid of her. They wouldn't want her back. They were probably throwing a nationwide celebration now that she was out of their hair. Hmm, maybe he should threaten returning her. They would undoubtedly send him the soldiers he needed, then.

The two knocks on the opening door startled him. "My lord, I've news." Andrei didn't bother shutting the door behind him, so it couldn't be military in nature.

"What is it?"

"While you were on Discovery Island, a patrol outside the kingdom walls found three refugees. A gladiator, a woman, and a baby. They were in poor condition. They've been taken to the welcome center and have been provided medical attention. They've been bathed, fed, and clothed as well. They are waiting for you in the throne room."

"They can't be refugees. A baby couldn't survive three months in arctic temperatures to get here. They must be from one of the lowland villages. Perhaps it's a trap." He glanced out the window expecting to see raiders scaling the castle walls. All was quiet on the training field and beyond.

"I don't think so. The man was much too assertive. He demanded on being taken directly to you. He insists you owe him your freedom."

Kedric's head snapped around. He fixed his gaze on Andrei. "What's his name?"

"The guards didn't say."

"What color are his eyes?"

"My lord?"

"Are they bright green?"

"I don't know. The guards didn't mention it."

This interrogation was getting him nowhere fast. "Send in the gladiator."

"Yes, my lord." He stepped back into the hallway and called for the guard to bring forth the gladiator.

A moment later the man entered. His sharp, emerald-green eyes glanced around the office, no doubt locating exits and improvised weapons. He stopped in the center of the room and stood in his relaxed battle-ready stance, feet apart, knees slightly bent, chest out, and hands at his sides but prepared to fight.

Kedric's throat thickened and began to ache. He drew in a deep breath through the nose and pressed his lips together to keep the stupid grin off his face. "If anyone could escape HuBReC twice, I knew it would be you. Welcome to freedom, Max."

The hard angles of his friend's face softened. His shoulders rolled forward to a neutral, relaxed position. One corner of Max's mouth turned up. Was that a smile? Max didn't smile. Ever.

He indicated his thanks with a slight nod. "Five years I've been telling Duncan you'd made it into the refuge. I'm relieved to know I wasn't lying."

They greeted each other with a hardy whack on each other's shoulder, and Max inhaled a sharp breath as if in pain.

"You okay?"

He nodded and then exhaled the breath he'd been holding. "Yeah. Multiple stab wounds. I'll live."

Max's injuries must be extensive. An alpha gladiator wouldn't divulge a weakness in front of two strangers—the guard and Andrei. He wouldn't even divulge it to his friend, unless he was downplaying major damage. If his sentries had attacked him, there would be hell to pay. "My guards?"

"No. Regan. Remember him? Arrogant, blond-haired little bas-tard? He's alpha in HuBReC now. Or was. Or still is."

"Was or is?"

"Not sure. We killed him, but don't know if it was his ultimortem or if he's been reawakened." Max ran his left hand through his short black hair, which was odd considering he wielded his sword right-handed.

His injuries were definitely extensive, then. Kedric moved to the window and peered out so no one could see him grimace. Should he heal Max? He'd passed up healing so many others for fear of being locked up and abused as a blood bank again.

Max had sacrificed himself for Kedric. Surely he could give the guy a little blood in return. If he did, would his secret be safe? A man could change in five years. What did he really know about Max now?

Kedric shook his head and turned around. "You said *we killed him*. Who is *we*?"

"Your sister."

Adrenaline rushed through his body. His heart raced as he crossed the room to stand in front of Max. "She's here? Tess is here? Well, don't just stand there, Andrei, bring her to me."

Andrei bowed and hurried out of the room.

He turned back to Max who had his mouth open to say some-thing, but he cut him off. "They told me there was a child, too. Is Tess a mother? She always wanted to be a mother."

Max frowned. He reached his hand out and rested it on Kedric's shoulder, like an older brother would do, and then fixed his gaze on Kedric's eyes. "You have more than one sister. Be kind to her." His last words sounded more like a warning than a request.

The sound of footsteps entering the office caught his attention, and he turned around to see a beautiful woman cradling a baby.

His stomach knotted. He tried not to let his disappointment show.

The fingers on his shoulders gave a hearty squeeze. "This is Addy. My mate and your sister. Well, half sister, really."

Though her long hair was strawberry blonde rather than the red that he and Tess had, her eyes were the same gray color. But eye color confirmed nothing.

"Prove to me we're siblings." He didn't mean for it to come out so harsh sounding.

"Um, okay." She shifted her weight onto her other foot as she bounced the baby in her arms. Since the child hadn't been fussing, the motion must have been to soothe her nerves rather than the child's. Max joined her at her side and slipped an arm around her waist, which seemed to give her confidence. "Well, Duncan, your father—well, our father—traveled to Earth with his Hyborean master Ferly Mor and fell in love with my mother…I'm not sure if that was before or after the experiment…maybe during…but anyway, he left her pregnant and returned—"

"Forget the story, Addy. Show Kedric your birthmark."

"What? No way." She leaned into Max and lowered her voice. "You know where my birthmark is."

"Never mind your modesty and just—"

"No."

"Hell, Addy. If you won't show him, I will." Max reached for the silk veils at her hip. She smacked his hand—hard, by the sound of it. Kedric could almost feel the sting. Addy had spunk. And apparently could hold her own against an alpha gladiator. Kedric felt the grin tug his lips. He liked her already.

"What's wrong with you?" she said. "Husbands don't go around unveiling their wives in front of strangers. Even if those strangers are family."

Clearly she had no idea of her birthmark's significance, which was understandable considering she came from Earth. "Your birthmark is a genetic brand," Kedric said. "The Hyboreans encode them into their studs' DNA. All the descendants of that stud will bear the same mark."

If she were indeed its mother, the infant in her arms would also carry her genetic brand. There was no need to match the baby's markings with Max's. The kid's emerald eyes proved without question he was the father.

"You mean I'm branded? Why?"

Her horrified expression almost made him chuckle. "Familial birthmarks are pedigrees in the flesh. They easily identify lost or escaped humans, and they prevent the Hyboreans from inbreeding us."

Addy shook her head. "I will never get used to this planet." She offered the baby to Max, who took it with no question.

Never had Kedric imagined Max—an alpha gladiator, a loner who'd slain hundreds of men—kissing a baby's forehead and holding it against his chest. It was the most human he'd ever seen his friend. And it made him smile inwardly.

Addy turned away from Andrei and the guard so only Kedric could see her part the veils and lift her undergarment to reveal her birthmark. There on the tender crease between pelvis and thigh—in the same place as his—was the familial birthmark. Duncan was indeed her father. And she was indeed his sister.

Heat radiated through his chest. A lump formed deep inside his throat. He hadn't had family in five years, and now he had a half sister, a brother-in-law, and a nephew. "Andrei, set them up in our best room and make quick preparations for a celebration. The whole kingdom will feast tonight in honor of my sister's arrival. You, guard. You're dismissed."

"Yes, my lord," they said in unison. Andrei bowed deeply and exited with the guard.

Kedric opened his arms and embraced Addy. "Welcome home, little sister. We've much to discuss, aye?"

"Yes, we do. You have no idea of the hell we just went through." She looked up at him, eyes shining with tears. "I'm so tired of running and living in fear."

"Rest assured, you will fear no more. You're safe here. I promise you that." He turned his attention to his nephew in Max's arms. He tousled the baby's silky hair. "You must be one tough kid to have survived an escape from HuBReC. What's his name?"

"Noah," Addy said. "Though I call him superbaby. You're right. He's very tough. He should have died a few times out there, but he managed to hold on."

"A born survivor." Max's tone carried nothing but pride.

"I'd like very much to hear his story." Kedric would also like very much to find out if Noah carried the same healing DNA that he and his father did. Tess never had it. He'd figured it was a male only trait.

If Noah carried the same genetic anomaly, and someone found out, it could mean disaster for Kedric, the future of his kingdom, and his war.

Chapter Thirteen

The Spirit Lights danced above the courtyard in a clear, starry sky. They were in a far happier mood than Myia, sitting here on Kedric's right at the head of his banquet table. Fifty people were seated between her and the other end where she'd rather be.

On second thought, she'd rather be seated at a different table.

They hadn't talked the entire trip back from Discovery Island. He'd gone to his office, and she'd gone off to heal some of the soldiers. Unfortunately, her soul hadn't been calm enough after their argument to heal anyone, so she'd spent the rest of the evening meditating in the garden.

It had worked, too. After her soul had recharged, she met with a group from her village and worked with them until Andrei found and brought her to the banquet table.

What if her presence at Kedric's side gave people the wrong idea? She didn't want anyone believing she supported his war.

Though if she were honest, she'd have to admit part of her annoyance was due to Kedric's demeanor. Their argument had left him untroubled. He showed nothing but smiles and joviality as he scooped the first helping from each serving bowl and then passed them down the table.

Yes, he deserved to be happy, celebrating his new family's arrival. But a little selfish part of her wished he'd show some remorse over their fight.

She'd have to meditate on that.

The aroma of spicy meat set her mouth watering. Hopefully a full belly and some lively music would help her regain balance.

Kedric got up from the table and headed over to Wren who had just arrived. Queasiness fluttered inside her stomach. She couldn't look at either of them without seeing enslaved Hyboreans.

Or her failing quest.

Okay, so that was her real problem. If her father were here, the kingdom would be healed by now.

She turned her attention to Kedric's new sister sitting to her right on the long side of the table. Her mate, Max, was next to her, and their baby lay on a pillow between them. She couldn't see him but heard his sweet coos.

Myia passed Addy a bowl of sea turtle roe.

She took it, frowned, and then handed it right over to her mate. "I thought I'd seen the last of black goop in HuBReC."

Max took two big helpings before sending it down the line. "You should really give it a try, Addy. It looks gross, but—"

"Tastes great," she finished for him.

He smiled at her as if she were the only woman at the table. The love radiating between them wiped clean Myia's annoyance. Her heart warmed.

These two were true soul mates. Their intertwined auras glowed with a devotion she'd never before witnessed. It intoxicated her spirit, making her light and dizzy.

If this was what it felt like sitting next to true love, imagine what it would feel like to be *in* true love.

"Hello. May I present myself? I'm Myia, shaman-aprendi." She bowed her head in greeting.

Addy seemed confused but then bowed her head in return. "I'm Addy. This is my husband, Max, and our son, Noah. Are you Kedric's wife?" She bit into a roll and chewed.

"Heavens, no. I'm his prisoner."

Addy choked on her bread. Without taking his gaze off the baby lying between them, Max handed Addy his goblet of water. She took it and drank until she stopped coughing. "What do you mean, you're his prisoner? I thought people in the refuge were free."

"Well, the lowlanders are free. That's where I come from. But the Highlanders mostly stay inside the kingdom walls. Kedric claims it's because they don't want to leave." She shrugged. Kedric was probably right. She hadn't met anyone interested in giving up their modern conveniences, including her tribesmen who'd only been here three short days. "Anyway, Kedric intends to keep me here until I, too, fall in love with the Highlands. When I do, he will allow me to go home for the sole purpose of convincing my people to join his army."

Addy stared at her incredulously. "And you're okay with this?"

"Well, I'm content as his prisoner. Everyone's been so nice and generous. I'm not, however, content with his plan. In fact, my own plan is to heal your brother's heart so he stops this war."

Max turned his attention to her. "What war?"

"On the Hyboreans. Kedric is creating an army to kill them all."

A single eyebrow rose. His head came forward. "Seriously?"

She nodded.

Max shook his head in blatant disbelief. "That's the stupidest thing I've ever heard."

"What's the stupidest thing you've ever heard?" Kedric slapped Max on the shoulder as he came to rejoin the table.

"That you're planning to attack the Hyboreans. Did someone

leave a piece of your splattered gray matter on the battlefield the last time they reawakened you?"

Addy tossed her fork onto the table in disgust. "Nice visual, Max."

"Sorry." He kissed her freckled nose, and Myia felt Addy's repulsion vanish.

Kedric took his seat at the head of the table. "I don't see how freeing your fellow man from torture is stupid." He kept his voice low. He probably didn't want to upset the other dinner guests with war talk.

Max matched his volume. "Freeing men is a noble cause. A global attack on the Hyboreans is suicide. They're an advanced race with advanced technology with a population of what, billions? What do you have? Spears, rocks, and a few hundred men who have to hump it by foot three months before they reach the nearest Hyborean city?"

Kedric chuckled and dismissed Max's concern with a wave of his hand. "We're much better equipped than that, my friend. You'll see."

"I'm telling you, Kedric. You send people out there to wage war, and you send them to their graves. All you'll end up doing in the process is piss off the Hyboreans."

"That breaks rule number one," Addy whispered to Myia.

"Exactly." Max winked at Addy before returning his attention back to Kedric. "Hell, Ked. Don't you think the Hyboreans could nuke Pele if they wanted to?"

Myia glanced from Max to Kedric who seemed to be considering his strange words. "What is this word, nuke?"

His green eyes focused on hers for a moment as if deciding how to answer. Finally he said, "It means decimate."

She gasped. The food in her stomach congealed into a hard lump.

Kedric leaned over the table to get closer to Max, and in the process got unnervingly closer to Myia. Why did he have to smell so good?

He whispered, "I have explosives and an incredible secret weapon. Two actually. I'll show you tomorrow. You'll need to know what's at your disposal since I'm appointing you general of my army."

"The hell you are," Addy shouted and half the table turned their questioning gazes at her. "I'm sorry, but we just traveled thousands of miles out of that hell. We fought for our lives every miserable step. Max is staying here with me and our son, and we're going to raise a family and finally be happy. You are not taking my husband out of his refuge."

Max's arm encircled his mate, and he hugged her to him. "Relax. Everything will work out."

Kedric's eyes smoldered. His aura burned red, but he remained calm. "You may be my blood relation, but I am lord here. You will not talk to me in such a manner."

Addy buried her face into her husband's shoulder. "Your sister," Max emphasized the word *sister*, "means no disrespect. It's her protective instincts talking. You must admit they run strong in your family."

A smirk came to Kedric's lips, as though he and Max had shared a private joke. The lines of tension in his face smoothed. "Aye." He tilted his wine goblet in salute. "Aye. That much is true."

Myia wasn't sure exactly what had passed here tonight. But if Addy and Max were against the war, then they were just the people she needed to help convince Kedric to give up his suicide mission and free the enslaved Hyboreans.

* * *

The next morning Kedric sat at his office desk feeling surprisingly well after the amount of alcohol he'd consumed last night. Must be the healing DNA in his body. No matter what he tried telling himself, downing goblet after goblet of wine hadn't been because of the celebration. It had been a consequence of his fight with Myia.

He'd been so stupid for showing her the Hyboreans. That terrible idea had backfired from the moment she saw them. It seemed the harder he tried to get her to join his side, the more she resisted.

Damn infuriating woman.

The door opened with two knocks. Andrei entered with Max close behind. "My lord." Andrei bowed deeply and gracefully. Kedric had to admit the formality was really quite respectful and nice. He should probably thank Myia, but that would only encourage her to heal more of his staff. "May I present Max, alpha gladiator."

"Not anymore," Max said.

"Thank you, Andrei. That will be all." Kedric waited for Andrei to leave before speaking. "You'll always be a gladiator, Max. You can make a new life in polite society, but you'll never forget what you've been through. You'll never forget your training or your survival instincts."

Max didn't argue. He must have realized Kedric was right. Max strutted to the oversized window and peered down at the A team training three stories below. The profile of his mouth turned down.

Where to begin? "I'm not sure how I feel about your mating with both of my sisters."

The quick turn of Max's head proved he hadn't expected that statement. "You don't seem particularly angry."

"It's not like gladiators choose who they're paired with in the breeding box."

"You know I've never hurt Tess."

He nodded. "She told me you were kind. Hell, if you hadn't been, I'd have let you drown when our canoe capsized. You were a crappy swimmer. You floated like a lead iceberg."

"I've since learned how to doggy-paddle." His hands scooped the air in front of him in illustration.

Kedric sniggered at the absurdity. Max had always been a loner. Even during their escape, he rarely talked and never cracked jokes. "You've changed."

"Yeah, well, women will do that to you."

The wooden chair legs scraped against the floor as he stood. He moved from behind the desk to its front corner and leaned against it. "Why did you do it? You were so close to freedom. Why did you save my life instead of your own?"

"If I hadn't, we both would have been captured."

"Then you wouldn't have had to deal with the punishment on your own. I know Xanthrag's rage. He would have tortured you for your escape and then torture you more for mine." By the pain in Max's emerald-green eyes, he knew he was right. Max never could hide his emotions very well. Though his two favorite emotions in the past had been brooding and rage. "Why did you sacrifice your own—"

"Hell, Kedric, I had my reasons. Okay?" He strode back to the window and leaned a hand against the stone wall. His head hung lower than before.

"It's not okay. I've carried around the guilt of your torture for five years. I've been planning this war to save you as well as my family. Now that you're already safe, I don't know how to make it up to you."

Max's gaze locked on his. "I do."

"Name it. Anything you want, it's yours."

"I'm not fighting your war."

"Anything but that."

Max didn't say a word. He pulled himself up to his full six-foottwo height, his green eyes sharpened, and his gaze hardened in challenge. He was posturing. Establishing the dominance hierarchy.

"You're serious?"

"Damn right, I'm serious."

"You're a survival race champion. You escaped from HuBReC. Twice! No one knows more about fighting, survival, and tactics than you. You're the best warrior I know. My army needs you, Max."

"Hell, Kedric, I just escaped from HuBReC. My battle wounds haven't even healed yet."

"Fine. Take some time to recover and then—"

"You don't get it, do you? I'm not asking permission."

"It's my sister, isn't it?"

"Hell, yeah, it's Addy. She doesn't see me as the beast this planet had turned me into. She actually loves me. *Me.* God knows I don't deserve that, but I'll be damned if I don't do everything in my power to make her happy. And I guarantee that risking death or recapture will piss her off."

"You really love her."

"She's everything to me. She and Noah are my life's breath."

Max loved her. For all that Max was a fearsome killer and lethal survival race competitor, he'd never been able to mask his thoughts. Of course, there had never been a need to when every man understood the others were out for blood.

Today, a radiance glowed in his bright green eyes. Addy had not only changed him, she'd transformed him from beast to man.

What would a love like that feel like? Myia popped into his thoughts.

He covered his pause in thought with a forced chuckle and derision. "I never thought I'd hear an alpha gladiator wax poetic."

"Don't underestimate me, Kedric. I may not fight your war, but I'll sure as hell fight you to defend my family and our newfound freedom. Your skills haven't gotten rusty living in luxury these past five years, I hope." The cold-blooded gaze of the beast in Max's eyes sent a chill whooshing up Kedric's spine.

He refused to shudder. "Retract your claws, Max. Your devotion to my half sister and nephew is commendable. I only wish your devotion was to freeing mankind." He joined his friend at the window and gazed out. Beyond the training field wall, his countrymen walked or rode bicycles over packed-dirt streets. Their baskets were filled with materials and goods they needed for their jobs. Every task was as important as the next in keeping his people healthy, happy, and safe.

"Look at them down there." Kedric pointed to the soldiers practicing archery. "Nine out of ten people have been born in Pele. They've never even seen a Hyborean. They haven't a clue what it's like to be a captive, to be an alpha gladiator trained to fight to the death for entertainment, and yet they practice and prepare for war because they understand all men should live free."

"Don't assume I'm against freeing mankind." Max turned to look him in the eye. "I'll train your soldiers and assist you with strategy and tactical planning, if you wish. But I will not leave this refuge or my family to fight."

If that was all Max could give right now, he'd take it. With Max training his army, they would be an elite fighting force in no time.

"Fair enough, *General*." He placed two fingers on his lips before slapping his open palm on Max's chest. When Max did the same, Kedric covered his hand. The accord was sealed.

Max removed his hand. "Now for that favor you owe me."

"You not leaving for battle was the favor."

"I told you I wasn't asking permission on that."

Typical Max. He crossed his arms over his chest. "What do you want?"

Chapter Fourteen

After the midday meal, Kedric strolled with Addy through town. She wore Noah on her chest in a baby sling and a floral sarong similar to the one Myia had on last night. Why that thought popped into his mind, he didn't know.

In the marketplace, they stopped at a jewelry maker's boutique where he picked out an anklet with little tinkering bells.

"What's this?" she asked when he handed it to her.

"It's an ankle bracelet. Highland women love to wear these."

She shook it and made an unpleasant face. "It reminds me of the jingle bell on my cat's collar. Or worse, a cowbell."

Whatever that was.

"I'm sorry, Kedric. I don't mean to be rude, but I can't wear anything that reminds me of being an animal. Not after I was forced to be a broodmare in HuBReC."

"Aye. I understand." Earth women were different entirely from Hyborean-born women. She returned the jewelry to the table before moving on.

They walked out of the town and then turned down the road leading to the ocean. He had asked Addy about her abduction and escape, but she hadn't divulged details. Her pain was still too raw.

"Perhaps you should seek Myia's assistance," he said. "She's a shaman and can help heal your pain."

"I don't know. That sounds a little hocus-pocus to me."

Not only was her Earth accent unusual, so were her words. "What's hocus-pocus?"

"You know, magic?"

"There's no such thing as magic. Everything has a logical, scientific explanation. Myia is most likely a gen-alt. Like Max and Noah."

"What's a gen-alt?" She rubbed her baby's back and kissed his head as if to soothe him from the nasty word he'd just been called.

"Genetically altered human. Max had been enhanced with exceptional vision. Noah's eyes are the same unnatural green so he must have inherited it. Myia probably had an ancestor in captivity whose DNA was diced and spliced to form a telepath. I don't know the science behind it, but trust me when I say she has a way of getting into your mind and soul."

Addy smiled conspiratorially. "Is that why you're keeping her as your prisoner?"

"Who said she was my prisoner?"

"She did."

"She's not my prisoner. She merely isn't permitted to leave the Highlands until she sees things my way."

Addy snickered. "And how long do you suppose that will take?"

Forever at this rate. When they'd first met, he had assumed Myia was weak and frail like Tess, but she was so much stronger. "I don't know. Like you, she's feisty and fearless. She's also strong willed, determined, and exasperating as hell."

"Yup. You're right. I'd say she most definitely got into your mind and soul."

He didn't like what she was insinuating. It might be true, but he didn't like it. "Tell me about Tess. Is she okay?"

"Your not-so-subtle change of subject reveals everything I need to know." She rubbed Noah's back and then used that high-pitched voice women always used around babies. "Doesn't it, Noah? I think Uncle Kedric's in love." She kissed the baby's head.

Thankfully no one was on the road to hear that. "I am not in love. Though I wouldn't mind her naked body writhing with pleasure beneath m—"

Addy covered her ears. "Oh my god, this is *so* not an appropriate conversation."

It was his turn to snicker. She'd sure as hell change the subject now.

She uncovered her ears slowly as if making sure it was safe to listen again. "I see what you did there. Fine. I won't talk about love anymore. And I won't tell you based on the way she looks and acts around you, I think it's mutual. Oh, wildflowers." She hurried off to the firewheels blanketing the ground up ahead.

Women. He shook his head in defeat.

"Tess was very kind to me," Addy said when he caught up. "She taught me about HuBReC, and we became friends. She was there for me when I thought Max had—well, that's not important now. Anyway, I didn't know she was my sister until a few days ago. I don't think she knew, either."

He doubted it, too. What would be the point in their father telling them they had a sibling on Earth?

Addy carefully knelt down with Noah and picked a firewheel. "Tess was happy for the most part. Ferly Mor treated her better than most Hyborean masters treated their pets."

"What do you mean 'for the most part'?"

"She wanted desperately to have a baby. She didn't care that the Hyboreans would take it away when it was big enough to swing a stick. If only for a little while, she wanted to experience motherhood. But she remained the only childless woman in a facility dedicated to breeding humans."

Kedric's heart sank. Tess could never have kids. She'd been to the breeding box numerous times but would always miscarry and die in the ninth week. After the last time she was reawakened, her Hyborean master never sent her to one again.

"She would have been a great mom."

"I think so, too." Addy stood. When her callused hands found his, she gave him a comforting squeeze. Her hands were so different from Tess's. Addy was a strong and athletic woman. Her muscular physique made her an obvious mate for an alpha gladiator like Max. Their offspring would have the perfect build for a warrior. Tess on the other hand was frail, always so thin no matter how much she ate. She wasn't athletic, and her body was too delicate for breeding. She didn't have the healing DNA that their father and he shared.

That reminded him. He'd better test Noah today.

"She likes HuBReC, Kedric. She has friends there, helps out in the school. Her master is good to her, feeds her well, and gives her love. She's brave. She helped me escape, even though it went against Duncan's wishes. When I was in the infirmary after—well, that's not important now, either—but she gathered the supplies I needed to escape."

He searched Addy's gray eyes so like Tess's. "Why didn't you take her with you?"

"I think we both know the answer to that question."

He glanced down, kicked a stone to the side of the path a little harder than necessary. Tess was incapable of surviving the perilous journey.

"She didn't want to escape. She really was happy in HuBReC."

"You keep saying 'was.'"

Addy inhaled and let the breath out slowly as if she had something important to say and was gathering the necessary strength to say it. She stuck the scarlet-and-gold flower in her hair. "During our escape, Duncan and a gladiator named Regan tracked us."

"I know Regan." He ground his teeth in disgust. That cocky rookie murdered him once.

"Regan told our father if he didn't do as he commanded, he'd make HuBReC his 'daughter's living hell.'" She raised her hands and curled two fingers on each as if that somehow emphasized her last words. "I'm not certain if he was referring to me or Tess, but—"

"You fear it's Tess."

She lowered her gaze and nodded. A lock of red-blonde hair fell in front of her face. She tucked it behind her ear before looking up at him with sorrowful eyes. "I'm so sorry."

"Tess isn't strong enough to withstand a gladiator's brutality."

"Neither was I, which is why I escaped."

"How long ago did this happen?"

She shook her head. "I don't know. So much has happened, I lost track of the days. A week? Maybe two?"

"I have to go back. I have to save her."

"Duncan is there to protect her and Ferly Mor. The alien really does love her, you know. I'm sure he wouldn't let Regan hurt her."

"Don't. I know you're trying to make me feel better, but you forget I was once an alpha gladiator. I know what they're capable of and how sneaky they can be. Besides we both know damn well the Hyboreans don't pay close attention to what goes on inside that Yard. There's no hope for her or anyone if I don't do something. I have to save my sister."

He turned and started back to the castle, his strides long and quick. Addy caught up. "What are you going to do?"

"I'm going to debrief the troops. This war starts now."

Chapter Fifteen

Myia!" Naomi's voice called through the crowded marketplace. Her friend pushed past and weaved through shoppers, a large basket tucked under her arm. "We have to talk. Where it's quiet." Naomi yanked her hand, pulled her through the street as she stumbled to keep balance, almost losing a moccasin to keep up.

Once they were alone and out of earshot, Naomi stopped and Myia caught her breath. "What is it? Are you in trouble?"

"We're all in trouble. I'd thought now that Lord Kedric had found a good woman to occupy himself with—"

Heat crept into Myia's cheeks.

"—he'd forget about war. But he hasn't. He's getting ready to deploy the troops to the Human Breeding and Research Center."

Her heartbeat raced faster than from the sprint of a moment ago. Her belly fluttered. "I knew something was wrong. Ever since Kedric came back from his walk with Addy yesterday, he'd spent all night and all day today in meetings." And spent no time with her unfortunately, but Naomi didn't need to know that.

Naomi glanced around, sending her thick curls bouncing, before leaning her head close and lowering her voice. "I'd been called to a secret gathering this morning with all the other garment makers to create more thermal suits for the soldiers. Lord Kedric wants fifty suits completed by the end of the week! I've been sewing like mad all day."

Myia stole a glance at the material in Naomi's basket. The fluttering grew heavier, like her stomach was sinking. She took a breath and kept her expression neutral. "How long until deployment?"

"One week."

"That's not enough time. I can't heal him that quickly. I need more help."

"What about his new sister? I heard they had words over dinner. Someone said she was against the war."

"I've already talked with her. She hates the Hyboreans. She wants Kedric to take them out. Her words." She shrugged. The saying was self-explanatory. "She's proud of Max for training the soldiers. And he's happy to train them."

"Yeah, but she doesn't want her mate to leave the island."

Myia couldn't fault Addy for that. "She wants to protect her man. And I want to protect all the men. But it seems everyone is so bloodthirsty. I can't do this alone."

"Have you asked Griffin for help?"

The tower bells rang indicating nineteen o'clock. Time for the marketplace to close. In an hour it would be dusk, and everyone would be home eating the evening meal.

"I'm late. I've got to go. Good luck, Myia." Naomi raced toward the castle.

Well, perhaps not everyone would be eating the evening meal.

Myia smoothed her hair and pulled it behind her shoulders before walking back through Market Street. She entered the crystal shop where an elderly man was straightening a display of crystal jewelry. "Excuse me. I'm sorry to bother you, but would you know where I could find Griffin?"

Twenty minutes later, Griffin opened his front door. His dark eyes widened. "Myia?" He glanced past her, searching for something. Or someone. Probably looking for Kedric. She hadn't seen Griffin since the night of the party when Kedric had struck him and carried her away.

"May I come in," she asked, before she could think any further about hanging upside down over Kedric's perfectly naked body that night. Oops, too late.

"Yes. Of course. Come in, come in." He moved to let her pass while holding the door for her.

She slipped off her dirty moccasins and padded barefoot across the floor, instantly regretting her decision. Grit and stone dust covered the hardwood. It needed a good sweeping. The front room was brilliantly illuminated and very cluttered with strange equipment, and all different shapes, sizes, and colors of rocks.

That explained the stone dust.

"I was about to eat. Are you hungry?"

When was her last meal? The aroma of fried fish coming from the kitchen set her stomach growling. She was starving. "Smells delicious."

He shrugged off her compliment. "Striped bass. Freshly caught. I'll fix you a plate. Have a seat in the garden, and I'll be right out." He indicated the open rice-paper sliding door.

The inside of his house might have been cluttered and dirty, but the garden was impeccable, beautifully landscaped with a manicured lawn, vibrant flowers, and ornamental grasses. Water trickled down a rock formation. Handcrafted wind chimes jangled in the warm evening breeze.

Enclosed on three sides by a tall wooden fence and on the fourth by the house, Griffin's garden was a private oasis.

The perfect place to meditate.

She found the small dinner table beneath a wooden canopy with flowering vines climbing across the overhead beams, giving it shade. Not that it needed shade now that the sun was setting and the Spirit Lights graced the skies. She sat in the grass at the table, which was already set with a plate of fish and mixed vegetables and a glass of wine.

Griffin appeared with her meal and a crystal goblet. He placed everything in front of her. "Cold tea."

It was sweet of him to remember she didn't drink alcohol. She picked up her fork. "Thank you, Griffin. Your garden is beau—"

"Does Kedric know you're here?"

The fork slipped from her fingers and clanged onto the table.

"I'll take that as a no." He blew out a breath and reached for his wineglass. "Not looking forward to *that* visit."

Surely Kedric wouldn't accost him again. She cleared her thickening throat. "Actually, I'm here because of Kedric. I need your help to stop this war."

"Sorry, Myia. War's inevitable. I've come to terms with it." He dug into his dinner.

"You've come to terms—how can you say that?"

"Because our ruler is a gladiator. A natural-born killer. What else would the brainless ape do?" The light of his aura darkened. Griffin's contempt for Kedric ran deep. Whatever happened between the two of them had caused great pain. She could remedy that.

"You're very angry with Kedric. He's hurt you somehow. I can help heal your pain."

His lips pursed. "The last time we tried that, I ended up with a bloody nose. I'll keep my emotional pain, thank you. It hurts less."

It was her turn to purse her lips. He wasn't ready for healing now. She'd revisit that in a few days. "Don't you want to stop Kedric?"

"I did. But like a friend of mine used to say, 'Insanity is banging your head against a rock over and over again and expecting different results.'"

Griffin wasn't supposed to talk like this. He was supposed to be on the side of peace. He was supposed to agree to assist her. How was she going to heal the nations if no one would help? Time was running out. "But if we work together, we can—"

"They're going to war, Myia. We can't stop it. I hypothesize two possible scenarios. One: Kedric deploys his troops, gets them all killed, and then we overthrow him. Two: Kedric deploys his troops, gets them all killed, and then we suffer the consequences." He shoveled a forkful into his mouth.

"What do you mean consequences?"

He took his time chewing before he swallowed and answered. "Retaliation. We've been left in peace here because we're not bothering anyone. But all that's going to change once Lord Stone-for-Brains picks a fight. All the Hyboreans need to do to wipe us out is torch the island. How many people could survive a wildfire?"

Her muscles tensed. Everyone, everything on the island would be destroyed. She swallowed the bile rising in her throat. "We need to explain this to the people. Make them understand."

"I've tried. Haven't you heard? I'm the doomsday prophet. I'm the selfish bastard spewing hate and fear out of greed for the throne." He shook his head in disgust and then drank deeply from his wineglass. "Kedric has the nation so brainwashed, they think they can kill a Hyborean bare-handed."

Though his aura had darkened, their talk didn't seem to bother his appetite. She on the other hand could only manage a few small bites. Her stomach churned, and she tried to settle it with a sip of tea. "You seem very calm for a person who believes our world is about to end."

"I've made contingency plans. If the worst should happen, I might have a chance to survive. Then again, who knows if I've accounted for every possibility."

"You really think it will come to that?"

"Honestly? No. I'm betting on my first hypothesis. The Hyboreans will see them coming and capture every last soldier." His brown eyes gazed into hers for a long moment, and his expression softened. "Look, I can see you like the guy, but once Kedric loses the troops, the country will turn on him and a pick a new leader who can rule in peace."

"You?"

"Maybe."

She took another sip of tea to combat her nausea. Her world was off-balance. Tipping toward disaster. Icy chills slipped down her spine every time she thought of war. Pain and grief loomed on the island's horizon. If she failed her quest, hell would consume Pele. She could sense it. She could feel it. "I think you're wrong. I think if I don't heal Kedric, he'll send that ship to kill the Hyboreans, and your second hypothesis will come true."

Griffin put down his fork, rested an arm on the table, and leaned closer. "What ship?"

"The Hyborean ship."

His eyebrows rose as if surprised she knew about that. "The subaquatic?"

She nodded.

"They can't pilot the subaquatic. They can't even get inside the subaquatic."

"You haven't heard the news? The scientists have created a mind control device. They are using it on Hyborean captives to sail the ship."

He leaned away and narrowed his eyes at her. "Mind control. They figured out how to create synthetic telepathy?"

She nodded again.

"Unbelievable! He kicks me off the science team, continues *my* research, and is successful? How the hell is that even possible?"

Myia picked at the grass. Now wasn't a good time to explain her role in the development of mind control.

"Synthetic telepathy," he said with awe in his voice. He leaned back on his hands and gazed up at the night sky for a long, silent moment. He seemed to have lost himself in deep thought. "This is incredible. Do you know what this means? It means—" He glanced at her. His grin faded and eyes widened. "It means you've got to go."

He pulled her to her feet, took her by the elbow, and ushered her into the house, across the gritty floor, and to the front door. "You were never here, okay? If Kedric finds out—" He made a show of shuddering.

"But—but what about stopping the war?"

He shoved her moccasins in her hand and then opened the front door. "Keep working on it, Myia. You'll figure something out."

He pushed her over the threshold. The door shut in her face.

Myia stood there in her bare feet, shoes in hand, blinking in utter disbelief.

Her last hope for preventing this war had just kicked her out of his home.

* * *

Salty sea air whipped back Kedric's hair as he seethed on the dock awaiting the approaching motorboat. The fast-moving cloud coverage obscured both full moons, which cast minimal light on the choppy inlet.

The driver eased into the dock, cut the engine, and threw a rope to the ferryman who tied it off. Griffin climbed out of the boat with fishing pole and tackle box in hand—as if anyone was stupid enough to believe he'd been fishing alone in the dead of night.

Kedric folded his arms across his chest. "Catch anything?"

"I had some success."

"I bet you did. Search him," he commanded the two guards at his side.

Griffin held Kedric's glare as he put his hands up and away from his body in a nonconfrontational pose. One guard took his gear and then searched through the tackle box. The other patted him down.

If Griffin stole so much as a paper clip from Discovery Island, he'd personally escort him out of the refuge and suspend him from a tree. Let the poachers have him.

"He's clean, my lord."

"Nothing in here but lures, line, and bait," the other guard said.

"Search the boat."

"What are you looking for, Kedric? Can't a man enjoy a little night fishing?"

"Not when he commandeers—"

"Borrowed."

"—my watercraft."

"You mean my *father's* watercraft, which should've become mine after he died."

The boat belonged to the king. Kedric was king. Boohoo. "What were you doing on Discovery Island?"

"Who me? On Discovery Island?" He feigned innocence. "I'm banned from there. Remember?"

"Cut the crap, Griffin."

"You're not going to believe anything I say anyway, so why don't you save us both the aggravation and ask the science team if they saw me there. When they tell you no, and you assume they're lying, maybe you can torture them like you did Red."

The comment was meant to unnerve him. It pissed him off. Kedric swaggered over to Griffin, who didn't seem intimidated. He focused straight ahead as Kedric stopped behind him and breathed down his shoulder. He mustered up his most menacing voice. "You are swimming in treacherous rapids. Tell me what you're scheming before I snap your neck right here."

"That's what gladiators do best, isn't it? Fight when they're scared."

The kid didn't back down. Any other day Kedric would have given him props for that, but not today. He was in no mood and had neither the time nor tolerance to deal with a pissant like Griffin. "My patience is wearing thin."

"You're scared I stole the tech-rings, aren't you? Or that I sabotaged the mind control devices? It would be a shame if they broke while in the middle of the ocean. No way to pilot the subaquatic. You'd probably sink into the abyss."

Heat flamed up Kedric's neck. His temples throbbed. Griffin was baiting him, and he refused to bite. He inhaled slow, steady breaths like Myia always did and carefully controlled the tone of his voice. "Did you?"

"Of course not, Kedric. I don't need to sabotage your army. All I need to do is wait. And unlike you"—he turned to face him—"I'm an extremely patient man."

He was also an extremely arrogant man, and arrogant men enjoying hearing themselves talk. Especially when showing off how smart they were. A few more questions and he'd have Griffin bragging about his entire scheme. "So what are you waiting for, Griffin? A set of balls to grow?"

Snickering came from the boat.

Griffin's nostrils flared, his chin rose higher, and his eyes darkened to near black. "Soon you and your army will be captured or killed, and the nation will need a new leader. I might be willing to take the job if they ask nice. Oh, and don't worry about the shaman girl. I'll provide her with a shoulder to cry on. And a warm bed."

Kedric's blood pumped and spiked with adrenaline. His hands clenched into fists. If Griffin so much as looked at Myia, he'd tear him apart. Hell, he should tear him apart now just for standing there with that cocky smirk, clearly enjoying himself.

"I have no idea what she sees in you. I guess she likes brainless apes. Or maybe she gets off on lost causes."

It's as if he wanted Kedric to beat the crap out of him.

Why?

Because the rat bastard was trapped and knew it. He was redirecting the focus of the conversation because he wanted to avoid answering the questions. What the hell was he hiding? It must be damn important if he'd take a beating in order to keep it secret.

Kedric released his pent-up energy through a hearty laugh. He could play this game. "If I die, don't think it will be so easy to take my place. You don't have the strength to lead a nation. Or the intelligence."

"Says the man with an intellect of a worm. You don't even realize what you have in your possession."

Aha, now he was getting somewhere. "Enlighten me."

"I can't. You're incapable of understanding that technology." He pointed in the direction of Discovery Island. "You're incapable of looking to the future. You see synthetic telepathy as a weapon. I see it as—"

"The boat's clean, my lord," the guards said jumping back onto the dock. "Just a couple of striped bass on ice."

Griffin shut his mouth tight.

Damn the guards.

"Are you going to let me pass, or are you going to beat me up for fishing?"

"I'm going to take you into custody until the men on Discovery Island can corroborate your story. Lock him up until further notice."

One guard shoved Griffin from behind to get him moving. The other flanked his side. The three of them disappeared into the night.

"Take me to the island," he said to the ferryman.

* * *

Sitting on the bed in her room—which hadn't been locked again after that first night—Myia took off her moccasins. She wiggled her toes and then flopped back, letting the soft mattress cradle her. She'd spent dawn until dusk—twenty exhausting hours—healing the soldiers. With a good ten hours of sleep, she'd be able to begin again at dawn tomorrow.

As tired as she was, she couldn't close her eyes. Tomorrow was going to be as busy as today, especially since she had three big obstacles to overcome. The first being the increase in the amount of time the soldiers trained. She couldn't very well heal them on the practice field.

Then there were the men refusing to be healed. The soldiers who had lived in the villages had no problem with her work, but the Highland men feared her touch. Perhaps Kedric had gotten to them.

Even the men who had gone through a session of spiritual healing wouldn't necessarily change his thoughts or behavior immediately. Rebalancing one's spirit takes time and effort on their part. Especially when they have strong conflicting feelings about what is right and just.

How many times had she been asked if it was okay to kill someone or something to save someone else?

Since she couldn't sleep anyway, perhaps she should meditate on it. She sat crossed-legged on the rug covering the hardwood floor, closed her eyes, listened to her breaths, and turned inward to the tranquil—

The bedchamber door burst open and crashed into the wall. Kedric stormed into the room. "What the hell are you doing?" He was livid. His eyes were as wild as his red hair sticking out in different directions.

"Meditating."

He slammed the door shut. "I mean with my men. My soldiers are deserting their posts. Some refuse to train. You know I need them for this mission, and yet you deliberately obstruct everything I've worked so hard for."

She stood and approached him slowly, as one would approach a trapped and frightened animal. "You're upset. Let me help—"

"Help? That's the problem, Myia. Your *help* is causing havoc. I won't stand for it. You will not heal another person in the Highlands." He stormed to the door.

How dare he tell her what to do? Or not to do, as the case may be.

She'd been sent here to do a job, and now that she knew it was working, she would not quit until every man in his army refused to follow him into battle.

"No." She spoke the word with defiance and conviction.

He stopped with his hand on the doorknob. His spine straightened as he drew himself up taller. Slowly he turned. "No?" His voice was calm. Too calm for the flaming-red aura burning around him. Why couldn't she do that when angry?

He sauntered toward her. "Do you really believe you have a say in the matter? I can lock you in your room until the war ends. Or better yet, the dungeon. No one would hear you pleading to be set free down there."

She met his gaze and puffed out her chest. "You don't scare me, Kedric. But I do find your hypocrisy disgusting. You claim to want to free mankind, yet you keep them behind your kingdom walls. You want to liberate gladiators from having to fight to their deaths, yet you command your soldiers to do just that."

"Freedom is worth dying for."

"And life is worth protecting."

"Which is exactly what I'm doing."

"No, that's what *I'm* doing by healing people's desire for war."

"What you're doing is weakening my forces. I need more men."

His eyes narrowed. "And I know just the place to get them. All of them."

He was threatening to go back to the villages, where her father was still recovering from his injury. If his condition hadn't improved, he wouldn't be able to survive the journey. "You wouldn't."

"The hell I wouldn't. Half my army originated in the lowland villages."

She shook her head in disgust and then tucked the hair that fell in her eyes behind her ear again. "You know I'm not the only one in the Highlands who believes Pele will suffer from your war."

His lips pinched together into a hard, distinctive line. "Stay away from Griffin."

"It's no secret he dislikes how you run the kingdom."

"That gutless wonder has no idea what it takes to run a country. Even his own father, a king, thought so. He wants everyone to worship him like a god. He's nothing but trouble. Stay away from him."

Myia shifted her feet. What would he do if he found out she took supper with Griffin? She gazed at the woven area rug, taking a sudden interest in the diamond patterns.

"You already saw him." It wasn't a question. She couldn't hide her guilt.

"I'm sorry, Kedric, but I can't prevent this war by myself. I need help."

"Oh, Myia," he whispered. "Tell me you're not the one who informed him about the mind control device."

Her silence and inability to meet his gaze would incriminate her again, but there was nothing she could say. She wouldn't lie to him.

"Dammit, Myia." His biceps bulged as he rubbed both hands over his head. "You've no idea what you've done. I should throw you in the dungeon. Maybe then you'd stop causing trouble."

Trouble? She was trying to protect the people!

Heat flushed through her body as her muscles tensed. She wanted to smack the attitude off his face. "Go ahead and imprison me, barbarian. Sooner or later, when you discover your army hasn't returned because your mission failed, you'll come let me out. You'll need me to mend the pulverized fragments of your spirit."

"If the mission fails, savage, you can rest assured I won't be seeking you out." He strode to the door. With one hand on the handle, he turned to face her again. "I'll leave you with this comforting thought. Wherever my men are. That's where I'll be. Captured, tortured, or dead."

Her gut twisted. "What? No."

He flung open the door.

She ran to him as he crossed the threshold. "You never said you were going into battle with them."

"I never said I wasn't." The door slammed.

The lock slid into place with a click.

Chapter Sixteen

General Sebastian entered Kedric's office. "My lord."

"Ready C and D companies. You leave on the hour." Kedric had assigned the capture of the lowlanders to Sebastian, as he couldn't afford taking Max away from the elite forces preparing for the attack on HuBReC. They'd been training in the arctic temperature in the Yard, each man getting up close and personal with a real live Hyborean. They needed to be comfortable around the creatures if they were going to infiltrate HuBReC.

Sebastian would lead the charge on the lowland invasion and capture.

"My lord. The winds have picked up. I fear a storm will be upon us before daybreak."

"Good. The lowlanders won't hear you coming. Don't return here until every last man, woman, and child are liberated."

"Yes, my lord." Sebastian gave a bow and left the room.

Kedric poured himself a shot of whiskey. The amber drink went down much smoother than the stuff his father used to make. What he wouldn't give to be drinking his father's brew.

He downed another shot, taking comfort in the liquid heat

warming him from the inside out. He poured a third and downed that, too, but nothing seemed to erase the argument with Myia from his mind.

She was right about him being a hypocrite. How could he think about saving the human race when he'd captured so many people? Including her.

He was an ass for locking her in her room again.

But Spirits be damned, her meddling with his soldiers had pissed him off to no end. She refused to cease and desist with her spiritual healing. He admired her spunk and her passion, but not when it opposed him.

And now she'd turned to Griffin. How the hell did that happen? Knowing she, of all people, told his enemy about the mind control device was like taking a Fleasheater to the heart. He could just see that prick coming to her rescue. Putting his sleazy arms around her, comforting her. Convincing her to help him overtake the throne.

Kedric punched the desk. The pain in his knuckles did no better than the alcohol to dull his grief.

Why couldn't Myia see things his way? Their relationship would be much less complicated if she did. She had wanted him. Hell, she wanted him still. Her eyes said as much when she learned he was going into battle. It took all his strength to close and lock the door when what he really wanted was to take her into his arms and make her his.

He wanted her so much it hurt.

Never had a woman consumed him. Or affected him like this. She was so wrong for him, yet he couldn't stop thinking about her. Wanting her. They had nothing in common. Except for a passion for their respective causes.

Her power as a healer was fantastic. He should know; she turned his whole world inside out with every person she touched. It was aggravating and yet inspiring. She wasn't ashamed of her ability. She didn't hide it. She didn't fear the consequences or costs of sharing it. To her, it was a gift to the world.

To him, his healing ability was something to hide. Hoard. Fear.

She was a much better person than he was.

Perhaps if their philosophies weren't so polarized. Perhaps if he gave into her view and forgot the outside world, there'd be no wedges between them, then. There would be nothing in the way of him running up there and making love to her like he'd wanted to since the first day she lay in his bed. Drive her crazy with his tongue. Make her beg for mercy. Bring out her passion that he craved.

But that would never happen.

His chest tightened, a prelude to his old pal guilt. He tried to relax it with another shot of whiskey.

If he kept Myia locked in a windowless room until his return, he'd snuff out that passion he had come to love. But if he let her out, she'd thwart his objectives and side with Griffin.

Thunder rumbled in the distance.

He poured himself another drink and slumped into his chair. What the hell was he going to do?

* * *

From the moment she awoke, Myia spent every minute in reflection and meditation. Relaxing into her trance had been difficult at first. She hadn't been able to stop thinking about last night with Kedric. It was as if anger and fear had taken up permanent residence in her heart. But she'd kept inhaling her cleansing breaths and repeating her chants until she was finally able to let go of selfish emotion and listen to the world around her.

The process was like being a beginner student all over again.

Eventually, focus was restored, and her soul received the wisdom of the Spirits. When her meditation ended, balance and tranquillity prevailed.

She didn't know what time it was when Kedric came in to see her. He closed the door so gently the sound of the latch was almost inaudible. Such a difference from last night. But last night he'd been frustrated and irate. Today his expression was somber. His aura was marbled with conflict and pain.

Her shaman's heart latched onto his distress and went out to him.

"You starving yourself in protest?" He indicated the table where her untouched breakfast remained. Someone had brought it in while she was in her trance.

"I fasted. For prayer."

Kedric nodded. He seemed deep in thought. Yesterday's anger had been replaced with worry and anguish.

She stood and crossed the room, meeting him halfway. "What's wrong?"

His eyebrows rose as if he didn't expect that particular question. "How can you ask me that with such sincerity after my deplorable behavior last night?"

"Meditation. You should try it."

"Yeah, I probably should."

Had he come to tell her he changed his mind about the war? Was he ready to begin his journey toward spiritual awakening?

With both hands, he pushed his long red hair out of his face. It was loose today, not plaited as usual. He blew out a breath. "I have bad news. I came here as soon as I found out. I thought I should be the one to tell you."

"Tell me what? What's happened?"

"We've taken all the lowlanders. They're here in the kingdom. In the welcome center. Getting food and medicine."

Her fingertips went numb. Her tribe would be no more. Kedric was right; the people enjoyed the easier Highland ways. "My sister and father are here, too?"

He nodded, his face still somber.

"What aren't you telling me?"

"The shaman—your father—is very sick, Myia. The doctor says it's a disease of the lungs called pneumonia. He also has a very bad infection from his broken leg. It has spread into his body. My men almost left him in the village, but they had strict orders to leave no one behind. I'm so sorry. He's dying."

Pain gripped her heart, and she grabbed hold of Kedric to keep from collapsing. He steadied her, as she gasped for breath. "Where is he? I want to see him. Please let me out to—"

"Of course." He ushered her to the door and then stopped before they left the room. "I was wrong for locking you in here. You have my word it won't happen again."

The strength of his sincerity almost knocked her over. "I accept your apology."

By the way he nodded, he didn't seem sure he believed her. She placed her hand in his. "Bring me to my father, Kedric."

They crossed the threshold together and then made their way to the first-floor medical chamber.

Her father lay on a low raised bed. He shivered even though blankets covered him and the room's temperature felt quite comfortable. Dried blood coated a gash on his head. She let go of Kedric's hand, ran to his side, and fell to her knees.

"Father, it's Myia. What happened to you?"

"That's not important right now." His breaths were shallow and erratic. Heat from fever radiated off of him. "What's important is that I help you heal these clans. Our people are fighting among themselves. Last night they fought the Highlanders."

"And lost." She couldn't stop her trembling chin. Kedric had mentioned they were receiving medical attention. The raid must have gone wrong this time.

"All who fight lose."

"Yes, Father."

"We must heal this land, or I fear the worst. Help me out of this bed." He coughed and didn't stop for at least a full minute.

"No. You must rest. I've been healing the people. Not quickly enough, but I'm trying."

"Myia, I am weak. I need your strength to help me so that I might help the people."

"Let's take one step at a time, Father. Give me your hand."

* * *

From just inside the doorway, Kedric watched the intimate scene, feeling like an intruder, yet he couldn't turn away from Myia. Her eyes glistened with unshed tears. The tender compassion she showed for her father made his heart ache. It was because of his war and his order to capture the lowland people that her father was sick and dying. He never would have broken his leg if he hadn't been fleeing from the prior invasion. Kedric tried to ignore his guilt. It had been an accident. In the long run, he knew he was doing the right thing.

Treating the shaman here was for the best. The medical knowledge and drugs his people had were far superior to lowland herbs. In fact, if it hadn't been for his latest command, the shaman would most certainly die in his hut. Now he had a fighting chance in the castle infirmary.

So why couldn't Kedric bring himself to feel better?

"Excuse me, my lord," Andrei said in a near whisper. "General Sebastian would like to make his report to you."

Kedric wouldn't take his gaze from Myia. Her eyes were closed. Her forehead was on her father's. Their hands were intertwined. He hoped her spirit was giving her father's spirit the comfort he needed. "Send Sebastian to my office." He kept his voice low lest he break her trance. "I'll be there shortly."

"Yes, my lord."

He didn't want to leave, but he was lord, and there was still much to prepare before the war.

* * *

It had been another exhausting day of spiritual healing, but at least she'd been able to procure the special herbs from the different people she had worked with. It wasn't easy keeping them dry as she walked from place to place in the pouring rain, but somehow she'd managed. Outside the castle's kitchen windows, lightning lit up the evening sky. The rain hadn't let up in over a day.

Myia poured hot water over the herbal blend. The tea should help Father's cough. And the poultice she made should help his infection. The medicines the doctor had given her father didn't seem to be doing much.

"Excuse me, Miss Myia." Andrei's voice echoed in the quiet and empty room. "You have a visitor."

She set the kettle back on the stove and turned to see her little sister's bright eyes. "Kimi." She raced to her sister, who met her halfway in a hearty yet wet embrace. She was soaked from hair to moccasins. Having her sister's arms around her again was like being home. "Thank the Spirits you're okay."

"I'll leave you two alone." Andrei exited the room.

"I'm so happy to find you, Myia. But I'm worried about Father. He wasn't in the welcome center with us. He's very sick. I don't know—"

"He's here. In the castle infirmary. A medicine man—a doctor—is taking care of him, but I fear Father's health is declining."

Tears came to Kimi's eyes and fell onto her cheeks. "I'm so sorry. I couldn't heal him. I tried everything I knew, but he only got worse." As she sobbed, her body shook from grief. "He'd lost so much blood from his leg wound. He was too weak—"

"Shh." She smoothed Kimi's wet hair. She hated seeing anyone this upset, especially her little sister who gave so much of herself for others. "You did the best you could."

"The Highlanders were wrong to have moved him. He shouldn't have traveled so many hours through a storm."

"I know. Come." She walked her sister back to the counter where the herbal remedy steamed. "I've made Father a brew. Let's bring it to him together."

Kimi nodded, wiped her eyes, and then followed Myia through the stone corridors of the castle into the infirmary where Father lay coughing on his bed. Pillows propped up his head and shoulders.

Myia sat on a floor pillow on one side of her father, and Kimi sat on the other. Each placed a hand in his. He opened his eyes, and his pale lips gave them a ghost of a smile.

It was a bittersweet family reunion.

And unfortunately evoked memories of Mother's deathbed. If Myia listened, she was sure to hear her mother's spirit whispering nearby.

"I have some tea for you, Father." Myia took the cooled cup; placed it to his dry, cracked lips; and gently tilted it into his mouth. She wiped the dribble from his chin.

The effort to drink a few ounces grew too much, as evidenced by his labored breaths and closing eyes. Father drifted into sleep, each deep breath accompanied by a wet, rattling sound inside his chest.

"He's even worse than last night." Kimi kept her voice quiet. "I blame the Highlanders. They're evil."

They weren't evil. Myia had lived here long enough to realize that. They were only following their lord's orders. If the blame for their father's condition should fall to anyone, it was Kedric. "Did the Highlanders mistreat you in the welcome center?"

Kimi seemed to think about that before shaking her head. "No. They fed us well, let us bathe in an indoor waterfall, and supplied us with clean clothing."

"The colors are rather beautiful, aren't they?"

Kimi crossed her arms over her chest. "I hate to admit it, but yes."

"What of the women and children? Did they reunite them with their husbands and fathers?"

"They did. Oh, Myia. It warmed my heart to see the families together again. The joy was enough to make me cry. The men took their families to their homes. The rest of us had to stay in the center."

"Why?"

"That's where our bedding is. They said we would live there until they find suitable homes for us. They promised we'd have a better life here. They said we'd all get jobs tomorrow based on our talents. And as long as we contribute to the kingdom, our needs shall always be met. This can't be the truth, can it? Surely, the Highlanders don't capture people only to give them a better life. There must be something sinister they want in return."

"They want our men to fight in their army. They want to make war with the Hyboreans."

Kimi's gasp woke Father. His eyes fluttered and then closed once again. "What are you doing about it?" she whispered.

"I'm trying to heal the people. I'm trying to heal the leader." Her face grew hot as she forced back threatening tears. She couldn't cry in front of her sister. She had to be strong. She had to provide Kimi with hope. Even though she had little hope left to provide.

* * *

Myia didn't know what time it was when Kedric entered the infirmary. It was pitch black outside the window and silent in the corridor. He placed a blanket over Kimi, who had fallen asleep with her head on Father's bed. The weight of a blanket fell around Myia's shoulders, too. It was nothing compared to the weight on her heart.

Father's breathing had become even more labored. He gasped for breath. "Myia."

"I'm here, Father." Her cry woke Kimi. Myia interlaced her fingers with Father's cold, clammy ones. His were the icy fingers of death.

She had to relax. She breathed in and out deeply, but the rhythm was uneven. She tried again. And again. But the more she willed herself to become tranquil, the more tense and upset she became.

"Concentrate, Myia," Kimi said. "Be one with the Spirits. Take away Father's pain."

"Don't you think I would if I could?" she snapped and immediately felt terrible for letting the words slip. Frustration took up residency in her heart, and she didn't know how to kick it out.

Again, she slowed her breathing down. She listened to the sound of air filling her lungs and then expelling from them. She called upon the Spirits. Their energy entered her soul.

Her father's coughing fit scattered her concentration, breaking the trance she had barely begun. "Father, I'm here."

"My time has come, child."

"Don't talk that way. You'll get better."

"No, I feel the poison in my blood. It has spread throughout my body. It is too late for me. You are the shaman now."

"But I can't be. I haven't received my full powers."

"You are the last of our kind."

"No. I need you. You're the only one who can teach me. You need to save the clans. I can't do it. I keep failing."

"Failure comes after you fall and choose not to rise again. Rise, my dear, like the Spirit Lights in the sky. I believe in you. And shall watch over you always." His eyes closed.

Tears streamed down her face. She glanced at her sister who was sobbing uncontrollably. She turned to Kedric at her side. "I shouldn't have come to the Highlands. I should have stayed in the village and taken care of him."

Kimi's body crumpled. Her head fell onto folded arms on the bed as she cried louder into the crook of her elbow.

Myia's heart ached. She hadn't meant any disrespect to her sister's medical care. She reached across Father's body to place a hand over Kimi's softer, smaller one. "I should have stayed with you. Together our healing powers would've been greater than each one of ours alone."

Kimi nodded, but Myia wasn't sure that her words gave any comfort. The guilt piled onto Myia's already burdened soul. "How can I save the clans when I can't save one man?"

Kedric tucked a strand of her hair behind her ear and gazed into her eyes. "You're doing the best you can."

"Am I? His connection to each person in our village is so strong that their fear, aggression, and capture has shattered his soul. I've been trying to repair it, but his spirit is dying. I can't heal him because I'm not a true shaman."

"It's not his spirit that needs repairing. It's his body. His physical ailments are beyond your power."

"I've given him every herbal remedy I know. Nothing has worked."

"Except for the pain medication, none of ours have worked, either."

"Your medicine takes away physical pain. I'm supposed to take away his spiritual pain, his heartache. But how can I when I can't be calm enough to go into a trance? I can't join his spirit. I can't give him the love he needs to get his strength back. My lack of tranquillity is killing him."

"You must stop blaming yourself."

"Why? It's true. I can't heal his broken heart. And I can't heal your pain or lust for war."

She hugged her legs to her chest and let her head fall onto bended knees. The tears couldn't stop. "I'm not a shaman. I'm a sham."

Chapter Seventeen

Y ou can do it, Myia," her sister said through her sniffles. Kedric had forgotten her name, but wouldn't forget her excitement in the welcome center when he'd told her he would bring her to Myia. It was the same excitement he felt inside every time he thought about freeing Tess. "Try again."

Myia wiped her tears on the blanket he had brought her. She intertwined her fingers with her father's and then closed her eyes in precisely the same manner she'd done with him on Discovery Island.

Perhaps he should leave. This was a private family matter too intimate for him to witness. But he couldn't. He didn't want to leave Myia's side. She needed his support.

"I am earth and the sky," she chanted. "I am wind and sea. May the peace of my tranquil spirit join in harmony with all nature's spirits."

She inhaled and exhaled, but her face was not relaxed. The lines were deep where she held her tension and fear. She breathed again and repeated her chant over and over, but each time her eyes squeezed tighter and her breathing grew faster and shallower as if she were exercising too hard.

"It's not working," she said. Her open eyes filled with tears. She wiped them away with her fingertips. "I can't call the Spirits. They won't answer me. Why won't you answer me?" she screamed, and her voice echoed off the stone walls.

"I could be mistaken," he said, "but I don't think yelling at Spirits will win them to your side."

"You." She turned narrowed eyes filled with hate toward him. Her jaw trembled. "This is all your fault."

"Myia!" The disbelief in her sister's voice was clear. Myia probably never blamed anyone for anything. Until she'd met him. He'd wanted to seduce her to his side. Apparently, he'd corrupted her instead.

"Our people never did anything to you. We wanted nothing more than to live in peace. But you barbarians"—she spat the word out with disgust—"keep attacking us and taking our men for your army and stealing our women and children. He's dying because of you."

"Myia. Stop it. You don't mean that."

Her sister was wrong. Myia did mean it, and she was right to yell at him. Good for her for finally getting up the nerve to say it to his face. It wasn't healthy to remain calm all the time. She needed to get out her anger and frustration and direct that energy to the one person who really was to blame.

Him.

"It's your fault he was injured during last week's invasion. And your fault he was in a rainstorm for fifteen hours." She slapped and beat his chest over and over.

Her sister was crying and hugging her herself.

He remained as motionless as their father lying on his deathbed so that Myia could strike him for as long as she needed. Her physical exertion would make her feel better. The blows didn't hurt much. It was her anger toward him that caused the real pain.

"You did this. Your lust for war and revenge did this."

She was right. And he could say nothing. Anguish emanated from her eyes. And the sight of it ripped out his heart.

The strikes came slower and with less force. Her face was red and blotchy.

He grasped her soft hands and held them to his chest. She struggled to hit him again, then stilled and gazed up into his eyes, realization at what she'd done dawning in hers. They widened. Her chest heaved as she sucked in air. "I'd say I'm sorry for hitting you, but you know it wouldn't be the truth."

"I know." When he reached for the hair stuck to her wet cheeks, she flinched in fear. His heart shattered. Did she really think he would strike her? Gently, he pushed the black strands off her face and then released her hands.

She wiped her eyes. "Though you may have caused his condition, it's my fault he can't be healed. I can't become one with the Spirits. I can't find forgiveness in my heart, for you or for myself."

Her sister came to her other side and wrapped her arms around her. He wished it were his arms around her. Myia pulled free from the embrace.

"Don't, Kimi. Father lies dying because I'm a fake."

"Don't say that. You are a gifted healer. You've—"

"Failed my test. And the kindest man, the true and last shaman, will die because of my failure." She crawled past her sister to her father's side, folded her arms on the bed and lay her head on them, and sobbed.

The failure she harbored killed him. She was too blinded by hate to see clearly, and unfortunately, no one else could heal that. Her heart was full of rage, and rage couldn't call upon the Spirits.

The ache in Kedric's chest was unbearable. How could he stand there and watch her blame herself? Watch her give up the fight. She wouldn't even try channeling the Spirits again. How could he stand her suffering when he knew there was one simple thing he could do to stop it?

He had the power to save her father but was too scared to use it. Her father needed his blood. Needed a lot of it to mend the broken leg, clear up the infection, and cure his pneumonia.

If he gave it to him, Kedric would lose consciousness for two days, maybe more. Plus it wasn't as simple as cutting his arm and smearing his blood over a small wound like he'd done to Myia. Collecting his blood via a syringe to his vein wouldn't work, either.

The shaman required a full transfusion, which meant someone else would have to transfer it.

His blood would save her father's life, but it would render Kedric unconscious, helpless. While he lay in sleep, news of the shaman's miraculous recovery would spread throughout the kingdom. His secret would be revealed. His advantage, his ability, would be known to all. Anyone—including Myia and Griffin—could use that knowledge against him.

That's how things worked here. He remained in power because he was the strongest. Because he could fight anyone and win and recover quickly. If he was out of commission, Griffin could overtake the kingdom and his whole plan for attacking the Hyboreans could end. His family would never be freed.

"I'm so sorry, Father," Myia whispered. "I've failed you and our people."

Perhaps there was still a way to save her father and his kingdom.

Kedric strode out of the room, and then climbed the stairs. It might actually work, too. As long as he could get everything together fast enough. He quickened his pace.

At Max and Addy's bedroom door, he reached for the doorknob, ready to barge in, when the sounds of lovemaking—very enthusiastic lovemaking—stopped him.

Shit.

After three days of nonstop training and planning, he'd promised Max a night off to spend with his family. He couldn't interrupt them now. He'd just have to go to Discovery Island himself.

He couldn't trust anyone else to do this.

The trip took thirty minutes through the rain and choppy seawater before he returned to the castle with Finn and his medical supplies. They went straight to Max's chamber.

By the sounds on the other side of the door, the two of them were still going at it. What'd they think this was, the breeding box?

"Okay, Finn. Come with me." They went back downstairs to the first-floor medical chamber. Myia hadn't moved from her spot. Kimi was curled up in the blankets on the floor, asleep.

"Set up the equipment. I'll be back with your donor in a few minutes."

Myia's head came off the bed. Her face was wet with tears. Her eyes were red and puffy and blinked as if bothered by the light. She sniffled and wiped her nose with the back of her hand. "What's going on?"

"You couldn't heal him because he isn't suffering from a spiritual wound. He suffers from a physical one. Your father's blood is poisoned and needs a transfusion."

"I don't understand this word. What does it mean?"

"Finn is a medical scientist. He knows how to take blood out of a healthy person and give it to a sick person. If it works properly, it will save your father."

"Give him my blood." She said it with no hesitation. He admired her for that.

"It's not that simple. The two blood types must match. And we don't have time to test your blood or his."

"My lord. If she's his daughter—"

"There is no guarantee the blood types are a match. Besides I already found a universal donor."

"Who?" she asked.

"Don't worry about that now. I need you to take your sister and leave the room."

"No. I can't leave Father's side. If something should happen, I must be here."

"Myia, please."

"No. I'm not leaving."

When had she gotten so assertive?

"My lord, we need to get on with this as quickly as possible. This man is barely holding on."

Kedric scratched his head. "Fine. I'll be back with the donor. Set everything up."

For the third time that night, Kedric stood at Max and Addy's room. He put his ear to the door. All sounded quiet inside. Thank the Spirits they were done. He turned the knob and let himself in.

Max and Addy were lying naked in bed, feeding each other fruit. Addy screamed and scrambled for the bedcovers.

He'd forgotten Earthlings were prudish when it came to nudity. He turned his back, but didn't leave.

"Don't you knock?" The frustration in Addy's voice was clear over the rumpling of bedcovers. The sounds quieted down and he faced them again. She'd covered them both.

"I'm lord here. I don't need to knock."

"You do if you want to remain lord," Max said. "What the hell's so important that you came to our door three times?"

"He came three times tonight?"

"He and I both." Grinning like the devil, Max wiggled his eyebrows at her, and she blushed.

Kedric rolled his eyes. Did Max really find it necessary to spout his virility at a time like this? The shaman's life hung by a silkworm thread, Myia gave up on her destiny, and a blood transfusion could end Kedric's reign as Highland lord.

He needed his sister's and Max's help. "Get dressed, both of you, and follow me."

"Why?" they said in unison.

"I'll tell you on the way."

Chapter Eighteen

Kedric returned with Max and Addy. Max, carrying a broadsword in his hand, remained by the door, looking formidable. Everything about his demeanor screamed warrior, and fear raced through Myia's heart. "What's going on?"

"I found you a blood donor."

After placing her bag on the floor, Addy knelt at her side and slipped her hand into hers. She smelled of fruit and musk, her lips appeared red and swollen, and the essence of love filled her aura. It couldn't be more obvious what she and her mate had been doing before Kedric returned with them. No wonder Max looked like he wanted to murder someone.

"Oh, thank you, Addy. I can't tell you how much—"

"I'm not the donor."

"Who is it, then?" Finn snapped. "I need to hook them up quickly. There isn't much time."

Kedric lay down on the empty bedding they'd brought in. He was an arm's reach from the shaman. "It's me. Let's do this."

Addy shook Kimi awake. "Come with me," she said, putting her arm around her shoulders. "We need to give the men privacy."

"Myia?"

"Go with Addy. I'll stay here with Father. Get some sleep."

Addy ushered Myia's reluctant sister out of the room. Myia turned her attention back to the men.

Her heart raced as Finn inserted a needle—a cannula he'd called it—into Kedric's arm, like he'd done to her father a moment before. He attached a clear tube to Kedric's cannula, which ran into a small machine and back out the other side. Finn turned a switch on the machine, and blood slid through the tube. Once filled with blood, Finn inserted the other end of the tube into Father's cannula.

Could this really work? Could inserting the blood of a healthy man into the body of a sick man heal him?

Her heart pounded so hard in the silent room she was sure Finn could hear it. Heck, Max probably heard it standing guard outside the door.

The process was slow and the minutes ticked by.

The door opened and Addy entered again. She came to sit by Myia's side; her hand slipped inside hers and gave a reassuring squeeze. The support and solace was comforting.

Kedric's eyes closed, and his breathing slowed. He'd fallen asleep.

The rhythm of his breaths was so relaxing that Myia closed her eyes, inhaled and exhaled in sync with his slow tempo, and prayed to the Spirits.

Okay, pleaded was more like it.

Though there was a balance to life, and death was a natural part of that balance, she prayed for her father to be healed. She needed him. All the people of Pele needed him. He had to live so that he could save the clans.

She couldn't save them.

Please, let this work.

Finn turned off the machine and unhooked his patients. "It will be a while before we know if the transfusion is successful," he said.

The doctor wiped sweat from his brow. "But there doesn't appear to be any complications. I hadn't expected Lord Kedric to fall asleep, though."

Addy was quick to respond. "That must be because you did a fine job making him comfortable. Plus, I think he had a busy day today. Perhaps we should let the men rest. I'll show you to your room, Finn."

"I need to check the shaman's pulse." After a moment of counting, confusion crossed his features. He counted again.

"What is it? Is my father okay?"

The shaman's chest rose and fell. His breaths were deep.

"I don't understand it. His pulse is returning to normal. This never happened so quickly before."

Addy pulled her hand free and then raced to the door. She opened it and then grabbed Max, pulling him inside while whispering something into his ear. She seemed nervous. His mouth set in a hard line of determination.

"What is it?" Myia said. "What's happening?"

"I think he's getting better," Addy said. "Isn't that wonderful? The blood transfusion worked. Come, doctor, you must be exhausted. I'll show you to your room." She reached for Finn, but he moved out of the way.

"Look at his face," Finn said. His color has returned. And his wound, it's—"

Disappearing in front of their eyes.

Addy's aura filled with nervous energy. "Max?" Her voice rose in an unspoken question Myia didn't understand, but apparently Max did. He shook his head no. What did they know that they weren't saying?

Finn checked Kedric's pulse and grimaced. As he checked it again, color drained from his cheeks. "His pulse is very low. A transfusion might weaken him, but not this much. I haven't taken enough blood."

"Doctor, surely my brother's pulse is low because he's sleeping," Addy said. "It can't be easy ruling a kingdom and planning a war. Let's not get excited. I should take you to your room now." She snaked an arm around his shoulders and began walking him away from the bed.

"Myia," her father whispered. His eyes were open.

Her heart leapt. A sound that was a cross between a gasp and a laugh escaped her lips. Tears came to her eyes. She sniffled and grabbed hold of the hand he reached out to her. "I'm here, Father."

His smile was fleeting. His grip slackened. His eyes closed once again.

"He's okay." She knew in her soul it was true. "He's fallen asleep, but he's going to be okay. I can feel it."

Finn freed himself from Addy's arm and came to Myia's side. The wound on her father's head was closing before their eyes. "It's a miracle." The awe in his voice was clear. "Did the Spirits do this?"

"Yes," Addy and Max shouted in unison, as she said, "No."

"I couldn't call upon them. I couldn't connect—"

"A normal blood transfusion wouldn't cause his wound to close up like that. You must have great healing power."

"But—but I couldn't connect with the Spirits. I didn't do this."

Addy was at her other side. "Of course she did this. Don't be modest, Myia. Come, doctor. Let Myia and her father have some time alone."

By Finn's expression, he knew Addy was lying. What did Max and Addy know that she and Finn didn't?

"I don't believe you," he said to Addy. "It's him isn't it?" He pointed to Kedric. "Your brother has something to do with this."

"How could he possib—"

"You're trying too hard to cover it up. Lord Kedric wanted to be the donor because his blood has the power to heal. Doesn't it?" He moved to Kedric's bed to get a closer look at him.

"You're talking nonsense," Addy said. She turned pleading eyes on Max.

"He's a gen-alt, isn't he? Superhuman. With the ability to heal. But it zaps his own energy." Finn shook his head in disgust and then looked back at Myia. "So many of our people have died, and he had the power to save them all along. He could have saved Alex Graham, but he didn't. Because it makes him weak and vulnerable. Powerless. The coward."

"That's enough." Max pointed his sword at the man. "You know nothing."

"I know everything. And soon so will everyone in the kingdom."

Max lunged, his sword tip pressed against the fleshy part of Finn's neck.

Finn froze.

Myia gasped. What was happening?

"One more sound, and I'll give *you* a blood transfusion. Gladiator-style."

Finn's eyes were as round as both full moons. Fear shot through his aura. Her heart went out to him, but she made no move to connect to his spirit. Max and Addy had Kedric's best interest at hand. They wouldn't hurt this man.

Would they?

"Cuff him, Addy."

She pulled out shackles from the bag she had brought. "Put your hands on the back of your head." When Finn obeyed, she preceded to grab each arm behind his back and shackle him. "You have the right to remain silent."

Max chuckled. "Miranda rights? On Pele."

Addy shrugged. "Old habits."

"Let's take a walk," Max said, and Finn shuffled toward the door. With a shove on the back to get him moving faster, Max escorted him out of the room.

"What's going on?" Myia finally found her voice. "I don't understand what's happening."

Addy returned to her. "Kedric gave up a lot of special blood for your father. He told us that he'd be unconscious for twenty-four to forty-eight hours. He fears that if the people learn of this, someone might take control of the kingdom. We must keep him hidden and make it appear he is healthy and in charge."

"What about Finn? Max won't hurt him, will he?"

"Max will keep the doctor locked up and away from everyone until after Kedric recovers. He must not learn how long Kedric is out of commission. The question is are *you* on board with us?"

"On board?"

"Will you tell anyone Kedric's secret?"

"No. I promise I won't breathe a word of it."

"Not even to your sister." It wasn't a question.

"You have my solemn word that I won't tell Kimi."

"Will you help us keep the appearance that everything is normal with Kedric? That he is out and about and leading the kingdom?"

"Yes. Of course I will. I've been so cruel to him. It's the least I can do to make up for the horrible way I've treated him."

"I believe you. I'm going to check on Max and make sure he doesn't get carried away with that sword."

"Thank you, Addy." Myia hugged her tightly and felt the goodness inside her new friend.

"Take care of my brother, will you? He's the only one I have. I think." Her face scrunched up in thought. She probably wondered if Duncan had been at stud in one of those breeding boxes they'd told her about.

"I will. Perhaps I can help his recovery. I'll call upon the Spirits."

Chapter Nineteen

It didn't take long before Max and Addy returned to the infirmary. "The doctor is taken care of," Max said. "We need to get Kedric to his room without anyone seeing us."

Myia glanced at Kedric's unconscious body. "How?"

"I'll have to carry him. You two keep watch. Make sure no one is coming."

Judging by Max's solid build, there was no doubt he was a strong man, but Kedric was a couple inches taller, had more muscle, and was very heavy as Myia recalled from being pinned beneath him in bed.

Heat crept into her cheeks. He'd been so alive, so virile then, but now he lay helpless.

Could Max really carry him up three flights of stairs to his chamber? What if he stumbled or dropped Kedric? They'd both tumble down the stone. Probably crack open their skulls. Her gut tightened.

"What if someone sees you carrying him?" she said as Max yanked Kedric by the arms into a seated position. His limp head propelled forward and drooped on his chest. She had to turn away. She couldn't stand seeing Kedric like this.

"We should come up with a cover story," Addy said.

"Fine." Max grunted behind her. There was a rustling and shuffling of bodies. "Kedric and I were drinking heavily. He passed out."

Max strode past her with Kedric's body over his shoulder. "Addy, go down the hall to the stairs. Make sure the area is clear. Myia, close the door behind me, and keep anyone from coming down the hall. We'll take it one section at a time until we get to his room."

The castle was quiet as it should be in the middle of the night. Everyone was sure to be asleep. Except maybe a guard or two.

Every little sound, every little creak amplified in Myia's ears. Thunder boomed and stopped her heart for a moment.

Please don't let anyone see us. Kedric had risked so much to save her father. She didn't want him to lose his kingdom because of it.

They climbed the three flights unnoticed. One more corridor and they would be in Kedric's room.

Addy disappeared around the corner and then returned, gesturing *come here* with her hand. "Clear."

Myia glanced behind them again. No one was on the stairs. It probably only took sixty seconds to walk the final corridor and enter his bedchamber, but it felt like fifteen minutes had passed.

"We did it," Myia said, closing Kedric's door behind the other two.

Max deposited Kedric's limp body on the bed. Rubbing his shoulder, he turned to her.

"Thank you both so much." She gave Addy a hug and then gave one to Max whose spine stiffened at the contact.

"We have to keep watch over him," Max said. "Make sure he isn't disturbed tomorrow. Keep up the appearance that he's awake and in charge."

"You two should get some rest," Myia said. "I'll sit with him tonight and comfort his spirit."

"We'll leave you to work your magic, then." Max's arm encircled

Addy's waist. He pulled her to him, and his smoldering eyes glanced down at her. "We've a little of our own magic to work."

Addy pushed him away with the palm of her hand. "It'll have to wait. It's time to feed Noah." The disappointment on Max's face was priceless. "Good night, Myia. Take care of my brother."

"Lock the door behind us," Max said.

After the two left, she locked the door, returned to Kedric's bed, and covered him with a blanket. She wished she could say he looked peaceful, but he didn't. He looked ill. Inert. Comatose.

His body wasn't resting. It was struggling. No one had said it tonight, but she knew there was a chance he wouldn't come out of this. His aura was too dim. Max and Addy seemed confident that Kedric would be better after two days, but she'd seen too many dying souls to believe it.

Kedric probably had told them there was no danger so that they wouldn't worry.

He needed her help. She needed to call upon the Spirits and pull him back. She needed to make him fight his way back to consciousness.

Climbing into the bed, she slipped beneath the blanket, laid her head on his pillow and took his hand in hers. She closed her eyes, sunk into the soft mattress, and listened to his slow, steady breaths. Inhaling and exhaling in time with him, she lulled herself into tranquillity. The Spirits answered her quickly, and her soul entered into a darkness that was Kedric's soul.

He was too weak to create a visual for her, not even the stone wall barriers she had seen the last time their spirits had intertwined.

"Thank you for your trust," her spirit voice spoke into the emptiness. It wasn't really trust that allowed her access to his soul, it was his debilitated and vulnerable state. But it was proper to show good faith by thanking his spirit anyway.

She waited for a reply, but none came.

Either he was too weak to answer or he didn't want to talk.

"You did a brave thing giving the shaman your blood."

Again she listened and waited quietly for any kind of response. There was nothing but a cold void. She shivered. Where was his essence? His soul? Calling upon the Spirits, she gathered their energy and dove deeper into Kedric's darkness. At his core, she found a dim glow from a dying ember. It was all that remained of a once great fire. It was all that remained of his spirit.

An ache formed in the back of her throat as she choked back the threatening sobs. Until this moment, she hadn't realized exactly what Kedric had given up for her father. "Why did you save the shaman when you knew it could kill you?"

Silence.

Come on, Kedric. She was about to demand an answer when a whisper cut through the darkness. "My...pain."

The grief she'd been holding back burst out in a strangled cry of relief. Tears welled behind her eyes as her heart rejoiced. Kedric's spirit had communicated with hers. She could latch onto it and coax him back to consciousness. "I'm here to help heal your pain."

"Myia's pain...is my pain."

Her spirit fluttered as though the wind had been knocked out of her. She never expected such a declaration, especially after the horrible way she'd treated him. But Kedric had feelings for her, strong feelings that radiated from his soul. He was dying, yet his essence didn't grieve for his own hurt. It grieved for hers.

Tears sprang forth, and her spirit wavered. Breathless, she refocused her energy and regained control of herself before losing the connection.

She had a soul to save.

"Come with me back to the world," she said.

"Too tired."

"Find your strength. You can come back with me."

"What for? Myia hates me."

The dejection in his whispered voice broke her heart. If he didn't have a reason to live, she'd lose him to the spirit world. His essence was nearly extinguished. He wasn't even aware he was talking to her spirit. "Myia thinks you're very brave and kind."

"Thinks I'm a barbarian."

Her belly knotted. She'd been so cruel to him. She'd caused him so much anguish. "Myia's anger had blinded her. She was upset for not being tranquil when she needed it the most. She was wrong to take it out on you. I was wrong, Kedric. Please, forgive me."

"Myia? That you?"

"Yes."

"Show yourself." It wasn't a demand, but an appeal. She could sense his anticipation as the ember of his spirit glowed brighter.

In the darkness she conjured her fantasy image in the same white thermal suit she'd worn the last time their spirits had intertwined.

"So you've entered my body," he said. "I knew you couldn't keep your hands off me."

His teasing sent a warm rush through both of her bodies—the fantasy and the flesh. He wasn't angry about her intrusion. Thank the Spirits. Not only would she be able to coax him back to consciousness, but also he was sure to go willingly. Rejuvenated, her fantasy image couldn't contain its grin. She relaxed and reciprocated the banter. "It was only a matter of time before you lowered your defenses and let me in."

"I didn't let you in, savage. You forced your way in."

Savage. In the past, her blood boiled every time he'd said the word, but now she could feel his lighthearted connotation marking it clearly as an endearment. Who would have thought that? "I would hardly call it force when the doorway to your soul was gaping open as wide as the mouth of Grand Pele Caves."

"Fine. I'll give you that, but you did trespass."

"Yes, right past your sleeping guard." Myia's fantasy image placed her gloved palms together and rested them against her cheek, closing her eyes in emphasis.

He chuckled, and the light from the embers spread. "I'm glad you're here. Your spirit is comforting. Stay with me a while?"

"How about if you come back with me instead? Come back to the conscious world. Find your strength again."

"I can't. I'm too tired."

"Then I'll stay here with you until you get your strength back, okay? I have so much to make up for. You have sacrificed so much for my father."

"For you, Myia. Your pain is my pain."

Spirit is honest. Always.

Her heart soared with the knowledge of his admission. Kedric cared deeply for her. But with his admission came more guilt for treating him so poorly. "Can you find it in your heart to forgive me for my behavior? I've been so cruel to you."

"There's nothing to forgive."

"There is. I am sorry for blam—"

"There's nothing to forgive."

Spirit is honest. Always.

He truly harbored no ill will toward her. None. The relief was enormous. Like a weight lifted off her body enabling her to float on air. She wanted to do something more for him. Take away his anxiety. Heal whatever he had been about to share with her in the science building that day. "Kedric, while I'm here, will you let me heal your—"

"Do you remember telling me that I couldn't enter your body without you entering mine?"

A deliberate change of subject. Since he was still weak, she'd humor him and drop the thought. For now. "Yes. I remember."

"I find this rather unfair that you've entered my body while I'm unconscious. You could be doing all sorts of wonderfully nasty things to me right now, and I wouldn't even know it."

"You would know."

"I don't believe I would. I could be naked right now."

"We'll, you're not naked. You're fully clothed in your own bed. With a blanket covering you," she added. She left out the part where she was beneath said blanket, too. He didn't need to know everything.

"And you're holding my hand?"

"Yes."

"In bed with me?"

Had he meant it to sound as sexy as she'd interpreted it? "Yes."

The glow from the embers spread wider as more and more of them caught heat. "Are you naked?"

Her mouth went dry. Fantasy Myia shook her head until she found her voice again. She swallowed. "No."

"Damn. That would have woken me up."

"I'm sure it would have. The thought made your embers grow."

"Really? What do you know of my growing member?"

Heat crept into her flushing cheeks. "That is not what I said. At all."

His spirit was quiet for a moment. "I have an idea. Perhaps we should try an experiment."

"You want me to undress to see if it awakens you." It wasn't a question.

"You read my mind."

"Haven't we discussed this already. The mind and spirit are not technically—"

"You're stalling. It's just a little experiment. Undress for me."

"I don't think it would work. Aren't you too weak to see my fantasy image? You haven't conjured your own image to join me."

"I can see your fantasy image just fine. Though I'd prefer you to be wearing something else."

"Then imagine me in it." If he concentrated hard enough, he'd start waking up.

Her image wavered. The tight thermal suit faded and changed into the rose two-piece veiled skirt and halter top she wore when she'd danced for him, except the skirt hung so low on her hips there wasn't much left to the imagination. Not to mention her breasts spilled out of the very low-cut top. Silky, black hair hung loose down her back. And her gold eyes shone in the dark as if a sunbeam had caught them. Fantasy Myia was beautiful—more so than what she interpreted of her reflection in the mirrored glass.

The conscious sees flaws. Spirit sees truth. Always.

Like a gentle breeze, his energy moved briefly around her, stoking the embers of his soul. Her heart swelled. It was working.

Fantasy Myia began rocking her hips. She closed her eyes and swayed to unheard music. Even without the song, Myia knew exactly what dance her fantasy performed.

Something entered into his spirit. It was just a wisp of a feeling too frail to recognize. And then it was gone.

Fantasy Myia vanished along with the glowing embers.

"Kedric." She kept the shake out of her voice. "Are you all right? Your spirit dimmed."

"Too weak."

The fantasy had been working. If only he had the strength to carry it out, she'd be able to bring him out of the coma.

Well, she would just have to help him with it.

Myia took a deep breath and conjured her image again exactly how he had conceived it. Ample cleavage. Low-riding skirt. After all, it was his fantasy.

She thought about the music the Highland women had played

when teaching her the mating dance. It was a song about renewal and love and sexual joining. The rhythm filled the darkness.

Naomi had explained that if a woman dances this privately for a man—which they did often—neither partner was obligated to uphold a union vow. In order to be legal mates, the dance must be performed during mating season at a ritual gathering in the castle courtyard. The women seeking a mate would dance for the men around a huge bonfire.

A bonfire appeared behind her.

Fantasy Myia swayed her hips. She moved her feet and arms, setting the bells on her ankles and wrists jingling in time to the music's sensual beat. It wasn't long before Kedric's energy surged again. He was still weak but definitely enjoying her dance.

Slowly, as the music played, she untied a veil and let it drop to the darkness beneath her feet.

Kedric's spirit grew stronger. She could feel the excitement and desire of his being surrounding her, and in an instant he materialized before her, lying on his side on a bed of long body pillows. He wore nothing but a rumpled, nearly see-through silk sheet draped over his manhood. Fantasy Kedric was perfect and muscular and as sexy as she could have imagined.

"I don't really look like that, aye?" His spirit chuckled.

"That's exactly the way you look."

"Well, who am I to argue with your dream of me."

"My dream?" She pulled her spirit back, distancing herself for clarity. Fantasy Myia, fantasy bonfire, and fantasy Kedric lying on the pillows naked—save for the sheer red silk draped over his groin—all disappeared.

"Hey. Where'd everyone go? Should have kept my mouth shut," his voice grumbled in the darkness, and his disappointment overwhelmed her.

Apparently she'd conjured all of it while having no idea she had shared her spirit so freely. She had been lost in the sensuality of the dance.

"Relax." She brought the fantasies back, though she started again at the beginning with all veils in place. There was no grumbling from Kedric as she'd thought there would be. She felt only his anticipation.

The music started again, and fantasy Myia swayed her hips. Fantasy Kedric lay on his side, propped up on an elbow, appreciation evident in his hungry grin and lustful eyes—both manifestations from his spirit. Not hers. A sign he was regaining some strength.

The music beat on and she fell in perfect timing with it, gyrating her hips, reaching for him, using her arms to call him to her over and over again. Raising arms over her head, she pivoted round provocatively and then cast a glance over her shoulder, locking it directly into his moss-gray eyes. Last time she'd done this, she couldn't meet his gaze for fear of what he thought. This time she knew.

He enjoyed watching her. And Spirits help her, she enjoyed having him watch.

When her image bent over to untie the first veil, she could see what Kedric saw: her breasts falling forward giving a perfect view of her—well, her fantasy's—cleavage.

An excited thrill shot through her. It was a spark of energy as the embers of his spirit ignited into a flame. He licked his lips.

One by one, sheer silk colors floated to the floor as she untied veils, danced with them, and then cast them aside.

His energy surged with excitement and anticipation. It was a slight surge, but a surge nonetheless.

At the start, the dance had been a means to bring him out of the darkness, but now there was no denying the sensual pleasure she experienced from performing it.

Fantasy Myia turned her back, untied her halter top, and let it fall to the floor. Heart thundering, she faced Kedric again. Her long, straight black hair covered her breasts. The silky strands felt nice against her skin, and when they swept across her nipples sent a thrill through her. It made her feel beautiful. Sexy. Confident.

Fantasy Kedric watched her every move. His spirit had taken control of his own image now. It was safe to release it fully to him. When she withdrew, his image didn't fade or falter. His growing strength lifted her spirit, and she danced with enthusiasm. There was no doubt he would follow her back to the conscious world.

He longed to take her into his arms. She could feel his desire mounting, just as she could feel her own. But Kedric restrained himself. Men weren't allowed to grab or touch any woman until such time as the ritual dance allowed.

But this wasn't a true ritual dance. Would it really matter if he didn't wait until the right time to touch her? Maybe she should step into his arms. Spirits knew she ached for him. Of course, this wasn't about her. This was about him and bringing him back to consciousness. She pressed her lips together to refrain from asking him to hold her and then untied the final veil directly below her navel.

Wearing nothing more than the scalloped belt that held the veils and pink G-string panties, she twirled in the firelight, allowing him glimpses of her naked breasts and behind. Light and shadow danced over her warm flesh.

A powerful charge from his sexual energy flashed between them like a lightning bolt. Desire thundered though his soul. The emotional storm sent shivers over her skin, heightening her own desire. He wanted her.

And she wanted him, too. Not just her fantasy, but also her physical body lying in bed next to his.

The music's tempo changed, marking the time for the woman to dance within arm's reach of her desired lover. Then, to accept her, the man would get on one knee and offer her his hand. Slowly she inched closer and closer, gyrating to the music, caressing her breasts, turning her backside to him, and wiggling in enticement.

Who cared if it was over the top for an actual mating dance ceremony? The fantasy was working to drive him out of unconsciousness as evidenced by the small fire representing his soul. Besides, it felt right and natural to touch herself in front of him. Her breath quickened, knowing in a few short moments, his hands would replace her own. She craved his touch. And yearned for their union.

Dear Spirits was she dancing for him or for her own lustful desires?

Lovemaking would launch his sexual energy over both of Hyborea's moons, fueling him with the strength he needed to wake. His sexual excitement was that palpable.

As was hers. After she brought Kedric back to consciousness, she'd lock herself in her bedroom and find her release. Alone.

Fantasy Kedric got up on one knee, his covering slipped to the floor and her heart thundered. The two times she'd seen him naked, he hadn't been overcome with lust. Who would've thought a man could triple in size when aroused?

It was amazing. Astonishing really.

Excited and more than ready to take the next step in the mating ritual, fantasy Kedric reached out his hand. "I want you, Myia," he rasped.

Her inhale caught in her chest. No one had ever before spoken to her with unmitigated seduction. She couldn't breathe, which was odd since she was a spirit. But this connection was different than any other. It had never felt so real. So authentic.

Was she really ready to go on to the next level when their spiritual joining embraced this level of physicality?

Don't overthink it. You've come this far, you can keep going. She was doing this for Kedric.

Oh, who was she kidding? She was doing this for herself, too.

She placed her trembling hand in his, accepting his proposal.

Wasting no time, he pulled her to him and sat her on his thigh. Soft hair tickled her mostly bared bottom. Her arms encircled his neck as his hands slipped around her waist. Pressed skin to skin against his chest, heat seeped into her breasts. His head tilted up, and he licked his lips in anticipation. She bent her head and brought her mouth down onto his. As if forged of fire, his lips seared hers.

His tongue flicked hers, and she deepened the kiss unable to get enough.

Lightning crisscrossed through the darkness surrounding them. Charged particles of energy heated the air. The fire grew larger. Since they'd no need of two bonfires, she snuffed out the one she had originally conjured.

She ran her fingers through his hair; fisted his thick, fiery mane; and then pulled him back so she could gaze at his beautiful face: gray eyes drunk with passion and sensuous lips swollen from their kiss. She wanted more, but his mouth moved down her neck to her collarbone, sending a delicious thrill through her.

Panting, she ran her hands down the back of his neck and over his muscular shoulders. He'd carried the weight of so much on those shoulders. Her fingers worked the tension from the muscles before continuing her exploration down his magnificent chest. She wanted to touch him everywhere, to explore him, but he had other ideas. The warmth of his breath moved slowly up and down her neck.

Her flesh tingled with anticipation, but no kiss came. Perhaps he couldn't reach. She leaned closer and was rewarded with only the touch of his nose.

"Kiss me, Kedric," she cried in frustration.

A hot current of sexual energy passed between them. Apparently, driving her wild was driving him back from the brink.

A light brush of his fingertips over her breast left jittery little bumps in its wake. Her nipples hardened into little tight pearls. How could he be so tender and gentle when she wanted more? A caress. A squeeze. So great was the need for his touch, she grew hotter than the bonfire flames rising behind them. Maybe he wasn't strong enough yet. Or maybe she needed to show him what she wanted.

In demonstration, she cupped and fondled her heavy breasts, showing him what she liked. What she longed for him to do. Her hands were pleasant enough, but she yearned for his touch. What would that feel like?

"Oh, Myia," he said, voice strained. As he watched her, his desire mounted, his arousal pressed against her leg. "My sweet, sweet Myia. Let me."

Again with a light touch that sent chills over her flesh and drove her mad. Would he stop teasing her and put his hands on her already?

And then he did.

Her heart thundered. Or was that his heart? The sound grew louder, stronger. Pounding all around them as energy from her life force flowed into his. He harnessed her power, gathered strength. The bonfire spread.

His hands ran over her bare back, up and down her ribs, and then over the curve of her hips. To get away from the tickle, she wiggled her butt on his thigh, which must have been hurting by now. He couldn't be comfortable kneeling on one knee, but he didn't complain. He didn't want to move from where they were. He feared she would stop. But she wouldn't stop, not when she had to bring him back to consciousness.

And certainly not when he made her feel so incredibly good, with his warm breath on her nipples.

He didn't take her into his mouth, though, and the need mounted. She thrust her breasts closer to him, but he didn't take the bait. He kissed the swell and then his lips were on hers again. His hands caressed her ribs, up to the outsides of her breasts, and then down to her waist. Over and over.

The pleasure was sweet torture, and it heightened her need, making her wet in want of him.

She'd never felt this way about anyone before. But it was right and natural with Kedric. Well, fantasy Kedric. Was that why it had been so easy to let go, because there was no conscious or unconscious mind to hinder their spirits? All they had between them was unadulterated honesty. True essence. Two spirits behaving as if they were two halves of the same whole.

Fantasy Kedric scooped her up in his arms and carried her back to the pillows. He laid her on them and then rolled over so that she was on top, legs straddling his hips. Her heart pounded. Could she go through with this?

Oh yes!

She bent her head to kiss him.

"No," he said. "Let me look at you." His gaze and hands roamed over her body. She'd never imagined she could feel this good, yet frustrated at the same time. He was too gentle. She wanted him to really feel her. To suckle her nipples.

Enough of this taking-it-slow stuff. She pinned his hands on the pillows and leaned a breast over his lips so he had no choice but to taste her.

She was rewarded with his hot mouth and tongue on her nipple. The sensation sent liquid heat into her sensitive, most private place, readying her for what she knew would be coming. Her core ached with the need to be touched. To be filled.

Fantasy Kedric suckled her other breast. His hands escaped hers and squeezed her rear end. She rocked on him, and the friction sent waves of pleasure through her.

"You are so wet, Myia." By his tone, she knew it turned him on and it wouldn't be long before he lost control.

"Make love to me, Kedric."

That was it. In a surge of energy, she was on her back, and he was between her legs. He plunged deep inside her, filling her with the remedy to her aching need.

Energy sparked between them. Visual currents of green-and-red light passed over them, around them, through them. Nerve endings she didn't even know she had tingled, as if electrified.

His need to move inside her was great, but his restraint even greater. He didn't want to hurt her, and his compassion took her breath away. "Are you okay?" he asked, stalling, giving her time to get used to him.

It was unnecessary. Her spirit felt no pain, only the delicious pent-up ache that needed release. "I'm wonderful." She thrust her hips in encouragement.

He didn't disappoint. Every move he made sent her higher and higher. Her spirit soared. Lightning cracked overhead. Thunder rumbled. Green-and-red sparks of energy sizzled around them. His life force grew stronger.

Her heartbeat—her real heartbeat in her physical body—thundered. Her real lips tingled with the need to kiss him.

It would be wrong of her to take advantage of his body, but she couldn't help herself. What if he didn't let her kiss him after he awoke? It would be torture to crave him so much and not taste his soft lips.

She rolled onto her side in his bed and pressed her mouth on his. He didn't kiss her back. He couldn't. He wasn't conscious yet.

"You're a naughty girl, Myia," fantasy Kedric said. "Taking advantage of a wounded man. I know you kissed my physical body."

"Because I want you. I want your body as well as your soul. Wake up for me."

Again and again he thrust deep inside her, and although it was only a fantasy, the pleasure she received was real. The bonfire popped and sizzled and spread farther around them. His energy was awakening, but it wasn't enough. He hadn't reached conscious thought yet. She needed to do more for him.

"Touch my body, Kedric. My real body." She kept the spiritual connection going by holding his wrist while unlacing her fingers from his. She removed the blanket and rolled on top, straddling him like her fantasy had done earlier. She guided his hand inside her halter top and rubbed his palm over her nipples aching for his touch.

Okay, so maybe she was doing this for herself as much as for him.

"You little savage," his fantasy image said with great satisfaction. "You're taking full advantage of my immobilization to have your way with me."

"I'm healing you."

"Aye. Aye, you are."

The warmth from his hand on her was even better than their spirit sex. But it wasn't enough. Not when he was powerless to touch her of his own volition. "I want your mouth on me."

"Trust me, I want that, too." Fantasy Kedric rolled her on top of him again so that in spirit and in reality they were in the same position. He held onto her hips as fantasy Myia rocked against him. The bonfire completely encircled them.

"Make love to me, Kedric."

"I am."

She giggled at the simplicity of his answer. "I don't mean our fantasies. I mean our flesh. Wake up and make love to me."

"Dammit, I can't wake up." Sweat glistened on his forehead. "Touch me, Myia."

She brushed her fingertips over his beautiful, muscular chest and twirled his hair around her finger.

"Mmm," his fantasy moaned in appreciation of her physical touch. "That's nice, but that's not what I meant, aye? *Touch* me."

And by the deep guttural words, she knew exactly the place he wanted her to touch.

Her heart thundered. It had been so much easier for their spirits to do this. There was no conscious thought inhibiting her. But now, in the flesh, she feared, never having touched a man there before. What if she did it wrong? What if he didn't like it? What if she hurt him?

"Please, Myia. Touch me. Heal me."

As their fantasies continued their lovemaking, in the real world Myia reached a trembling hand behind her and slipped it inside Kedric's pants, taking hold of his rock-hard penis.

Her heart raced. She gulped in air. Slowly, she moved her hand up and down his silky shaft.

"Holy Spirits," fantasy Kedric said, and the bonfire flames rose higher as they made love inside walls of fire. Lightning shattered the darkness above them and thunder boomed.

Her spirit image rocked faster and harder. No matter how deeply he thrust inside her, she couldn't get enough. Sweat glistened off her. As the intensity built, fantasy Myia moaned from the pleasure of it, and he clutched her hips tighter so that she couldn't get away. Not that she had any desire to do that.

Faster, harder, in the real world she stroked his penis in time with their spirits' lovemaking.

He grunted with pleasure, and she knew he wasn't far from release. Her spirit could feel the strength of it. He was nearly over the top. Nearly back.

"That's it, Kedric. Come back to me." The flames shot higher and bent inward over them, creating a dome of raging fire. Thunder boomed from beyond the dome. Red-and-green flashes of energy exploded around them.

Spirit Kedric thrust deep inside her and held her tight, immobilizing her hips as he pumped her harder, reaching climax.

He needed release.

Now.

His fantasy cried out with it.

Kedric's eyes opened. A grunt escaped his lips as he climaxed physically.

"You did it," she shouted, not caring if she woke everyone in the castle. Tears streamed down her cheeks. Her body trembled as she wiped her eyes. "You came back."

"Oh, I came all right." Breathless, he gulped in air. "That was the most incredible thing I've ever experienced. You were amazing, Myia. Your spirit is phenomenally powerful."

Should she tell him she'd never connected this deeply with anyone before? That she'd never felt sensations this intense? This connection was on a level she never even knew existed, let alone mastered.

Her cheeks ached from grinning, but she couldn't stop. "How do you feel?"

"Exhausted and energized at the same time."

"Good." She removed her hand from his pants and rolled off him.

"Wait, where are you going?" He grabbed her wrist as she got out of the bed. "Was this nothing more to you than a ruse to reawaken me?" The hurt in his eyes almost made her cry. He thought she was abandoning him.

"I need to clean up."

"Don't leave. Please." He sat up slowly, as if testing himself to be sure it didn't make him dizzy, and then placed his feet firmly on the floor. Seemingly satisfied in his seated position, he wiped her hand with the rumpled-up bedsheet and then tossed it onto the floor. "I'm not finished with you. Aye?"

Her heart flip-flopped. While she'd worked so hard to bring him to completion—both his fantasy and his body—she hadn't found her release. That was something she'd planned to remedy in private.

But if Kedric wasn't finished with her, she had no problems climbing back on top and making love to him in the flesh. Her mouth dried.

Wetting her lips, she leaned down to kiss him. Energy surged into her body, charging her nerve endings, setting them sizzling from the heat of their intertwined auras. Something sprang to life inside her core. Rejuvenating her. Energizing her. Completing her.

They had kissed before, but never like this. Never with sensual hunger. With the desire to become one in the flesh. To claim and be claimed.

If he did nothing more than kiss her, she'd die in sweet bliss.

He eased back, and they separated just long enough for him to strip off his shirt. Her breath hitched. It's not as if she hadn't seen him bare chested before or even ogled him before. But somehow when she looked at him now, she was seeing him with new eyes.

Gently she traced his muscles, and his eyes closed and head fell back. Heat surged through his aura and seared her fingertips.

"Your turn," he said, and her belly dropped. Would he like her body? Would she know how to please him in the flesh? She trusted he would be gentle and guide her.

He lifted her shirt over her head and let it fall to the floor. His palms slid the undergarment straps off her shoulders. When his warm mouth found her neck, the room spun.

She grasped his solid shoulders, steadying herself until the dizziness passed.

When the heat from his lips disappeared, she opened her eyes. He'd unhooked her undergarment and was waiting for her. She let it slip off her arms and resisted the urge to hide herself with her hair. The hunger in Kedric's eyes was the encouragement she needed.

It had been much easier and less frightening baring herself, letting herself go in spirit.

Kedric eased her onto the bed and did as he'd promised, tracing the curves of her breasts. Her heart thundered. If she didn't die from it beating out of her chest, she was sure to die from his sweet touch. Her body burned. Her nipples tightened.

When his mouth gave her equal attention, her core grew wet with need.

Her body tingled with excitement and anticipation, and when his hand slid beneath the sarong and pulled down her panties, she almost came undone.

He brushed her most sensitive place, and hot excitement shot through her. She couldn't help but make appreciative sounds and hoped Kedric didn't think her a fool. But with each little moan, he increased her pleasure.

How could he make her feel so good? So sensitive? And yet so frustrated at the same time. She ached for more. She didn't just want his fingers on her, she wanted them inside her.

She widened her legs.

He didn't take the invitation. He pleasured her sex until she thought she'd die from the eroticism. Would he just fill her already? She needed him.

"Please, Kedric."

He slipped inside her, and she almost came undone.

"You are so wet." The approval and sexiness in his voice set her body tingling. He moved in and out of her.

Heart thundering, excitement mounting, she took his touch. The pleasure increased, and pressure built until she could stand it no longer.

"I want to make love to you, Myia."

"Wait. Don't stop, Kedric. I'm—I'm—" She lost all control. Her body spasmed and trembled in sweet ecstasy.

Her legs went numb all the way to her toes. She'd never experienced an orgasm that powerful before. She could close her eyes right here, right now, and sleep for a week.

Kedric's lips found hers again. He caressed her jaw with the back of his knuckles and then kissed her once more.

"I think you wore me out, Kedric. I'm exhausted."

"Stay with me tonight?"

She nodded. "I was hoping you'd want me to." She snuggled into him and closed her eyes.

Chapter Twenty

What the hell? He was ready and willing for another round. He was full of energy, vim, and vigor. What they'd just shared was only a warm-up, yet here she was falling asleep in his arms.

Her black hair spilled down over his pillow. What he wouldn't give to run his hands through the silky strands, but she looked much too peaceful to disturb. It must have taken great strength and energy for her spirit to enter his body and bring him back from that cold, dark place. So near ultimortem.

He'd never given that much blood before. Not even that time during his escape from HuBReC when he stole a canoe in the Tuniit village and gotten clubbed in the head. When his faster than normal recovery had raised suspicion, Kedric traded blood for his attacker's canoe. Though it had taken a few days to regain consciousness from the blood loss, he hadn't been as deeply entrenched in the abyss that Myia found him in today.

If it hadn't been for her, he never would have regained consciousness. He kissed her lips once more and settled into bed next to her. "Thank you for bringing me back."

Her soft murmuring wasn't decipherable, except for the names

Max and Finn. She snuggled closer to him, intoxicating him with the scent of perfume, woman, and sex. In a few minutes, she'd be asleep. He'd wait until then to clean himself up and check on Finn.

He'd hoped the guy would've left the infirmary quickly after the transfusion, but he had anticipated a problem, which was why he instructed Max to imprison the doctor if he overstayed his welcome.

That must have been what Myia tried to communicate.

Satisfied she was asleep, Kedric slipped out of the bed, covered her with a blanket, and then took a quick shower, after which he dressed in clean, pressed clothes.

He wanted to make sure he looked as healthy as possible for his visit to Finn. Only five hours had passed since he'd lain down on the hospital bed. It was an unremarkable duration to be out of commission and hardly notable of a mention.

Thank the Spirits for small favors. He'd have enough trouble if Finn mentioned his unique blood to anyone.

Especially to Griffin.

After retrieving the dungeon's keys from his office and tucking his Flesheater knife into the back of his waistband, he followed the toasted aroma of freshly ground coffee beans into the kitchen. It was nearly dawn, and a steaming pot of caffeine awaited the castle's early morning crew. Cook poured him a mug and then offered him a fist-sized banana muffin still cooling on the rack. Kedric thanked him and carried the breakfast down to the dungeon.

As he descended the stone steps, heat and moisture assaulted him. It was like walking into a steam bath. The natural underground hot springs made the humidity so thick, not only could he taste the musty, dank air, but he could chew it.

Perhaps it was time to put in a ventilation system and dehumidifier. And while he was at it, more lighting. Someone was liable to trip and hurt themselves in these gloomy passageways. Eh, but that would defeat the whole purpose of the creepy, underground prison atmosphere, wouldn't it?

No guard was posted in the dungeon, as there were no prisoners other than Finn. And no one knew about the doctor except for him and Max.

He unlocked the solid wood door leading into the prison.

The last time he'd opened this door, it had been to carry out the suspension of General Bathas's murderer. He'd offered the red-bearded man his freedom in exchange for revealing the name of the mastermind behind the crime. It had to have been Griffin. Unfortunately, no manner of persuasive techniques had resulted in a name. The red-bearded man had been an alpha gladiator, and thus had a great tolerance for pain.

Finn was a medical scientist. His gift was brains, not brawn. It shouldn't take much to procure his cooperation.

He placed the muffin and coffee mug on a shelf, pulled the sheathed knife from his pants in order to tuck in his shirt, and then tied the sheath around his hips so the knife was clearly visible.

The interrogation probably would go smoother if he'd gotten Max's story first, but he had already bothered his brother-in-law enough after having promised him family time. He'd get Max, Addy, and Myia's account after they rested.

Right now, he'd make Finn talk.

Kedric found the doctor in the cell farthest from the door. He was awake on his bedding in the corner, staring at the ceiling. A fresh, dark red scab—most likely the consequence of Max's sword—contrasted against his pale neck.

Finn leaped to his feet and nearly tripped as he ran to the prison bars. The young man's bow was deeper and held more respect than he'd ever shown before. "My lord. How good it is to see you well."

"Is it, Finn?"

Still bowing, the man glanced up at him with confusion in his eyes. "My lord?"

"I've heard the others' account of the night," he lied. "Now, I will hear yours. Explain yourself." His tone was menacing. He spoke as if holding great anger in check. The ploy worked, too. Finn's eyes grew round as he backed away from the bars, probably thinking he'd be safer out of the warlord's reach.

Smart thinking.

"I was confused and upset. I didn't mean it, my lord. Please, you've got to believe me."

"I'm not sure that I do. Convince me."

"I didn't mean to call you a coward. My anger got the best of me. I-I just don't understand why, when you have this incredible healing power inside you, you didn't save the others. Like Alex Graham. He was a brilliant scientist who had so much more to teach us. And General Bathas was your best friend. And—and you could've saved the king. Why would you choose not to?" Finn stopped short. Realization dawned on his face.

No doubt he believed Kedric's nonintervention regarding the king's death was because of selfishness. He'd be right, of course, but not for the reasons Finn suspected. "Is that all you've got to say for yourself?"

"My lord, I apologize for my outburst and rage in the infirmary. Please forgive my inability to rein in my curiosity now. I am, after all, a scientist. A seeker of truth."

"I can forgive your outburst. I can understand your curiosity. I can't, however, allow my secret to be known." He unlocked the door and entered the cell. The steel bars slammed closed with a rattle.

Finn backed away. His head turned from left to right searching for any means of escape. There were none. "What do you intend to do to me?"

"I intend to keep you quiet." He pulled the Flesheater from its sheath.

Finn's knees smacked the stone floor. "Please, Lord Kedric. Spare my life. I won't tell a soul about your blood. I swear it!"

"I know you won't, Finn." Even to his own ears, his patronizing voice sounded cold. It was a cruel thing to do, but it had to be done.

"I beg you, my lord. Please don't do this." Tears glistened in his eyes as he cowered and crawled backward across the dank floor.

Never had a man been so terrified of him and so unwilling—or perhaps incapable—of fighting for his life. It was pathetic really. At least it told him what he needed to know. Finn was the sort of man who, when threatened with pain or death, would keep a secret.

Unfortunately, he was also the sort of man who'd spill a secret under an enemy's threat of pain or death.

"I swear it. I swear I won't tell. Have mercy. I beg you!" Finn backed himself into the corner. Unable to move farther away, he squeezed his eyes tight, screwed up his face, and turned his head away.

Kedric switched the Flesheater to his left hand and drew his right index finger over the sharp blade, feeling no sting until he squeezed the skin to produce a blood bead. When he knelt down and swiped the sticky fluid over Finn's sword wound, the doctor inhaled a sharp breath and wrenched back, hitting his head against the wall with a dull thud.

It sounded like it hurt.

Kedric stood and then stepped back, giving Finn some much-needed breathing room. His rapid and shallow breaths of this stale, humid air couldn't possibly allow enough oxygen into his lungs. If he didn't calm down, he was sure to pass out. That wouldn't do at all.

Finn's eyelids fluttered open. Disbelief, fear, and confusion shone in his wide and unblinking eyes. His hand rose with jerky, uncertain movements like it was mechanical. He was about to touch the blood on his neck when Kedric slapped his knuckles. "If you wipe it off, rest assured I won't be cutting myself for you again."

Finn's mouth moved, but no sound came out. His Adam's apple bobbed up and down as if trying hard to swallow. Finally he managed a thank you.

If Kedric were a real bastard he would've insisted the reason for healing him was so that no funeral guests would question the neck injury. But he'd put the kid through enough hell for one night. "You keep my secret, you keep your life. Understand?"

"Yes, my lord. Thank you. I won't breathe a word of it to anyone."

"Then make your accord."

It must have taken a full minute before Finn was able to pull himself off the floor. Standing on visibly shaky legs, he recited his promise and then touched his lips with two fingers before placing his palm on Kedric's chest to seal the deal.

The touch was so light Kedric barely felt it. Kedric covered the man's hand. "I'll hold you to your promise." On his turn, Kedric put his fingers to his lips. "If you so much as hint to anyone about my ability, I *will* kill you." He'd no reservations about slamming his palm into Finn's chest, emphasizing his brute strength.

Finn's hand shook as it covered Kedric's. "So be it," he whispered.

According to law, the accord was now legally binding.

"Have a seat, Finn. We've more to discuss." The doctor shuffled to the cot while Kedric remained standing. "You've been practicing with the mind control device?"

"I have."

"Dunna tells me you're competent with it."

"I am. Very."

Kedric didn't doubt that. The kid had more empathy than the older scientists and therefore communicated more efficiently with the Hyboreans. He also had a heightened curiosity that led him to experiment further with the machine's capabilities and limits. Finn would serve his mission well. Plus, Griffin couldn't manipulate Finn if Finn were safe at war with Kedric.

"I've decided to assign you to military duty. You'll be one of the Hyborean's "brains" on the subaquatic to HuBReC."

This time when Finn's eyes grew round, it was due to excited enthusiasm. "Thank you, Lord Kedric."

"We leave in two days. You'll remain here until then. It's best if you stay out of General Max's sight for a while, aye?" In reality, staying in the dungeon had nothing to do with Max, and everything to do with preventing Finn from seeing the shaman up and about in full health.

Though Finn knew Kedric's blood had healing properties, he didn't know the extent of it. Plus, it wouldn't hurt to keep him out of the public and away from anyone who might ask questions about his whereabouts last night. Finn might be agreeable to swearing an accord to keep quiet, but why tempt fate?

Kedric locked the cell with Finn inside and then retrieved the muffin and coffee for his prisoner. He handed them to Finn through the bars. "Coffee's cold. It's probably better that way. It's damn hot down here. I'll collect you later. Oh, and wipe that blood off your neck. Your wound is healed."

"Yes, my lord. And thank you for your generosity."

Kedric made his way to the prison door satisfied with the situation. Now he would return to Myia and satisfy another need.

Chapter Twenty-One

Myia woke to the twitter of birds in the courtyard down below. The early glow of dawn's light filtered in through the oversized windows in Kedric's bedchamber. How wonderful to wake up to natural light again. The small interior room she'd spent the past few nights in had been dark and lifeless even though the lightsticks had illuminated the room beautifully. It's just that artificial light didn't emit the organic spirit she craved.

She yawned and stretched and glanced about the room for Kedric. There was no sign of him. No sound came from the bathroom, either.

After all his body and spirit had been through last night, he should have slept until midday. Maybe even longer. He needed that time to recoup his strength. She must have dozed off for an hour or two. Had Kedric been awake the whole time? Could the night they'd shared together made him restless? Because it made her absolutely relaxed and at peace. When had she ever experienced this kind of unadulterated serenity? She'd never been this tranquil.

Ooh. She should meditate.

As she sat up in the bed, the covers slid off her breasts and pooled in her lap. Cool morning air swept across her naked skin like her lover's soft caress. Her nipples tightened. She crisscrossed her legs, relaxed her arms on her thighs, and closed her eyes. Air rushed into her lungs. Air expelled. In and out. In and out.

Focusing on her deep breathing had never been so easy. There were no distractions. There was only the sound of her inhales and exhales. And the sound of her heart. The rhythm of her life's blood pumped slowly and steadily.

Her spirit rose, releasing itself from the corporeal body to float freely about the room. Never had it felt so light. So liberated.

Floating overhead, she gazed down upon her body, meditating in the bed, simultaneously a part of the spirit world and the living. Her soul danced on air, climbing higher and higher on the wings of birds, soaring over the kingdom. Over the jungle of Pele. Climbing higher still up into the golden dawn, joining the Spirits of the sky, her essence bathed in red-and-green light, she danced on the wind and soared through the heavens with them. If she'd wanted to, she could keep on soaring right out into the ether.

From this place, she gazed upon the entire outline of the island.

The energy of those who've gone before her welcomed her. They intertwined in her soul and wrapped her in comfort and love.

Thank you for your trust and confidence, she said and was immediately enveloped in joy. *Please, as shaman-aprendi, I seek your guidance and wisdom. Will you help me find a way to heal Lord Kedric. Show me how to bring him peace, and I will act as your humble servant.*

A gust of wind blew her out of the arms of the aurora tropicos. She sailed farther over the land, crossing over the river separating Pele from the continent of Southland.

Had she angered the Spirits? Had they sent her out of their midst because she was not worthy of her proclaimed status?

Breathing in deeply, she remained calm and allowed the Spirits' power to whisk her away. Her home continent fell into the distance behind as she soared over ocean waves and gathered strength from the sea's mighty currents. The ocean soon filled with huge chunks of floating ice beyond which lay a frozen land covered in snow. The air was as bitter as the Hyboreans' special Yard on Discovery Island, which was odd since she had no physical body in this place. Her body—meditating in Kedric's bed—shivered.

Though she'd perceived physical sensations when connected to another person's spirit, she had never felt them during an out-of-body experience. Not to mention she'd never engaged in an out-of-body experience with such clarity.

This was a truly unique encounter. One that only a true shaman should witness.

Thank you, Spirits, for choosing to share this world with me. I am your humble servant. Please show me how to serve you.

Another gust of wind, and her spirit soared past an ice mountain and a village with houses made of snow, where humans and Hyboreans lived in harmony—for the most part. For a quick moment her spirit rejoiced in the harmony. She soared farther north and came to a city with enormous buildings. Starships took off to the heavens, while still more landed. She hovered over a place with much light and noise and confusion, and then all at once her spirit was sucked downward through the walls of a building where a great pain begged to be healed.

Someone's spirit was filled with agony and heartache. A woman. With red hair and gray eyes, bathing in a pool set in a lush garden. Somehow she knew it was a Yard. A place where the Hyboreans kept their human pets in their appropriate habitat, similar to the special chamber on Pele where Kedric kept the Hyboreans in a habitat suitable for them.

The woman's skin was so light it was almost see-through. Her blue veins were clearly visible. Her spirit was clearly troubled. Water droplets glistened on her face. At a second glance, Myia realized they weren't water droplets from the bathing pool. They were tears. A terrible wrong had been done. Pain and grief clung to her like the bruises on her wrists and face.

When she washed the residue of men from between her legs, Myia's heart ached for her.

"Please, God, help me," the woman cried. "Make him stop."

Fear not. I've been sent by the Spirits to help you.

The woman glanced around her as if searching for where the sound had come from. Her eyes were wide and her fear was palpable.

Will you let me enter your spirit and help heal your pain?

The woman looked around again. "Who are you? Where are you?"

I am Myia, shaman-aprendi, I've been brought here by the Protecting Spirits. I want to help. Open your hand, and I shall enter your soul and take away your pain.

Slowly, the woman's hand came out of the bathing pool, her thin fingers opened, water dripping off them. Myia touched the woman's hand with her spirit and entered into her body.

The woman was too broken to put up a guard and more than willing to have her pain vanquished. Her spirit image showed the reasons for her distress. A huge and menacing gladiator held her down and raped her violently while three other gladiators looked on and cheered. She never struggled. She'd only closed her eyes and withstood the torture. After he finished, the others each took their turn with her, none of them gently.

This hadn't been the first time, either. For the past few weeks, she'd been preyed upon by the alpha gladiator and forced to perform humiliating sexual acts. Only once—the first time—had she refused and fought back, but the alpha gladiator had beaten her to near death. She went into premature labor and almost lost her baby boy. A Hyborean attached the preemie to lifesaving equipment, and the gladiator threatened to kill the baby if she ever fought back again.

She'd acquiesced every time. Suffering in silence, her soul grew bitter with suppressed rage and hate.

Myia wouldn't be able to heal the woman in one session. It would take much time. But she'd been brought to this place for a reason, and she knew she would be able to revisit. Her shamanic powers had grown to a new level. There was no doubt she'd be able to come back again.

As for now, Myia called upon the Spirits of the sky and sea and land for healing strength and began to reassemble the pieces of the woman's shattered soul.

* * *

Kedric balanced the breakfast tray in one hand and opened the bedroom door with the other. The scent of eggs, bacon, coffee, fruit, and chocolate—Myia's favorite—made his stomach rumble. Now that Finn had been taken care of, he could spend some time with Myia before starting his duties as Highland lord.

He closed the door and placed the tray on the table. Myia was sitting up in bed. Her perfect bared beasts were missing something, his mouth on them. His groin stirred.

"Good morning, love." He set up two plates and cups and left the food on the tray in the center of the table. Hmm, perhaps they should eat in bed instead. Too bad the chocolate wasn't melted. He'd pour it over her and then lick it off. "Would you rather eat here or in bed?"

Myia said nothing. He repeated himself louder. Still she remained silent and unmoving. His heart jumped into his throat. Was something wrong with her? He raced across the room to the bed. "Myia?"

Her eyes were open but unblinking. He waved his hand in front of her face. "Myia? Are you okay?"

Her chest rose and fell very slowly. Something wasn't right. Had wrenching him from near death last night weakened her? He reached for his Flesheater, ready to let his blood and smear it over her body to heal whatever it was that ailed her.

"Myia," he shouted while shaking her. He gazed into her unseeing eyes. What the hell was wrong with her? He unsheathed his knife, poised it over his hand, but before he cut himself, her eyes blinked.

"Myia? Are you okay? Your eyes were open, but you were unresponsive. It's like you weren't here."

Her eyes blinked rapidly and seemed to have trouble focusing on him. Then her lips broke into a huge smile, and her eyes focused on his face. They were filled with wonder and awe.

"I wasn't here." The enthusiasm in her voice set him at ease. Whatever had happened to her was apparently something she was excited about. He sheathed the knife. "I was somewhere across Hyborea. A lost soul called out to the Spirits, and they brought me to her. I traveled thousands of miles away. It was the most incredible experience I've ever had."

The most incredible experience, huh? Why should that admission bother him so much? Except that he'd hoped her most incredible experience had been what they'd shared together last night.

Okay, so apparently his ego wounded easily.

"I've never been that deeply entranced before. I think it's happened."

Her soft, warm hand on his arm melted his macho resolve. He sat next to her on the bed. She was so beautiful wearing nothing but a thin sheet. He wanted nothing more than to crawl beneath the sheet and make love to her in the flesh this time. "What's happened?"

"My spiritual powers must have reached maturity. I think I've become a full shaman."

Aha. So she'd gotten her full shaman powers after one night of passion. Damn, he was good. A self-satisfied grin pulled at his lips.

"What's that look for?"

"You can thank me now."

"Thank you for what?"

"For my expert skill as a lover."

As she leaned her naked back against the headboard, the sheet had slipped below her hips. Just one little tug was all it would take. "Well, yes, that was very enjoyable, don't get me wrong, but I've just had the most powerful out-of-body experience. I think I've passed my test. I've become a full shaman."

"Because of my potent, virile sexual mastery."

"Your—" She giggled. "You claim that your mastery gave me a spiritual awakening?"

"You didn't have global telepathic capabilities before entering my bed, did you?"

"Well, no."

"But you have them now?"

"Yes."

"Draw your own conclusion."

The gold in her eyes seemed to glow, and her lips curled into a coy grin. "Perhaps we should experiment once more."

"Tsk, tsk." He shook his head in playful admonishment. "It's shameful, really. Using the Highland leader's virility to gain more spiritual power. For that, I should take you over my knee." He reached for her, but she grabbed his wrists to stop him.

"I was thinking we could join again so that I might heal you."

"You already have."

"I healed your loss of consciousness. I didn't heal your heart. Open your soul to me, Kedric. I want to know all of you. I want to heal you."

Maybe if she saw his pain, she would finally understand the need for this war. Maybe then she'd stop trying to change his mind. Maybe she would change hers. "Okay."

Her eyes beamed and sparkled. She scooted closer to him and clutched his hand before he could change his mind. The sound of her excited giggle melted his heart.

He offered no resistance as she closed her eyes and entered into his soul.

Their two fantasies stood together in the darkness inside his stone barriers. He leaned down to kiss her lips, but her image stiff-armed his in the chest.

He winced, not from pain but from disappointment. "What? Aren't we going to have sex while you heal me?"

"Not this time."

His stomach dropped. What did he get himself into here?

"Thank you for your trust, Kedric."

He grumbled. Why couldn't they have sex while she healed him? If she heard his mind's question, she ignored it.

"Why is it so important that you make war on the Hyboreans? What are you fighting for?"

The sound of rocks moving over each other drew his attention to the stone barrier at his left. A small section of wall crumbled. Taking her by the hand, fantasy Kedric led her through the opening. On the other side of the wall stood Tess and his father.

"Who's that woman?" Myia's question was barely audible. It came out as a frightened whisper.

"No need for jealousy, Myia. She's my sister."

"Oh, Kedric." Her hand squeezed his in reassurance. For what, he didn't know. Her gaze met his, and the worry in her eyes sent his heart racing. "Your sister was the girl in my vision."

Chapter Twenty-Two

Y ou saw Tess? Why didn't you tell me?"

"I didn't know who she was."

"Well, what did you see? Is she okay?"

Fantasy Myia turned to him and took his other hand in hers. Her eyes glistened with unshed tears. He couldn't stand the torture waiting for her to speak. She seemed unsure of what to say.

"I'm sorry, Kedric. Tess is in a great deal of pain emotionally, spiritually, and physically. She's been abused by men. Gladiators."

Fantasy Kedric's eyes blazed with a fierce heat. His lips curled with ferociousness. "I'll kill them."

Myia's spirit wrenched from his body.

He blinked his eyes and focused on her face wrought with concern. She scooted closer to him on the bed and reached for his hand. "Let me back in, Kedric. I can help take away your pain."

"No. Tell me everything you saw."

"I'm confused about what I saw. There was your sister...and a baby. Tinier than any newborn I've ever seen. He shouldn't be alive, but somehow he is."

"Is the child Tess's?"

"Yes."

"Is Regan the father?" Addy had said that Regan would make Tess's life a living hell. His gut tightened into a hard lump. He hated thinking the child Tess had been yearning for, for all those years, belonged to her rapist.

"I'm sorry, Kedric. I don't know."

* * *

Kedric was halfway across the small room when Max jumped naked from his bed, angry green eyes glowing in the dark. Before Kedric could say anything, a vise of fingers clenched his throat. He stumbled backward. Stone wall smashed the back of his head.

Addy screamed from the bed.

Myia screamed from the doorway.

"It's me," he wheezed. In the future, he'd remember to knock. Max had always been the type of gladiator to kill first and ask questions later, which made him the perfect warrior to train his troops.

And the perfect warrior to lead his attack.

"Jesus, Kedric. What the hell's the matter with you? You know better than sneaking up on a sleeping gladiator. I could have killed you again."

The tension on his throat eased as Max released his grip. "Apparently my five years of freedom have tamed the beast I once was. Don't worry, Max, in time, you, too, will learn how to relax."

"How the hell can I relax when you keep barging in? Aren't you supposed to be unconscious for two days?" He picked up a pair of rumpled pants from the floor and put them on.

"You sound disappointed I'm not."

"If you were, I might actually get some sleep around here. I'm putting a lock on that door as soon as you leave."

"Why are you here, Kedric?" Addy held a sheet to her breasts with one arm and rocked the cradle next to the bed with the other. Noah had awakened during the commotion, and the gentle rocking seemed to be settling him down to a whimper.

"I need your help."

"I'll say you do." Max sat on the edge of the bed. "You forgot the fundamentals of your gladiator training. It's a wonder you haven't been slain yet."

Myia gasped behind him. She grew up in a peaceful village. She wasn't used to the casual talk of killing.

"In my defense, I didn't think my sister or the man who'd saved my life five years ago were a threat. But I've since reconsidered the notion."

Max chuckled. "So what's so damn important that you couldn't wait till morning? You need to give another blood transfusion?"

Addy tapped Max's shoulder. "It is morning. There's light peeking through the drapes."

There was no easing into this conversation. Kedric had to come out and say it. "Myia's spirit visited Tess."

"And?" The impatience in Max's voice grated on his nerves.

"And"—he directed his gaze to Addy—"you were right. Regan's been brutalizing her. In every way."

"Oh, god." Addy's voice was choked with tears. She reached for Max who pulled her tight to his chest. She buried her face in his neck and cried.

Kedric reached for Myia. Her soft hand slipped into his palm and gave him a reassuring squeeze. Knowing she was there for him was an amazing comfort.

Max kissed the top of Addy's head, smoothed down her hair, and then glared up at Kedric. If looks could slaughter, Kedric would've been butchered. "Why the hell would you tell her this, Ked?"

He meant, *Why would you upset my mate when there is nothing that can be done about Tess?* That's where he was dead wrong. "I'm sorry. I thought she should know."

"Bullshit. You want something."

"Damn right, I want something. I want to kill the bastards who abused my sister. I want to blow HuBReC off the face of the planet. I want to exterminate the Hyboreans."

Another squeeze from Myia. This time harder. It wasn't meant for comfort so much as it was meant to snap him out of his rage. He shouldn't be having this conversation in front of her.

"I need your help, Max. I need you to lead my army into battle." With Max leading the men, they had a greater chance of succeeding.

"I can't. I won't go back there. Not for your sister. Not for revenge. I'm staying right here in the refuge with my mate and my child. You can go to hell yourself."

"You'd go back to HuBReC if Cameron were there." It was a low blow, but it was the truth. When Max had asked him for a favor, it had been to search the Highland records for his kid brother.

"But he's not there, is he?"

It wasn't a denial. "There's nothing I can say that will convince you to join me, is there?"

"No."

"So be it."

That seemed to satisfy Max. His posture relaxed, and he kissed Addy's head again.

"I'm still going to need your help. From here," he added when Max's eyes narrowed.

"With what?" By Max's tone, he didn't sound as though he really cared to hear the answer.

"I need you to oversee the kingdom while I'm gone. I don't want to come back to a regime change."

If he came back at all.

Of course he'd come back. His warriors had prepared for this. The science team had prepared for this. His men would attack HuBReC, kill the Hyboreans, and save the humans.

In six hours, the troops would be loaded onto the subaquatic and everyone would move out.

Chapter Twenty-Three

Whuile Kedric was with his troops, Myia decided to visit her father. She opened the door to the infirmary. An empty breakfast tray sat on a low table at Father's side.

The sight made her heart swell. He'd had a healthy appetite today.

Father wiped his mouth on a cloth before placing it on the tray. He gave her a warm, loving smile as she approached.

The wound on his head had healed. He had no more cough, his breathing and pulse were normal, and his leg was mending nicely. Not only were his ailments gone, but the deep lines in his face seemed to have diminished. When she had left the village on her quest, he had been old and sickly, the antithesis of the health he now exuded.

Could Kedric's special blood have reversed the aging process?

Father reached his hand out to her. "My aprendi." She cringed at the name. He shouldn't call her that. She didn't deserve the title. "Tell me why your heart is heavy."

Her father was the one person who could always see through the masks she wore. Her smile and happy façade couldn't screen the distress glowing much too brightly in her aura.

"I must renounce my position as shaman-aprendi." The tears were hard to blink back. The decision wasn't a difficult one to make. It had to be done as evidenced by her complete and utter failure of the calling. What she hadn't counted on was the complete and utter heartache giving up her dream caused.

Father sat up in his bed. He didn't seem upset, angry, or worried. His face was peaceful. After a week of suffering and nearly dying, he had regained strength, focus, and balance. He'd been healed physically and spiritually and could now take over as shaman.

That would be a weight lifted off her soul.

"Sit with me." He moved over giving her room on the bedding at his side. "Now then, why have you come to this decision?"

"I've failed, Father. In every way possible. You'd sent me here to heal the warlord's heart, but instead I've propelled him into battle quicker than he would have if I'd never come. It's my fault he learned how to use mind control on the captive Hyboreans. It was my healing of his soldiers that provoked him into invading the village for more men. It was my vision of his sister that triggered his decision to attack the Hyboreans today."

He kept quiet as he let her collect her thoughts. There was so much more for which she'd been responsible, she didn't know what to tell him first.

"I can't keep my emotions in balance. I mean, you know I've always had a difficult time with that, but I'd been able to control—okay, conceal—it for the most part. But not when it comes to Kedric. I've physically struck him more than once. I've given in to temptations. I-I've given him my body without the promise of a union." The fantasy mating dance didn't count since their spirits had performed the ceremony rather than their flesh and blood, conscious bodies. They were not legal mates.

The last admission wasn't something she wanted to share with her father. In fact, the humiliation of verbalizing the loss of her virginity set her cheeks aflame. But the man she was purging her soul to wasn't just her father, he was the shaman, and that's who she needed to talk to right now. Besides, he would have seen by reading her aura that she was no longer pure. When their fingers intertwined, he'd see it in her soul as well.

Spiritual healing trumped shame. Though, truth be told, she wasn't ashamed of giving herself to Kedric. She loved him. It didn't make sense that she should love a man so different from her, but Spirits help her, she did.

Giving herself to Kedric hadn't been wrong. Nothing had ever felt so right. However, the consequences it brought to both of their positions were a nightmare. He wasn't just entering into war, he was going to his slaughter.

What was she going to do without him?

She raised her hand, fingers spread, waiting for Father to place his hand in hers. His spirit would cleanse hers and help her return to balance.

"You've much turmoil in your soul, my little shaman-aprendi."

"Yes." A tear cooled her cheek as it slid down.

"Which is why it pains me to refuse my assistance."

She blinked. There was nothing else she could do in response. Did he just say he wasn't going to heal her spirit? "Father?"

"My daughter, my shaman-aprendi. This is your vision quest. You cannot receive my spiritual guidance. You must find it within yourself. Seek the help of the Spirits and your totem. Do what you know to be true in your heart and soul, and you will find enlightenment for yourself, for the Highland lord, and for all the people."

"I've failed, Father. I have renounced my calling. You are well now. You can heal the people."

"You cannot renounce your destiny, my aprendi. You must see it to fruition. A desert cannot decide to become an ocean merely because it rains. It must live out its destiny providing an environment hospitable for the creatures in its care. You too must live out your destiny and find a spiritual environment hospitable for the people in your care."

"Haven't I already proved I failed my vision quest? Don't you see my destiny is not in becoming a full shaman?"

"Has the Highland lord made war yet?"

"Well, no."

He said nothing more. She knew what he was thinking. If Kedric hadn't made war, then she hadn't failed. Yet.

"So my vision quest is to prevent this war?" Wasn't it to heal Kedric's heart? Perhaps those two goals were one and the same. If she healed his heart, he would no longer desire war on the Hyboreans. Everyone would be safe. Was there something else she was missing in all of this?

His silence was unbearable.

"Father, please. Guide me."

"I cannot interfere with your vision quest, my aprendi."

The frustration overwhelmed her, and she wanted to pound her fist on the mattress and demand he guide her.

"I will only say that you are doing much more good than you believe. I have faith in you. You must find faith in yourself. You must believe."

That was the whole problem, wasn't it? She'd lost faith in herself. She believed that she would fail. She believed that she already had failed. Kedric was leaving for HuBReC today.

How was she going to convince him to forget this war in three hours?

Chapter Twenty-Four

Myia spent the next two hours searching for Kedric. He'd been with the troops for a good part of the morning, but his guards wouldn't let her see him. They had even refused to give him a message that she wished to speak with him. She had waited for him to finish on the training field, but he must have left through a different gate from where she lingered. Andrei had come to inform her Lord Kedric was at the dock leaving for Discovery Island.

So now she waited at the dock for his return.

If he returned.

He had to. He wouldn't leave without saying good-bye. Would he? She kept pacing back and forth, trying to think of what she would say to him. The minutes ticked by agonizingly slow.

With one hour until deployment, the motor ferry finally returned. She stood and strained her eyes to see if Kedric was on board. Nerves fluttered in her stomach.

As the boat came closer, she saw red hair whipping in the breeze. Her heart leaped. She'd finally be able to talk to Kedric. Or plead with him if it came to that.

"Myia," he shouted as the boat docked. "What are you doing

here?" The pleasure in his voice sent a thrill shooting through her. He jumped onto the dock, wearing his thermal suit and boots, and strode right over to her. A muscular arm encircled her shoulders. He pulled her to him and planted a hearty kiss on her unsuspecting lips.

My, he was in a good mood. "I've been trying to see you all morning."

"I've been busy. Walk with me to the castle."

She tried to fall in step beside him, but his strides were long and hurried. He pulled ahead of the five military men who had exited the boat with him, and she had to jog every few steps to keep up. "Kedric, we need to talk."

"So talk."

"It's kind of hard when my breathing is labored from keeping stride with you. This is a very steep hill."

He laughed. His mood was too good. He was too excited. Too happy. Everything must be going according to his plan.

She had to stop it now. Spirits help her. "Please don't do this, Kedric. Please don't go to war."

"You're going to miss me, aren't you?"

She was in no mood for his teasing smile. Did he not understand the seriousness of this matter? "I'm afraid for you and the men. I don't have a good feeling about this."

"I knew you cared about me. Maybe when we get to my room, you can show me just how much you care." He wiggled his eyebrows. "Though we'll have to make it quick since we don't have much time."

"This is serious, Kedric. I have to stop you from going."

He chuckled again. "How do you suppose you'll do that? Did you rally an army?" He made a show of looking in every direction to be sure no one was going to jump out at him or the military men falling farther and farther behind.

She was sucking in air faster and harder. As soon as she'd brought up the impending war, his already swift steps quickened even more. "I thought I'd plead with you."

"Myia. We've been through this before. There is nothing you can say or do that will make me change my mind. The Hyboreans are evil and must be destroyed. I know I can defeat them."

"What if you can't?"

"For a spiritual leader, you have very little faith." He halted on the bottom step of the castle, and she smacked into his back. He turned sharp eyes on her, and his mouth formed a hard line. "Or maybe it's just me you have little faith in. You think I'm too weak to stop this, don't you?"

With his last words, his aura surged with displeasure. There was something else in there, too. Inadequacy? Guilt?

"It has nothing to do with weakness. It has to do with killing and dying. It has to do with the annihilation of Pele if all goes wrong. And most important it has to do with your soul."

"If you're worried about my residence in the afterlife, you can rest assured I've reserved a room in hell years ago." He continued up the steps, taking them two at a time.

She watched him go, unable to get the last glimpse of his aura out of her mind. Some deeply rooted hurt was driving him toward this mission. If she could figure out what it was, she could figure out how to heal him, and he'd stop this attack.

Myia ran up after him, but couldn't catch him. What was he doing, sprinting? She finally reached him as he opened the door into his bedchamber. She entered behind and shut the door. She didn't wait for her breath to return before speaking. "What are you fighting for?"

"Freedom." The answer was an automatic response. No pause for thought. No pause in his movements as he gathered his gear.

"No. What are you *really* fighting for?"

"We've been through this. I'm going to save my family."

"Why? Why didn't they escape with you five years ago?"

"Dammit, Myia. I don't have time for this." The same colors sparked in his aura as before. He was definitely feeling guilty about something. Could that guilt be behind his motivation for revenge? Was he leading people into a war over his own survivor's guilt?

"I just want you to be honest with me. Why now?"

"You know what you saw in your vision. I have to save my sister. I have to protect her. No one deserves to be abused."

That was true. Though no one deserved to be led to their slaughter, either. Even with his mind-controlled Hyborean slaves, the odds of winning were...well, zero. He had to know that. According to some of the soldiers she healed, the Hyboreans had advanced technology and weaponry. They could detect the Peletians coming from miles away and could either destroy or capture everyone on the ship. They may even annihilate Pele for good measure.

Why didn't Kedric see this for what it really was? A losing battle.

But Kedric was certain his Hyborean mind control would be the secret weapon that would allow him to execute his mission exactly as planned. He believed he would save his sister. He wouldn't be convinced otherwise.

His soul wouldn't be healed even if he did save his sister. Or all of mankind.

What was the true reason he wanted war? The reason he kept hidden from everyone, perhaps even from himself. *That's* what she needed to heal.

"If I can't convince you to stay, then I'm going with you."

His eyes lit up. His arms went around her, and he pulled her to him in a solid hug. He looked down, relief on his face. "I'm so glad to hear you say that. Your visions will be useful. We'll be able to locate my sister quickly." He planted a kiss on her lips and then pulled away to finish packing.

It wasn't the response she'd expected.

One part of her was glad he didn't oppose her. She didn't have time to convince him she was going. His agreement was much easier.

The other part of her hoped he'd tell her to stay home. Tell her he loved her and wanted to keep her safe. Apparently he had great confidence in his strategy and his soldiers. He also thought she'd be safe on the subaquatic with him.

Unless he was less concerned with her safety and more concerned with her ability.

She disliked being used as a pawn in his war. Her visions had already propelled him into this mess.

If her destiny had been to assist the war efforts, she was doing well.

But her destiny was to stop it. So she'd get on the subaquatic with Kedric, his troops, and the Hyboreans and take the eight-hour ride to the Human Breeding and Research Center, praying they wouldn't be taken or killed.

"You better pack," he said. "We move out in thirty minutes."

Right. She'd gather her things and meet him on the subaquatic. Then she had only one thing left to do.

Get him alone and give him some sexual healing.

Chapter Twenty-Five

Applause and cheers followed Kedric as he stepped off the rock he'd used as a stage. The speech had been short yet grand. He'd encouraged the troops, reassured the people, and named his sister Addy as acting lord in his absence. He roused the crowd with talk of freedom and fighting spirit and unity of all mankind.

It was inspirational and motivational if he did say so himself.

Nearly eight hundred people lived in the Highland kingdom now, and from the look of the crowded rocky shores, nearly all eight hundred had turned out today. Some people came to see the warriors off. Most came to get a glimpse of the subaquatic surfaced between Pele and the little island. This maiden voyage would be historic.

Dressed in their thermal suits and boots, the warriors, subaquatic crew members, and three scientists—including Finn—were saying their good-byes to their families.

Kedric kissed Addy's cheek. "You're in charge until I return tomorrow. Follow the instructions I left. Don't trust anyone and you should be fine." He turned to Max. "Keep an eye out for Griffin." Kedric hadn't heard from Griffin since the night he caught him "fishing." After the science team swore they hadn't seen Griffin on Discovery Island, Kedric had to release him from prison. "The man is bad news. Guard Addy."

"With my life," Max said.

"Griffin won't hurt her. That would turn the people against him, but I wouldn't put it past him to assist Addy in having an accident."

"Why don't I just dispose of him?"

"The consequence for murder is suspension, Max. From a tree across Sanctuary River until dead or poached. Your job is to keep Addy safe. I'll be home tomorrow."

"And if you're not?"

Though the odds were in his favor, there was a possibility he'd die, be captured, or both. "If I'm not back in sixty hours—that's two days," he clarified for Addy, "as acting lord you have the power to decide what course of action to take. You can remain the ruler, appoint someone else lord, or do that voting thing I've heard you Earthlings talk about."

"I won't have to do any of that because you *will* be back." Addy embraced him. For a little thing, she sure did have a powerful squeeze.

The warriors were being ferried one group at a time out to the subaquatic. The large craft was unable to maneuver into the shallow waters at the dock for loading. Kedric and Myia would take the last ferry ride. He had a few more minutes to say his good-byes.

He gave Max a friendly whack on the back. "I wish you were coming with me as my right-hand man."

"I'll be your right-hand man right here. Oh, I have something for you." He pulled a sheathed knife from his waistband and presented it. "Your Flesheater. It served me well in my escape. May it do the same for you."

He took the fighting knife he'd lost five years ago, wrapped his gloved fist around the finger grooves, unsheathed the nine-inch recurved blade. The weight felt wonderfully familiar in his hand. He'd slain many a man and beast with it in the survival races over the years, preferring the one-handed close combat weapon over something that required two hands to wield like a claymore or a bow. Holding it was like holding an old, reliable friend.

"I never thought I'd see this again." He replaced it in its sheath. "Thank you."

Myia, who had been nearby in the crowd saying her good-byes to her father and sister, joined them. She hugged Addy and then turned to hug Max.

"Be careful," Max said to her. "Stay on that ship no matter what. It's the only safe place."

"I will."

"You better. I need a lot more healing. No offense to your father, but if someone's going to get all touchy-feely with my soul, I'd prefer it to be you." Max put his arms around her, and Kedric had to restrain himself from pulling them apart. He didn't like to see another man's hands on Myia. Not even his brother-in-law's.

Myia turned to Addy and bowed deeply, giving the new lord the respect due her status.

"It's time Myia." Kedric escorted her away from the group, ushered her down the dock and into the motorboat.

"So," he whispered as the boat pulled away from the dock, "you were healing Max?"

"Of course. That's my job. Poor man has so much pain. It's going to take quite some time to heal him."

"You didn't, you know. Connect with him?"

"Of course I did." Her devilish smile indicated she clearly enjoyed his discomfort.

He'd never been the jealous type before. He didn't like the feeling. "You do the naked dancing thing for him too?"

Her hand slipped into his and her spirit reached out to his fear.

"Search your heart," her spirit-image said. "You already know the truth."

Aye. He knew. Myia used her healing powers on the warriors, but not in the same way she used her powers on him. Theirs was a different bond, a different connection and since they had eight hours to HuBReC, maybe they could connect again.

A barely clad fantasy-Myia appeared in his mind and he knew she was thinking the same thing he was.

He kissed her soft lips. The spray of the sea misted them as the boat drove faster to the subaquatic.

"Mark my words, savage. Once we're underway in the subaquatic, you will dance for me. I don't mean your spirit. I want to watch *you* dance for me. In the flesh."

The ferry slowed and docked at the subaquatic. It didn't take long before Kedric and Myia passed through the sublimated hatch and climbed down into the ship.

The Hyborean captives were already chained in place at the helm. A good feeling came over him. Confidence flowed through every fiber of his being.

The ship would be able to sail into port without suspicion. The troops would be able to get into and out of HuBReC with the help of the mind-controlled Hyboreans. The battle would be a success because the Hyboreans would never know what hit them until it was too late.

The soldiers would plant their bombs and detonate them after they got the humans to safety in the subaquatic. The ship had room enough to take about a hundred passengers, maybe a few more if they all squeezed in.

The best part was that a journey that had taken him months on foot and canoe would take only eight hours in the subaquatic.

Aye, indeed, this would be a historic day. When they returned home in thirty hours—exactly one full day later—the tears on the shores would be tears of joy, and the kingdom would have a grand celebration.

After tomorrow there would be no way anyone would doubt his leadership. No one would dare try to overthrow him. Those who'd opposed him were sure to join him now, for who didn't like siding with the winners. This war would continue one Yard at a time.

Chapter Twenty-Six

Myia waited for Kedric in their sleeping compartment, as she had no wish to see the Hyboreans being used like machinery. Mind control made her uncomfortable, especially now that they were deep in the ocean and it was a necessary tool for keeping everybody alive. A slight chill tingled up her back. Having to rely on something she didn't believe in was unsettling.

Mind control wasn't good or bad.

It was both.

Once she healed Kedric, he would turn the ship around and then free the Hyboreans. And that would be the end of mind control.

An agonizingly slow hour and thirty minutes of waiting, thinking, perfuming her body, and painting her face the way Naomi had taught her passed. There was no doubt that Kedric would return to their sleeping compartment. He'd promised he would.

Plus, he'd made it perfectly clear he wanted sex.

Myia wanted it, too. But she would have to push her lust aside. Tonight's intimacy was reserved for healing his fear and stopping this war. She'd have only one chance to get him to change his mind and turn the craft around. The question was, should she be honest from the get-go or should she infiltrate his spirit when he wasn't expecting it and summon his pain?

Deceit would only make him close off again. That would be the end of it. It would also be the end of their relationship.

Whatever that relationship was.

Her spirit had performed the mating dance for him, and his spirit had accepted. Then when he had awakened, she gave herself to him with no mating promise. She was nothing more than—to use the term she'd heard before—a castle wench. Someone he could call upon to satisfy his urges.

Not only would she be a complete failure as a shaman-aprendi, she'd be a complete failure as a woman in love.

The warriors would go into HuBReC with hate in their battle-ready hearts. They'd be captured or killed or worse.

Deception was not the answer. It never had been. If she were to get Kedric to turn around, she would do it with honesty and integrity.

And a little sex appeal.

She paced up and down the small bedroom. Even if Kedric allowed her access into his soul, how would she be able to heal him in one session?

While in the Highlands, she'd begun healing a few escaped gladiators. Their despair and pain ran deep in their tortured souls, causing her great sorrow. They all needed more time for healing. Especially Max. While Addy's love had helped shepherd him from tortured beast to devoted mate, he still had nightmares. His soul suffered because the torment ran to his marrow. Those scars wouldn't heal overnight. He needed much more time and spiritual guidance in order for him to relinquish his hate.

The same would be true for Kedric.

Unfortunately, she didn't have the necessary time it would take to heal him little by little.

Speaking of time…the clock Kedric had placed on the floor near his gear bag read 13:30. Where was he?

She found her brush, pulled it through her hair harder than necessary, even though her hair was already smooth, shiny, and tangle-free. She adjusted her breasts so that they swelled beneath the skintight thermal suit. She peered again into the little mirror she'd brought.

If he didn't find this outfit sexy, then the man was already dead. If only he'd—

The door sublimated from solid to gas, and Kedric strode through the fog. He hit a button on the other side, and the door solidified once again with a crackle.

Though the Hyboreans opened doors by telepathy, the Hyborean slaves had been commanded to install manual controls on board the craft so no person could get trapped inside.

How could the humans ever beat an advanced race like this?

Her determination grew.

She stood in front of Kedric in her ice-blue thermal suit. "I'm ready to dance for you."

His mouth, which had been set in a straight line when he entered, now curled into an eager grin. His eyes smoldered. "Well, then. I'm ready to watch."

"Would you like to lay on the bed? It would be more comfortable."

He strutted to the bed and then dove onto it, landing on his side. His elbow propped up his head. "You may begin."

Since there was no music, she hummed a tune. She loved to dance, to let her spirit soar free with the music, and this time was no different.

Relaxing into the rhythm, she didn't worry about connecting to his spirit. That was a no-brainer. He was excited and horny, and he anticipated a sexual encounter like the last. He would welcome her into his soul, but would he allow her to find the core of his pain?

Would he allow her to heal his fear?

"What dance is this?" His lips pursed and eyes narrowed.

She stopped. Stepping back, she rubbed a forearm. "You don't like it?"

"It's—well, to be blunt, it's not what I was expecting."

She couldn't meet his eyes. He didn't like her dance. Her awkward freestyle movements turned him off. Suddenly feeling exposed, she pulled her hair over her breasts.

In an instant, he was off the bed standing in front of her, sweeping her hair back. His finger pressed into her chin to make her look at him. "I didn't mean for it to come out that way. I'd thought you'd want to perform the other dance for me."

"You want me to perform the mating dance?"

"Aye. I do. For real this time."

Her mouth went dry. Her heart pounded.

"I love you, Myia. I want you to be my one and only mate. If you'll have me."

"Yes!" She couldn't contain the laughter or stop herself from jumping up and wrapping her arms and legs around him. Her full weight propelled him backward. He staggered and fell with her onto the bed. Her mouth covered his, and she unleashed her pent-up passion in the kiss.

His returned kiss set her heart aflutter. She couldn't get enough of his mouth, his tongue, his lips.

His fingers tightened around her upper arms as he gently pushed her away. "Hold on, savage. I know you can't keep your hands off me, but we need to do this properly. With ceremony. If you want me to be your mate, dance for me."

What was she doing attacking him like that? Why couldn't she ever control herself? "I'm sorry. This is not proper shaman-aprendi behavior." She climbed off him and off of the bed and then inhaled deeply, letting the cool air quench her desire.

Kedric sat up. His head tilted, and his long hair fell to the side. "Why do you do that?"

"Do what?"

"Suppress your emotions?"

"I'm not suppressing anything. I'm maintaining balance."

"Your balance is all out of whack. You're a passionate woman. Yet every time you let yourself go, you immediately repress your feelings. You feel guilty. I can see it."

He wasn't wrong about that.

"You do know that you're human and that humans have emotions, right? It's okay to feel."

"I know it's okay to feel. But a shaman is supposed to remain clear and focused. I can't do that if I act upon emotion. I need to stay in balance."

"Lack of emotion isn't balance. You have a passion, Myia. I love that passion. I love your spirit, your drive to succeed—even if your goals do conflict with my own. It's who you are. Embrace your passion. Give in to your feelings, even those that say you need to scream or hit something, because trust me, sometimes you really need to."

"Kedric, hitting you was wrong."

"I disagree. I deserved it."

"No one deserves to be hurt. Trust me. It was wrong."

"For the sake of argument, let's say it was. Does that mean that the feelings inside you were wrong, too? Do you tell the people you heal that their feelings are bad?"

"Of course not. Their feelings are natural."

His eyebrows rose. "So their feelings are natural, but yours aren't?"

"Right."

"You really believe that?"

"Yes. My father never has extreme emotions. He always remains in balance."

The look on his face was hard to place. Suspicion lurked in his eyes, yet he smiled as if he knew a secret.

"What?"

"How do you know what his emotions were? Were your spirits intertwined every time he felt something?"

She shifted her feet. "Well, no, but I could read his aura. He maintains a very peaceful aura."

He shrugged that off as if it weren't important. "You're not your father, you know."

"I know." With a loud sigh, she flopped onto the bed. If only she could sink all the way into the mattress. "I've tried so hard to be like him, but I'll never be as good. A shaman must remain calm if she's to be one with the world. I'll never find that kind of en-lightenment."

The bed compressed beneath his weight as he moved closer. She rolled downhill toward him. He leaned over her. The tips of his hair tickled her cheeks. "You've seen many souls. Do all of them react with the same emotion to a stimulus?"

"I think you've been spending too much time with the scientists. You're starting to sound like them."

"Answer the question. Please."

"You're not trying to pump me for more information that would somehow enable you to control the Hyboreans better, are you?"

"Tsk, tsk, tsk. So suspicious." His words admonished, but his smile and eyes were light with teasing. "I'm merely trying to heal you, savage."

The warlord was playing spiritual healer? The giggle bubbled up from deep inside her. "Well, barbarian, I shan't stop your desire to heal. No, all people do not react with the same emotion to a given stimulus."

"Good to know. Now, do all people react with the same intensity to a stimulus?"

"No."

"So what might upset one person may not, in fact, upset another?"

"Correct."

"Have you ever given thought to the fact that your father may be impassive not because he's a shaman, but because that's his personality?"

Perhaps he had a point. Her father's lack of shown emotion may very well be due to his nature and not necessarily something she could attain.

"Just because a stimulus doesn't affect him, doesn't mean it wouldn't affect you. However you personally feel in any given moment is okay. Maybe you're right about not acting upon certain emotions. Maybe your meditation is the correct course of action. But feeling guilty about having natural human emotion is unhealthy. And absurd."

Isn't that what she'd always told her people? What made her believe that she should be immune to emotion?

"All this time I thought I'd lead you to enlightenment, but it turns out you're leading me to it." He was a remarkable man, and she couldn't love him more. He'd healed her father physically. He was healing her spiritually. Now he needed to heal himself and end this war. He couldn't do that until she healed him first. "Let me into your soul, Kedric. Let me do for you what you have done for me." She offered her hand, fingers spread and ready for him to grab hold.

"If you enter my body, savage," his voice deepened into a sexually suggestive voice, "rest assured I will enter yours."

The promise sent adrenaline rushing to her core. He'd already confessed his love, he had made a commitment to her. If they were to join their bodies, they'd do so properly this time. "You will not enter my body, barbarian, unless you accept my proposal."

"Then dance for me, Myia. Please."

She hummed the music of the mating dance.

The first time she had danced for him was because she wanted to heal his spirit. The second time, to save him from ultimortem. This time, she danced for both those reasons plus one more.

Love.

She held nothing back as she enticed him with her body, gyrating close enough to feel desire sparking between their auras. Deliberately taking her time, she unzipped the thermal suit, giving him a glimpse of her cleavage before dancing some more. Teasing him, tempting him to take her before the proper time.

He was on the edge of the bed leaning forward, smacking his lips. She giggled at the sound. Turning her backside to him, she stripped off the thermal jacket and let it drop to the floor. Refusing to cover her naked breasts with her hair, she faced him again. She flashed him a sultry gaze, daring him to touch her.

Sexual energy charged the room. Her body flushed from the heat.

Dancing topless in front of him, she could feel his restraint breaking down. Without even touching him, she could see into his spirit. He wanted to rip off her clothes, throw her down on the bed, and bury himself deep within her.

She wanted that, too.

As she peeled the skintight pants over her bottom and down her legs, her core grew wetter. There was something incredibly sensual about dancing naked in front of her fully clad Highland lord.

He looked dangerously sexy.

His gaze burned with pent-up desire. The moss-gray thermal suit hugged his bulky physique. Power emanated from him like an active volcano. At any moment he could erupt and consume her.

His control was amazing. He waited until the proper time to get down on one knee and hold out his hand. The instant her fingertips slipped into his gloved hand, he sprung up and covered her mouth with his. Bodies pressed together, she couldn't get enough of him. His lips, his jaw, his cheeks, anything she could kiss.

The smooth material of his gloves moved over her skin. "Stupid suit," he grumbled. In a flash, he stripped off his thermal suit.

His naked, muscular body was exquisite. And all hers.

Fevered hands squeezed and caressed her body, her backside, her breasts. Never had she experienced such intense heat. Her nerve endings sizzled with electricity.

She couldn't tell if it was her desire for him, his for her, or both together. Why hadn't she noticed it before? The strength and energy of their combined auras? Their spirits were united as one.

It could only mean one thing. Kedric wasn't just her life mate.

Kedric was her spiritual mate.

"Aye," he said out loud. "I feel it, too, Myia. The power. The pleasure. We are meant to be together. Soul mates."

"So what does this mean for us now?"

"It means." He smirked wickedly and then tumbled with her onto the bed. "We must consummate our sacred union."

His words sent a thrill to her core. She wanted him more than he knew. She was ready.

Body burning, heart pounding, she couldn't get enough of him. He touched her all over. He suckled her breasts. She squirmed with delight as he kissed and touched and teased her most sensitive places.

He made love to her with his hands, and the pressure mounted inside her, building, building, waiting for release.

She rocked against his fingers and closed her eyes to the pleasure. Her head spun with dizziness. She raked her fingers through his fiery hair and then fisted it when unable to stand the intensity.

His fingers dipped in and out of her faster and faster. She'd never been so wet or so hot or wanted anything as badly as she wanted him inside her.

"Aye, you're ready for me." His knee nudged her thigh, and she opened her legs for him, pulse racing, belly tingling.

Kedric thrust into her and claimed her cry of pain with his hot kiss. His tongue dipped into her mouth and the sting vanished, but the ache for him remained.

While giving her body time to adjust to him, his mouth made love to hers.

The waiting was sweet torture. Dear Spirits, if he didn't rock his hips soon, she'd die from need. "Make love to me," she said against his lips.

"Patience, my little savage."

He was being too gentle. She wanted him to move inside her, to satisfy the aching need. She thrust against him, taking him in fully, and he moaned into her mouth.

Rocking slowly at first, and then faster and faster, their bodies fell into an easy rhythm. She'd never felt so light. So free. Her spirit soared high over the ocean waves and danced on the air. She swirled and dove and plunged into the water again and then rose up higher and higher on the wind until she lost her breath from the deprivation of air. She crashed back into her body as it trembled with lovely spasms of ecstasy.

Kedric's body shuddered before his full weight collapsed on top of her.

"Can't breathe," she said, and his weight lifted to a comfortable pressure.

"Sorry." He kissed her again.

They held each other for some time before Myia gathered the courage to ask the most important question. "Would you let me into your heart?"

"You already are," he said.

"No, I mean would you let my spirit into your heart? Would you allow me to heal the anger in your soul?"

"Your spirit joined mine a moment ago. Why didn't you sneak in and heal me then?"

"Because I don't want to deceive you. I want you to *want* to be healed."

"Why is this so important to you? Does your destiny hang in the balance on whether you can stop a warrior from going to war?"

"At first maybe that was the case. Honestly, Kedric, I want to heal you because you deserve to let go of your pain. I don't want your pain to control you. I love you."

"And I, you." He kissed her. "Aye then, soul mate. Take your best shot. But I warn you my wounds run deep. Just promise me one thing."

"Anything."

"Please don't blame yourself when you realize I'm a warrior to the core, fearless in the face of any danger. My battle scars cannot be remedied."

"It's true not everyone can learn to heal. However, you are wrong about being fearless. Fear is the root of hurt. Once you conquer your fear, your scars will fade. Because you, my love, are a warrior with the blood of a healer."

"Well, then. Let's get to it, shall we?"

Chapter Twenty-Seven

Fantasy Myia stepped with fantasy Kedric through the fog and into a house. In front of them stood a low table maybe two feet off the floor. Thin pillows were stacked neatly underneath. To her right was a kitchen sideboard with a decanter of gold liquid that contained a pungent scent of fermented fruit.

She sensed Kedric's longing for the alcohol and could almost feel it burning her tongue as he dreamed of its taste. Farther into the room was a couch and chair covered with a thick fabric she'd never seen before.

"It's from Earth," he said. "The fabric is called polyester."

Had his answer been coincidence or had he heard her confusion?

"Most everything in Da's house is from Earth. He travels there frequently with his Hyborean master, Ferly Mor. He brings back anything he can."

She could see he was right by the knickknacks scattered all over the place, especially the statues of little bearded men with pointy red hats.

"Garden gnomes. For some reason Da likes to collect them."

Two little bedrooms were off the main room, and she knew one was Duncan's and the other Tess's. "Where did you sleep?"

"With the gladiators." Duncan's house wavered, and a new image appeared around them. They stood in a corridor with small, cramped rooms lining the right and left sides, reminding her of stalls the Highlanders kept their livestock in. Each room contained a burly and ferocious-looking gladiator, a rumpled blanket on the floor, and maybe a trinket or two each had collected. There really wasn't much more space for anything more.

Fantasy Kedric hit a button on the wall, and the solid white wall sublimated just like the walls did on the subaquatic. He held Myia's hand, leading her through the vapor and out into the sunshine. The vapor swirled behind them and then solidified again.

"Most doors are controlled by telepathy to prevent escape. Some have a control to let humans come and go as they please. They can't escape from the Yard because it's not really outside."

"I know. My visions have shown me the outside world. It's frozen. Kedric, this place brings you pain and sadness. Physically, emotionally, and spiritually, you've suffered great abuse. I believe there's more. There is something even deeper within you causing your greatest pain. I feel it. You must face it. Please share it with me."

"I can't."

"You can. I won't lie. It will hurt. It will be painful, but you are strong and I'm here with you." She kissed his lips for reassurance.

He deepened the kiss, and she tasted his apprehension and desperation. She hoped he tasted the love and courage she held for him.

When their lips parted, he gazed into her eyes. They shone with moisture. He was ready. He would finally confront his pain.

"I escaped without my family," he said in a near whisper. "I left them behind because I wasn't strong enough to stay in that hellhole any longer. I wasn't strong enough to save them. I was a coward and saved only myself."

Her heart ached for him and his pain. But she sensed more, and she needed to coax it out of him.

"There's something more you're not telling me. What is your greatest fear? What deep wound are you covering up? You use your strength and influence over all the people of the kingdom for a reason, Kedric. I feel it. What are you refusing to let me see?"

"Nothing. We're done here. Disengage your spirit." His words weren't angry, they were fearful. He wanted to tell her, but didn't know how. He didn't trust himself. If he really wanted her out of his spirit, he would have purged her soul from his like he'd done so many times before. She was so close to the truth now.

His fingers loosened their grip. She held on tighter. "You are not alone. I'm here with you. Your fear drives you to attack the Hyboreans. Your fear has put the lives of all the people on this ship in danger. Please, tell me why. What wound are you sheltering yourself from?"

"Abandonment. I abandoned my fami—"

"Kedric, the truth."

"All right. They abandoned me!"

"Who?"

"My family. They refused to escape. They'd rather stay in HuBReC. My own father would rather live in captivity with Ferly Mor than live free with me." His spirit image collapsed to his knees. "He abandoned me, Myia."

His grief consumed her. It weighed heavily on her heart, and she asked for all the strength of the Spirits to enter into Kedric's heart and take his grief and pain away.

"The true, deep-rooted aim of this war isn't to save your family, is it?"

Fantasy Kedric hung his head and shook it no.

"You want to kill the creature who captured your father's love."

"Aye." It was a whisper.

"You've hidden your selfish desire from your countrymen. You've stolen innocent lives and lied to them in your freedom speeches.

You want to destroy this one Hyborean because your father gave him the love you desperately desired."

"Aye."

Dark, furious clouds engulfed them. A tempest of terror, resentment, and hatred churned within his soul.

"You are not alone, Kedric. I feel your grief. I will ease your pain. Release your anguish."

"As a gladiator, I was powerless against my father's master. Not this time."

The storm raged. It gathered strength. It whipped about their spirit images like a hurricane.

"Let go of your vengeance," she yelled over the whipping wind.

"This time I will storm HuBReC, kill the beast, and take back my family."

"Is that what you really want?"

"Aye. It is."

"Search your soul, Kedric. What is it that you really want?"

Tears filled his wild eyes. He blinked them back, but they escaped and ran down his face between his nose and cheek.

"Say it, Kedric. You have the power to heal yourself."

His chin trembled. His resolve was breaking down. He was so close to purging his grief. She took hold of both his hands, gave them a squeeze for encouragement.

"I want my father's love." She almost didn't hear him over the storm. "He abandoned me, Myia."

"Perhaps he was afraid to escape with you and Max. The journey was perilous."

"No. Before then. When I became of age to wield a knife. He brought me to Xanthrag to be trained as a gladiator."

In the eye of the hurricane, a memory appeared. Five-year-old Kedric held his father's hand as he skipped along in the grass. Beside them was a gray Hyborean. "That's my father's master, Ferly

Mor." A large black Hyborean approached the three. "That's Xan-thrag. Survival race master. He owns HuBReC and most of the gladiators."

Duncan lifted five-year-old Kedric up, but he didn't hold him against his chest like usual. He offered him up to the race master. Xanthrag's leathery fingers encircled Kedric's waist as he grabbed him from his father's hands. Screaming and crying so hard his nose ran, young Kedric squirmed and kicked and tried to break free.

Why wouldn't his father rescue him?

Xanthrag's powerful squeeze crushed the breath from Kedric's little lungs. He gave up the fight. As the black Hyborean carried him off, Kedric watched his father walk away, hand in hand, with Ferly Mor.

Duncan never shed a tear, and he never glanced back.

The hurricane unleashed its fury in a downpour that drenched Kedric and Myia's images. A torrent of rain and tears surged down Kedric's face. "My father gave me away. He couldn't love me when his heart belonged to Ferly Mor."

"That is the pain and the fear you must heal, Kedric. You need to forgive your father. Allow peace to enter your soul. It isn't the Hyboreans you hate. It's your father's emotional and physical aban-donment."

Myia lifted her face skyward, her hair whipping about her, and spread her arms apart as if embracing the hurricane. "Protecting Spirits enter this man's heart. Take away his pain. Let him receive your grace and peace."

Light radiated from her body. An aura. Small at first and then growing in intensity. She harnessed all the spiritual energy she could and released it into the bitter torrent. She projected love, and com-passion, and forgiveness. It radiated from her soul.

Light and heat grew in intensity, expanded, reached out into the emotional upheaval. The winds lessened. Rain eased up.

"That's it, Kedric. Feel the love inside you. Let the forgiveness penetrate your soul. Receive peace. Return to balance."

Slowly—very slowly—the rains lessened. The winds died down. Rage and revenge decreased in intensity.

Fantasy Kedric got up onto his knees and joined her—head up and arms out. Rain fell on his face. The light of forgiveness radiated from him, warming the bitterness, melting the hurt. The winds died. The rain shower eased up and calm followed.

When peace returned, Myia gently untwined her spirit. Her image faded as she slowly slipped back into her own body. She didn't release his hand. He needed to know she was still here for him.

She waited quietly for his eyes to open before she asked, "How do you feel?"

He swiped a hand over his wet eyes and cheeks. "Like I dropped fifty pounds."

"Your heart is lighter without your fear weighing you down. And your aura is brighter."

He searched her eyes as if seeing all the way into her soul. "You're an amazing woman, Myia." The awe and love in his voice squeezed her heart. He embraced her, and she melted into his warmth. Never had she felt so relieved. "Thank you for healing me."

She pulled back from his embrace to look at him as she spoke. "I helped you face your fear and gave you support to confront and forgive it. You healed yourself. I'm sorry to say it won't last. You've been carrying around this burden and rage for so long, you'll need to do this again when the pain reemerges. You don't need me, though. Now that you know what fears to face, you can mend them on your own. Of course, I'm always here if you prefer not to go it alone."

He reached for her again and held her tight. His body was warm and solid, his lips so soft and tender. Enlightenment always made her essence soar. Healing Kedric—her soul's mate—sent her spirit soaring to the highest heaven.

There was only one thing left for him to do. Return home and free the Hyboreans. "You best tell the crew to turn the ship around before we get too close to the Hyboreans' world."

"I can't."

"Why not?"

"Because we're not heading home."

"What? Why?" She had to push him away in order for him to stop kissing her.

"Because now I know how to beat the enemy." He kissed her fast on the mouth. "Thanks, love. You're the best." He ran to the door and slapped the wall button. A white swirling cloud appeared.

"Wait. Where are you going?"

"To debrief my A team. Thanks to you, I have a new plan of attack."

Kedric disappeared through the fog before the wall solidified.

Her throat closed. Her chest tightened. She couldn't tamp down the frustration welling up inside her. Anger balled her hands into fists and, unable to settle her rage, she repeatedly punched the bed and screamed.

Yes. She failed as a shaman on so many levels.

Chapter Twenty-Eight

A kiss on her forehead woke her. When had she fallen asleep? She glanced at the clock. Two hours had passed since Kedric left the room with his new attack plan that she'd somehow inspired. The knot in her stomach tightened.

Kedric's gray eyes were inches from hers. "Are you okay?"

Of course she wasn't okay. She felt nauseous and hot. Her head ached and her body was sluggish as she sat up. She masked her anger with a light, casual tone. "Why do you ask?"

"Because your face is red and your eyes are bloodshot. Have you been crying?"

"Crying, screaming, throwing a temper tantrum. You know, the usual tranquil feelings of one who's in harmony with the world." She wasn't a shaman, why hide the sarcasm now?

"What's gotten into you? Besides me earlier?" He grinned a sexy, devilish grin, but she was in no mood for his innuendo. In a release of pent-up frustration, she slapped his face.

In the next instant, her back was pressed into the bed as he pinned her down. She struggled to get free, but couldn't move beneath his full weight. "What the hell's gotten into you?"

"As if you don't know."

The fire in his eyes extinguished. His voice softened. "Did I do this? Did my anger get transferred into you while you were healing me?"

Why did he have to be so sweet and worried when she was enraged? "I didn't heal you. That's why I'm angry. Don't you see? All I've ever wanted to be was a spiritual healer, but every time I've tried to heal you, I've made things worse."

"No, you haven't. You've healed me."

"Right. That's why you fled here excited to share your new attack plan with your war party."

"Myia, I didn't commission a new attack plan. I—"

"Don't you dare lie to me. You said the words yourself as you were leaving."

He released her wrists and sat back, giving her the space she needed to sit upright. He looked thoughtful. "I meant that figuratively. I'm a warrior. That's the vernacular I use. But it's not what I meant."

"Then what did you mean?"

"I left to inform the troops of the change in game plan. We're not attacking the Hyboreans." His shoulders straightened, his chest puffed out, and pride gleamed in his eyes. "We're rescuing the people."

She pressed her lips together and squinted. No glowing light or color outlined his body. "This is the truth?"

"Read my spirit. You know it is."

Her stomach dropped and she glanced away. Heat crept into her face and behind her eyes.

"Myia?" By the question in his voice, he knew something was wrong. The light pressure of his fingers beneath her chin turned her head toward him. "What is it?"

Tears blurred her vision. Unable to hold her head up, she let it drop to her chest. "I can't read anyone's aura when I'm angry. I'm a complete failure."

"Look at me." He tucked a knuckle under her chin again and lifted it until her gaze met his compassionate eyes. "You're not a failure. You set out to heal my heart, and you did it. I promise you I won't wage war against the Hyboreans. My A team and I have been working the last hour on a new plan of atta— Er, action. We're going to infiltrate HuBReC's Yard and covertly free our people. No bombs. No war. No mess."

Warmth radiated throughout her body, and tears streamed down her face. She'd done it? Had she really healed the warlord's heart?

"Oh, Kedric. I'm so relieved." She wrapped her trembling arms around him. He squeezed her so tightly she felt his heart beating against her chest. "Can you forgive me for doubting you? And...and for striking you?"

"You don't need my forgiveness, love. You need your own. You're a great shaman and should trust your work. Besides, if anyone should be asking for forgiveness, it's me. I didn't mean to have upset you, but it seems to be something I excel at."

She laughed and hiccuped at the same time. It didn't matter if his actions provoked her negative reactions or not. The fact remained that she was a pacifist with anger issues. It was something she needed to work on. If she were to heal others, she had to heal herself. "I promise you I'll never again raise my hand to you in anger."

"I promise you I'll never again give you a reason to be angry." The soft warmth of his lips kissed the top of her head. When he broke the embrace to gaze into her eyes, his expression turned serious. Whatever he was about to say was important. Her heartbeat sped up. "I must be completely honest with you, Myia. If something should go terribly wrong during the rescue, my men and I are prepared to fight our way out of there."

"I understand."

"By any means necessary."

She nodded, saying nothing more. Though his admission weighed on her heart, self-defense could be accepted over pure antagonistic aggression.

His lips pressed against hers. His solid arms were steady and reassuring around her. He hugged her as though he didn't want to let her go. Honestly, she didn't want him to, either. She kissed him back with longing. If only they could hold each other forever.

Protecting Spirits, please let this rescue go off without a hitch.

After Kedric saved his family, his restless soul would be able to live in peace. She wanted nothing more than to share that tranquillity with him.

A pounding on the door interrupted their kiss. Kedric got up and sublimated it. General Sebastian emerged through the vapor, breathless and sweating. He bowed quickly.

"My lord, we've got a problem."

Chapter Twenty-Nine

The worry and fear in Sebastian's eyes set Kedric on full alert. "What is it, General? Have we been detected by the Hyboreans?"

"No, my lord. Worse." Sebastian glanced past him to the bed, his expression indicating an uncertainty of how much information he could reveal in Myia's presence.

She'd already seen Kedric's dark soul and the bowels of his secrets, and didn't fear them. He'd no desire to hide anything from her again. "Say what you've come to say."

"My lord, Dunna requests your presence right away. One of the Hyboreans is not responding properly to the mind control. It—" He glanced at Myia again, obviously uncomfortable stating the problem.

"Go on."

"It's starting to resist. Dunna fears it's waking up."

The hair on his arms rose. They'd considered this possibility. The scientist had no way to know if the EM fields had irrevocably damaged their brains. The Hyboreans had never demonstrated a regeneration of brain activity on the training runs, but they'd never been taken this far from Pele before. Nor had they been off the island for this long. "Where are the Hyboreans now?"

"Chained and in their positions."

"Alert the troops. I need every man ready to defend our mission."

"Yes, my lord." After a quick head nod, Sebastian disappeared through the smoky door.

"What does this mean, Kedric?"

A sour taste formed in his mouth. He tried to swallow, but couldn't. The back of his throat ached. He had to get himself under control. It wouldn't do Myia or anyone else good to see their leader shaking with fear. Everything his army had trained and worked for could come crashing to a halt before they even reached land.

If the Hyboreans regained consciousness, they were all doomed. His men would be sold as survival race gladiators.

Myia would suffer the fate of a broodmare. Or worse.

His chest tightened. How could he have let her come? How could he have been so stupid to think she'd be safe on this ship?

"Kedric?" She was standing in front of him now.

He had to pull himself together. He was lord, dammit. He had to fix this. He pulled her into his arms for reassurance. Who was he attempting to reassure, her or himself?

"Everything in the subaquatic still runs on telepathy. If the Hyboreans wake up, they could trap us and take over the ship. Stay here where you're safe. I have to see Dunna." He kissed her hard, tasting her lips as if it were for the last time. Though he didn't want to let go, he had to pull himself away to confront the Hyborean.

"Be safe," she called after him.

He ran down the corridor to the bridge and then entered through the sublimated door. The vapor crackled as it solidified behind him. The chained Hyborean at the controls seemed to be in a blissful stupor, calmly doing his job. The instrumentation the scientists had added to the helm—since humans couldn't read Hyborean equipment—appeared to be running on course.

"Where's Dunna?" Kedric asked Finn.

"With the other Hyborean in the cargo hold, my lord."

"Is this creature giving you any trouble?"

"No, my lord." There was a questioning hesitation in his voice. Apparently, he didn't know what Kedric was talking about.

"Carry on, then." He left the room in search of Dunna in the cargo hold. What the hell was going on? The impression General Sebastian gave was of a wild Hyborean, but Finn didn't seem to know anything about it.

Could he be walking into a trap? Was Dunna working for Griffin? Was Sebastian? He unsheathed his Flesheater, tightened his grip around the knife. If this story was a lie to get him alone for a mutiny, he'd be ready to strike down anyone foolish enough to cross him.

At the cargo hold, he stepped through the vaporous door. Only a guard and Dunna were in the large empty room. The chained Hyborean sat quietly, eating its meal.

"What's the meaning of this? I was informed your Hyborean was regaining consciousness, yet he looks comatose to me."

"Lord Kedric." Dunna stood, removed his tech-ring from his head, and then bowed. "Before its feeding I commanded this Hyborean to sit as usual, but he didn't."

"That's your complication? You couldn't get a Hyborean to sit? I thought they were trying to break free from their chains."

"That may happen yet, my lord." Dunna's gaze wouldn't leave the creature for more than a few seconds at a time. His anxiety around the beast was new. Even the guard, Bigby, seemed to be on high alert as he watched the creature. "I've never had a Hyborean disobey its mind control device even when asked to perform the most complicated tasks. However, it took eight tries to get this one to comply with one simple command. I fear this creature is waking up."

There was no mistaking the worry in Dunna's tired eyes. The man was telling the truth. Kedric sheathed his weapon. He moved to the Hyborean for a closer look. It seemed as it always had in the research habitat. "Could there be a problem with the tech-ring?" After Griffin had mentioned sabotaging the equipment that night, Kedric had inspected the rings. Three separate times. They were fine.

"No, my lord. I swapped the controls out for the other one, and they both had the same result. This Hyborean refused to sit and eat as an act of defiance. It took a while, but his mind finally obeyed mine."

Fantastic. His stomach clenched. "That answers that question."

"I fear the longer we are away from the island's electromagnetism, the more their brain waves will repair themselves."

"How long before they become free thinkers again?"

"I don't know. I first noticed the Hyborean wouldn't sit when told, then it elevated into refusing to eat. If we can't control these beings, how are we going to get into the city?"

"Have you charted the progression of its dissent?"

"Yes, my lord. The computer is compiling and plotting the data now. It should be ready any moment."

The door sublimated and in rushed Wren. "The data is finished," he said. "If cognitive function continues to increase at a steady rate, this Hyborean will be able to fully override our thought control in three hours. It will have fifty percent of its brain capacity back in about ninety minutes."

How the hell could Kedric conduct a rescue mission with their secret weapon only working half of the time? When the Hyborean wasn't working, it would be fighting against them for its freedom and their capture. "How long until we reach land?"

"About fifty minutes, my lord."

"Plus another fifteen to infiltrate HuBReC's Yard. That only gives us twenty-five minutes to find the refugees and bring them back to the ship."

"That's assuming the Hyborean doesn't disobey my commands,"

Dunna said, rubbing the back of his neck. "Every minute he fights me is a minute lost for the rescue."

Did a 50 percent regeneration of brainpower translate to a 50 percent loss of rescue time? If so, that gave Kedric only twelve minutes to find his family and get out. That might be doable if Tess and his father were home. What if they weren't? The Yard was over twenty-eight hundred acres. He'd never find them in time.

His muscles bunched. He needed to move. He needed to do something. He strode to Wren. "Inform Finn at once to push the subaquatic to its max. Every second counts."

"Yes, my lord." He bowed and raced out of the room.

"What if the Hyborean tries to escape while we're trying to gain access to the Yard?" Dunna said.

"I'm sure he will." Kedric turned to the guard. "Bigby, inform General Sebastian of the situation. Team Alpha Two will stay on board and keep the Hyborean in line and under control."

"Yes, my lord." Bigby bowed and then raced out of the room.

Having finished its meal, the Hyborean sat in its place, watching Kedric with its beady, black iridescent eyes. Though it was quiet, it was alert. He'd seen that look in a Hyborean's eyes before. It was thinking.

No, it was calculating.

Its eyes glazed over once more. Its head dropped as if it couldn't hold it up any longer.

"The real problem is whether the waking Hyboreans will have the ability to communicate telepathically with their kind."

"With fifty percent brain capacity, he'll likely be able to," Dunna said, taking the creature's food bowl away from it. "I won't be able to stop him from calling for help. Do you think it wise to continue? Perhaps we should retreat. We could continue studying the creatures, find a way to keep their minds scrambled, and try again."

"They will be fully conscious in three hours whether we abort the mission or not. I'd rather take our chances returning with one Hyborean on a subaquatic full of refugees than two Hyboreans on a cargoless ship."

"Only one, my lord? Surely you don't mean to dispose of this creature."

"Aye. I do. It's a liability now. After it grants us access into the Yard, it will be tranquilized, drugged, and hidden. Soldiers will be stationed at the exit points, ensuring each man and his refugee group escapes the building. Everyone returns to the subaquatic before the countdown ends. At T minus zero, the Hyborean pilot—"

"Cavy, my lord."

Kedric narrowed his eyes at the scientist for interrupting him. Who cared what the Hyborean's name was? He was giving orders here. "Fine. At T minus zero, *Cavy* sets sail back to Pele."

It was a sound plan. Assuming nothing backfired.

"What if Labrat's brain function returns to full power before we return with the refugees?"

His chest tightened as a painful lump formed in his heart. Myia would hate him, but it had to be done to save their people. "The men must make him obey the old-fashioned way."

"My lord?"

"Pain compliance. Torture."

Chapter Thirty

After Kedric returned to his quarters, he stripped naked so Myia could lather him with thermal cream. The scientists had found tubes of the warming balm, along with thermal suits, gladiator boots with retractable crampons, and human cages, when they'd searched the subaquatic days ago. Summer in Handakar City, where HuBReC was located, meant temperatures around thirty degrees below zero on the Fahrenheit scale. Though the troops wouldn't be outside for long, the thermal cream would prevent shivering, thereby helping the men conserve much-needed energy.

Myia's soft, feminine hands rubbing cream down his back and over his buttocks were pure heaven. His penis reacted to her touch. It stood at attention like a proud warrior. "Make sure you don't miss any spots."

Myia's hands slid over his shoulder and arm as she moved to face him. "I see one part of you eager to be rubbed with cream."

"Aye. It wouldn't do to have him getting frostbite."

"It most certainly would not." Her lips pressed together in an apparent attempt to hide her impish smirk. It didn't work.

Her hands were glorious, sliding over his chest, abdominal

muscles, and down to his manhood. He drew in a breath. She stroked him much longer than rubbing in thermal cream required. If only he could lay her on the bed and plunge himself deep inside of her.

It took all his strength to remove her grip from his cock. "I think that's enough, aye?" It pained him to speak the words, and the result was a raspy voice. "I have a rescue mission to lead, and if you keep at that, I might miss it."

Myia's sigh held disappointment and something else. Fear? He wrapped his arms around her back and hugged her to his naked body. "What's the matter?"

Her embrace tightened. "Return to me, Kedric."

"That I will, love. That I will." He kissed the top of her head. "However, returning necessitates me to leave first. And I can't do that until I'm dressed."

She gave him a sad, little smile as she nodded in acquiescence before continuing her thermal cream journey down his thighs and legs. When this was over, he'd return the favor and rub lotion all over every inch of her golden body. Not thermal cream. Rather some floral-scented lotion made up of her favorite Peletian flower. He'd take his sweet time exploring every tanned and nontanned part of her.

The white thermal suit she handed him brought him back from the daydream to cold, hard reality. Having donned so many of these in the past, the mere sight of it had his adrenaline pumping and heart racing. Stepping into the thick, close-fitting material was like stepping into a second skin. Gladiator skin.

Battle armor.

His muscles bunched. His senses awakened. Shrugging into the sleeves and zipping up the thermal jacket completed the transformation from king into warrior. Only this time he wouldn't be killing as many as possible. He'd be saving as many as possible.

Unless, of course, someone or something came between him and the rescue of his family.

* * *

Kedric looked formidable. Powerful. Sexy in his thermal suit with every bulging muscle visible beneath skintight material. His body moved with strength and fluidity. Heat spread from her core to her flesh. It wasn't right having lustful thoughts at a time like this. Not when faced with the possibility that Kedric might never return.

He pulled white gladiator boots up to his knees and then stashed his knife inside. His aura radiated with confidence.

Though unable to predict the future or today's outcome, she knew in her spirit he'd be successful. If anyone could rescue these people, it was Kedric.

He pulled the thermal suit up over his plaited hair, concealing his red locks. "I need your help."

"With what? Your thermal suit looks fine to me. White is a good camouflage for the city."

"Not with the suit. With the mission."

Her heart beat a little faster. "Really? What help could I give?"

"My A team is made up of ex-gladiators. They'll be in the field with me. The rest of the men have been born on Pele. They've never seen a fully alert Hyborean before. I'm not sure how they'll react if the pilot wakes up."

"You want me to help them remain calm?"

"Aye. That's part of it."

Something else was troubling him. It was obvious from the way his lips pursed as if unsure how to tell her something. "What's troubling you?"

He took hold of her hands. "I don't know if any of these men have loyalties to Griffin. If they do, I wouldn't put it past anyone to—"

"Leave you and your men behind?" It was a good thing he was wearing gloves. It prevented him from feeling her clammy palms. Inhaling a breath, she resolved to be strong for him and masked her fear.

He nodded. "You're the only one I can trust, Myia. If anyone gets any ideas about turning tide and sailing out before the return rendezvous time, use your ability to make them stay."

"Don't worry, Kedric. No matter what happens, I won't leave without you."

His brows knit together as he searched her eyes. "That's not what I meant. If the timer reaches zero and I'm not back, you *will* leave without me."

Her breath hitched. She couldn't move. It was as though her moccasins sprouted roots anchoring her to the floor. She clutched Kedric's arms. "I can't. I won't."

"You can and you will." His hand cradled her cheek, his fingertips reached into her hair, and she wished she could feel his skin beneath the thermal suit. "My life is worth no more than the men, women, and children about to board this subaquatic. You must see them safely home."

"Kedric—"

"Promise me my rescue will not be in vain."

"Don't talk like this. You'll return. I know you will."

"Promise me, love. I need to hear you say it."

Her blurred vision cleared as she blinked away tears. The smooth pad of his gloved thumb wiped the tears from her cheek. "I promise," she whispered.

His mouth was on hers in ravenous hunger. With a need just as great, she returned the kiss as if it were their last.

Chapter Thirty-One

Minutes later on the subaquatic's bridge, Myia stood silently at Kedric's side as the ship surfaced. Daylight streamed through the clear walls. Observation walls Kedric had called them. He'd explained they were made out of special one-way transparent material in which those on the inside could see out, but no one on the outside could see in. Ocean lapped against the ship below eye level, giving a unique perspective of the drift ice's submerged chunks and floating shelves.

The chained Hyborean pilot seemed docile and under control. Finn's face glistened with perspiration that couldn't have been due to his thermal suit. Hers kept her warm in the room's subzero temperature, but not warm enough to induce sweating. Poor Finn was laboring in deep concentration as he navigated the Hyborean through frozen obstacles.

Hopefully he wasn't laboring against it waking up. As much as she'd like to see the creature regain consciousness, it would be a tragedy if it occurred before their return to Pele.

Not one of the fifteen people gathered on the bridge spoke a word. They most likely shared in her fear of distracting Finn.

Her heart pounded as the ice dock grew nearer and nearer.

Finn gripped the arms of his chair. He leaned forward, his spine straightened. His excited cry shattered the dead silence. "Lord Kedric! I can't believe this. I've just received telepathic communication from a Hyborean on land. I think it's a harbormaster."

"All hands ready," Kedric shouted.

The two teams of soldiers unsheathed their weapons ready to spring into action. Spirits willing, neither a fight nor a retreat would be necessary.

Kedric nodded to Finn. "Reply."

"This is so cool." He turned back to the observation wall in front of him.

"The moment of truth," Kedric whispered, and Myia's heart leaped into her throat. "As long as Finn can pass this mindless animal off as a functioning member of society, we're golden."

"What do you mean?"

"Social norms. You know, Highlanders greet each other with a bow. Earthlings shake hands. Gladiators establish a dominance hierarchy."

"What do Hyboreans do?" She kept her voice as quiet as his for fear of interrupting Finn's concentration.

Kedric wouldn't meet her eyes. He kept them on the scientist, the Hyborean, and the transparent wall in front of them. "Finn better figure that out fast."

It seemed there was a collective breath holding on the ship. Everyone was deadly silent. Would Finn be able to communicate with the harbormaster via their pilot? Would he be able to fake social etiquette?

Finn's arms punched the air above him. "We have permission to dock!"

The crew's collective sigh of relief probably caused the room's carbon dioxide level to double. The men cheered and slapped each other's backs as the subaquatic slid through the water to an empty berth at an ice jetty. Outside, a Hyborean waited for them to cut the engine before mooring the vessel.

"We're in," Finn said.

A thrill shot through her. Step one was complete. They'd safely docked in Handakar City. Hopefully the Hyborean and soldiers about to depart the ship would be able to get away with anonymity.

"What are the chances the Hyboreans will do a background check on this water craft?" a crewman asked. Myia didn't know his name.

Kneading the muscles on the back of his neck, Finn turned to the crewman. "As Alex Graham had said, New York City parking attendants don't run the plates of the vehicles. They just park cars and collect money. Let's hope the same holds true with these guys."

"Aye." Kedric pressed a button on the silver tech-ring hiding beneath his long hair. "Dunna, is Labrat ready?" He paused for a response Myia couldn't hear and then directed his men. "Alpha Two stand guard. Be prepared for backup. Alpha One to the cargo hold. Load the hovercraft cage."

Labrat and Cavy had used a ten-by-ten-foot cage to contain their poached humans. Kedric said fifty people could be crammed inside and would transport the refugees through the city. Modified for safety, some bars had been cut and then reattached with low-bond glue so that no man would be trapped inside. With little effort they could pull out the bars and escape.

"Start the countdown."

She bit back the sudden urge to grab him and beg him not to leave. To demand he take them all back to safety. Of course, that would only distress everyone on board and frazzle the men's already tense nerves. Such behavior from a shaman was generally frowned upon.

Finn pressed some buttons on his computer. Bright red digital numbers lit the wall clock. The seconds began ticking down from thirty-five minutes. When it reached zero, the subaquatic crew had been ordered to leave no matter who was—or wasn't—on board.

What if Kedric was caught? What if he didn't return in time? Could she really stand by while the crew left him here?

She ran to keep up with him as he strode into the cargo hold.

"Open the hatch," he called. The subaquatic's wall sublimated into swirling white fog, beyond which lay a dangerous alien world.

Her heart pounded uncontrollably. She blinked back tears. He needed her strength right now. He needed to know she had faith in him. That she believed in him.

Wanting desperately to kiss him good-bye, she forced herself not to lean into his body. Not to tell him how much she loved him. He couldn't afford any distractions.

Yet she couldn't let him leave without saying anything. She repeated her plea from the bedchamber.

"Return to me, Kedric."

* * *

Myia stood there proud and poised, the way a queen should stand as her men answered their call of duty. Beneath those confident golden eyes, she feared for his life. He knew his little savage well enough to recognize that hidden pain.

Or maybe he was projecting onto her his own pain at leaving.

"Aye. I'll return. I promise you that."

Labrat and Dunna were situated in the hovercraft's cab. The hovercraft's bed held the cage. One by one, the seven-man team climbed the ladder to the cage's top and then jumped through the gaseous door, landing inside.

He'd stay if he could and make love to her over and over again, but he couldn't shirk the mission. He'd thought about commanding one of his men to rescue his family in addition to his assigned mark, but there wasn't enough time. Each man had to get in, grab his people, and get out within minutes. They didn't have a moment to spare searching for Tess and Duncan or convincing them it was safe to escape.

Kedric was his family's only hope of rescue.

With seconds left before his turn to climb, he kissed Myia's trembling lips. It wasn't a passionate kiss or a long kiss good-bye. It was a *be-right-back* kiss. A confident, *see-you-in thirty-four-minutes* kiss. A kiss meant to reassure her everything would work out all right.

The floor of the cage met his feet as he landed inside. "Commence operation freedom," he shouted. As the hovercraft glided to the hatch, he glanced back at Myia, searing into memory her beautiful face and the warmth from her loving eyes.

Fog passed around him as he emerged into the frozen Hyborean world.

Chapter Thirty-Two

Dunna, acting as Labrat's brain, navigated the hovercraft out of the marina and into the city streets. HuBReC wasn't far, only two miles away, but Kedric couldn't get there fast enough. His heart pumped knowing he'd see Tess in only a few short minutes. Then he'd save her from the Hyboreans and gladiators alike. If he encountered Regan or her other rapists, he would slit their throats.

Above frosted skyscrapers, distant spacecraft lights twinkled in the dusk as they arrived and departed one of Hyborea's busiest cities.

The seven men of Alpha One remained silent. They all seemed deep in thought, perhaps contemplating their fate should the mission go wrong or perhaps remembering the last time they'd seen this place. Every one of them had either lived in or visited HuBReC at some point, which was why they'd been hand selected for the rescue.

Covered head to toe in thermal suits, it was unlikely a Hyborean would recognize any of them, though it remained a possibility.

Their advantage came in knowing the layout of the Yard. According to Max and Addy's drawings and accounts, the Yard's landscape hadn't changed much over the past five years.

The hovercraft slowed to a halt in an alley behind HuBReC.

In a few moments they would enter the building the same way he'd escaped: through the refuse bunker. More accurately, through the maintenance door *next* to the refuse bunker. Now that he had a Hyborean slave to sublimate the door, they needn't step foot in garbage.

What was taking Dunna so long? He and Labrat should be letting them out of the cage by now. He checked his watch.

T minus thirty-one minutes.

"Where the hell is he?" Bigby mumbled. The other men voiced their frustration as well.

"Quiet."

A thud came from the vehicle's cab. It sounded like a body hitting the wall. An animal screamed and snarled in his mind. It wasn't a real sound. It was his brain's interpretation of the Hyborean's anger. His adrenaline spiked. "Bigby, sever the bars. Labrat's awake."

In seconds Kedric was out of the cage, running to the cab where Dunna struggled with the Hyborean. The scientist's eyes were closed in concentration, his lips were moving, shouting commands to the Hyborean.

There was no way inside. The door was solid. In order for it to open, it had to be sublimated.

Dammit, Kedric hadn't accounted for this scenario.

"Fight him with your thoughts, Dunna."

Thank the Spirits, Dunna wasn't wearing a collar. The Hyborean couldn't shock him into submission.

The creature grabbed for the scientist's tech-ring, but Dunna covered the band, pinning it to his head with his arms. The Hyborean's fingers fumbled as it tried prying Dunna's arms off his head without success. It lacked full control over its fine motor skills. It also lacked an understanding that removing its own tech-ring would sever the mind connection.

"Orders, my lord?" someone shouted.

He sensed the entire team's presence behind him. He couldn't spare them a glance. "Find a way into HuBReC. Now!"

Their footsteps retreated. Kedric pounded on the cab's door, gaining the Hyborean's attention. Maybe Labrat would sublimate it to grab him, giving Dunna a chance to escape.

No such luck.

At least they were in an alley. If they were parked anywhere else, this scene would have attracted attention by now.

The struggling inside settled. Kedric placed his hands on the cab to peer into the window, but his arms gave out. He nearly fell through the sublimation cloud into the cab. Quickly righting himself, he backed away as the Hyborean—with eyes glazed over once more—emerged.

Dunna followed sweating and panting.

"Are you all right?"

"Yes, my lord." His breathing labored. "Let's go rescue our people."

At HuBReC's maintenance door, Labrat took up the team's leashes and then sublimated the door as commanded. The fight with Dunna might have exhausted his mind, but who knew how long before his strength regenerated.

They were treading dangerous territory now.

The men entered the building calmly, though Kedric's insides were anything but. Especially when a red-and-brown-furred Hyborean approached.

"He wants to know what we're doing here," Dunna said.

"Tell him we're Xanthrag's new gladiators." Xanthrag was the wealthy survival race master and owner of this building, and a nasty son of a bitch.

"He doesn't believe me," Dunna said. "He wants to know why Labrat entered the maintenance area."

"Tell him Xanthrag's orders. These warriors are to be kept secret until the next survival race."

The Hyborean glanced down at the group of leashed gladiators. The men's backpacks wouldn't raise a red flag. All gladiators used one in the survival races to hump their gear. Of course, the only gear the packs contained at the moment were thermal suits for the refugees and a few weapons.

Kedric glanced at his watch.

T minus twenty-nine minutes.

"Tell him if he detains us any longer, you'll call Xanthrag and he'll have to deal with the boss's anger."

After a quiet moment, the creature's eyes widened. Kedric sensed its fear as it backed away. Neither humans nor Hyboreans wished to piss off Xanthrag.

Ever.

"Permission to enter granted," Dunna said.

Kedric's clenched hand relaxed. He hadn't realized he'd made a fist.

Suppressing the impulse to run inside and find Tess, he strode calmly through the door at Labrat's furry feet.

The group passed through the maintenance area and then hurried down a dingy corridor, up a flight of stairs—each step twice the size of human steps—and down another corridor in less than three minutes. The only thing separating them from the human habitat now was a one-way transparent wall.

Observation walls like this one made up the Yard's perimeter. Luckily, HuBReC was home to over a thousand people and hundreds of Hyboreans. Anyone peering through his apartment's observation wall into the Yard wouldn't question the men's presence. They'd assume the men belonged to someone else in the complex.

Regardless, to be safe, they would keep to the shadows as much as possible.

Kedric couldn't take his leash off fast enough. He threw it on a pile with the others.

Dunna commanded the Hyborean to sublimate the door, and a twelve-foot-tall smoke cloud appeared.

"Stay here with the Hyborean," Kedric ordered Dunna. "Drug him enough to keep him quiet and under control but not enough to knock him out. We'll need him to get out of the building."

"Yes, my lord."

"The rest of you, move out." He turned back to Dunna. "Place a leash across the threshold to trip the door sensors so it won't completely solidify." If Labrat caused problems again, they wouldn't have to waste time fighting him to open the door.

Kedric was the last to leap through the smoke. For the first time in five years, he was back in the Yard.

It looked just as he'd remembered: holographic sun setting behind Xanthrag's training field and a dirt path cutting through the forest that would lead him to his father's house.

He sprinted toward it. He could run the mile and a half in less than nine minutes. Unfortunately, Tess and Da couldn't do the same. If it took them longer than twelve minutes to return, they'd miss the shuttle back to the subaquatic. He pushed his pace, racing through the darkening woods.

Every turn and every small incline came back to him as if he'd never left. The heady scent of forest and earth brought back bittersweet memories of gladiator training. As well as memories of pain.

After five years, he thought he'd have lost some familiarity with the way home. Not that Duncan's house had been his home for long. His father had given him away at five.

What was going on with all these thoughts? He shook his mind free of the past in order to focus on the present.

The path soon emptied into a grassy meadow. His heart leaped at the sight of Duncan's house twenty yards away.

He sprinted the final distance to the hologram wall, slapped the little black button on it, and then entered though the sublimated door into a dark, quiet home. In less than thirty seconds, he'd searched the tiny house calling for his sister and father.

They weren't there.

He was about to go through the back door to Ferly Mor's apartment when he noticed a woman's thermal suit and Duncan's cloak hanging on a wall peg. Unless these were extra clothes, they wouldn't be in Ferly Mor's apartment. The temperature was unsuited for humans unless they had the proper clothing. Still he refused to leave without checking.

Upon entering Ferly Mor's apartment, the room illuminated on its own. The giant house was quiet and empty.

No one was here.

Outside the window, the sky had grown dark. Ferly Mor would be returning from work anytime now. Kedric couldn't be here when that happened.

Where would he search for his family? The Yard was twenty-eight hundred acres. If only Myia was able to reestablish a connection with Tess. But she couldn't. He'd asked, and she had tried. Apparently her long-range telepathic connection had nothing to do with his sexual mastery. Too bad they couldn't figure out what had caused it.

His heart pounded so hard, his head throbbed. Or maybe it ached from tension. His family could be anywhere. What if Ferly Mor brought them to work today or took them on vacation?

They couldn't have been taken outside the building without their thermal suits. They were somewhere in the Yard.

He ran back through Duncan's house and into the woods. He kept running, though he wasn't sure where to go.

"My lord," Dunna's panting voice came through the tech-ring's earpiece. He sounded like he'd been the one running. "I've good news and bad news."

Kedric's stomach dropped. He knew exactly what news Dunna was about to report. The man sounded just as winded as he did after fighting the Hyborean in the hovercraft. "Labrat woke up, and you tranquilized him."

"Correct, my lord."

Shit.

Alpha team's pissed-off swears and curses blasting through the tech-ring nearly split his eardrum. "Silence on the line."

The men quieted down.

He needed to be careful how he worded his next sentence. Aboard the subaquatic, the crew and Myia listened in. He didn't want to frighten her, but there was no delicate way to ask the question. "Are we're trapped inside the building?"

"No, my lord. That's the good news. Amazing news, in fac—"

"Spit it out, Dunna."

"You see, I've been recording all the Hyborean's thoughts in my tech-ring. I played back the one he used to sublimate the door, and it worked! It changed from a solid to a gas."

Adrenaline surged through him. Chills tingled down his arms. This was a huge breakthrough. "Can you do the same with the hovercraft? Can you drive it?"

"No, my lord. I'm afraid that's too complicated. All I can do is open a door."

"Transmit that file to the team's tech-rings. No one will be trapped inside this building."

"Transmitting now, my lord."

Without the hovercraft no one would make the two miles back to the subaquatic before the countdown ended. "General can you give us more time?"

"No more than twenty minutes, my lord. We must get back to Pele immediately. Cavy is waking up."

"Okay, boys, we've lost our ride back to the marina. You have twenty minutes to rendezvous at the subaquatic. Get the refugees out now." He may have given the order, but he wasn't about to follow it. He'd come too far to leave now without Tess.

Splashing water and feminine laughter drew his attention to a bathing pool beyond the brush. Maybe he'd get lucky and someone would know where to find her. Weed fronds rustled against his thermal suit as he barreled his way to the bathing pool where three wet, naked, and giggling young women bathed a strapping gladiator. By the unnatural size of the man's muscles, he had to be on some kind of steroids.

"I'm looking for a woman."

"These are taken." The gladiator snickered as he pulled a woman onto his lap.

Their orgy didn't affect Kedric. He'd witnessed plenty in his captured days. "Her name is Tess. She has the same color hair and eyes as me. Our father is Duncan."

The gladiator was sure to know his father. He made the best whiskey in HuBReC. There wasn't a gladiator who didn't pride himself on getting drunk from it. A half-empty bottle with his father's mark balanced on the grassy ledge.

"Get lost." From beneath the water, the gladiator pulled out his claymore and pointed the tip at him.

A woman gasped.

"If you think that sword's big," her friend said to her, "wait until he pokes you with his other one."

"Run him through," the woman on his lap goaded.

These people weren't worth the time it would take to tell them about the rescue. "Carry on," Kedric said, before racing through the forest again, ducking low-hanging tree branches and jumping over rocks. Thanks to them, he knew just where to search.

He leaped a stream and came upon an old still chugging away near the mouth of a small grotto. A white horse hitched to a wooden cart was tethered to a nearby tree. His heart soared. Da and Tess always borrowed Walter's horse to transport their alcohol.

"Da," he shouted. "Tess. Where are ye?" Funny how his old accent returned the closer he got to his father.

A sickly, pale woman with red hair and a whiskey bottle in each hand darted out of the grotto. "Kedric? Is that you?" She dropped her bottles in the grass and ran toward him.

"Tess!" He raced to her, snatched her into his arms, and kissed her cheek. He couldn't let her go. Not even to look into her gray eyes. He just wanted to hold her trembling body.

Or was he the one trembling?

He hadn't realized precisely how much he'd missed her until he held her. He heard her sharp intake of air from the pain his hug evidently caused.

"Are you all right, Kedric? Have you been captured again? Is Xanthrag your master?"

Black-and-blue marks wrapped her wrists like bracelets. More bruises were sure to cover her body beneath her T-shirt. Yet she held no concern for her own discomfort. She worried over him.

If only he had the time to hunt down Regan and slaughter him for assaulting his sister. At least he had the power to heal her with his blood when they got back to the ship.

"Kedric, me boy. Ye've come back." Duncan stood at the cave's mouth, whiskey in hand. With deliberate care, he placed the bottles down before ambling over. If only Duncan's slow gait could be blamed on an injury rather than a lack of enthusiasm. But it couldn't be. They had the same healing DNA.

So why hadn't Duncan used it to heal Tess?

Had she refused his offer? She could be stubborn like that. He'd ask them about it later. After giving his father a quick one-armed hug and whack on the back, he said, "I've come to free ye both. I've a subaquatic at the marina waiting to take us to Pele."

"That's wonderful," Tess said.

Duncan sputtered and harrumphed. "Are ye daft, lad? I canna leave my home." He wouldn't meet Kedric's eyes.

His chest tightened. He knew the ten-foot furry reason why Duncan wouldn't leave. "Ye mean ye won't leave Ferly Mor."

"He's my master. I love him."

The scab covering his wounded heart ripped clean off. Old hurt poured out tender and raw. "I'm yer son." *Ye should love me.*

"Ye're a gladiator. And a damn fine one, too. That's what ye were born for, lad. Ye should stay here and fight in the survival—"

"I'm no' a gladiator. I'm the lord of Pele. A free man. I came back to free ye, too." Damn how his accent thickened the angrier he got. The way he rolled his r's he almost sounded like his father. He had to regain control of himself.

"When do we leave?" Tess's excitement tempered his imminent rant.

"Right now."

Her eyes bulged. Shaking her head no, she backed away as if he were animal control.

"What is it, Tess? What's the matter?"

"I-I can't leave."

"Don't be afraid. I promise I'll keep ye safe. Trust me. Everything has been carefully planned. In twelve minutes we'll be in a sub-aquatic heading to Pele." They would never make it back in time on foot. They'd have to take Walter's horse.

He unbuckled the leather strap to unhitch the cart. While it was a sturdy Hyborean animal, the horse couldn't carry the three of them, which was fine. Da would never leave Ferly Mor anyway. Though Kedric had held out hope otherwise, he'd known his father wouldn't escape. According to Max and Addy, Da had caught up to them at Sanctuary River a few weeks ago. He could have crossed the river into Pele's refuge but instead of freedom he chose to return to HuBReC with his master.

He backed the cart out of the horse's kicking distance, set down the handles, and then returned to his family. Duncan's arm was around Tess as she rested her head on his shoulder. Tears glistened in her eyes and streamed down her face.

Kedric reached for her. "We have to go now."

"You don't understand."

"No, you don't understand. If we're not at the rendezvous point in eleven minutes, we're stuck here. Come on." Ignoring Duncan's objections, Kedric grabbed her hand. Pulling her was like pulling dead weight.

She yanked out of his grip and dug in her heels, which couldn't have been easy in moccasins. "I'm not going."

"The hell you're not." It didn't take any effort to pick her up, throw her lithe body over his shoulder, and carry her to the horse. Duncan chased behind protesting.

"Put me down, Kedric." Her fists pounded his back and her legs kicked with more strength than a malnourished, frail woman should've had. "I can't leave without my son!"

The horse shied.

Kedric dropped her onto her feet. "Where is he, inside?" He started running back to the grotto.

"In the infirmary." Her cry pierced his heart like Hyborean steel. A chill colder than the arctic winds swept through his marrow.

There wasn't enough time to rescue the boy from the infirmary and return to the rendezvous point.

Hell, there was barely enough time now for the two of them to make it back.

All her life she'd wished for a baby. Now that she was a momma, there'd be no way to convince her to abandon her child, even if Regan was its father. Yet he had to try. "Leave him behind." It was no more than a whisper. "Please."

"You know I can't. I'm sorry. I won't leave Gem."

"He'll be taken from you when he's weaned anyway. You can't save him from a gladiator's fate. Trust me on that. You must save yourself. You can have another baby in the refuge. Spirits know, there are plenty of men to choose from there."

The tears streamed down her face. "I can't have another baby. You know pregnancy kills me."

Her frail body wasn't meant for breeding. She'd miscarried and died every time. No wonder she'd named the boy after a precious stone. Gem was her treasured jewel. "If it worked this time, surely it could work again. We've wonderful doc—"

"It didn't work, Kedric. I died. Ferly Mor reawakened me and saved the baby. He put Gem in an incubator. He's so tiny and helpless. I can't leave him." She fished something out of her shorts pocket and then held up her closed fist. Her fingers uncurled. Floating above the hologram chip in her palm was the image of a tiny naked baby boy connected to wires and tubes.

Kedric's throat constricted. His words could barely squeeze past the lump inside it. "He's beautiful."

"Aye," said Duncan, beaming.

He'd never seen his father so proud. More old heartache resurfaced. Maybe if Duncan had been that happy and proud of him, his father wouldn't have given him away to Xanthrag so freely. "He looks like his cousin."

Duncan's eyes shone with question.

"Aye. Addy, Max, and Noah are safe in my kingdom."

Tess smiled a sad smile. "I'm so happy for her. I miss her. Tell her that when you go back, will you?"

"You can tell her yourself. I'm not leaving without you."

"And I'm not leaving without Gem." Her hand curled into a fist around the holograph chip. "I'll fight you if I have to, Kedric. You're not taking me from my baby."

He almost laughed. She couldn't fight him, though he did admire her courage and conviction. Arguing was pointless. If he carried her off against her will, she'd be safe, but she would never forgive him. Being responsible for taking away her one happiness would destroy him. So would leaving her in this place to be used and abused by Regan and other gladiators. That knowledge was a pain worse than any physical torture he'd endured. Including being skinned alive.

Maybe if he stayed, he could protect her.

Yeah, right. When Xanthrag found out he was here, he'd be tortured and killed for escaping. Then he'd be sold to the subclass for blood sport. Staying would only lead to his ultimortem. He couldn't protect anyone when dead.

Not to mention the woman he loved awaited his return on the subaquatic. If he didn't get to the ship in eight minutes, he'd never see Myia again.

Could this horse even run three miles that fast?

His heart slammed into his rib cage. He would not lose the one person who loved him and believed in him.

General Sebastian's voice came through his tech-ring. "My lord, Dunna and four soldiers have returned with their refugees. The other two soldiers are heading back on foot now. You must hurry. One of them spotted animal control's vehicle."

"How many people are in the streets now?"

"Seventeen, including the soldiers."

Fantastic. Nothing like seventeen humans running loose through the city to attract animal control's attention. At least his soldiers knew enough to split up. Hopefully the darkness would give them enough cover.

Curse Labrat for gaining consciousness.

"Go," Tess said. "You must leave without me. Lead the other refugees back to Pele."

Kedric nodded in acquiescence, untethered the horse from its branch, and then mounted. "Can I at least get one last hug from my sister before I go?"

Tess stood on tiptoe and stretched her arms up to him. Leaning down, he reached around her tiny waist, grabbed, and then yanked her up onto the muscular horse. A swift kick, and it took off running faster than anticipated. Apparently, the animal didn't require much force to get it going.

"Kedric, stop!" Bouncing up and down on her stomach couldn't be comfortable in the least, but at the moment he didn't care. If this was the only way to save her, then so be it.

Duncan's shouts faded into the distance.

"Stop, Kedric, or I swear I'll knock us both off. You'll never make it back in time without the horse."

She didn't have the strength or the leverage to make good on her threat. He pushed the beast faster.

Chapter Thirty-Three

Dunna entered the bridge of the subaquatic. "The sixth group has returned to the ship, General. All refugees are loaded into the cargo hold. We are only awaiting Lord Kedric."

General Sebastian's gaze darted to the clock—T minus six minutes—and then to Myia.

Used to faking poise in stressful situations, she kept her expression calm, posture relaxed, and remained silent. Inside, she was dying. Her stomach churned. Heart pounded. She wanted to scream into the communication device for Kedric to hurry. Not that it would do any good.

He couldn't go any faster than the animal carrying him and his sister.

"Thank you, Dunna." The general's gaze shifted to Finn. Conflict flickered within Sebastian's aura. His lips pursed, and he glanced at the clock once more.

He was contemplating leaving Kedric before the clock timed out. She wouldn't let that happen.

Kedric would be here. Would Tess be with him?

She'd listened in on the entire exchange between Kedric and his sister. The communication device had captured every heartbreaking word. Their relationship would require a great deal of healing. Tess was sure to resent Kedric. Kedric would surely blame himself for Tess's resentment and inevitable bitterness. He'd constantly wonder if he had or hadn't done the right thing.

"Myia," Dunna said, "some of the refugees are panicking. The warriors are trying to calm them, but they lack…well…tact. Would you mind healing their fears?"

"Kedric's instructions were to stay on the bridge." *To make sure no one left him behind.* That was an order she didn't want to disobey. Not with General Sebastian's nervous glances at the clock. Besides, how well could she help anyone when her nerves were on edge, too?

"I doubt Lord Kedric would mind if you healed the refugees' fears. The more upset they become, the louder the soldiers are. I don't want anything bad to happen in there." The sincerity of Dunna's plea matched his aura.

How could she say no to healing someone's fears? That's what she'd been born to do. It's what she trained for all her life.

"Of course," she said. "But you must promise to stay here and make certain we don't leave before the timer reaches zero."

* * *

"Going silent," Kedric said before switching off the tech-ring's com-link. The transmission had to be shut down for the Hyborean's telepathic recording to work. He'd be radio silent until he opened both doors. Once outside, he'd reestablish communication with the subaquatic.

As the Yard's maintenance door sped closer, Kedric pulled out the earpiece and retrieved the file Dunna had sent. With the push of a few buttons, the door sublimated. He slowed the horse to a trot and then a walk before crossing the threshold from the Yard into the chilled corridor where Labrat lay on the floor, tranquilized.

Tess slid off the horse and ran back to the door. The crackle behind him signaled it was solidifying.

"No," she cried. She pounded on the solid door. "Let me back in, Kedric. Please. I beg you."

Her despair would not get to him. He was saving her life. He dismounted, shrugged out of his backpack, and retrieved a thermal suit. "Put this on."

Her body slumped against the transparent door in defeat. Slowly she turned to him, body still pressed against the wall as if she needed the support to keep from collapsing. The anguish on her face tore his heart apart.

"Have you ever loved someone with all your heart and soul?" she said. "Have you ever loved them so much you'd do anything to be with them?"

What the hell kind of question was that? His blood boiled. Of course he did. He was here wasn't he? "Aye. I have. I love my sister so much that I've risked everything to save her. Everything. My life, the lives of my men, my kingdom, the woman I love." He tried keeping his anger in check so as not to draw attention from the Hyboreans, but emotions he'd thought long buried erupted from deep inside. "Except instead of escaping with her brother, she'd rather be abused and raped by gladiators, bond with a son who she'll be stripped of in four years, and be forced to watch him die repeatedly in the survival races."

She sobbed. "I love Gem. I can't leave him."

"Don't you see, Tess? Loving a son is torture!"

And there it was. In the silence of a dark Hyborean corridor, he'd shouted the answer to the deep-seated pain plaguing him his entire life. The reason for his father's abandonment.

Loving a son was torture.

A person couldn't feel sorrow or loss if they never gave away their love in the first place.

Wasn't that what he was trying to do for Tess? If he separated her from Gem now, he'd save her the heartache of watching her son become an animal, fighting to the death in the survival races.

This was the same thing his father had done. Remaining detached was Da's only means of coping with his son's gladiator existence.

"He loves you, you know," she whispered. "Da does."

Had she read his mind, or had his face depicted his grief? He wiped a hand over his blurry eyes. He sniffled and choked down a sob. This was not the time to go all emotional. He'd do that later with Myia's help in the privacy of their bedroom. Spirits knew, he'd need her healing power.

Wallowing in anguish would have to wait. Right now he had to get them both back to the subaquatic.

His watch read T minus four minutes.

They'd never make it.

If Tess wasn't going to dress herself in the thermal suit, he'd have to do it for her. He stuffed her arms in the sleeves and her legs in the pants. She offered little resistance. She knew she'd been defeated.

Tears flowed down her cheeks. He tamped down the guilt. After all, he was saving her life.

After they mounted, her arms tightened around his waist, and he felt her head against his back. He maneuvered the animal around Labrat's body.

It pained him to leave the Hyborean behind. Under the influence of mind control, he had been a huge asset to his cause. But conscious, Labrat was dangerous.

The corridors and maintenance room were unoccupied as the Hyboreans were sure to be in their homes eating their evening meals. Outside, the streets would be quiet, too. Hyboreans were nothing if not creatures of scheduled habits.

The door to the alley sublimated, and Kedric pushed the horse out into the icy night. Hyborean horses were hearty, no question. He'd ridden a few in the survival races. Hopefully this guy was no exception and would fare well running in the twenty-degree-below-zero summer temperatures.

T minus one minute to departure.

He turned his comlink back on. "Hold the door, General, I'm on my way."

"My lord," Sebastian yelled through the earpiece. Men hollered and chains rattled in the background. What the hell was the commotion about? "Cavy's fighting us. He's resisting the crew. Finn is injured."

His mouth went dry. The Hyborean woke up quicker than anticipated. "Did you shock him?"

"It only made him angrier. We must tranquilize him before he kills us all."

"Do not tranquilize him! We'll never get home. Give the mind control device to Myia. Let her talk to the creature."

"My lord, she'll be killed."

* * *

Myia was in the cargo hold, helping to relieve the fears of the people when the Spirits around her grew restless. Something felt very wrong. Had Sebastian decided to leave without Kedric?

"Myia." Dunna raced over to her. "You're needed on the bridge immediately." His hand gripped her upper arm and pulled her away from the woman before Myia could protest. "Cavy is awake and lashing out." He handed her a tech-ring as they ran down the corridor. "Talk to Lord Kedric. He wants you to calm the beast."

She placed the tech-ring on her head and inserted the earpiece, which wasn't easy while running. "Kedric? Where are you?"

"On my way. You must calm the Hyborean. Make him drive us home."

"I don't know if I can, Kedric. I'm not exactly tranquil at the moment."

"Forget tranquillity, Myia. That's only one part of your spirit. What about your fire and passion? Use that. Channel that to talk to the Hyborean."

Her father had always used tranquillity. Then again, calm was his true nature. Her true nature was volatile. Her emotional state constantly changed. Why fight it when she could use it?

"Engage all of your spirit, Myia. Like you did to save me."

Could it be so simple?

Approaching the bridge, the sense of danger and foreboding loomed. The feeling was unlike anything she'd received from the Spirits. On the other side of the door, she'd find a snared beast trying to escape. The sensation vibrated around and within her. She could hear it roar, though no actual sound came to her ears except for the men hollering.

It was merely her perception of the Hyborean's rage.

She rushed through the sublimated vapor.

Cavy, fully awake, yanked on his chains to break them.

The warriors hit him with clubs, Tasered him to submit, but the creature refused to give into the pain. He was aware he was in his frozen land, and escape was his only thought. If he could only break his chains, he'd be free.

He swiped a warrior, knocked him across the room. The man didn't move, though his rib cage expanded and contracted. He was knocked unconscious but not dead.

Cavy cried out in pain as he was hit and shocked again.

"Stop it," she screamed. "Stop it now. Let me talk to him. I can help."

"This is no place for a woman," Bigby said. "The creature is out of control. You need to leave before he lashes out at you."

"No. I can make him stop fighting. I can heal him."

"How? He's conscious now."

"I can communicate with his soul even while he's conscious."

"Hyborean bastards don't have souls."

"Stop hurting him, and let me be the judge of that."

Bigby stood defiantly.

"Stop," General Sebastian said. "She is to communicate with him. Lord Kedric's orders."

"Then her blood will be on Lord Kedric's hands."

"Back away from the beast, men." The warriors did as their general commanded. Without interference from the men, Cavy yanked at his chains.

Myia inhaled a deep breath, but rather than reducing her heartbeat and finding her inner tranquillity to communicate through the tech-ring, she stoked the fire in her soul and ignited into his mind.

Get away from me, you little, puny humans. I will destroy you all.

She voiced her thoughts for the men's sakes. "Fear not." If they knew what was going on, they'd be less inclined to do anything foolish. "I am a shaman. A spiritual healer. I won't harm you. I want to talk."

Won't harm me? Ha. That's all humans know how to do.

"The men were wrong for hurting you. They were scared. Just as you are. They won't hurt you now. See, they're putting down their weapons."

General Sebastian nodded, and the men slowly, carefully placed their weapons on the floor.

Release me.

"I can't do that until we come to an understanding. Place your trust in me." She moved closer and stretched out her hand toward him. "Touch my hand. Let me heal your pain."

She sensed Cavy's desire to use her as a pawn. He wanted to pull off her arms to make the others fear him.

Her stomach convulsed. She resisted the urge to vomit. Though sickened and frightened by his thought, she was determined to get through to this creature. An entire nation counted on her ability to heal him. She would not let down her people. She would not let down the man she loved. The man who believed in her. The man from whom she drew strength.

If Cavy wanted to rip off her arms, he'd have to touch her first. As soon as he did, she'd jump into his spirit. He wouldn't hurt her, then. She hoped.

It was a risk worth taking.

Heart pounding, she shuffled closer, keeping one arm at her side and one reaching out to him, palm up in a gesture of peace. One more step, and she'd be within his arms' reach. She moved forward.

He snatched her up and her spirit dove full force into his.

Around her blurred a vortex of bitter emotion—chilling anger, humiliation, and hate. Gale-force winds meant to drive her intruding spirit from his soul knocked her down. She refused to leave. She could be stubborn that way.

Gathering her passion and love for Kedric, her spirit image erupted into a radiant blaze. Her literally fiery spirit stepped into the eye of Cavy's raging storm.

Her heat would melt his icy winds.

"I'm here to help you. Thank you for your trust." Not that he trusted her yet. But the fact that he hadn't ripped off her arms was a good sign.

Chapter Thirty-Four

Kedric had kept to the shadows as best he could while pushing the horse to its limit. No one had followed him on the quiet city streets. If they noticed him, they didn't give chase. Hopefully, they didn't call animal control, either.

The marina's entrance came into view. He'd have to let the horse go. If they hadn't already, the Hyboreans would start searching for the eighty-seven humans missing from HuBReC. They'd start in the Yard, of course, and then branch out from there. A horse at the marina would lead them right to Cavy's subaquatic.

That couldn't happen. Myia needed time to convince Cavy to help.

If he let the horse run free the way they came, someone would find it and return it to its rightful owner.

He dismounted first and then reached for Tess. Her spine was straight and rigid, and she glanced back at the direction they'd come.

By the look in her eyes, she was weighing her options. Escape with him and live free, or return to Gem and a life of abuse. All she had to do was give the horse a squeeze and she'd be gone. She glanced down at him and then back at the city.

Did her heart ache as much as his right now?

No, her pain was sure to be greater.

How the hell could he take her away from her son? If the thermal suit wasn't covering his head, he'd rake his hands through his hair.

What was it that Addy had said to him? If you love someone, set them free.

Everything he'd done for the last five years had led up to rescuing his sister, and now that he had her, here he was contemplating letting her go.

He exhaled a long, white cloud. "I love you, Tess. I was wrong to take you against your will. The choice is yours. Come with me or take the horse back to HuBReC. I won't force you to take one more step."

"Oh, Kedric." Tears dropped from her eyes and froze on her cheeks. "I love you, too. I want to escape to the equator. I do. But not without Gem. My baby needs me."

His heart shattered. If only she chose freedom. He nodded in understanding, even though he wasn't sure that he did understand. Maybe he would if he were a parent. If he were anything like his father, maybe he wouldn't.

"I'll come back for you both. I promise. I don't know how soon, but I will come back for you."

She bent down and kissed his cheek.

He hugged her. "Good-bye, Tess."

Alone, Kedric crossed beneath the lights of the marina's entrance. If Myia couldn't get Cavy under control, he might be back in HuBReC sooner than he wanted.

He turned around for one last wave good-bye.

Hovercraft headlights grew bigger as it raced down the streets toward him. An icy chill slid down his spine. He sprinted to the parking lot, weaved in and out of parked vehicles, and then ducked down between two.

When the craft hovered beneath the marina lights, his stomach roiled. A sour taste formed in his mouth.

Labrat was in the driver's seat.

* * *

Exhausted and groggy from the coma, Cavy didn't take long to calm down. Once he did, his story poured out. The lack of resistance wasn't surprising given the fact that his cognitive brain function probably hadn't repaired itself fully. Not that Myia cared why he freely shared his feelings with her. It only mattered that he did.

He and Labrat had been poaching humans and selling them for profit on the black market. Their most lucrative business came from selling men, women, and children for deadly games like saber-toothed smilodon fighting. This illegal sport was a favorite pastime of the Hyborean subclass. In a given death match, they'd gamble on which creature—human or tiger—would kill the other first.

When she asked why he did this, the answer surprised her. His life mate had contracted an illness that the Hyboreans' advanced medicine could cure only if he had the means to pay for it. He was a subclass and couldn't afford it so turned to the illegal but lucrative endeavor of poaching humans. He was a few credits shy of payment when Kedric's people had captured him. In the months he and Labrat had been held captive, his life mate was certain to have died her ultimortem.

I could have saved my life mate if it weren't for you cursed humans.

Anger and resentment tore through his soul like bitter arctic wind.

Thawing his heart would not be easy.

Nor quick.

* * *

"Kedric to base. I'm inside the marina. Labrat is here. What's your departure status?"

"Myia is working her magic. Cavy has calmed. No word yet if he'll drive this thing."

The hovercraft turned in his direction slowly gliding over the frozen ground. No doubt searching for Kedric. "The second you can, get the hell out of here. I'll buy you as much time as possible."

"Yes, my lord."

No matter what happened to him, he had to prevent Labrat from reaching the subaquatic. Gripping the Flesheater knife in one hand and his backpack in the other, he ran from his hiding place behind the passing vehicle. With everything he had, he hurled the backpack over the craft.

It hit the windshield.

The craft jerked to a stop, and Labrat scrambled out.

If Kedric wanted to save his people, he had to kill this Hyborean. So what that the creature was four feet taller, possessed immense strength, and was angrier than a starving smilodon? Kedric had the Flesheater, the gladiator skills to use it, and a shipload of humans to save.

No beast would ever take Myia captive. Not while Kedric had breath left to fight.

His adrenaline spiked, his muscles bunched in anticipation of battle.

The Hyborean strolled toward him, caution evident in his beady eyes.

Thunder rumbled deep and low, signaling a coming storm. Not a real, physical storm. It was the Hyborean's anger simmering beneath the surface. A warning that, at any moment, lightning would strike.

"Come on, you mindless lab rat. Let's see what you're made of."

The Hyborean charged, swinging his large three-fingered hand.

Kedric lunged left, slashed his blade against Labrat's leg, making contact just below the knee.

Thunder boomed.

His heart pounded with a new fear. Did anyone hear Labrat's cry of pain?

Dammit. He had to kill the beast quickly and quietly. He couldn't risk attracting another Hyborean.

Labrat swung at him again. Kedric dodged it. For a quick and quiet death, he had to somehow slit the thing's throat.

His gut clenched. Myia would be upset if he killed the Hyborean.

Sudden pain registered in the entire left side of his body. He sailed through the air and then landed hard on his right side. He gasped for breath.

Okay, Myia would be more upset if the Hyborean killed him.

He had to concentrate.

He had to get his knife back.

Hell, he had to breathe!

His lungs wouldn't fill. He sucked in shallow breaths and then rolled away from Labrat's foot stomping at his head. His Flesheater glinted off the snow behind the Hyborean. He couldn't get to it.

Another stomp. Another roll farther away from the knife.

The ground vibrated under his back as thunder rolled louder and louder.

Wait. Not thunder. Hooves.

The underside of a horse soared overhead as Tess jumped it over him. Labrat stumbled backward to avoid getting trampled.

Kedric scrambled to his feet and ran for the knife.

Tess turned the horse around and galloped back toward the Hyborean. This time, Labrat postured in anticipation for the collision. Seconds before impact, he sidestepped the horse and shoved her off it.

"No!" Watching her fall was like seeing it in quarter speed. Time stood still. Her body seemed to hang in the air longer than humanly possible before hitting and tumbling across the hard, packed icy ground.

She didn't move again.

Fire erupted inside his soul, fueling his strength. His fist tightened around the Flesheater. His vision blocked out everything but the Hyborean he was about to murder.

* * *

Cavy grew weary, which was just as well. The more tired a being got, the more vulnerable its spirit. It would be so much easier if he'd revert back into a state of unconsciousness so that Finn could make him drive them all home, but that wasn't going to happen. He was awake now. And would remain so.

She had to convince him to help them. How much longer could they stay docked before someone came looking for the people they had taken? How much longer before Kedric returned?

Cavy lowered himself onto the floor, leaned his back against the wall, and splayed his legs out in front of him. He sat her on his leg, and she stroked the furry arm holding her. He enjoyed the contact. It had been too long since anyone touched him with kindness.

His heart was open.

Reaching deep into his spirit, she found memories of the people he'd poached, caged, and delivered to the underground market. Then she showed him his captivity and humiliation.

"What is the difference between what you have done to the humans and what they have done to you?"

His spirit gave no answer. He knew it was wrong.

"The Spirits have given you a gift. They allowed you to be captive so you can experience firsthand what my people have felt for centuries. No creature should live in captivity when he desires freedom."

A heaviness fell upon his soul. It was the weight of remorse. The emotion she'd been waiting for.

Now he could be receptive to change. He could be receptive to the idea of repentance by way of helping.

What you show me is the truth, his spirit said. *What I have done has been done to me. I never saw humans as a race before. You were animals. Animals that loved to fight even when not provoked. But you're so much more than that. You've language and emotion and intelligence I never knew existed in another species. I must admit your ability to control our brain waves was most impressive.*

The first healing stage was accepting the two species shared commonalities. And now he was processing that he'd been wrong to capture and poach. But the humans had captured him, too.

Let me go free, and I shall not tell anyone what happened.

"You will go free. I promise. But first we need your help driving this ship back to our island."

I can't go back there.

"I know you're afraid. You have my word no harm will come to you."

His spirit went silent. She sensed him weighing the pros and cons of going back. Though she felt his trust in her, he wasn't certain if he could trust the men around her. Going back to Pele meant going back to captivity and a mindless existence. Would they turn him loose or lock him up again?

"Everyone on board wants their freedom. You and us. But we can't be free without your help. Please. We need you to pilot this ship. Put your trust in us, as we've put our trust in you not to call the authorities and not to sell us on the black market."

He cringed at what he'd done to the humans in the past, trapping and selling them into blood sport. Humans may be a simple and primitive species, but they were not, as every Hyborean believed, soulless.

"Please bring us to Pele. Then you are free to return."

Unchain me and I will bring you as close as I can to your island. I refuse to get within range of those electromagnetic fields.

Spirit was honest always. Though Cavy was awake and, therefore, wasn't merely talking with his soul, could he be saying all this to be set free?

No. Everything that made up her being believed he told the truth. He wanted to make up for his sins. He wanted to bring the humans home and then return home himself.

"Shall we make an accord?"

Their spirit images made the gestures of a Hyborean accord, binding each other to the deal.

"Thank you for your trust." She disengaged her spirit before hopping off of his leg to the stares of fifteen mute, wide-eyed warriors. "Unchain him, and he will take us home."

"All hands prepare for departure," General Sebastian shouted.

Why wasn't Kedric giving that order? "Where's Lord Kedric?" She emphasized the word *lord*.

The general ignored her. "Finn, get that Hyborean to power up this hunk of junk and get us out of here."

"Where is Kedric?"

"Fighting Labrat. Giving us time to escape. We must go now. Finn, command that Hyborean to set sail."

"Yes, sir."

Heart thundering, Myia ran to the dockside transparent wall, pressed her face against it to look down the jetty.

Kedric balanced at the edge of the dock. One step back and he'd fall into ice water. The knife in his hand dripped with blood. Only a few feet away from him, Tess lay unmoving, a dim glow of her aura the only indication she was still alive.

Labrat staggered closer to Kedric. His aura held one thought. Vengeance.

"No!" Myia raced for the hatch. "Open the door." She felt no pain as she pounded the solid wall. "Open it. Let me out! We can't leave him."

"It's too late for him," Sebastian said.

"How can you be so obtuse? That's your king!"

"I'm sorry, Myia. His orders were to get all these people to safety. Don't compromise his rescue mission by allowing their recapture."

"The line's been cut," a voice came across the intercom. "We're clear to depart."

"Engage engines."

She turned back to see Kedric on the ground unmoving. "Kedric!" Her scream went unanswered.

Her heart shattered. A weight crushed her spirit. Helpless, she could only watch as Labrat picked up Kedric's limp body and carried him toward the subaquatic.

The solid door vanished beneath her fingers. She fell through the sublimation cloud onto the deck. A gray blur ran past her.

It was Cavy.

"Capture him!" General Sebastian shouted.

Five men raced to the door.

Myia stepped in front of the door, blocking their exit. "Wait. He's not escaping. He's helping us."

The group watched as Cavy and Labrat approached each other on the dock.

"You men. Collect the unconscious woman and bring her to the sick bay. Use the cargo door. And do it quietly."

"Yes, General."

"What are they saying?" Sebastian asked.

"I don't know." Myia was too busy calling upon the Spirits to heal Kedric. He had powerful blood that healed faster than normal. She just hoped he didn't sustain too much damage for it to work.

"I'm still connected to Cavy by the tech-ring, sir," Finn said.

"He's telling Labrat that it's over. He doesn't care how many credits the humans will bring. He's taking them—well, us—back to the wildlife refuge. They've suffered enough. And so have we." Finn paused for a moment. "There's silence now. He must be listening to Labrat. I can't hear what he's saying."

Labrat dropped Kedric's body in obvious disgust. Whatever he was saying, he wasn't happy. Hitting the ground must have woken Kedric. His aura brightened. Myia's pulse quickened.

"Cavy says he's already lost his life mate. He doesn't want to risk banishment or worse if the Human Gaming Commission finds out about them. He says he can't blame us for what we've done when they've done so much worse."

Kedric's eyes blinked open. Thank the Spirits he was going to be okay. She couldn't concentrate on Finn's interpretation when her focus was on Kedric.

With minimal movement, he glanced around. No doubt assessing the situation.

Sebastian spoke into the communication device. "Lord Kedric, can you hear me?"

Myia's heart thundered as she waited for a reply.

"Can you hear me, Lord Kedric?"

She couldn't hold her breath any longer without passing out. Why wouldn't he answer? Was he in too much pain?

"Aye." The word was a whisper.

Myia exhaled.

"Everyone is on board except you and Cavy. He's made an accord to be our pilot. Labrat is enticing him with profit from selling us. If we engage Labrat, I fear retaliation from Cavy."

"Aye," he said again, this time with more strength. "Stand down, but be alert. Let's see how this plays out."

Kedric stayed on his back, either to rest or so that Labrat wouldn't take notice of him, she wasn't sure. Maybe both. Neither

Hyborean would notice him if he stripped naked and dove into the ocean, they were that intently focused on each other. Staring each other down.

Finally Cavy turned his back on Labrat and strode toward the subaquatic. The bridge erupted in cheers from the warriors and crew.

Myia knew better than to cheer. The Spirits around her grew restless. Labrat's anger was palpable.

Kedric must have sensed it, too, because he hadn't moved from his spot on the ground, probably wanting Labrat to believe he'd been beaten into submission.

Labrat glanced around the dock searching for someone, but no one was around that she could see. Just then, he lunged at Cavy, whose spine arched back and twisted. His painful howl penetrated the depths of her soul.

He staggered, trying to reach Kedric's knife sticking out of his furry back. Crimson drops of blood fell on the snow. Labrat punched him in the temple. The tech-ring flew off as Cavy fell on his side directly in front of Kedric.

Kedric leaped to his feet, pulled the knife from Cavy's back.

Ten gladiators rushed past her and tackled Labrat before he could reach their lord. They used their bodies to pin his arms and legs to the ground. Kedric sauntered over to Labrat. His head came off the ground as he struggled to get free, but the men held him down.

With eyes colder and bitterer than the arctic temperature, Kedric squatted down and slit the Hyborean's throat.

Bile rose. She covered her mouth to prevent vomiting. She inhaled a deep breath and then swallowed repeatedly until she was sure nothing would come up. Tears welled in her eyes from the unfortunate slaying Kedric felt he had to do.

"The six of you take Labrat's body into the subaquatic," Kedric shouted, seemingly unaffected by the murder he committed. "You four, kick the bloody snow into the ocean. Don't leave any evidence of foul play."

Myia retreated inside the subaquatic, her shaman's heart aching with the sorrow of violence and death. As Labrat's body was dragged past her, she prayed, "Mighty Spirits, retrieve the soul of your precious creature. His life was taken so that others may live."

A large gloved hand slipped inside hers, giving a quick squeeze before moving on. It was Kedric. If he and Finn hadn't been helping Cavy to the pilot seat, she would have thrown her arms around him and kissed him hard on the lips. Welcoming him back would have to wait.

Bleeding and breathing heavily, Cavy worked the holographic controls as Finn busily administered to his wounds. The ship slipped away from the jetty, leaving Handakar City in its wake.

Kedric approached with a grim slant on his lips. His usual silver-gray eyes had darkened to charcoal. They seemed serious, bleak.

Afraid of what she might see in his aura, she refused to read him.

"I don't regret my actions, Myia. I do regret that you witnessed the beast's death."

Why wasn't he touching her? She took a step closer, reached out to hold him, but he stepped back. Her stomach tensed. What was going on?

"I'm sorry I disappointed you."

"Oh, Kedric. I—"

"I know you can forgive me, seeing as how you're a shaman and all, but—" Why did he sound like he was about to break off their relationship? "Well…I may not desire war, but I'll always be a warrior."

She cupped his face in both hands and gazed into his eyes. "I know that."

"Then"—he gently removed her hands from his face—"you must know you deserve so much more than I'm able to give."

"But you've given me so much already. Without you, I never would have found my full potential. You taught me to channel all of my emotions when healing. You taught me that fire and passion are good."

His lips twitched, and a spark lit his eyes. "Aye, that they are."

"If you taught me to embrace all that I am, why wouldn't I embrace all that you are? I love you, Kedric. Unconditionally." She stepped into his outstretched arms. The strength of his embrace affirmed a mutual sentiment.

"I love you, too, Myia. Unconditionally."

In his arms, ear pressed against his chest, taking comfort in his steady heartbeat, there was nowhere on this planet she'd rather be.

Chapter Thirty-Five

Myia had already changed into her Highland garb and folded up her thermal suit when Kedric returned to their room. His face looked tired and peaked. Her heart went out to him. "Is Tess okay?"

"She will be. I washed her wounds—the new and the old—with my blood. They'll heal before we get to Pele. I don't know about her heart, though. She didn't want to leave HuBReC." He plopped onto the bed and unzipped his thermal suit.

Myia slinked behind him to help remove the jacket. "I know. I heard through the tech-ring." She rubbed his bare shoulders. Little tight knots held his tension. "I also heard you let her go. It was her choice to come back."

"She only did it to save me. My whole mission was to save her. But instead I've crushed her. I've taken her away from her one true happiness."

"It wasn't your fault. She knows that."

"I don't know that she does."

"Give her some time."

He pulled off his boots and then his pants. "Would you talk to her? Heal her spirit?"

"Should I do that before or after her working hours, my lord?" She giggled.

He gazed at her over his shoulder. "You mock me, savage. Shall I take you over my knee?"

Her core grew warm at the thought. Before she could reply, he pulled her onto his lap and kissed her lips. She reached behind his head and held him tightly. Wouldn't it be bliss to hold each other forever?

The pounding on the door was an unfortunate reality check. "Lord Kedric," Dunna shouted. "Cavy's condition is worsening."

Kedric pulled on his thermal suit in seconds. She did the same. A minute later they were on the bridge. Myia ran to Cavy, who was slumped over in his chair, and then dove into his spirit. A moment later she reported, "His spirit is very weak. He's dizzy and disoriented from the loss of blood. He can't concentrate on operating the subaquatic."

"I patched him up the best I could," Finn said. "But his breathing has gotten worse. I fear he has an injured lung from his puncture wound."

"If he dies we're all trapped aboard this ship. We can't pilot this thing."

"Aye. Stating the obvious is very helpful. Thank you, General."

Myia shot Kedric a disapproving look. Snapping at his men wasn't exactly helpful, either.

He ignored her reproach. "Can you talk to him, Myia? Can you help him pilot the ship?"

"No. He's incoherent."

"There's only one thing left to do. Clear the room," he ordered. "Finn, go get your medical equipment. You're doing another blood transfusion."

The young man's eyes widened. "Will it work, my lord? He's an entirely different species."

Aye. It would work. Kedric had been drained of blood for sick Hyboreans before. This time, though, he wouldn't fight. This time he wouldn't be strapped down. This time he'd give it freely. "We'll find out soon enough, won't we?"

"Yes, sir." Finn hurried away to do Kedric's bidding. General Sebastian ordered the men out of the room. The door solidified behind them.

The room was quiet.

Too quiet.

Suddenly cold, Myia crossed her arms and hugged herself. "Kedric, in addition to repairing yourself, you've given blood to Tess. Are you healthy enough to give more?"

He didn't respond. He just stared through the observation wall into the darkness of the ocean. There was nothing to see outside. He was avoiding talking to her.

An ache formed in the back of her throat. "How much blood will you lose to Cavy?"

His shoulder shrug was meant to convey his ignorance, but the mere refusal to respond verbally proved he knew. He just refused to tell her.

"He's a large creature. He'll require more blood than my father did. Won't he?" Tears formed behind her eyes, blurring Kedric's stoic stance. "You nearly died from the amount of blood required to save my father."

His head dropped, which only made her tears fall faster.

"This isn't a transfusion, is it?"

He shook his head no.

"This is a sacrifice." Her whispered voice cracked.

He reached for the wall and leaned both palms against it, bracing himself. If he needed support, she should be the one holding him up. Wiping her eyes, she ran to him, ducked under his arms, and then hugged him like she'd never let go.

He clutched her to him. "No sense keeping my healing powers a secret now."

If he were trying for a light tone, he failed. "You don't have to do this," she whispered into his shirt. Heat from his body seeped into her skin, yet couldn't warm the numbing cold inside her.

"If I don't, we'll remain in the middle of the ocean until taken by Hyboreans or death. Since Hyboreans rarely travel this far south unless they're poachers, death is imminent."

Finn returned with the transfusion equipment and went to work prepping Cavy. He diverted his eyes from the two of them, giving them their last bit of privacy.

"Do you think I'll become a spirit, Myia? That my energy will float over the Highlands in the aurora tropicos?"

The sob she held back formed a painful lump in her throat. She didn't trust herself to speak without breaking down and bawling into his shirt. Kedric was a courageous man. He deserved her to be brave for him.

His lips pressed against the top of her head. "I'd watch over you, of course." His whispered breath swept through her hair. "Maybe visit your bed and engage in some spirit sex."

The mischievous tone was probably meant to lighten the mood, to make her laugh. Though crying would make her feel better. She hiccuped.

"Or do you think I'll be snuffed out completely, like a lightstick beam when shut off?"

"My lord," said Finn. "It's time."

His embrace tightened and then loosened before his mouth was on hers. Kissing her. Not quickly like he'd done before the rescue. And not with a lover's passion. The kiss was urgent, desperate, filled with a need to hold on to love and goodness.

A last kiss good-bye.

"Let my life be taken so that others may live."

* * *

It was impressive how quickly Finn hooked up man and Hyborean to the transfusion machine. On the hard floor at Kedric's side, Myia sat between Kedric and Cavy holding each of their hands. Her spirit kept the Hyborean's company. He feared death. He knew he was slipping away.

Kedric feared death as well. Only it wasn't his own. He feared death for every one of his people on board if his blood didn't heal Cavy.

She'd been tasked with keeping the Hyborean awake. Keeping him engaged long enough for Kedric's blood to heal his wounds and fatigue. If he slipped into a coma…

She shuddered the thought away. She had to remain positive.

Spirits, fill these men with your grace. Grant them your love and healing power.

Crimson fluid filled the tube. When it invaded Cavy's body, he jerked. His distress was heart wrenching. It took trust to allow the humans to do this to him.

"Shh." Fantasy Myia wrapped her arms around fantasy Cavy. It was easy to do. Cavy's spirit manifested at half its height. A sign of his depleted strength. Sitting next to his now five-foot image, fantasy Myia rocked him. Soothing thoughts of calmness and love flowed into the darkness around them.

Her spirit image wavered and transformed into a female Hyborean. His deceased life mate.

It wasn't just a memory. She was channeling the female's spirit.

We are all one with the universe. One with the living and nonliving. Made up of the same energy. Accept the life-healing blood of this man.

Who knows how long she chanted that over and over before Cavy's fear dissipated. His spirit image began to grow. A sign of returning strength.

Her heart soared. Her soul rejoiced.

It was working.

In the physical realm, Cavy's hand twitched in hers. She opened her eyes. "Stop the transfusion. It's working."

"How could that be?" said Finn "I haven't given him nearly as much blood as I'd given your father."

"He doesn't need it. Check his vital signs."

Finn read his instrumentation. "He's recovering." In a scurry of movement, Finn stopped the transfusion and unhooked the tubes. "Lord Kedric is weak yet stable."

She sat back on her heels and closed her eyes. Thank the Spirits.

Cavy's chest rose and fell with great strength.

Kedric's didn't. His face appeared sallow. Sickly. But not like the night he'd saved her father. He was not marching upon death's door.

Her spiritual healing had worked in harmony with Kedric's physical healing to save Cavy. Together they were more powerful than either one alone.

Her body felt like it could float on air. Giddy excitement bubbled within her. She wanted to dance and twirl and sing with joy. Why not? It was right that a shaman should display her emotions.

But perhaps Sebastian and the three men who had returned to the bridge—in the event Cavy became uncooperative—wouldn't appreciate her pirouetting around their sick king's supine body.

"I've taken a lot of blood from Lord Kedric," Finn said to the men. "He'll need to rest. Carry him to his bedchamber so he can sleep where it's quiet."

Four men scooped up Kedric. Cavy rolled to his side. "The Hyborean is waking," one shouted.

"His vital signs are getting stronger." Finn cleaned up the medical instruments. "I believe he'll be able to drive the ship within the half hour."

"Take Lord Kedric to his room," General Sebastian reiterated, probably because he didn't like Finn giving orders. "And then man your stations. We're going home."

Myia took the tech-ring off her head and handed it to Finn. "Thank you."

"No, it's us who thank you, my lady." He bowed with reverence before standing once again to accept the tech-ring.

"Take good care of that Hyborean. He's not a hundred percent yet. Your empathy will help get us all home."

"Yes, my lady. And you take good care of our lord." His meaning was clear. She wasn't to care for him as his shaman. She was to care for him as his life mate.

And she would, too.

Starting with a little sexual healing.

Chapter Thirty-Six

Though Myia had healed Kedric hours ago, they didn't leave the bed for the remainder of the voyage home. They'd spent hours making love and plans for the future. After returning home and seeing to the new refugees, Kedric would host a grand celebration in the courtyard that would include a ritual mating ceremony.

Her heart leaped with joy. She had so much to prepare for tonight. She hoped Naomi would be available to help.

The ship surfaced near the shore of Discovery Island. Cavy was taking no chances on getting any closer. Myia didn't blame him. He trusted her and Kedric and Finn, but some of the other men kept staring at him like he was evil. He didn't want to give anyone an opportunity to force him back into mindless slavery.

They waited in the ocean for some time as one of Kedric's men swam ashore and called for the boat to come out and ferry the people to Pele.

It took nearly an hour before the only people left on the subaquatic with Cavy were Finn, General Sebastian, Tess, Kedric, and Myia.

They stood on the deck of the subaquatic watching the shores grow packed with loved ones running to meet the ferry. It seemed as if the entire nation came out to welcome everyone home. Father and Kimi were sure to be among them. Myia couldn't wait to see them again. It was as if they'd been gone for weeks rather than a day.

The sun warmed her face. Salty sea air whipped her hair off her shoulders. There was nothing like the taste of the ocean, the colors of the Protecting Spirits in the sky, and the love of her life in her arms.

If only those around them could be as happy.

Tess's broken heart consumed her aura. She hadn't spoken a word to Kedric since she'd been taken aboard the subaquatic after he had set her free in the streets of Handakar City. Despair colored Cavy's aura a mottled brown. Finn was communicating with him via tech-ring.

"What's he saying?" Kedric asked.

"Cavy's lost. He can't return to Handakar. He fears his people will learn of his involvement in the HuBReC thefts and Labrat's death. Great punishment falls upon any Hyborean who harms his own people."

"He can stay here," General Sebastian said. "Be our secret weapon for the next mission."

Kedric raked his red hair back out of his eyes. "He's done enough. I'm letting him go."

"What?"

"He was free in Handakar, General. He could have escaped at the marina. Instead, he helped us. His blood was spilled saving us."

"And you've repaid him by giving him your own blood."

"Aye. My *blood brother* is free to go. And so are our people. When we return, I'm opening the kingdom gates. Anyone who wants to leave may."

"The barbarian king is healed," Myia teased.

"Thanks to his savage little shaman." His arm around her shoulders drew her closer to his body. She couldn't wait to get back to his bed and show him just how savage she could be.

"What of the army, my lord?"

"General," Kedric said. "The only people who will populate my army will be those warriors who desire being part of my cause."

Myia glanced up at him. "What cause is that?"

"Human rescue. I still have a nephew to save."

Turn the page for an excerpt from the first book
in the Survival Race series,

Captive.

Chapter One

Dawson," the dispatcher's voice crackled through the radio, "the fire jumped the line. Get to safety, now."

"I'm evacuating the two mountain bikers as we speak. We'll be in Happy Camp in about twenty minutes." Officer Addy Dawson raced her Ford Expedition through the tight turns and narrow roads of Klamath National Forest.

In her rearview mirror, an orange beast raged in the distance. It devoured the mountain. Its smoky tongue licked the night's sky clean of stars and moon.

Wildfires were commonplace in California, especially during hot, dry summers that turned her world into a giant tinderbox. Unfortunately just as commonplace were recreationists who didn't respect Mother Nature's awesome power. Case in point: the two shaken teenage boys in the backseat who had ignored the evacuation so they could record the inferno for YouTube.

And were still recording it.

Thank God she had found them before the wind shifted. They never would have survived.

Addy turned north onto Bigfoot Scenic Byway—the main road that ran along the Klamath River—and rounded one of its many bends. Her headlights caught a large hunched-over body darting across the road.

She swerved to avoid hitting it, slammed on the brakes. Pain ripped through her chest as the seat belt tightened, crushing her between it and the boy hurled against the cage behind the driver's seatback. After catching her breath she asked, "Everyone okay?"

"What happened?" It was the kid with the "Beam me up, Scotty" T-shirt. She guessed he was about fifteen.

"Dude, we almost hit Bigfoot," the older one said.

"That wasn't a Sasquatch." Addy reached for the flashlight in her glove compartment. "It was a man. And by the way he was limping, I'd say he's hurt."

"Hey, lady. Where you going?"

She tossed her hat onto the front seat. "To save him, of course."

"Are you tripping? News flash: there's a big-ass fire headed this way."

"Guys, I need you to calm down. We're a mile ahead of the fire, which gives us ten minutes. I only need two. Sit tight."

She shut the door, muffling their hollers of protest, and aimed the flashlight into the trees whipping angrily in the blazing wind. The pungent smell of burned and scorched earth made her nose crinkle.

"Hello?" she called. "Sir, can you hear me? You must evacuate the forest immediately. I can drive you to safety."

No answer.

She entered the woods where the injured hiker had run. What did he do, vanish? She called out again, flashed the light through the trees and brush, climbed deeper into the forest.

"Sir, you're putting yourself in grave danger out here. You must come with me. Now."

The wind gathered strength. Branches struck and scratched her arms and cheek. Powerful gusts of hot air blew her French braid back off her neck. The air tasted of ash. The conflagration was approaching fast.

She'd better get those boys to safety.

Her heart wrenched. She hated leaving the hiker behind, but what choice was there? She couldn't risk four lives when she could save three. Addy pushed through the undergrowth, making a quick retreat back to her vehicle.

A motor revved. Tires squealed on the pavement.

"Oh, no you don't!" She sprinted out of the forest in time to see the Expedition's taillights disappearing into the darkness. "Come back here." She chased after it, waving her flashlight until she was alone on the empty road.

Stranded.

How the hell did the boys escape from a locked backseat? They couldn't have. The hiker must have stolen her vehicle. Dammit. Happy Camp Ranger District was as deep in the wilderness and as far from civilization as anyone could get...and eight miles away. The chance of rescue was less than slim. And there was no outrunning a forest fire.

"Dawson to dispatch. My vehicle has been hijacked and is heading your way. I'm stranded on Bigfoot Scenic Byway."

"Dispatch received. Stand by."

"Addy, it's Pierce." Her ex-boyfriend was the last voice she expected to hear on her radio. He sounded breathless, like he was running. "Head south. I'll be there in ten minutes."

Great. He'd be there five minutes too late.

Above her, white lights blinked through the smoky haze billowing and swirling in the sky. It had to be smoke jumpers or a water plane. Her heart raced with hope. "I'm here! Down here!" She waved her arms and flashlight, but there was no sign they noticed her on the ground.

"Dispatch, I can see lights overhead. Inform the craft I'm directly below them."

"I'm sorry, Officer Dawson, there is no aircraft—"

Her smoke-induced coughing fit and the crackling radio static drowned out the dispatcher's reply. "Repeat," she said.

"Dispatch received. There is no aircraft in your vicinity."

"Then what are these lights hovering above me?" Ash and blackened material fell around her. Sticky residue landed on her arms and caught in her eyelashes. Thick, acrid smoke enveloped her, made her eyes water, choked her. The firestorm raged forward with the speed and shrieking sounds of war bombers.

Adrenaline exploded in her veins.

Addy raced down the embankment of the Klamath River, slipping on the steep slope, riding an avalanche of pebbles. She had been born to the wilderness and always knew she'd die there.

But not today.

She'd escape in the current. Assuming she could survive the rapids.

She splashed into the river and dove beneath the cool water. Her belt was a twenty-pound weight, sinking her, pulling her deeper and deeper down. When she finally managed to get it off and swim to the surface, she gulped a breath of smoke and ash. Coughed.

Swept backward in the current, she watched the inferno tear down the mountain like a fiery tornado. Or a bloodred beast, ripping apart the earth, consuming everything in its path. Huge trees silhouetted against the blaze spontaneously combusted as superheated air hit them. The explosions screamed in her ears.

Or maybe it was terror.

Rapids broke over her head as she struggled to keep above the white water. She couldn't stop swallowing water, sucking in charcoal air. Coughing. Gagging. Hacking.

Whack.

She smashed into stone, and pain ripped through her shoulder. Her leg. White water pummeled her eyes, ears, mouth. She was turned around. Submerged into the silence beneath the water. Reemerged into thunderous chaos. Pitched into unseen obstacles as she tumbled through a rock garden. Chaos. Silence. Chaos. Silence.

Can't breathe. Lungs on fire.

It seemed like forever before she broke to the surface again. The forest crackled behind her in the distance. She had escaped the fire. Now to escape the rapids. Fatigued, she willed her aching body to swim for the bank. Water crashed over her again. And again.

A huge, shadowy figure stretched out an arm to her. Pierce? She reached for him.

Whack.

Darkness.

* * *

Addy bolted upright and gasped a deep breath of fresh air. She opened her eyes. The dying orange glow of embers from three fireplaces spun before her. A few blinks later, the images converged into one.

A woodpecker drilled for breakfast inside her skull.

Lifting weak and heavy hands to massage her temples took way more effort than it should have. Odd. She felt no abrasion or pain from being pitched headfirst into the rocks. She checked her shoulder: no bruise. But the light was dim, and her eyes kept pulsing in and out of focus.

Checking her legs, Addy hiked the blanket past her ankles, shins, and— Wait. Where had the blanket come from? Where was she? Besides sitting on long body pillows on the floor. Naked.

Pierce. Of course the guy would take off her sodden clothes after rescuing her, but you'd think he'd have the decency to give her something to wear. It wasn't like they were dating anymore.

She tried calling his name but no sound came out. She licked dry lips and peered into the room's darkness. Her vision wavered and her head spun as if in the aftermath of one god-awful hangover. She closed her eyes, waited for the dizziness to pass. When she finally opened them, a thick, white fog clouded her vision. Before she could wave it away, the fog crackled as it dissipated, revealing a sleeping man.

A very large, very naked sleeping man.

There must have been some potent wacky weeds burning in that forest. Men with chiseled bare chests and six-pack abs did not materialize in her bed. Not even in her dreams. She was too practical for that kind of fantasy. Well, if she had to hallucinate, a hot hunk was a better pick than pink elephants on parade.

A dark line of hair trailed down his belly and under a strategically positioned royal-blue satin sheet. One hip and a well-defined thigh were bared. Still asleep, he rolled toward her onto his side.

His heavy leg draped over her thigh. Warm breath tickled the hair on her arm.

Every muscle in her body froze. Every muscle except her heart. That was beating double-time. This stranger was no hallucination.

As quietly as she could, Addy eased out from beneath his leg, then rolled off the pillows comprising her bed on the floor. She snatched her discarded blanket and—despite the weakness in her body and fumbling fingers—managed to wrap it around her in strapless toga fashion. Her heart now rapped in time with the woodpecker in her skull.

She held her pounding head and stared at the stranger. His black lashes rested peacefully above sharp cheekbones. He had a clean-shaven, square jawline; thick lips that appeared a bit chapped; and a dainty, silver necklace that was way too effeminate to be on this guy.

Nothing about him jogged her memory. Who was he? Had he

pulled her from the river? Had he stripped off their wet clothes believing their body heat might prevent hypothermia?

Or had he believed their body heat might prevent a lonely night?

Well, he'd be in for a disappointment. She had three rules about sex: it was never casual, never used as a weapon, and never, ever given as a thank-you gift. That's what fruit baskets were for.

She'd send him one as soon as she got out of there.

Addy glanced around the dimly lit room—if you could call it a room. Actually, it looked more like a ten-foot box. There were no doors. No windows. Nothing.

Except for a miniature fireplace and logs centered on one wall, the body pillow bed in one corner and a large terra-cotta flowerpot in the opposite corner, the room appeared empty.

She crept to a wall and drew her hand up, down and across it, searching for a hidden doorknob or lever.

"If you're looking for me, I'm over here."

She jumped and spun to face the stranger but was tripped up by her hangover and stumbled into the wall. Righting herself, she tried for a casual smile but knew it didn't pass for anything more than a nervous tic.

When the room stopped spinning, she noticed he had propped himself up on one elbow. His dark, shoulder-length hair and sleepy eyes enhanced his wicked attractiveness. He made no attempt to move closer. Of course, he made no attempt to cover himself, either, and his sheet had slid farther down.

She forced herself to look at his eyes. Eyes that shone eerily in the dark like a cat's. Eyes that appeared emerald.

Odd choice for colored contacts.

"Come here." He lifted the sheet with one hand and patted the pillow bedding with the other.

Her heart rate revved as she stared at the parts of him beneath the sheet. "I…uh…I…umm."

"Skittish little thing, aren't you?"

The only way to stop gawking was to squeeze her eyes shut. "Who are you?"

"You don't know?" His voice oozed disappointment.

Apparently they had gone through this already. So why couldn't she remember? What else couldn't she remember? "Did I—? Did you—? Did we—?" There was no polite way to ask if (a) she'd given herself to him under duress or (b) he'd violated her while she was unconscious.

"Mate?"

Okay, that was one way. Odd word choice but it sufficed. She nodded.

"No."

She relaxed.

"Not yet." There was no menace or presumption in his words. He spoke them casually, matter-of-factly, as if they'd already discussed sex and concluded they'd sleep together. When had she given him that idea? Her head ached trying to remember.

"I'm sorry. You seem like a nice guy, but I can't…you know…do this."

"Oh. First time, huh?"

"What?"

"Though judging your age, I wouldn't have pegged you for a virgin."

"Excuse me?"

"Relax." The sleep in his voice gave the word a husky sexiness. "I'll make sure you enjoy it, too." He got up and strode toward her, eyes hungry and body very ready to make good on his word.

If her pulse was a car, the turbo just kicked in. "Stop right there," she said, and he did. The surprise was evident on his face. With a body like his, he probably wasn't used to rejection.

"Woman, this won't work unless we're closer. Much closer." He winked.

She turned back to the wall, frantically feeling for that doorknob. But it was too late. He was behind her, towering over her. Sweeping the hair off her shoulder. Brushing his lips down the side of her neck.

A tingling sensation slid down her spine. "Stop it. I'm warning you."

"I understand your hesitation," he said between kisses. "But it's going to happen sooner or later."

Like hell it is. She pivoted around and kneed him in the groin. Swearing, the man grabbed himself and fell to his knees as she ran to the other side of the tiny space.

Ready to defend herself, she looked over her shoulder, expecting to see him lunging at her. He hadn't moved from his spot on the floor.

"Hell, woman, what's wrong with you?" Pain and confusion filled his eyes.

He'd obviously expected her to be a willing participant. Probably figured it was the least she could do after he'd saved her life.

Her head lolled, amplifying the drone in her ears. She wrapped both hands around her skull to make the pounding stop. "God, I need extra-strength aspirin."

"You and me both." He slowly got to his feet. "If you needed some time after reawakening, you should have just said so."

"Reawakening?"

"Don't tell me it's your first time for that, too."

"You mean resuscitation?"

The lines of his forehead wrinkled. He stared at her in puzzlement, as if trying to figure her out. "You don't have a clue what reawakening is, do you?"

She shook her head no. "Should I?"

"What Yard are you from?"

"Yard?" What was he talking about? "You mean Ranger District?"

He didn't answer. And he didn't bother to get dressed or cover himself. It wasn't that she didn't care for the view, but it was one more thing compounding her inability to focus.

"Did you pull me from the river? Did you give me CPR? I can't remember anything that happened after hitting my head."

The man paced, seemingly lost in thought. Maybe she shouldn't have told him she didn't remember his heroism. Bruising his ego only moments after bruising his manhood couldn't be good.

"Look." Addy tried hard to ignore the muscular definition in his legs and butt as he strode back and forth across the floor. "I'm really very grateful that you saved my life. Resuscitated me. Whatever. But if I said or did anything to lead you on while I was in shock, I apologize. So how about you give me my clothes and show me the door."

"Where are you from?" he asked.

Why should that matter? What did he want to do, track her down? Well, she wasn't about to give him a Google map to her front door. "Northern California," she answered, as unspecific as she could be without appearing to be unspecific.

"You live there. Right now. That's where you live."

"Uh. Yeah."

"Son of a bitch."

The hair on her body bristled. "Where are my clothes? I want to leave."

He rubbed his eyes with his fingers and thumb, the same way her patrol captain did when agitated. Though this man was a foot taller than her captain, twice as broad, and three times as menacing.

"I said I want to leave. Now."

He stopped, made a show of looking around the empty room, and with palms up in front of him, shrugged. "You can't."

Addy clutched her toga and yanked it higher. "Why not? Where am I? Who are you?"

"You don't remember how you got here?"

What was wrong with this guy? Didn't she just tell him that? Did he expect her to give him a reward or something? Or maybe he wanted a ransom. Great. That's another thing her mom could blame her for. She could hear her mother now. *Some cop you are, Addy, getting yourself kidnapped. Now we have to waste our retirement money getting you back.*

"Are you holding me for ransom? What kind of single-celled pond scum takes advantage of the person he saved? You did save me, right?"

"Son of a—" he whispered, then shouted at the wall, "How the hell do I explain this?"

Addy stepped back.

He drew out a long sigh, then locked his eyes on hers. "I didn't save you and I didn't kidnap you."

"Then how did I end up trapped in this…this box with you? Who are you?" *Please don't be a serial killer…please don't be a serial killer…please don't be a serial killer.*

He stepped toward her, then stopped when she flinched. Raising his hands in front of him, he pointed to the fireplace. "I'm going to throw a log on the fire. Okay?"

She hesitated. Brighter light would make it easier to see him. That way she could give a more detailed description to the police artist. And if it was a trick, she was ready to fight. Her fingers curled into a fist. She nodded.

The man moved to the small woodpile next to the fire. The three identical logs, each about one foot in length and four inches in diameter, appeared way too cylindrical to be real. Damn. If she could have identified the tree from which they'd been cut, she might have gotten a clue as to where she was.

He tossed a log on the embers and the fire sprang to life.

Addy stepped sideways—back sliding against the cool wall and bare feet squishing into soft pillows still warm from where he had slept—until she stood behind him. She stuck out her chin. "Okay, the log's on. I want answers."

"My name's Max," he said, still watching the fire. "They took me, what, fifteen years ago maybe? I don't know. I lost count."

"Took you where?"

He turned to face her and searched her eyes. "You really have no idea, do you?"

She resisted the urge to shake her head. She'd do the interrogating, thank you very much. "You said *they* took you. Who's *they*?"

"The Hyboreans."

"Who are the Hyboreans? A cult? What do they want?" When he didn't answer, she started to ask again.

"Babies," he said. "They want us to make babies."

His reply was so preposterous, she laughed. "What is this, some kind of prank? Am I on some reality TV show? Pierce put you up to this, didn't he? Where is he?" She searched the wall for a hidden camera. Any minute the crew would open the door, and they'd all have a good laugh.

"If it is a joke, it's on me. This is the first time I've been with a female who didn't understand her role. Why would they throw you in here without bringing you to the Yard first?" He asked the question more to himself. "Well, hell. The only obvious reason is because you're ovulating."

"Excuse me?" The smoke from the fire reached her. Its odd scent seeped into her head, making her dizzy again. Warm. Flushed.

"You can't get pregnant unless you're ovulating. They probably examined you, realized you were ready, and didn't want to waste an opportunity."

"Y-you're not an actor. You're psychotic." *Oh my God, maybe he escaped from an insane asylum.* She pounded her fists on the wall. "Let me out of here," she hollered. "Let me out."

"Whoa." Max jumped up and grabbed her hands. "Settle down. Don't make them angry."

His words sent shivers through her, and a new fear exploded inside. She pulled her arms free, hit and punched him. "Don't touch me."

"Hell, woman, control yourself!"

Was that anger or panic flashing in his unnatural green eyes? What would he do to her? Was he capable of murder? She unleashed frightened fury on him in blow after blow, striking him with anything she could—fists, feet, fingernails.

He tried muscling her but couldn't get a solid grip on her limbs spinning wildly.

Pain like a bolt of lightning struck her neck and ricocheted through her body. She screamed and collapsed to the ground, every muscle spastic from the jolt.

Get up, Dawson. Weak and heavy, as if her body had been magnetized and stuck to a metal floor, she couldn't move. Max crouched next to her, keeping some distance between them. His lips moved, but she couldn't hear him.

An instant later, the spasms stopped. As she rubbed the pain from her neck, her pinkie got caught in a…necklace? Where did that come from? She wasn't wearing one last night. She rolled the thin, light chain between her fingers. Did it match his? Did he give it to her?

Hot anger pulsed through her veins, and she jerked the chain. The damn thing didn't break. Obviously, her strength hadn't returned.

"Don't." It sounded more like a warning than a command.

Locking a defiant gaze on his eyes, she slid four fingers between the necklace and her throat and yanked hard. The chain dug into the back of her neck. It still didn't break. What was it made out of, steel? She yanked again and again, each time harder than the last.

"Stop," he shouted. "Listen, woman, before they—"

Another jolt of electricity pierced her neck and shot through her body. She curled onto her side.

"Are you okay?" He moved closer, but still didn't touch her.

Addy's forehead slid back and forth on the floor as she shook her head no. "What's happened to me?"

"It's the Hyboreans. Are you hurt? Can you see?" She must have given him an odd look because he explained, "Too much voltage can blind you. Or worse. Hell, woman, for your own safety, don't anger the Hyboreans."

It wasn't until he wrapped the blanket around her that she realized it had fallen off—at what point that actually happened, she had no idea and, quite frankly, was too beat to care.

He scooped her up into his arms.

"I don't understand what happened," she said, unable to stop the trembling.

"Shock collar. It's their way of keeping us in line."

"No, I mean how did I end up here? Kidnapped. Into white slavery. Where on earth am I?" She could have sworn his face paled but couldn't be sure through her tears threatening to escape.

He eased her onto the pillows. "We'll talk in the morning."

Drained, yet unwilling to shut her eyes, she fought heavy lids. It was no use. Exhaustion owned her. A hot tear slipped from the corner of her eye, making its way to her ear.

The feathery weight of another blanket covered her. A finger brushed across her wet temple.

"I won't hurt you," Max whispered.

She drifted into darkness.

* * *

She was beautiful. Hell, what naked woman wasn't? Though this one didn't have the large breasts and wide hips typical of the women they had brought him in the past. This one was muscular, strong, and a ball of fire.

Max grinned.

She definitely could hold her own, with that knee to the groin and the kicking and clawing. He examined the stinging marks on his chest and knew he'd find the rest of his skin under her fingernails. The woman could draw blood. He'd give her that. But she'd never hurt someone if she didn't learn how to throw some weight behind her punches.

He watched her fight exhaustion…and lose.

She looked vulnerable lying in his bed with her reddish-blonde hair spilled around her. He imagined her sweeping that long hair down his chest and could almost feel the tickle. Blood pumped through him, bringing him to readiness.

He could take her right now. She wouldn't fight. She couldn't.

Their mating would please the Hyboreans. And happy Hyboreans didn't punish people.

Usually.

Her breasts rose and fell with each fast and shallow breath. A tear slid across her face.

Ah, hell. Only a beast would take a defenseless woman.

Inhaling deeply and then letting it out slowly, he commanded his body to relax. With a gentleness he forced himself to control, he pulled the blanket over her and then wiped away her teardrop.

"I won't hurt you," he whispered.

It wasn't long before her breathing slowed and its rhythm steadied. Her face relaxed and the lines of tension disappeared, making her appear younger than he originally guessed. Early twenties probably.

Poor kid. She had no idea what had happened.

It'd been so long, he'd forgotten what it felt like to wake up in a strange world. But it had all come back to him when he'd glimpsed the terror in her eyes. His gut tightened as he remembered the range of emotions that had crossed her face in a matter of minutes: confusion, fear, anger, helplessness, pain, and finally defeat.

There was only one thing worse than defeat. Accepting it.

Pulling the blanket over himself, he settled onto his side with head propped in his hand. He studied the curves of her face and the handful of freckles on her tanned cheeks. What would he do with her?

Besides impregnate her, of course.

Maybe he should explain where they were. No. She'd never believe him. The truth would only frighten her more.

Just keep your mouth shut, and do your job.

"How can I do my job," he whispered to her, "when you're so damn feisty?" He drummed his fingers on his head.

The other women had known their role and greeted him with open legs. Okay, so maybe one or two weren't quite ready at first, but they always responded favorably after a little coaxing and the aphrodisiac fire.

What if this one refused? Her spirit was strong. She was a fighter. Dread surged through his veins.

He hadn't been at stud in a year. And the year prior to that he'd only been in twice. He had to face facts. At thirty-five, he was no longer the young strapping alpha the Hyboreans wanted. Any noncompliance on the woman's part was sure to be viewed as his failure. And failure equaled torture.

Only at his age, he doubted he'd suffer a beating. Or starvation. This time he'd be sold on the black market.

Shit. That was a death sentence.

His head fell to the pillow and he stared at the ceiling. "You bastards," he said, keeping his voice low, "why didn't you take her to the Yard first? I can't afford complications at my age."

He knew of other studs who forced themselves on the females. His stomach turned and dropped into his bowels.

You're not an animal.

He cringed at his lie.

Not a *complete* animal anyway. That's why rape could never be an option.

Ever.

The breeding box was the only safe place he could act like a man. If he lost that last bit of humanity, he lost everything.

The heat of her body warmed his side. Rolling to face her again, he traced her soft lips with a gentle finger. There was only one thing to do.

"Woman," he said. "Prepare to be seduced."

Chapter Two

Waking to the dull clank of something hitting the floor, Addy opened one eye. Still naked, Max knelt by the unlit fireplace with his shoulder toward her. Two pitchers and three cereal bowls sat at his side between them. A citrus fragrance wafted over to her. He wiped the back of his hand across his mouth, then retrieved a bundle she hadn't noticed before from beside the fireplace, opened it, and ate whatever was inside.

He had no idea she was awake. Good. Maybe she'd have a few minutes to check out her surroundings in the light and figure out how to escape.

Her gaze shifted around a room void of light fixtures and windows. Large shadows moved across bright, translucent walls. Where was she? Inside a giant, plastic milk jug?

In slow motion so Max wouldn't detect her movements, she lifted her head off the pillow. Every sound grew louder; his crunching and sucking as he chewed, and her breathing that seemed to echo in her ears. She held her breath, listening.

From the other side of the wall came a dull clank followed by faint crackling. Rice Krispies? She cocked her head toward the sound.

"Morning."

Her gaze shot to her captor. He hadn't moved from his place except to turn her way and flash a crooked, sexy smile. "How you feeling?"

Let's see: there's confused, scared, angry, humiliated.

"Hungry?" he asked, a little too cheerful after the horrible night they shared. He pushed the larger bowl closer to her.

Holding the blanket tight around her, Addy sat up and eyed the bowl. Why hadn't he eaten from it?

Max crouched on the floor facing her. She couldn't stop gawking at his nakedness, fascinated how in its relaxed state it wasn't nearly as threatening. She felt his gaze on her. He knew she was checking him out, yet he didn't bother hiding himself. The guy had absolutely no shame.

"Go on," he said. "Eat."

What woman could eat with *that* staring at her? She pulled a sheet off the pillowed mattress and tossed it to him. "I don't suppose you'd mind covering yourself." She was parched and the words came out rough. She coughed to clear her throat but that only made it feel scratchy.

"Oh. Right." He wrapped the blue satin around the lower half of his body. "Better?" His smile held amusement.

Why was he acting so nice this morning? Maybe he wasn't a crazed serial killer. After all, if he hadn't strangled her in her sleep, he probably wasn't going to. She hoped.

He took a long drink from the pitcher, each swallow causing his Adam's apple to bob up and down, making her uncomfortably aware of her growing thirst. She tried to swallow, but couldn't.

"Ahh." He wiped his mouth.

She eyed the pitcher.

"Go ahead." He pushed it toward her. "I know you're thirsty."

Thirsty was an understatement. After a moment's hesitation, Addy slowly brought the pitcher to her lips and sipped. Cold water refreshed her tongue and mouth. She drank deeply, rehydrating herself.

Max picked a pink, juicy cube from the bowl of colorful fruit and held it out to her. "Here."

"What's that?" Her voice still sounded horse. How was she going to ask him the million questions rattling around in her brain if she could barely talk?

"Food. Try it."

She took her own chunk from the bowl and sniffed it; a citrus fragrance filled her nostrils. Her stomach growled, making her realize she wasn't just hungry. She was ravenous.

Seemingly unaffected by her snub, he popped his proffered food into his mouth and watched her study the cube.

Heat radiated inside her hollow stomach. It cried out again for nourishment. The fruit looked harmless enough and he did eat some, so it couldn't be poisoned. Besides, sharing a meal might make him more inclined to answer her questions.

She nibbled. Sweet nectar with a hint of spice trickled over her taste buds. Juice and saliva pooled in her mouth. She swallowed and greedily took a bigger bite. Juice dribbled down her chin. "It's good." She wiped her chin with her fingers. "And messy."

He grinned, and his weird green eyes brightened with the joy of a little boy showing off a new fishing pole. "Pop the whole thing in." He tossed another piece into his mouth.

She bit into another cube, squirting juice on him, and tried not to snicker as the pink liquid rolled down his chest into the nail marks she had left from yesterday's attack.

He drew in a quick breath, his pain giving her a perverse satisfaction. "Nice shot." He wiped his chest with his hand. "You might want to close your mouth before biting, next time."

"What's going on here, Max?"

"Nothing. Just breakfast," he said in a sorry attempt at feigning innocence.

"You know that's not what I meant. You said we'd talk in the morning. So talk. Where are we?"

He finished chewing before he answered. "Hyborea."

"Where's that?"

"I can't exactly say where it is, but I can tell you where it's not."

"Okay. So where isn't it?"

"It's not in the USA. Here, try this. It's my favorite." He handed her a cracker as long and wide as a graham but with the texture of a Triscuit. "Dip it in here." He indicated a bowl of little round black balls stuck in a heap of thick pasty stuff. Was it caviar? For breakfast?

"Eew. What the heck is that?"

"It looks gross but tastes great. Try it."

"No thanks." She bit into the plain cracker. "Do you know how I got here?"

He shook his head. "What do you remember?"

"There was a forest fire. I tried escaping in the river but was caught in the rapids. I was getting banged up on the rocks. The last thing I remember before losing consciousness was a huge shadow over me. Then I woke up here."

"Sounds like the Hyboreans pulled you from the rapids."

"Are the Hyboreans a cult?"

Max choked on his cracker. He covered his mouth and coughed. "Something like that." He coughed again. "More biscuits?" He offered another Triscuit thingy.

"Are the Hyboreans out there now?" She pointed to the wall.

He nodded.

"What are they doing?"

"Feeding us breakfast."

"Knock it off," she said with more anger than she intended to show. She folded her arms across her chest and glared at him. "I want answers. Real answers."

He stopped eating and looked her square in the eye. He dropped his shoulders slightly and leaned toward her. "If I explain everything, do you promise not to flip out?"

She nodded slowly, unsure if she'd be able to keep that promise.

"Okay. The Hyboreans want babies. They take people, put them naked in a room together, and let Mother Nature take her course. There is no escaping. Ever. If you do what they want, you'll survive. If you piss them off, you won't." He spoke as if he were explaining the rules of a card game.

Addy scooped another cube of fruit from the bowl and ate it, hoping this basic life function would ground her in reality. She had to keep her wits in order to figure out where she was and how to escape. "So what do the Hyboreans do with the babies?" She really didn't want to know but had to ask.

"Sell them."

"This is a baby ring? You mean instead of kidnapping newborns, they enslave adults to make the babies for them? Oh my God."

She couldn't wrap her brain around the idea. It was so crazy and disgusting—like that fertility doctor who gave his patients his own sperm in order to save money. "People are sick." She spat the words in disgust.

"Oh my God," she said again, covering her mouth. The weight of the conversation finally hit her full force. This wasn't some campfire ghost story. This was real.

She'd been kidnapped. By a baby-selling cult!

Tears prickled behind her eyes. Her throat constricted. Her breathing sped up. She was a Forest Service cop. A tree cop. She wasn't experienced in handling human trafficking. This was totally out of her jurisdiction. "There really is no escaping, is there?"

The sudden sadness in his eyes said it all. She was trapped here, probably until she died. Or until they killed her.

She'd never be set free. The cult couldn't risk anyone telling the FBI or the United Nations or whatever organization one informed about international kidnapping and slavery. Her body tingled with a cold numbness. She hugged her knees to her chest and rocked. She'd never again see her friends, her father, her home.

Shaking from the swelling rage bubbling inside, she wanted to scream. She wanted to pound on the wall. She wanted to demand they release her. But she couldn't. She couldn't stand that pain they'd shot through her yesterday. And she couldn't stand her vulnerability. A good cop knew how to manage her emotions under stress. So she just sat there, sitting and rocking and wondering how this had happened.

Dazed, she reached for more food, hoping it might fill the hollowness inside. Max snatched the bowl away and she flinched.

"Lesson number two: don't eat all your food at once, in case they forget to feed you."

She felt her eyes widen. She wanted to ask if that happened often, but was too scared to hear the answer. Instead, she asked, "What's lesson number one?"

He reached for her, hooked a finger around her choker, and drew her to him. His piercing cat eyes, inches away from hers, held a stern seriousness that penetrated her body and stopped her heart. This lesson was crucial.

"Don't piss off the Hyboreans."

About the Author

K. M. Fawcett writes sci-fi and paranormal romances and enjoys stories filled with adventure and strong, kick-butt heroes and heroines. K. M. holds the rank of *sandan* (third-degree black belt) in both *Isshinryu* karate and *Ryukonkai* (Okinawan weapons). K. M. and her husband own Tenchi Isshinryu Karate Dojo in New Jersey where they teach karate, weapons, and self defense. When not writing, working out at the *dojo*, or blogging at Attacking The Page, she is driving her children to and from drum lessons and ballet classes. You can visit her at www.KMFawcett.com.

Learn more at:
KMFawcett.com
Twitter, @KMFawcett
Facebook.com/km.fawcett